When you begin the trial, one Faerunian day hence, you will all observe the rules. Now, what charge have you raised against Cyric?

Tyr lifted his head and studied Cyric's dark eyes. "The charge shall be Innocence, I think."

"Innocence?" So loud and shrill was Cyric's shriek that several gods cringed. "But I am the Lord of Murder! The Prince of Lies! The Sower of Strife! The Master of Deception!"

"The charge is Innocence," Tyr declared. "Innocence by reason of Insanity."

FORGOTTEN REALMS
FANTASY ADVENTURE

The Avatar Series

FORGOTTEN REALMS

FANTASY ADVENTURE

CRUCIBLE:
THE TRIAL of
CYRIC the MAD

Troy Denning

CRUCIBLE:
THE TRIAL OF CYRIC THE MAD

Distributed to the book trade in the United States by Random House, Inc. and in Canada by Random House of Canada Ltd.

Distributed to the toy and hobby trade by regional distributors.

Distributed worldwide by Wizards of the Coast, Inc. and regional distributors.

Cover art by Allan Pollack. Interior art by Jeff Easley.

FORGOTTEN REALMS and the TSR logo are registered trademarks owned by TSR, Inc.

TSR, Inc. is a subsidiary of Wizards of the Coast, Inc.

First Printing: February 1998
Printed in the United States of America.
Library of Congress Catalog Card Number: 96-60817

9 8 7 6 5 4 3 2 1

8577XXX1501

ISBN: 0-7869-0724-X

U.S., CANADA, ASIA,
PACIFIC, & LATIN AMERICA
Wizards of the Coast, Inc.
P.O. Box 707
Renton, WA 98057-0707
+1-206-624-0933

EUROPEAN HEADQUARTERS
Wizards of the Coast, Belgium
P.B. 34
2300 Turnhout
Belgium
+32-14-44-30-44

Visit our website at http://www.tsrinc.com

For Matt and Josh

Acknowledgments

This story is rooted in events arising from the Avatar Trilogy and *Prince of Lies*, and I would like to acknowledge the original Avatar team, including (but not limited to): Ed Greenwood, Jeff Grubb, Karen Boomgarden, and all the creative people in the game department who worked on the project; Mary Kirchoff, who oversaw the novels; Scott Ciencin, author of *Shadowdale* and *Tantras* (under the TSR pseudonym Richard Awlinson); myself, author of *Waterdeep* (the "other third" of Richard Awlinson); and James Lowder, trilogy editor and author of *Prince of Lies*.

I would also like to thank the following people for their valuable contributions to *Crucible: The Trial of Cyric the Mad*: Peter Archer, for his patience and editorial insight; Brian Thomsen, for his invaluable advice; Julia Martin, for reviewing both outline and manuscript; Steven Schend, for disclosing early his work on the cultures of Calimshan and Amn; and most especially Andria Hayday, for her hard work in polishing the manuscript and salvaging Malik's voice.

It depends on me, of course. Everything does.

Who shall live. Who shall die. What is, what shall be.

Imagine I am watching from above, hovering in the sky as mortals are wont to think we gods do. The vast sea lies below, forever slapping at the rocky shore of the Sword Coast, where Candlekeep's towers of profane ignorance sit upon the pedestal of a black basalt tor. With a breath, I could blast that bastion of falsity down, powder the mortar between its stones and send its high walls crashing into the sea, scatter its twisted tomes to the bubbling mires and the deep, stinking oceans in the far corners of the world.

Now imagine I am standing. The sea hangs upright before me, a sparkling green tapestry stretched across the endless expanse of the heavens, its white-capped waves spilling down again and again to taunt the shore below. The world has turned on end, and Candlekeep's towers hang upon that basalt tor like warts upon the tip of a black, cragged nose. With a thought, I could release the fullness of the sea to swallow that citadel of corruption, to scour that library of lies from the face of the world, to wash its books of deceit into oblivion and rinse from Toril even the memory of their false pages.

It all depends on me, you see. Nothing is certain until I have beheld it and set it in place, until I have placed myself above it or below, before it or after. Let them keep their temple to Oghma the Unknowing, their shrines to Deneir the Prattler and Gond of the Forgestinking Breath, and even to Milil, Lord of Screeching

1

Racket! Let them scorn me if they dare. I am the One, the All, the Face Behind the Mask.

I am the Everything.

* * * * *

Thus spoke Cyric the All on the Night of Despair, and in my anguish, I could not understand. I was as a child; I heard with a child's ears and saw with a child's eyes, and I understood with a child's mind. I despaired and I lost faith, and for that I suffered most horribly, as you shall see. But know also that the One found me when I was lost, that he returned me to the Way of Belief, that he burned my eyes with the Flames of Glory and Truth until I saw all that occurred in the world and in the heavens, and that he did all this so that in the account that follows, I might set down all the things done by men and by gods in complete accuracy and perfect truth.

I am the spy Malik el Sami yn Nasser, a famed merchant of Calimshan and a welcome attendant to the royal house of Najron, and this is my tale, in which I relate the events that befell me and a thousand others during the Search for the Holy *Cyrinishad,* the most Sacred and Divine of all books, and tell of my faithful service to Cyric the All in the boundless lands of Faerûn, and reveal the Great Reward bestowed on me for my Valiant Labors and my many Terrible Sufferings.

Praise be to Cyric the All, Most Mighty, Highest of the High, the Dark Sun, the Black Sun, the Lord of Three Crowns, and the Prince of Lies. All Blessings and Strength upon his Church and his Servants, who alone shall rule over the Kingdom of Mortals and Dwell Forever in the Palace of Eternity in the time beyond the Year of Carnage! Look kindly upon this Humble Account, O God of Gods, though no passage can measure the expanse of your Might, nor all the words in all the tongues of men describe the Splendor of your Presence!

Prologue

In the City of Brilliance lived a young prince, handsome in all manners, but lacking in the virtues of restraint and good judgment. While I was out on business one day, the Caliph sent this prince to my home with a letter to be presented to none but me. My servants bade the prince wait in the shade of the anteroom, and my wife, being a gracious and most cordial hostess, brought him many refreshments and sat with him to keep him entertained. It was there that I found them when I returned.

Now it is true that no person of modesty would go about the streets dressed as were my wife and the prince when I returned. But, as they were not in the streets, I merely remarked upon the heat and adjusted my own dress to accommodate theirs. My informal manner was a great comfort to the prince, who had at first seemed flustered and unsettled. He presented his letter, and I invited him to take some refreshments while I read.

The letter was a trivial thing requesting some tariff I had forgotten to pay. As I composed a reply, we had quite a pleasant talk, which I am certain won me no small favor at court, the prince being the eldest son to the Caliph's first wife. After that day, I received many letters from the royal house, all delivered in person by the first prince. If I found it wise to knock upon my own door before entering the antechamber of my own home, it was a small price to pay for the esteem brought by the prince's frequent visits, and for the great honor with which he was to later repay my hospitality.

3

The day came when the Caliph received a letter telling of events in Zhentil Keep, once a great stronghold of Our Lord Cyric in the distant kingdoms of the barbarians. According to the letter, the Dark Sun himself had composed a sacred history of his rise to godhood, the *Cyrinishad*. So beautiful and brilliant were the words of the *Cyrinishad* that anyone reading them saw at once the truth and magnificence of all they proclaimed. In this great book lay the power to convert all the heathens of Faerûn to the True Faith—to drive all the pretender gods from the world and make Cyric the One True Divinity!

The Caliph's excitement was great, for it offended him that others failed to believe as he did, and he was always eager to guide them to the Path of Faith. Indeed, he ran about waving the letter and singing the glory of Cyric's victory for nearly an hour before his chamberlain could catch him and continue reading. I saw this myself, as I was a visitor to the palace that day.

The second page of the letter explained how Mystra (the harlot Goddess of Magic) and Oghma (the thieving God of Wisdom) feared the *Cyrinishad*'s power and plotted against Cyric. At the *Cyrinishad*'s first public reading, Oghma replaced the holy tome with a book of slander, and all who heard its lies lost their faith and turned from the Dark Sun. In that moment, Kelemvor Lyonsbane—a vile traitor whom Cyric had slain years before—escaped from his prison in the City of the Dead to lead a rebellion and steal the Throne of Death from Our Dark Lord!

Upon hearing these words, the Caliph grew so distraught that he drew his dagger and flung himself upon his chamberlain and cut out the poor man's tongue. There was so much blood the chamberlain's replacement could not continue reading until the royal priest made the words legible again.

The third page of the letter said Cyric's power was so great that even Oghma and Mystra together could not destroy the *Cyrinishad*. Oghma gave the tome to a mortal and bade her travel forth and hide, blessing her with a diamond amulet that would conceal her from all the gods of Faerûn. Oghma denied even himself knowledge of her whereabouts, for such was his fear of the One's cunning that he knew Cyric would trick him into revealing her location.

The last page of the letter asked the Caliph to send his most loyal spies to watch the temples of Oghma and all his servant gods, Gond and Deneir and Milil, and also the temples of Kelemvor and Mystra and her servant gods, Azuth and Savras and Velsharoon. He asked as well that the Caliph send spies to the places where the Harpers make their secret havens, and to the places where the dead are left for Kelemvor, and to all other places where the servant of thieving Oghma might seek refuge. All this the Caliph did, and more besides, sending word to even his most distant cousins to aid in the great vigil. He drew up long lists so they would waste no effort watching the same places. He said also that if their spies found the book, they should send word to him and not attempt to recover it themselves. This, he did not expect them to do, for any mortal who recovered the *Cyrinishad* would win great favor in the eyes of the One and All, but the Caliph did not wish to appear forgetful by neglecting the demand.

So it was that the Caliph summoned his loyal spies to his chambers. It was to the hospitality of my house that I owed the honor of being among them, for the prince suggested I be given the honor of a distant post, where I might endure the great hardships of my mission in the guise of a beggar. At first I was too humble to accept, protesting that my business and my family required my presence in the City of Brilliance. The kind prince replied that he would handle my affairs while I was away, and ensure that no harm came to my business or my wife. Seeing the high regard in which his son held me, the Caliph declared I would watch over the most important and dangerous of all the posts, the great library at Candlekeep.

At once, I knew I had been blessed. Was Candlekeep not Faerûn's mightiest bastion of learning, much beloved of envious Oghma and jealous Mystra? And was the *Cyrinishad* not Faerûn's greatest work of history, able to make even gods worship the One and All? The Fates themselves had decreed the *Cyrinishad* would come to Candlekeep—and when it did, I would be waiting.

Thus assured of my success, and confident that afterward I would be in a position to repay the kindness of the prince, I changed my merchant's silks for the flaxen rags of a beggar. I hacked all trace of grooming from my hair and dark beard, then smeared my face with mud and in great haste traveled north to the plain outside Candlekeep. There I lurked for years, filthy and unkempt, babbling like a madman and begging food and news from the monks who watched the gate.

Nor did I seek comfort from Our Dark Lord. The monks kept a temple to Oghma in their citadel, and I feared the Wise God would hear my devotions and have me chased off. So I closed my eyes to my master and lord and lived utterly alone year upon year. I prayed for no refuge from my hunger. I called down no curses upon those who pelted me with stones. I made no appeal, even in my thoughts, to the hallowed name of Cyric the All. I passed seasons huddled in the shelter of the Low Gate's archway, and pled alms from all who entered, and humbled myself before those who imagined themselves my betters.

And one evening when the patter of a gentle rain filled my ears with a sound so constant I feared I would go truly mad, there came two strangers splashing up the road, a warrior and a woman. Their tongues wagged in the accent of a barbarian land, and their packhorse snorted beneath a great iron lockbox all bound in chains. I went to beg a coin for my dinner, and the armored warrior gave me a copper to hold their horses. He spoke to the gate monks of close fights and hard rides and enemies left dead upon the road. The woman talked of dark nights and lonely journeys and aid from all who revered Oghma, and she opened her cloak to show a diamond amulet in the shape of Oghma's scroll.

Even had I not been watching for that unholy amulet, I would have known! I could feel the darkness welling up inside that iron lockbox and smell the musty fetor of human parchment and hear the whisper of dark truths rustling across holy pages. The *Cyrinishad* was reaching out to touch my mind and my body, and my ears filled with such a rushing I was seized by a fever!

At once, I could think of nothing but the book, of how Oghma's thieves stood facing the other way, of how I held the reins to their horses, of how the *Cyrinishad* lay within my grasp after so many endless months of waiting. With not a thought for my own safety, I slipped my foot into the stirrup of the warrior's horse, hoisted myself into his saddle, and jerked the reins around.

Had my father taught me more about turning horses than gold, my account would have ended here, with me earning Cyric's eternal favor and returning home to repay tenfold the prince's great kindnesses in looking after my wife and my fortune.

But this was not to be.

The war-horse would not turn. The harder I jerked his reins, the more he pulled back. When I thought to force the stupid beast by lashing him between the ears, he protested with a whinny so shrill it nearly burst my eardrums. In an instant, the warrior's swordtip was pressed beneath my chin. I could do nothing but tumble from the saddle and throw myself into the mud and beg his mercy, and still he spared my life only because a gate monk interposed himself and uttered many stern warnings against the killing of halfwit beggars.

It was nearly five minutes before the man sheathed his sword and kicked me away, and five more before his wretched companion finished assailing me with sharp words about taking the property of others. (And this from a servant of thieving Oghma!)

When at last the woman grew tired of her own voice, the monks opened the gate and led her and the warrior inside. I left that very minute to rush to Beregost and send word to the Caliph. As soon as he spread word of my great discovery, I knew that Cyric's Faithful would rush north to recover the *Cyrinishad* and punish the infidels for stealing it.

Surely, my days as a spy were done! The Caliph would call

me home and bestow on me a reward fitting for all I had endured, and I would be hailed throughout Calimshan and the world as the Finder of the Book. My name would be honored in temples from Athkatla to Escalaunt, and at last I would be in a position to repay the prince for the many kind attentions he had shown my household and my wife!

But mine was to be a different story.

One

On the morning of the storming of Candlekeep, I was given the honor of joining the command party atop a knoll some distance from the citadel. The Caliph had appointed me, as Finder of the Book, to stand in his place while his best swordsmen joined the Faithful on the plain below. These warriors formed but a fraction of the forces amassed in the name of Cyric, the One and All.

To my left stood Most High Haroun with his horde of black-armored bodyguards. He was a tall and hulking man in jingling chain mail, who commanded a great following of Faithful Warriors called the Black Helms. On my right stood His Deadliness Jabbar, with his own throng of bodyguards. His Deadliness was a pale man, shunning noisy armor in favor of a soft-swishing priest's robe. He commanded the Purple Lancers, a following of Faithful Warriors equal in size to that of Most High Haroun. Together, their troops were called the Company of the Ebon Spur. The warriors of the Ebon Spur were Cyric's shock riders, an elite cavalry from Amn who plunged into battle mounted on war bulls. And their leaders, Jabbar and Haroun, were known as the Dark Lords.

Across a thousand paces of open plain, high atop a jagged horn of black basalt that loomed a hundred feet above the crashing seashore, soared the impregnable towers of Candlekeep. In the soft light before dawn, I could see tiny figures standing in the embrasures along the outer wall, peering down on the road that circled up the tor. In my mind, I could even hear our foes up there laughing, boasting of the short work they would make of us as we climbed up the narrow path to the High Gate.

". . . stones will crack their skulls like eggs."

"Like spoiled eggs no dog would eat!"

"Aye, Carl, like old stinking eggs with gray rotten yolks, so slick and foul we'll be stuck up here till the rains come to wash their brains off the ramp!"

"Ha! Till the rains come! Ha-harragh!"

I was content to let them laugh. The almighty hand of Cyric the Invincible would shield our army during its long climb; I had seen this in a dream. Soon enough, the Ebon Spur would be cutting the smirks from their dead faces.

I nodded to the signal masters. It was but an honorary act of command, and my only one. Although the Dark Lords had an uneasy alliance, they were united in this much: on this day of glory, no Caliph's delegate from far-flung Calimshan would overshadow them.

The signal masters unfurled their dark flags, and a great clamor spread across the plain as our army made ready its weapons and shields. The fire giants of the Scarlet Fellowhood, hired for the cause at vast expense, took up their iron battering ram and formed a wedge. Behind them, the two troops of the Ebon Spur mounted their black-horned war bulls and formed their lines, the Black Helms of Most High Haroun to the left of the road and the Purple Lancers of His Deadliness Jabbar to the right. Together, all the riders of the Ebon Spur numbered several hundred strong.

Next came the Caliph's Sabers, led by the Caliph's second son, the prince (the first prince remained in the City of Brilliance to watch over my fortune and wife). Then came the Sable Daggers of Soubar, Tunland's Ravagers, the Invisible Axes from Iriaebor, and a dozen other foot companies sent by the Night Goddess Shar and Talos the Destroyer to win the favor of Our Lord Cyric. A tribe of Cloak Wood orcs had even joined our side. Truly, it was the mightiest Army of Belief ever assembled, and it filled my heart to think my own actions had brought it there.

When the companies had made ready, all eyes turned toward the Dark Lords. The Most High raised his staff of office, a golden scepter crowned by an iron starburst—which was half of Cyric's sacred starburst-and-skull. Jabbar did not raise his own half, for the two commanders of the Ebon Spur always refused to look upon one another directly, and he had not seen Haroun's signal. A young aide emerged from the throng of bodyguards and stepped to His Deadliness's side.

I could not hear what was said, but when the adjutant backed away, Jabbar spun upon his heel and looked toward the back of the hill, barking at his guards to give him a view. The mob parted. His Deadliness gazed out over the plain a moment, then whirled around and pointed his scepter at the signal masters.

"Hold!"

"Hold?" Haroun's head snapped around to glare at His Deadliness. "We agreed at dawn, you double-tongued coward!"

Jabbar accepted the insult with the softest sissing of breath, a sure sign he would have his vengeance later. "This is no treachery, fool. A column is coming down the Way of the Lion."

"More reinforcements?" Haroun growled. "Ours or theirs?"

His Deadliness raised his shoulders. "I can't make out their banners. But the company looks large. We dare not ignore it."

"Or so you say."

Haroun stomped across the knoll to see for himself. His bodyguards followed behind, amidst a great cacophony of ringing armor and rattling weapons.

From our impatient army below arose a din of snorting beasts and groaning men. The commanders of the foot companies scowled up toward the knoll, their lips curling with curses upon the names of Haroun and Jabbar. The captains of the Ebon Spur, more accustomed to the discord between the Dark Lords, simply ordered their troops to dismount—war bulls were not patient beasts; once mounted, they craved the charge.

I went to join the others across the hilltop. Although I was neither tall nor imposing—in truth, I was short and pudgy, with a round face and bulging eyes that made me look the exact opposite of menacing—the crowd let me pass. I was the Finder of the Book, the Sly One who had outwitted Oghma the Wise, and only the Dark Lords themselves cared to risk my ire.

I squeezed out of the throng and found myself standing in the no-man's-land that always separated Haroun and Jabbar. Both Dark Lords were gazing down the Way of the Lion toward a long file of foot soldiers. The white-clad warriors were mere dots of chalk upon the gray road, yet their company banners were so huge I beheld their symbol clearly. It was a nine-stranded whip entwined around a white staff, all against a crimson background.

"Loviatar?" I gasped.

"The Monks of the White Rod," said Haroun. "A good order, disciples of pain. The more they hurt, the harder they fight."

"Whether that is good or bad depends on whom they support," said His Deadliness Jabbar. "Loviatar has yet to declare."

"They must be ours," I said. Few men would have been so bold as to offer their opinion to a Dark Lord, but I had made certain 'special arrangements' with both Jabbar and Haroun that allowed me this freedom. "Is Loviatar not one of the Dark Gods?"

"She was also beholden to Bhaal, whom Our Lord Cyric slew during the Time of Troubles," answered Jabbar. "Whether she thanks him or curses him for that, who can say?"

"But, Your Deadliness, Loviatar would never aid the likes of Oghma!"

Jabbar's face reddened, and I realized my mistake even before the onlookers gasped. Only a fool or a caliph could suggest a Dark Lord was mistaken, and since I was no caliph . . . even my 'special arrangements' would not spare me the wrath of His Deadliness. I let my legs go limp, that I might prostrate myself and plead for mercy.

My knees never touched the ground. Most High Haroun seized my arm, and for a moment I hung as limp as a puppet.

Haroun said, "If the Finder does not fathom the intricacies of divine politics, Jabbar, we must forgive him. Do not forget that el Sami has, of necessity, been blind to the progress of the One Church over the last few years." The Most High jerked me to my feet, then turned to study the column coming down the road. "Nevertheless, we should assume that he is right."

"What?" Jabbar glared at me as though I had put the words into Haroun's mouth. "You have gone as mad as the spy!"

The Most High lifted his chin. "You speak as though that would be a bad thing, Jabbar."

His Deadliness glared at Haroun, grinding his teeth as he thought how to disguise his mistake. Cyric had claimed the mantle of God of Madness, and now no pious man would speak of lunacy as anything but a divine gift. This was one of many reforms that had occurred during my long sojourn outside Candlekeep, and while I was wise enough not to say so—or even to think it very often—my duty as a faithful chronicler compels me to admit that I regarded the change as dubiously as did Jabbar.

After a long silence, His Deadliness fixed a cobra's smile upon me. "We all revere Madness. That is clear by our respect for Malik. But the battlefield is no place for whimsy. If Loviatar sends her monks against us, we will be trapped against the tor—"

"Which will drive our men up the road all the faster." The Most High waved his scepter's iron starburst toward the east, where the sun now sat the full span of a hand above the horizon. "In the meantime, the morning is passing. We agreed to attack at dawn so the sun would be in our enemy's eyes. If we await the arrival of Loviatar's disciples, the time will be gone."

"Then we will attack tomorrow," said Jabbar.

"And call it off again when another column arrives?"

Seeing that the Dark Lords were falling into another of their arguments, I retreated into the throng and slipped away, as was my custom. I had not been away from court so long that I

13

failed to see my position in these matters, or why the Caliph had asked me to stand in his place instead of one of his many sons. The moment I showed favor toward Haroun, Jabbar would slay me out of hand, and the moment I favored Jabbar, Haroun would do the same. I had lived this long only because no one else had seen the *Cyrinishad* or its bearers—and also because of the special arrangements I had made, secretly promising each Dark Lord to help him recover the book before the other.

That I had sworn these things in Cyric's name bothered me not at all. As God of Strife, the One and All would applaud my resourcefulness. And the truth was this: that I thought neither Dark Lord worthy of the *Cyrinishad*.

I had returned from my years of spying to find the One Church splintered into many factions—just as the Ebon Spur was split into the factions of Haroun's Black Helms and Jabbar's Purple Lancers—and this filled me with a terrible disgust. I saw how this strife weakened the church and its men of stature, and I feared that all my suffering had been in vain, that I would never have it in my power to repay the kindness of the prince.

Then a vision came to me.

I saw myself standing beneath a roiling sky. Spread before me was a vast host of True Believers, the number of which far exceeded all the grains of sand in the Desert of Calim. The sacred *Cyrinishad* floated before me, opened to the first page, and I read from it in a voice like thunder. All who heard my words understood that I spoke in the name of Cyric, that I was the One True Prophet, and that the Fates themselves had chosen me, Malik el Sami yn Nasser, to bring all True Believers together beneath a single dark mantle!

Then the vision faded, and I perceived that my destiny lay in my own hands. All I wanted could be mine: to be lord of a hundred kingdoms, master of caravans beyond number, captain of all the fleets in the sea, to repay the prince's kindness a thousand times over. I had only to recover the *Cyrinishad* and spread its truth across the lands.

My thoughts still reeling with this vision, I emerged from the throng of Haroun's guards and stepped to the front of the knoll. On the plain below, the fire giants of the Scarlet Fellowhood had dropped their iron ram. The shock riders of the Ebon Spur stood beside their impatient mounts, struggling to calm them. The Cloak Wood orcs milled about, gnashing tusks and picking lice from their scalps. The wizards of Tunland's Ravagers stood behind the Sable Daggers, amusing themselves with will-o'-the-wisps and clouds of dancing smoke. The hour of attack had come and gone. A fan of golden light hung low over Candlekeep's copper-roofed towers, shooting out across the Sea of Swords to illuminate a flock of birds flying in from the bay.

As I watched, the flock wheeled and spiraled down toward Candlekeep, their wings flashing silver in the morning light. The descent seemed too slow; then I saw that they were much higher than I had realized, and so much larger—nearly the size of horses. Their bodies were square, and when their profiles were silhouetted against the darker sky of the west, some appeared to have two heads.

My stomach grew cold and full, for I knew of only one kind of bird that had two heads—the kind that carried a rider.

I spun round and hurried toward the rear of the hill, shoving through Haroun's guards with no regard for their curses. We had to attack that very moment, while the flying beasts were still exhausted by the long journey from whence they had come—Waterdeep, perhaps, or some place even more distant. The gods of our enemies were calling forces from all across Faerûn, for they were not idiots; while Oghma's magic denied them any knowledge of the *Cyrinishad*'s location, they had guessed the battle stakes as soon as the Ebon Spur rode north to siege Candlekeep.

I returned to find the Dark Lords still arguing.

"They mean to attack us!" boomed Jabbar. He pointed at the Loviatar's company, which had stopped ten arrowflights up the road. "Why else do they not send a messenger?"

"Because they are proud warriors who await an invitation!"

Haroun growled. I made to interrupt the argument, but stopped when the Most High exploded, "What I do not understand is your reluctance to do as we are charged! Did the Dark Sun not bid us destroy that Citadel of Lies and recover his sacred book?"

"He bade us bring Candlekeep low, not let ourselves be smashed against its walls."

"As I thought!" Haroun sneered. "You would wait for Candlekeep to fall of old age and call that obedience! Once again, you use the letter of the charge to ignore the spirit!"

"The spirit is not to get ourselves destroyed!" Jabbar huffed out his breath, signaling his unyielding resolve.

With no thought to the ire I was sure to raise in His Deadliness, I boldly stepped up to the Dark Lords. "If I may—"

"I'll order the attack without you!" exclaimed Haroun, drowning me out.

I waved my hand, but the pair failed to notice.

"Without me?" Jabbar scoffed. "Without me, you'll be lucky if your own Black Helms take up the charge!"

Again I stepped forward, and now I stood between the pair. My head came barely to their shoulders, yet so bold was the intrusion that both men fell to glaring at me. I turned to Jabbar and addressed him in a manner both firm and inoffensive.

"Your Most Lethal Deadliness, pray excuse my interruption, but as the Finder of the Book and he who stands in the Caliph's place, I must agree with Most High Haroun. The Monks of the White Rod pose no danger to us." I did not mention the flying cavalry; far be it from me to suggest I knew something the Dark Lords did not. "We must attack now."

Jabbar's eyes grew as empty as a fish's, and his brow wrinkled as though he could not understand why I thought my opinion mattered. My knees began to tremble, but I gave no thought to recanting my words. To let him delay the attack would be worse than death—it would be to lose the *Cyrinishad*.

Jabbar's voice turned as cold as a crypt. "Did you say something, Sly One?"

"I d-did." My tongue, never as brave as my heart, stumbled over the words. "Most P-P-Potent Deadliness, we must attack now."

Jabbar's mouth fell open, then he began to assail me with many insults, the worst of which are too terrible to recount here. "You fat little lunatic! You bug-eyed insect! You filthy, unwashed groveler of pig sties! Betray me, will you?"

I heard the swish of Jabbar's silken robe and glimpsed the rise of his scepter. Knowing I would not live to see my vision come true, I fell to my knees and began to pray. Time raced on, and yet it also seemed to slow, and all that happened next occurred in the space of a single instant: A streak of feathered darkness shot from the mouth of the iron skull on Jabbar's scepter, and Most High Haroun bent forward to seize my arm.

"Stand up, you—"

The Most High's command ended in a gasp, then he raised his hand to touch a small puncture in his neck. A ribbon of smoke was curling from the tiny hole, and the skin around the wound had already grown dark and puffy with poison. I grew queasy and weak at the sight, for I knew that Jabbar had meant his needle for me.

Haroun's anger poured forth in an incoherent rasp, then he flung himself past me, scepter raised to strike. A dozen of Jabbar's bodyguards leapt forward to intercept him, but they were too slow. The Most High's holy starburst found its mark, driving an iron point clear through the skull of His Deadliness Jabbar.

The starburst flashed crimson. Jabbar's mouth fell open and poured forth a cloud of vile-smelling smoke, all that remained of the matter that had once filled his head.

Then the Dark Lords came together, each as lifeless as the other, and before their bodies hit the ground, a wall of Haroun's bodyguards swept past me to crash into Jabbar's men. The hilltop erupted in a frenzy of clanging steel and screaming warriors. From all around came the slash of ripping flesh and the crackle of splintering bones and the thud of falling bodies. I covered my ears and pressed my head tight to the ground, trying to escape the terrible sounds—not because they sickened me or made me fear for my life, but on account of what they meant. With each death rattle, each prayer that died upon a warrior's lips, each drop of blood that trickled into the ground, the *Cyrinishad* grew more distant. This knowledge filled me with such an anger that I feared I would leap up and get myself killed!

Fortunately, a pair of armored bodies fell across my back and held me down. For a time, I lay half-crushed beneath them, wheezing for breath and waging battle with my angry heart. Haroun and Jabbar lay less than two paces away, the Most High still sprawled over His Deadliness, all but hidden beneath a mound of dead and dying bodyguards. I called a thousand curses upon their names, and prayed their spirits would simmer in the Boiling Sea a thousand years. Their rivalry had cost me the *Cyrinishad,* and in my ire I could not see why Cyric had suffered either one to command his Faithful, much less the pair together!

Then I spied two glints of yellow in the shadowy tangle beside Haroun and Jabbar. The glimmers came from their scepters of office, still grasped in their cold hands. I recalled my vision and saw again the great host of True Believers standing before me, and I perceived what a fool I had been to question the ways of Cyric the All.

I struggled to rise, but could not escape the press of bodies upon my back. The ground began to rumble as though it would open. Taking this to be a sign of the One's anger at my weakness, I clawed desperately at the ground—and dragged myself forward an inch. A deep lowing joined the rumble, and then an angry snorting and the clang of clashing weapons. My heart sank, for this noise was no holy sign; it was the sound of the Ebon Spur riding into battle.

With a fury born of panic, I redoubled my clawing and began to kick, and at last I freed myself of the corpses. Then, seeing that all the warriors nearby were too busy killing each other to pay me any heed, I crawled toward the Dark Masters. The stench of death was horrid, for bodies were never meant to spill all their contents, but I clenched my teeth and burrowed into the steaming heap like a dog after a badger. A bodyguard wailed in pain as I pushed aside his shattered leg. I slid between two breastplates slick with blood, passing faceless lips that moaned for help, and at last the golden staffs lay within reach. I stretched my hand forward and grasped Haroun's scepter.

It issued no warning scorch, nor did it discharge a heart-stopping shock. The scepter slipped free of the Most High's dead grasp, then gave a soft pop as I wrenched the iron starburst from Jabbar's head. I drew the staff to my chest and tucked it into the rope that served as my belt, then pushed Haroun's arm aside so I could reach Jabbar's scepter.

A hand, warm and slick with blood, clamped my forearm. I was so startled that I screamed and pulled away, but the hand held fast. I heard a heart beating, low and fast and mean, and I did not think it was my own. My blood cooled, for it was said that Dark Lords could come back from the dead to avenge themselves.

"I beg . . . you." The words were wispy and weak, and I had not spoken them. I felt a great relief, for Jabbar would never beg. "Help . . . me."

"As you wish," I replied. "But first you must let go."

Still the bloody fingers held fast. Lacking the strength to break the fellow's death grip, I slipped my free hand inside my beggar's cloak, then drew forth the small hooked dagger that I always carried in a concealed place.

"Here is your help!"

I slashed the blade across the clutching hand. The warrior cried out and loosened his grip. I twisted my arm free, then snatched the scepter from Jabbar's dead grasp and began to squirm backward. When at last I freed myself from the stinking heap, my ears filled with thunder—the sound of charging war bulls.

I staggered to my feet and turned. Less then fifty paces away, a pair of the beasts were pounding across the hilltop in my direction, their black horns rocking up and down, their hooves

19

pummeling the dead and wounded alike. On their backs sat two officers, one a Black Helm and the other a Purple Lancer, flailing at each other with an axe and a morningstar.

I scrambled up a pile of bodies and raised the golden scepters above my head. "In the name of Cyric the All, stop!"

The riders continued forward, and I saw that only a few of the Dark Lords' bodyguards still remained standing, fighting each other in scattered pockets all across the gore-strewn hilltop. But the two troops of the Ebon Spur were flooding onto the knoll, their blades and hammers filling the air with a clamorous din. I could not see over them to tell what the rest of our army was doing, but it alarmed me greatly to notice a dark line of the enemy's flying mounts streaming down from Candlekeep.

I brought the scepters together above my head, creating the sacred starburst and skull of Our Lord Cyric. The war bulls continued to pound across the hilltop, the lead pair still thundering in my direction. The riders were cursing and grunting, oblivious to anything except their clanging weapons, but the bulls fixed their eyes on the holy scepters and came charging toward me as though I were taunting them with red flags.

I stood where I was, weak in the knees but trusting in the protection of Almighty Cyric. "By this hallowed symbol, stop!"

So close were the bulls that I saw their nostrils spraying steam. My knees would have buckled, had a peal of thunder not broken across the sky and shocked the strength back into my legs. I glimpsed the enemy's flying beasts diving out of the sky—they were fantastic creatures with the heads of eagles and the bodies of winged horses—then I saw a silver bolt flash from the lead beast down toward the plain.

The bulls reached my gruesome pulpit and continued forward, veering apart only slightly as they plowed over the tangle of limbs and torsos. The riders leaned inward and continued their battle, creating an arc of flashing steel before my eyes.

"For the *Cyrinishad*, Mighty Cyric, make me brave!" I separated the two halves of the starburst and skull and, having no idea what magic might pour forth from the staves, pointed one scepter at each of the charging bulls. "Stop, I command you!"

There was nothing, for Cyric had turned his back on me, or so I believed. Before I could flee, the beasts were beside me, filling my ears with a booming tempest of hooves and hearts and snorting breath. I could not keep from cowering. The bulls, always quick to seize on any weakness, lowered their heads.

A searing pain lanced deep into my stomach. I rose into the sky and glimpsed below me a purple-clad rider sitting astride a bull. I closed my eyes and felt myself rise further still. For a moment, I could hear every sound in the battle with perfect clarity: every chiming blade, every crunching bone, every last gasping curse. I heard the feathers of the enemy's eagle-horses beating the air, the thrum of the foot companies scattering through the salt grass, the bellowing of fire giants lying scorched and torn upon the plain. I thought I would rise until I reached the heavens and never come down.

Then I heard the crash of my shoulders slamming into the ground, the crunch and hiss of my broken body rolling down the slope, the wail of my own voice:

"Why have you done this, Cyric My Lord?"

I smashed into a boulder and came to a rest bent around it backward, blood gushing from the wound in my stomach. By some miracle, my quaking hands still grasped the scepters of the starburst-and-skull. The sun had already risen high above the eastern horizon, and I felt it beating down on my face, a hot disk of mocking golden light. The sounds of battle grew distant, until the silence became so profound I could hear nothing but the low, dead pulse of my own heart.

"Why did you leave us, My Dark Lord?"

The disk of light vanished. I was foolish enough to believe Cyric had answered and turned my face into the darkness.

It was only an eagle-horse swooping across the sky, its outstretched wings blocking the sun like those of some great fiend risen from the pit to carry me to Cyric's palace. The beast wheeled low over my head, and I saw a man in leather

21

armor holding the reins. Behind him sat a smaller figure, her head swaddled in a purple scarf and her body cloaked in dark robes. I could see her eyes, rimmed in kohl and as black as the veil that hid her face, scanning the battlefield. Her hands began to move.

She was calling to me, I thought, casting her spell. I imagined her voice rustling inside my skull, beckoning to me, bidding the Finder of the Book to stand and show himself.

It might be wiser, I decided, just to close my eyes.

Two

I am but a man, and no man may perceive everything that occurs in the world and in the boundless heavens above. Only the gods see all, and when it serves their purpose, they will sometimes brighten a mortal's mind with their perfect knowledge. Know then that the following accounts, like many others describing events I could not have witnessed personally, are gifts of the One. Long after my days as a spy came to their end, Our Dark Lord graced my thoughts with an exact knowledge of all that occurred during the search for the holy *Cyrinishad,* whether or not I had seen it with my own eyes, and even if it happened in the heavens above where no man may see.

I bear no blame for the many blasphemies of speech and thought contained in these accounts. These lies belong only to those who spawned them, and I swear they are a great offense to my ears! I include them only because it is my duty to present a complete and faithful chronicle of the search for the holy *Cyrinishad.* I pray you, Almighty Cyric, One and All, do not torment your poor servant for doing as he is bound!

* * * * *

After the companies of Most High Haroun and His Deadliness Jabbar destroyed each other, what remained of Cyric's army fled across the plain in ten directions at once: south toward the Cloud Peaks and east toward Beregost and north toward the Cloak Woods, and in all directions but west, where loomed the towers of Candlekeep and the raging Sea of Swords. The eagle-horses wheeled over the field, their riders hurling fireballs and lightning bolts, True Believers scattering before them as sheep before wolves. Only the Company of the Ebon Spur did not flee, for it had become a crimson tangle on the knoll where Jabbar and Haroun had fallen. The bodies of men and beasts lay as deep as a man's shoulders, and their steaming blood cascaded from the summit in glistening streams. A dozen bulls staggered over the heap, lowing for their dead masters, while the warriors who had not yet expired prayed to Cyric in voices hoarse with pain.

All this did fickle Tempus, God of War, see from his home in faraway Limbo. The sight charged his heart with such a fury that he smashed his gauntleted hand against his iron throne, and fields of battle quaked all across Faerûn. Pikemen lost their footing and exposed whole flanks to the charging enemy. Loyal war-horses stumbled and fell, pitching their riders to the mercy of their foes. Castle walls crumbled and cracked, and besieging armies poured through the breaches to pillage and plunder.

The Battle Lord paid no heed to these calamities, for war is won as often through accidents of destiny as through acts of courage. But when he thought of the valiant warriors slain before Candlekeep, stilled by the blades of their own fellows, and of the epic contest that might have been, again Tempus felt his anger rising. It erupted with the rumble of a hundred thunderclaps, and the Numberless Hosts that did battle in his vast halls shrank from the ire of their god. They lowered their blades and turned to tremble before his throne. For the first time since the Time of Troubles, the Eternal War fell quiet.

A slender elf emerged from the shadows of a far corner and started across the debris. He wore a cloak of dark gloom, and though he crossed many heaps of crumpled armor and trod upon the shards of countless broken weapons, he moved in utter silence and never caused a sound. Nor did his feet leave any track, though he often walked through pools of fresh blood and stepped in piles of steaming gore.

The elf stopped before the throne of Tempus and bowed low. "When mighty Tempus is robbed, I would expect him to strike down the thief—not vent his anger upon the mortals who serve his cause." The words were as wispy as a yard of silk, and so soft they seemed a mere thought. "But I often expect more than I should."

Tempus, garbed as always in little more than his battered breastplate and war helm, regarded the intruder in sullen silence. Though the Battle Lord's visor was lowered and had no slits for seeing, his gaze sent a shudder down the visitor's spine. Such was the horror of War, that its face was too terrible to look upon and its stare too withering to bear.

Tempus leaned forward in his great throne and loomed over the elf, who stood no higher than the Battle Lord's knee. "What you expect is no concern of mine, Shadowflea." He did not ask how this visitor had passed through his castle's defenses; though Mask was feeble by the measure of gods, no ward or hasp could lock out the God of Thieves. "And when I am robbed, I shall strike *you* down before any mortal."

Mask rose from his bow, and his gloom-shrouded features changed to those of an elven female. "Then you shall be doubly robbed, first of what is already lost, and next of a loyal ally."

"You could never be loyal, and I take no allies." Tempus made no comment on his visitor's transformation, for he knew that the Shadowlord changed appearances constantly to evade his many pursuers. One of these pursuers Mask feared above all others, and the Battle Lord could not resist a taunt. "Perhaps you should say what you came to say. Is that not Kezef I hear baying?"

Mask cringed and looked over both shoulders, and Tempus chuckled darkly. Many years before, during the turbulent times of the *Cyrinishad*'s creation, the God of Thieves had tried to sic Kezef the Chaos Hound on Cyric. Of course, the One had countered this plan easily, nearly destroying the Shadowlord in a mighty blast. Kezef had arrived on the heels of the explosion, angered by Mask's bid to manipulate him and eager to take vengeance. The Shadowlord had fled so quickly that, for a time, even his fellow deities had thought him destroyed in the blast.

When Mask saw that Tempus had deceived him, his features brightened to the color of a fair-skinned girl. "The god of war makes a joke," said the Shadowlord. "How unexpected."

Tempus sat back, his eyeless glare still fixed on Mask's ever-changing face. "I have more humor than patience this day, Shadowcrab."

"As well you might, given what Cyric has stolen from you."

"Stolen?" Tempus noted the quiet that had fallen over his battle hall. With a mere thought, he ordered the Eternal War resumed, then snorted, "Cyric could not steal the feculence from my cesspits. That lunatic has done nothing in years but ponder his own lies."

"Just so, but Cyric has robbed you." Mask's visage changed to that of a long-snouted troll. "He has robbed you so well you do not blame him, though his guilt is as plain as the nose on my face. In too many places, diplomats are bargaining fairly, second princes are content in their positions, foes are keeping treaties made in good faith. This is Cyric's doing. Is he not the god of murder, strife, and intrigue? Is it not his duty to spread these things across Faerûn? And yet, they are vanishing everywhere—everywhere but within his own church."

Tempus nodded. "Peace has spread like a disease across the continent—and without the usual aid of Sune or Lliira."

A crescent of yellow teeth shone in the gloom beneath Mask's long troll nose. "We are in agreement, then."

"We have noted the same condition," Tempus said. "But to say we agree implies we are allies, and I remember how you betrayed both sides during the debacle of the *Cyrinishad*."

"You dare chastise *me* for vacillating? The God of War, who favors one side at dusk and another at dawn?"

Tempus folded his arms. "Such is the nature of war. I make no claim otherwise, and that is why I make no alliances."

"But you *are* unhappy with events at Candlekeep. You were robbed of an epic battle by Cyric's incompetence. His priests are more adept at murdering each other than at spreading

26

strife across the land." Mask had taken the stocky form of an orc, and nothing showed in his shadowy face except two gleaming pig's eyes. "Unless matters change, war will become a thing of the past on Faerûn—and you with it."

Tempus felt his anger stir once more, but he resisted the urge to pound the arm of his throne. If he tipped the balance of battle yet again and so quickly, he might dampen the fighting, and already there were too few good wars raging across Faerûn.

"I know what Cyric's incompetence has cost me," Tempus said. "And I know why you are here. But if I lash out in vengeance—"

"Not lash out," Mask said. "That would accomplish nothing, save to draw your foes into a battle there is no need to fight."

Tempus locked his visored gaze on the God of Thieves. Mask's form shifted from orc to dwarf, but the Battle Lord still did not see the meaning behind the Shadowlord's words.

"What are you suggesting?"

At that moment a howl echoed through the hall, and though its source lay outside the Battle Lord's palace, it was loud and shrill, piercing the din of the Eternal War as cleanly as the blare of an unholy trumpet. The Shadowlord's flesh rippled and turned pale. Tempus saw a puny halfling with pink eyes and skin as white as alabaster, then Mask remembered himself and took the form of an eight-foot gnoll.

"You must assemble the Circle of Twelve." Mask spoke rapidly and edged away from the direction of the howl. "Accuse Cyric of neglecting his godly duties."

"Call a trial council?" Tempus paid no attention to Kezef's impending arrival; the Chaos Hound was Mask's concern. "We cannot intrude upon Cyric's affairs. Ao would never hear of it!"

"He will—if enough of you ask." Mask's gaze darted over his shoulder. "You are not the only great god who suffers because of Cyric's neglect. After the debacle at Candlekeep, Talos the Destroyer and the Nightbringer Shar both have reason to stand against him. And you can be certain Mystra and Kelemvor will support you; their hatred for Cyric will blind them to how his incompetence benefits their cause."

Another howl broke over the hall, this one as shrill as finger bones scratching at iron walls.

Mask shuddered and became an amorphous blob. "Of the twelve gods in the Circle, you can already count the support of five. Just one more is enough to guarantee victory, for Cyric will never deign to attend, and Tyr will hold himself above the polling as judge." Mask raised his shadowy hand, and a parchment scroll appeared in his grasp. "I have spelled it out for you here. Even if Ao denies your petition, he will take action himself. He must, for the very Balance is threatened!"

"All you say is true enough." Tempus spoke slowly, for he enjoyed watching Mask twitch and ripple, and he wished to see whether the Shadowlord's fear of Kezef was greater than his hatred of Cyric. "Yet, your plots have a way of rebounding on those who take part in them."

Mask lowered his eyes. "In the past I have had a weakness for intrigue, I admit." His shadowy head took the form of a two-faced human, one visage turned in Tempus's direction, the other keeping watch for the Chaos Hound. "But I am better now. That is why I came to you directly, instead of trying to . . . 'arrange' the trial through other means."

A great moan rolled through the hall, echoing off the iron walls rather than passing through them, and Tempus knew the Chaos Hound had entered his palace.

Mask started forward, holding out the parchment scroll.

Tempus raised a gauntlet, bidding him wait. "And when Cyric is stripped of power, you will be there to claim what he loses?"

Mask glanced toward the dark corner from which he had come. "I want only what I lost to him—my dominion over Intrigue—and perhaps the small boon of Lies, if my service proves worthy."

"That is not in my power to grant," Tempus said. "Even if the trial goes against him—"

"I ask only that you suggest it." Mask's words were soft and quick, and his shadowy figure changed with every one, as though switching forms might hide him from the keen nose of Kezef. "And I ask that you stand by your charges. Once you lodge your complaints, it will be too late to change our course."

A deep, profane snarl rumbled through the battle hall and drowned out the din of clanging steel. A beast the size of a war-horse emerged from the far corner. It resembled a giant mastiff with black-crusted fangs and a shimmering coat of maggots.

Mask trembled so violently his form grew blurry and indistinct, but he did not flee. "Do I have your promise?"

The Chaos Hound cocked his head, then swung his massive snout toward the Shadowlord and snuffled. Threads of poison-laced drool fell from his chomping maw.

Tempus nodded. "I give you my word."

Kezef charged.

Mask tossed the scroll at Tempus and leaped over a pile of warriors and disappeared into a shadowy corner.

The Chaos Hound streaked between two ranks of charging cavalry, then bounded over a knot of grappling footmen. He shoved through a tangle of blood-spattered knights, flashed past Tempus's throne, and disappeared into the shadows after Mask.

The Battle Lord sat watching the Eternal War for a moment, then opened the scroll Mask had thrown him. The Shadowlord's plans always made him uneasy, but Tempus would convene the Circle of Twelve. The Battle Lord rarely gave his word, but when he did, he always kept it.

Three

The great gods of the Circle of Twelve gathered in the Pavilion of Cynosure—eleven in all, for Cyric the One was not among them. The Battle Lord Tempus arrived first, followed by Mystra, Lady Magic, and her lover Kelemvor, Lord Death. Then came Talos the Destroyer and Shar the Nightbringer, Goddess of Loss and of all the wicked things men do under cover of darkness—a pair upon whose support the Battle Lord was counting. And too there was Chauntea, Goddess of Bountiful Nature, along with her paramour Lathander the Morninglord, who appeared in a streak of golden light. Never to be outshone, Sune, Goddess of Beauty and Love, appeared in a flash of flame as red as her hair. Silvanus Treefather, God of Wild Nature, also saw fit to attend, as did Oghma, thieving God of Wisdom. Tyr, the eyeless God of Justice, came to act as judge. Though many called him Tyr the Evenhanded, this was something of a joke, as his right arm ended in a stump.

The gods did not "arrive" in the pavilion so much as turn their attention upon it, for deities are more energy than body and can manifest themselves anywhere with little more than a thought. By dividing their concentration, they can perform many tasks at once, or "travel" between locations in an instant. But their abilities are not entirely without limits; they can divide their attention only so many times, and the greater their exertion in any one place, the more of their attention they must concentrate there.

The Pavilion of Cynosure appeared different to each god.

30

Chauntea the Great Mother perceived it as a lush and fragrant garden, burgeoning with dew-kissed blossoms of impossible brilliance. Shar the Nightbringer saw a dark cavern where no light could shine, filled with barbed stalactites and hidden abysses that seethed with pains long buried but never forgotten. To Mystra, Lady of Magic, the pavilion was an alchemist's laboratory, strewn with simmering beakers and jars packed with arcane spell components.

The gods saw each other as differently as they saw the pavilion itself, each in accordance with his or her own nature. Mystra saw her companions as wizards of awesome power, cloaked in robes spun from the shimmering energies of the Magic Weave. In turn, Tempus envisioned her as a valkyrie armored in gleaming plate of the purest silver. Oghma the Wise viewed her as a young sage, while Talos the Destroyer saw her as an annihilating whirlwind of magic that left havoc wherever she went.

But Mystra did not know how Kelemvor, Lord of the Dead, saw her—perhaps as a skeleton of polished ivory, or a mummy wrapped in golden silk. She had asked him once, in a quiet moment alone, and he had refused to answer, saying only that he regretted some things about becoming a god.

When these eleven had come to the pavilion as gods do, they waited. Two places remained empty in the circle. The first was a large gap between Oghma and Chauntea; it was always left open in acknowledgment of Ao's eternal presence. A smaller space lay between Talos and Shar, the space reserved for Almighty Cyric, the One and the All. Although the Dark Sun had not deigned to attend any circle in many years, the gods stood in such awe of his power that they did not dare begin before allowing him a few moments to appear.

When it grew clear that Cyric had chosen not to grace their meeting with his presence, Tyr the Evenhanded gazed around the pavilion, lingering upon each of the gods until he caught their eye. Slowly, the chamber fell silent.

Tyr the Just turned his empty eye sockets in the direction of fickle Tempus. "I believe you called us here, Foehammer?"

Tempus walked to the heart of the pavilion, which he saw as a war room cluttered with maps and markers. Most of the other gods remained in their places, arranged in a circle, although some created chairs in which to sit or couches upon which to lie. Ever restless, Talos the Destroyer and Sune Firehair began to wander about, Talos tearing map corners and Sune pausing at every shiny surface to study her own reflection. No god scowled at their behavior, for it was no more in their nature to hold still than it would have been in Shar's to step into the light.

Tempus raised one armored fist and smashed it into the palm of the other. "I have had enough of Cyric the All!" he declared. "The time has come to strip him of his powers. Give me the word, and I will muster my thousands to storm the Shattered Keep and drag that mad god from his throne!"

Tempus offered no explanation of his charges and presented no evidence to back them up. He had done all that as he summoned the others to the pavilion, and the Battle Lord was not one to repeat himself. He spun in a slow circle, glaring at each god in turn. "Who will stand with me?"

Tempus turned to Shar and Talos, then waved his palm through the air before their eyes, leaving in its wake an image of the plain before Candlekeep. Though the battle between Jabbar and Haroun was not yet an hour gone, already Kelemvor's carrion-eating harbingers had turned the knoll black with their gleaming feathers. On the plain before Candlekeep, hundreds of bodies lay scattered through the salt grass, struck down from behind as they fled the madness that had seized the Ebon Spur. "Even now, your worshipers lie dying in the field, betrayed by Cyric's madness."

"You bound ahead of yourself, Foehammer," said Tyr the Eyeless. "We cannot levy the punishment without giving a verdict, and we cannot give a verdict until we have debated the charge."

"Speak for yourself, No-Eyes!" exclaimed Talos. He overturned a table, sending a parchment that was to Tyr a law scroll and to Tempus a war map fluttering to the floor. "We have had too much of Cyric already! We know the charge and we know the verdict. I stand with you, Tempus! My bolts and my quakes will level the Mad One's twisted castle, my winds scatter his Faithful to the thousand Planes!"

Tyr waved his stump at the Destroyer. "Your rancor has no place here, Stormstar. Our duty is to preserve the Balance, not annihilate it."

The Nightbringer Shar leaned forward in her chair, spreading a stain of darkness before her. "In this case, Blind One, it seems clear that what Tempus proposes is in the best interests of the Balance." Her voice was but a whisper, like a terrible thought that had lain long-buried until a moment of weakness. "It is not Talos's rage that threatens the Balance, but the Mad One's neglect. Cyric has fallen victim to the lies in his own book, and now he can think of nothing but himself."

Tyr sat back and made no reply. The discussion had swung to deliberating the charges, and he was content to let it proceed.

Tempus said, "Cyric fosters his creed only among his own Faithful and neglects his duty to spread his tenets to the rest of Faerûn." He faced Mystra's side of the table. "Strife and murder, lies and intrigue, deception and betrayal—all these are becoming things of the past. Even his own worshipers spend all their energy slaying and plotting against each other."

"And while the Church of Cyric devours itself, our Faithful suffer," added Shar. "If wives never lie to their husbands, nor husbands betray their wives, if men never covet their kin's treasure, nor clansmen murder one another in the night, how then can I nurture the hidden jealousies and secret hatreds that inspire men to greatness? How can I feed the dark bitterness of their souls, that ever keeps them striving for more glory, more gold, more power?"

"All you say is true," said Chauntea. The Great Mother spoke in a voice both warm and reassuring. "Yet I cannot support your solution. Would it not be better to help him, to guide him out of this maze in which he has wandered?"

"Absolutely not!"

It surprised Mystra to hear her own voice echoing off the pavilion's pillars, for she had not meant to shout—or even to speak. As much as she despised Cyric, the mere fact that Tempus, Shar, and Talos demanded his downfall made her reluctant to join the call. They formed a triad of war, darkness, and destruction, and whatever they were planning, she did not think it likely to benefit the people of Faerûn.

"Would you care to elaborate?" asked Oghma. He stood beside Mystra, on the side opposite Kelemvor, and he spoke in a voice as smooth and melodious as the strings of the bards who sang his praises. "Perhaps you want Cyric to stay the way he is?"

"Perhaps I do. He is more dangerous sane than mad."

"Dangerous to the Balance, or to the people of Faerûn?" asked Lathander. As always, the Morninglord stood beside the Great Mother Chauntea, eager to lend his support to her every word. "We all know how much better life has become for mortals since Cyric began to neglect his duties. Whether he is replaced or cured, their lot can only grow harder."

"A hard life can also be a good life," observed Chauntea. "Yet, Lady Mystra is like a mother who loves her children too well. She cannot bear to see them hurt, and so would prefer to keep matters as they are."

That was exactly what Mystra would have preferred, but she knew better than to say so.

"Well?" prompted Oghma.

"We all know what would have happened if we had let Cyric keep the *Cyrinishad*," Mystra replied. She turned a stern glare on Talos, who was casually splintering a chair with his fingernails. "Which only makes me wonder why Talos and Shar were trying to help him recover it."

"Yes," said Oghma. "I'd like to hear your explanation."

The Destroyer shrugged. "It was something to do."

"As for me," hissed Shar, "I was only trying to help. Surely, you can all see that our best hope of saving the Mad One is to lure him back with his precious book."

"I suspect you were less interested in saving Cyric than in

bribing him to support your war against the Moonmaiden," said Oghma. "That is a dangerous game to play, Night-bringer—a very dangerous game."

"Which is all the more reason to destroy him," said Tempus. He stomped across the pavilion to stand before Kelemvor, who had not yet spoken. "How say you, Death Lord?"

Before Kelemvor could reply, Oghma leaned in front of Mystra. "Think well, Kelemvor. Remember who you are, not who you were. Old grudges have no place here."

Of all the deities gathered in the pavilion, the God of Death hated the One most fiercely. Long ago, Kelemvor, Cyric, and Mystra, who was called Midnight at the time, lived on Faerûn as mortals. With them walked a priest named Adon, now the high priest of Mystra's church. Then came the Time of Troubles, when two gods stole the Tablets of Fate and Lord Ao grew so angry that he cast the gods from the heavens. Through a strange turn of events, the four mortals discovered the Tablets. Cyric saw at once that he and his companions might demand anything they wished in return for these arti-facts, but his cowardly friends did not share his vision. They tried to stop him, and the One was forced to kill Kelemvor. Ao rewarded Cyric by making him the God of Death, and the One arranged for the woman Midnight to become Goddess of Magic. Seething with jealousy, Kelemvor's dead spirit lurked hidden for many years, until the moment came when he took his vengeance by rising up and leading the spirits of the dead in rebellion against the One. Thus did Kelemvor overthrow Cyric and usurp the Throne of Death, claiming for his own the fickle heart of the harlot Mystra.

All this Kelemvor remembered when Oghma spoke to him, and his hatred grew hotter than before. "I stand with Tempus," he said. "Cyric must die."

Tempus turned to Mystra. "And you, Lady Magic? How say you?"

To Mystra's ear, the Battle Lord sounded too certain of him-self. He had thought this through with great care, and the rage he affected was not as spontaneous as he feigned.

"I say the matter is not for us to decide," she said. Mystra glanced at Kelemvor and saw the surprise in his face, but she knew he would not attempt to dissuade her. They were not as Chauntea and Lathander; they kept separate their passion and their business as gods. "When it comes to the Balance, Lord Ao—"

"Has made plain we must follow our own callings," said Shar. "*That* preserves the Balance. Stand with Tempus or Chauntea, but you cannot leave matters as they are."

Mystra glanced at Oghma, hoping to find some support in his dark-skinned visage. As God of Wisdom, his opinion often swayed the Circle's decision, and she flattered him often enough that he usually supported her. But not this time. Oghma met her gaze long enough to shake his head, then looked away and said nothing.

Mystra turned back to Tempus, feeling that he had put into her mouth the words she was about to say. "I have borne witness to Cyric's treachery too often to make the mistake of aiding him. Given the choices, Tempus, I stand with you. Destroy Cyric."

"As I thought."

Tempus turned away without asking Oghma's opinion, for he already knew it. In his arrogance, Oghma would not destroy what he believed he could control.

"We are getting ahead of ourselves again," Tyr protested. "We have barely discussed the charge, and still the Battle Lord is leaping ahead to the punishment."

"The punishment is all we need discuss!" boomed Kelemvor. "No one disputes Cyric's condition. The only question is what to do about it."

When no one disagreed, Tempus looked past Chauntea and Lathander, seeking out the final vote he required. He stopped at Sune Firehair, who was at that moment admiring her reflection in a shield of polished gold. The Battle Lord's choice was a surprising one. The Goddess of Love shifted her passions like the wind, but she remained constant in the disdain she displayed for the ugliness of war's destruction.

Still, Tempus seemed entirely confident. "And how say you, Beautiful One?"

Sune acknowledged the compliment with a gleaming smile, then turned back to the golden shield and spoke to her own reflection. "We must do something, I agree that Cyric has eyes for no one but himself."

"Yes, but what action do we take?" asked Lathander.

The Morninglord rose from his couch and went to stand at Sune's side, bathing her in the golden radiance of his own smile. Tempus amazed the other gods by remaining silent and allowing Lathander to have his say.

"It would be so much more caring to help him find his way, do you not agree—Most Radiant Star?"

The Morninglord's adulation evoked a snort from Chauntea, which drew in turn an icy glare from Sune. The Goddess of Beauty raised her chin and graced Tempus with her most ravishing smile.

"I fear the Mad One must be destroyed," she purred. "Even when he was sane, Cyric never understood the power of beauty."

"Thank you, Beautiful One." Tempus turned to Eyeless Tyr. "That makes six votes in favor of destruction—a clear majority, given Cyric's absence."

Tempus had barely spoken before a great trembling seized the Pavilion of Cynosure. The gods saw the chamber around them grow flat and begin to warp, unraveling like a tapestry. The ceiling cracked and shattered, and the columns and the walls melted away. Gasps of surprise arose, but no god cried out in fear or panic. The pavilion did not dissolve often, but every member of the Circle knew what followed when it did: Ao was about to make his presence known.

The gods found themselves floating in a vast sea of emptiness, surrounded on all sides by a twinkling infinity of whirling stars. They began to drift away from the thousand aspects of their minds, from the facets of their being that answered the endless prayers of their worshipers, fulfilled their godly duties, and kept vigil over Faerûn. At last, only the core of their intellects remained, drifting aimlessly in a void so vast that no mere god could comprehend its enormity.

Powers of the Cynosure, you have taken it upon yourselves to condemn one of your own.

The words came from both inside each god and without, from deep within their breasts and down from the countless stars. Lord Ao did not show himself—at least not in any normal sense—yet they could feel him all around, as if he were the fabric that enveloped them, the air itself.

Despite the rebuke in Ao's tone, Mystra felt almost relieved. Surely, he would prevent the gods from meddling in Cyric's affairs, from either curing the Mad One or replacing him with someone more effective.

You presume to judge what is best for the Balance.

"We thought it necessary, Lord Ao." It was Tempus who spoke, and *still* he sounded confident. "In his madness, Cyric has turned inward. He has grown so self-absorbed that he does not foster the precepts of his godhood outside his own church."

"Mad?" came the reply.

Like Ao's voice, this one had no certain source. It was shrill and piercing, like an arrow through the throat, and it rang out from everywhere at once. "You call me mad! You, Tempus? You who hide your face behind a steel veil? You are mad, not I!"

"Cyric," Mystra whispered. She shuddered, for she could not imagine how the Prince of Madness had traveled to Ao's realm without being drawn through the Pavilion of Cynosure.

"Yes, Midnight," sneered the One's voice. "I am beyond you now. I am beyond you all—you who dare think yourselves great enough to destroy me—or to 'save' me."

Mystra shot a glance toward Tempus and saw the Battle Lord's shoulders sink. Whatever Cyric was doing, it had surprised the Foehammer as much as it had her. She looked next to Oghma. The Wise God's face paled, and his jaw hung slack.

Mystra looked away. To catch Oghma in such a state of bewilderment was akin to spying Sune in an instant of ugliness. Without realizing she had reached for it, the Goddess of

Magic found herself grasping Kelemvor's hand.

"Lord Ao?" Mystra asked. "Did you summon Cyric?"

"Summon me?" scoffed Cyric. "Fellows do not summon fellows!"

Fellows? boomed Ao. *Fellows! You dare compare yourself to me?*

"With whom else?" demanded Cyric. "I have raised myself as far above *them* as you were once above me!"

The stars dimmed, as though a cloud of mist had filled the infinite void.

Mystra slipped her hand from Kelemvor's grasp, and at last she began to feel the proper fear of the One and All. If Cyric could dim Ao's sparkling light, what could he not do?

The mist cleared, and the stars began to shine as brightly as before. *I see.*

It was then that Mystra understood even Lord Ao had his limits. Until that moment, Ao had not known how dangerous Cyric could be—and neither had she. Tempus was right; there was nothing to do except destroy Cyric—before he destroyed them.

And that is why they wish to kill you, Cyric? Because you are more powerful than they?

Mystra dared to interrupt. "Yes, Lord Ao."

She felt Kelemvor grab her arm and squeeze, urging her to be careful. Mystra would not remain silent. She had to make Lord Ao see that they could handle the situation for themselves, or he might replace Cyric with someone more capable—or worse still, simply cure the One's madness.

"We must kill Cyric," Mystra said. "We must destroy him, for he has made himself better than us!"

A sphere of wavering light appeared before Mystra's eyes, and in it she fancied she could see Cyric's gaunt face.

"You see how they envy me?" asked the sphere. "Is it any wonder I refuse to grace them with my presence?"

No wonder at all, replied Ao. *You have made yourself so much more powerful than they.*

"You sense it, too?" Cyric's head became solid. The face was white-fleshed and almost skeletal, with sunken eyes that shone from their sockets like two black suns. "You can feel how much I have grown?"

Indeed. And I can see that you are capable of dealing with your inferiors.

"Of course, but—"

Yet, there is one matter that disturbs me. I trust you will forgive me for interfering. Ao paused, as if for emphasis. *Tyr!*

"My liege?" The Just One's voice held the barest quiver.

If you are conducting a trial, you must observe the formalities. You, of all gods, should understand this.

Though Tyr had twice tried to steer the proceedings along a proper course, he simply lowered his chin. "Yes, my liege."

Good. When you begin the trial, one Faerûnian day hence, you will all *observe the rules. Now, what charge have you raised against Cyric?*

Tyr lifted his head and studied Cyric's dark eyes. "The charge shall be Innocence, I think."

"Innocence?" So loud and shrill was Cyric's shriek that several gods cringed. "But I am the Lord of Murder! The Prince of Lies! The Sower of Strife! The Master of Deception!"

"The charge is Innocence," Tyr declared. "Innocence by reason of Insanity."

Four

By the One, there is no pain greater than that of a man dying Faithless! How long I lay in the wicked sun on that blood-soaked hill, I cannot say. Where the bull's horn had pierced me, there was an ache as hot as white iron. A fever had dried my mouth until my swollen tongue blocked my throat, and though I could scarcely breathe, from my lips came these terrible words:

"Cyric, you are a tapeworm in the gut of the heavens!"

I meant them to the depths of my agonized soul. For years I had stood vigil, watching for the sacred *Cyrinishad,* doing all any mortal could to return it to my worthy god. Now the *Cyrinishad* was lost through no fault except Cyric's, who had filled his Church to bursting with chaos and discord. I cursed the One again! Now my vision would never be. I would never stand before that vast host of Believers to read from the sacred book, never return home to repay the prince and reclaim my fortune and my wife. My Dark Lord had failed me, and I felt as foolish as the sheep that follows its master to the slaughter.

I swore my lips would never again sing his praises.

A terrible fear seized me then, and my eyes turned to fountains, pouring forth their tears. I was a Faithless man at the brink of death. Soon my spirit would let go my flesh and sink beneath the stones and go down to that place where the gods claimed the souls of their Faithful. But I had closed my heart to Cyric. He would not answer my cries, and I would be left to wait until Kelemvor fetched me to the City of the Dead. I would be marched before the Crystal Throne and judged according to the deeds of my life, and the verdict would be most harsh indeed.

I fell to trembling and begged Cyric to take me back, but he had no use for cowards and would not hear my prayer. The wicked sun burned hotter still, and I had to close my eyes against the damning light.

I dreamed then of the many torments of the City of the Dead. Kelemvor stacked me in the Wall of the Faithless, where my head was stung by a hail of sleet and my feet scorched by the fires of the World Forge. He threw me into the Pool of Fools, where my eyes melted and my flesh dissolved in the Boiling Acid of Bliss. He laid me into the Road of Betrayers, where my skull was crushed and my bones broken beneath the Iron Wheels of Duty. All this I dreamed and more, until I had suffered the thousand torments of Kelemvor's city and knew all the tortures that awaited me there.

Then I awakened to yet another.

Inside my belly came a tugging and a miserable pain, as if a new-forged dagger had plunged deep into my wound. I saw that I had rolled onto my back. Night had fallen and the air had cooled, but I took no comfort in these things, for upon my chest stood one of Kelemvor's black-feathered harbingers. The vulture was silhouetted against the moon, its white eyes rimmed in crimson and its naked head smeared with carrion. The filthy thing had stuck its beak into my wound, and it was trying to pull a string of entrails from the hole!

Seeing the great haste Kelemvor was making to claim my spirit, I screamed in terror and pummeled the bird with my bare hands. The squalid beast spread its wings and began to flap—though it did not pull its beak from my wound. Had a volcano erupted in my belly, I would not have felt such pain! I imagined the bird rising like a kite on a string of my own entrails. Then I sat up at once, grabbed the wretched creature, and wrung its neck and flung its filthy corpse down the hill.

The night was as still as a painting, save for the distant lights flickering in the high windows of Candlekeep. The air reeked with the stench of battle, of blood and offal and all else that dying men spill, ripened by a day in the sun. Counting myself lucky I was not yet part of the rotting mass, I turned my thoughts to how I might survive.

First, I needed water. My whole body was aflame, my throat raw and swollen. Having lived near Candlekeep so long, I knew where to find springs, but even the closest lay too distant for a dying man to reach. But atop the hill lay the fallen riders of the Ebon Spur, and I had seen plenty of waterskins hanging from the saddles of their bulls.

I started up the slope, crawling on hands and knees, whining like a child. Halfway there I had to rest. It seemed impossible to continue, but no rider had done me the courtesy of dying closer to hand. I pushed myself up and resumed my journey, for I had seen what awaited me in Kelemvor's realm if I perished on the hill.

I crawled, then collapsed, then crawled and collapsed again, until I lay just below the summit. I could lift nothing but my head. This I dared not lower, for if it touched the ground, my eyes would close and never open again.

At last I found the strength to roll onto my side and inch forward like a worm. I crested the knoll and saw a forest of black feathers flashing and gleaming in the moonlight as Kelemvor's harbingers feasted on the corpses of the Faithful. Just two paces away, three of the foul birds were dancing over the carcass of a mighty war bull. From behind the beast's shoulder protruded a rider's leg, the foot still caught in the stirrup. And from the saddle hung a waterskin filled with the sweet nectar of rivers.

I dragged myself forward. The three vultures hissed and raised their wings, then gave a great shocked cry and rose into the air. When they were gone, a silhouette stood behind the fallen bull where none had been before. The figure had the shape and white-gleaming eyes of a man, but the shadows of the high-piled dead clung to his shoulders, and I could not say whether he was a rider of the Ebon Spur or a Dark Lord's bodyguard.

"Thank the Fates!" My words were but a feeble croak. "Bring me some water."

"As you wish."

The shadow spoke not with one voice, but with a thousand, all as deep and rasping as a grinding stone. The rest of Kelemvor's flock took flight, drumming the air with their wings and blocking the light of the moon. I forgot my thirst and pushed myself down the slope, cursing the pride that had turned me from Cyric. Now I had no god to defend me from this fiend.

There came the slosh of water not far above my head, and the air cooled. My limbs shivered uncontrollably, and even the heat of my wound became the burning of frozen flesh. The phantom was upon me, and I could do naught but surrender.

"Malik, why do you tremble?"

His voice was as terrible as before, and I dared not look up. I wanted to ask how the apparition knew my name, but my cold lips would not part.

"Did you not beg for water? Come now, open your mouth."

An icy toe nudged my ribs, then I was on my back, my mouth stretched wide as a cavern—though not by my own effort. A stream of liquid gurgled from the waterskin and splashed upon my face and coursed past my lips.

The fluid was as thick and foul as a sewer! It was cold and salty, and it filled my nose with the stench of spoiled meat. My gorge rose and expelled the loathsome slime, but the rancid stream continued to pour and gush down my throat, until my belly was so full of the swill that it bubbled from my wound like water from a spring. In vain, I tried to close my mouth and roll away, but my body was not mine to command. My entrails grew chill and twisted in upon themselves. The scream that followed could not have been my own, for no man's voice had ever made such a sound.

"Ah—so this is why one does not let a man with a stomach wound drink." Again, the phantom spoke in a thousand voices, and still he continued to pour that odious sludge into my mouth. "But I am not to blame, am I? *You* ordered me to bring water."

The last of the vultures swept clear of the moon, and the hillside was aglow in silvery light. Above me I saw a grinning skull's face with black-shining eyes. A crimson film clung to his ivory cheeks. His body was a mass of veins and sinew covered by no skin of any kind, and it undulated like a wave upon the sea, as if it did not have a single bone beneath its gristle.

Nor was this the worst of what I saw, for now I could see the stuff that poured from the waterskin, and it was not water. It was full of clots and bubbles, and of a color so darkly red that it seemed almost black.

Now, when I was a merchant in the City of Brilliance, this would have caused my stomach to purge itself, which would certainly have killed me on the spot. But my years outside Candlekeep had much hardened me, as there were many times when I had kept myself alive by eating and drinking vile things, and so my discovery only returned my strength at once.

I rolled away from the phantom and, leaping to my feet, rushed down the slope. When I reached the bottom of the hill, I went to the Way of the Lion and turned toward Beregost, paying no heed to the lonely distance ahead.

And, indeed, it did not matter. Before I had taken two steps, the bloody wraith loomed before me. He struck my right eye a blow so savage that the lid swelled instantly shut.

My hand flew to my face, and I turned and ran with a strength that only grew with the agony of my wounds. Every breath was as a bellows, fanning the white-hot fire in my belly. After some twenty paces, the phantom still had not overtaken me. I stopped and looked around with my good eye, but saw nothing. It appeared the fiend had grown tired of his fun. Candlekeep loomed ahead, and thinking it wise to stay beyond the reach of the Low Gate's archers, I turned to leave the road.

At once the phantom blocked my path. His white fingers hissed through the air, and his curved black talons raked my neck. A fountain of hot blood erupted, drenching me from my robe to my tattered shoes. I turned back to the road and ran until the fear of Candlekeep's arrows grew stronger than my fear of the phantom. Then I slowed, daring to look over my shoulder.

Nothing.

Again I turned to leave the road, and again the wraith was there! He slapped the right side of my head, and it is a wonder my skull did not burst. A great surge of air rushed down upon my ear, then shot through my head from one side to the other. I grew dizzy and lost all hearing in the bloodied ear. A terrible throbbing ensued, but this new pain brought even greater strength. I turned and sprinted.

At last I realized the phantom was forcing me toward Candlekeep. Perhaps thieving Oghma had sent him to capture me, as I was the spy who had discovered the *Cyrinishad*'s arrival. My heart sank further, for I had denounced Cyric, and who else could I call to save me from Oghma's servant? I continued toward the Low Gate, wondering how I might save myself. My fear grew with every step, but my strength never faltered, which was good, as the wraith assailed me horribly whenever my pace lagged and would certainly have killed me if I had fallen.

At last I reached the Low Gate and could go no farther. The portcullis had been lowered against our army's attack and not yet raised. I grabbed the bars and began to climb, knowing the guards who watched from their spyholes would either take me prisoner or kill me, though perhaps less horribly than the phantom.

A band of ice closed around my ankle and jerked me from the portcullis. When I crashed to the ground, I was again lying at the fiend's mercy.

"Not yet," the phantom said in his thousand voices. "You have not heard my command."

"Whatever you desire." I turned my good ear toward him, for it would no doubt pain me greatly to miss his command. "But I beg you, let me live. I will be no use to you dead."

"More than you think," said the wraith. "But for now, it suits me that you are alive. Stop your trembling."

This news certainly came as a great relief. Even so, I could not obey his command. I had lost the use of an eye and an ear and ached from countless other assaults, and I could not stop shaking for fear of suffering more.

My disobedience did not seem to trouble him. "You have seen the *Cyrinishad?*"

I nodded. "It was in an iron box, bound with many chains."

In the blink of an eye, the phantom snatched me up by my bloodied throat and held me to his face. "An iron box?" His breath was as a dog's, foul and rancid from eating rotten things. "How did you see inside?"

"I could not. But I saw the bearers. The woman wore a diamond amulet shaped like Oghma's scroll."

The grasp of the wraith grew tighter on my throat, and the vision in my one good eye began to darken.

"Oghma could make a thousand of those baubles!"

I began to have unpleasant suspicions about the wraith's identity, and I grew eager to stay in his favor as much as possible. "I am certain it was the sacred *Cyrinishad!* Even through the iron, I felt its darkness, and I smelled a foul odor that could only have been human parchment."

The phantom did not release me, but neither did he crush my throat.

"And I heard it whispering!" The fiend's grasp loosened, and so I added, "Its voice was soft, no more than a rustle, but I know the sacred truth when I hear it!"

This last revelation seemed to convince the phantom, for his hand opened and I found myself slumped against the portcullis.

"Good. Then you will go and fetch it for me."

"Fetch it, Dark Prince?"

"At once," the phantom replied, and I knew without doubt that I was speaking to Cyric; no mere wraith would dare claim one of the Dark Sun's thousand names. "I have need of it."

I smiled with relief. Cyric had already punished me terribly for losing faith, but now he had taken me back. The worst had passed. "As you wish, Mighty One. I shall fetch it right away."

I turned and looked up toward Candlekeep, but saw only the

endless gray rise of the jagged tor upon which the citadel stood. The Low Gate was Candlekeep's only access. One could not go around it, for it was carved into the tor itself, creating a sort of tunnel, and the cliffs flanking it could not be scaled. Knowing the importance of the gate, its builders had made it impenetrable. The portcullis was made of iron bars no man could bend and no elephant could lift. Then came the gates themselves, gilded with tin and reinforced by a drawbar as thick as a fire giant's waist. The watch portals of the guards were too small to admit a pixie. I saw no way to break in, yet I continued to study the gate in earnest, so that I might appear eager to obey. I was certain Almighty Cyric would show me how to breach the impervious defenses of the citadel.

Fortunately, the sentries at the watch portals happened to be looking away, as though something inside had caught their attention. Then I noticed they never once glanced back or made any visible movement at all. It was as if they had been frozen solid by Cyric's cold aura. If this was so, I wondered why he did not walk into Candlekeep and recover the book himself!

When the One spoke, it was not to explain. "The instant you have the *Cyrinishad,* go to the nearest high place. Call my name three times and fling yourself over the edge."

"Over the edge, my lord?" I saw my body tumbling down, down toward the sea and shattering like a melon upon the rocky shore.

"And do not forget the book!" The One still spoke in a thousand rumbling voices, but the noise did not disturb the sentries. "The *Cyrinishad* is everything!"

"Of course, Mighty One. It is sacred. And am I to understand that it will it stop me from hitting—"

"Listen to me, fool!" Cyric grabbed me by the shoulders, and his fingers sank into my flesh to the depth of the first joints. "You must understand how much depends on you."

"Yes. I am listening." What else could I do?

The One's talons dug deeper still. "The *Cyrinishad* is my only defense! It will make them see. When they read it, they will bow before me and beg the honor of kissing my feet. They will plead for mercy, and even Ao will have no choice."

"Ao?"

"Yes. He will understand what I have made of myself. He will see that I can watch over Faerûn alone, that I do not need *them*—" Here, Cyric suddenly tore his talons from my shoulders and backed away, and he cast many furtive glances in all directions. Then he straightened, and hissed in a thousand whispers, "It depends on me, of course. Everything does."

"Mighty One?"

"Who shall live. Who shall die. What is, what shall be." His dark eyes flashed. "Imagine I am watching from above, hovering in the sky as mortals are wont to think we gods do. . . ."

What Cyric said here I have already told at the beginning, and there is no use recounting it, other than to describe how his words fed the doubts that had already risen in my mind. I listened in dumbfounded awe as he rambled on about how nothing is certain until he has beheld it and set it in place, and I heard with my own ears why all of Faerûn called him Prince of Madness. My despair grew as black and bottomless as the Abyss, and I cursed myself for ever praising his name.

When at last he finished, I stood gape-mouthed before him, so stunned I could not even tremble.

Cyric smiled as a father smiles when he sends his son into battle in his own place. "You must be fast, Malik. Very fast indeed. The trial begins at dawn."

"The trial?" I asked hoarsely. I had not yet learned of the events in the Pavilion of Cynosure, and so was greatly confused. "Am I to be tried for—" In my fear, I could not bring myself to repeat the blasphemies I had uttered that morning.

"*Your* trial?" His words exploded with such fury that I was hurled against the portcullis. "You dare worry about yourself? You are nothing to them!"

By what he had stated earlier, I took "them" to be his fellow gods. They were not "begging for mercy" now, and I realized the trial at dawn was to be Cyric's. But I did not see how the Dark Sun would save himself by recovering the *Cyrinishad*.

His fellows would never read it. They knew the awesome power of its truth and would go to any length to avoid looking upon its pages, for they were all vain and arrogant and had no wish to serve a master greater than themselves. Nor could they be tricked into reading the sacred book, even by the awesome cunning of the One. They were great gods, after all, and clever enough to avoid any hazard they knew so well.

I was wiser than to speak these doubts aloud, as Cyric would not suffer gladly the skepticism of a mortal. I merely inclined my head and awaited the Dark Sun's next command.

"Go on," he said. "Dawn is not far off."

Thinking he had created some passage for me, I turned to find it. The Low Gate stood as before. But now I could see the sentries turning toward me, ever so slowly. To say their heads were inching around would have been a great exaggeration. When one man blinked, the act took as long as all that had passed between the One and me.

"What are you waiting for?" asked Cyric. "Dawn is coming!"

My answer was sure to displease. Still, I had no choice but to give it, since I could not pass through the gate as it was.

"Forgive me, Almighty One, for I have the wits of an ass and just one good eye." Naturally, I made no mention of whose doing this was. "But I thought you might provide me some way to enter."

Cyric's burning black eyes flared in the empty sockets beneath his brow. "Idiot! If I could do that, I would get the book myself. If I were to endow you with my power, Oghma's magic would make you as blind to the book as it does me. Only a mortal—an unaided mortal—can find the *Cyrinishad*."

"Unaided?" I gasped. "But I am no thief, no warrior! Even if I get into the citadel, how am I to defeat the book's guardians?"

"*How* does not matter."

This was a terrible thing to hear, and not only on my own account. I was shrewd in the ways of cheating the scale and claiming one cargo is another, but I had never stolen a thing from another man's home, nor killed any person except through the exchange of gold, nor was I certain how to accomplish these things. Counting on someone like me in such a great and dangerous matter was more than folly—it was insane! Cyric could only be as mad as his enemies claimed, and if I obeyed him, I would certainly be killed.

I threw myself at his feet and wrapped my arms about his legs. "Holy One, I beg you! Find one more worthy! If you rely on me, you will never see the *Cyrinishad* again!"

"I will. Look what you have done already. Who else would have left his mansion to live in the mud? Given up his fortune to beg for his dinner? Forsaken the envy of his peers to grovel before strangers?" The thousand voices of the One spoke with unaccustomed gentleness. "You will do this thing not because I command it—though I do—but for the same reason you have done all these other things: because you have no choice."

The One reached down and grasped my arms with great delicacy, and I dared not speak as he pulled me to my feet. "And, Malik, you *will* succeed. Do you know why?"

I could but shake my head.

"You will succeed, because if you do not—if you fail me, or merely die trying—I will let Kelemvor take your Faithless soul."

Five

Mystra and Kelemvor manifested themselves outside Oghma's palace, which never looked the same on any two visits. Today, they faced a many-domed alcazar of snow-white stone, with a long garden pool to reflect its splendor. No wall enclosed the grounds, nor did any gate control access; the House of Knowledge was open to all who troubled to visit.

Mystra and Kelemvor squandered no time upon the beauty of the alcazar, for they had much to do before Cyric's trial. They floated down the alameda, past throngs of scholars engrossed in debate. Myriad bards pressed forward to sing ballads praising magic and death, and countless fiends and seraphim stopped to bow, their arms laden with charts and manuscripts. The two gods ignored them all. They reached the palace and passed through its arched entrance into a vast foyer, where the vaulted ceiling was inscribed with the names of the innumerable learned who had died and been taken into the House of Knowledge by their loyal god.

"Truly, the stars have favored my house today!" Oghma's voice was a song. He stood in the doorway to the next room, dressed in snug trousers, billowing tunic, and loose turban. "To have two visitors of such distinction!"

"Fortune did not bring us here, as you well know," said Mystra. She pushed brazenly past Oghma into the vast library beyond. "We have come to discuss the trial."

Oghma frowned. "We should do that *at* the trial."

The God of Wisdom turned and followed Mystra through

the door, and Kelemvor came behind. The library was a cavern of pillars and shelves, vast beyond limit and filled with volumes recounting every detail learned by Oghma's Faithful during their lives. Mystra twined her way through the maze in perfect ease, having visited the House of Knowledge often enough to know her way whatever the palace's form.

"It is not for us alone to decide Cyric's fate," said Oghma, still following Lady Magic. "That is for the whole Circle."

Mystra reached Oghma's throne, an alabaster seat surrounded by tables and benches of white marble, and turned to her host. "What I have come to say, I cannot say before the Circle."

"Then, my dear, perhaps you should not say it." Oghma stepped past Mystra and sat in his throne.

"And perhaps you should hear her out," said Kelemvor. "Unless your mind is not as open as you pretend."

Oghma cocked an eyebrow. "Touché, Kelemvor." He waved his guests to the benches beside his throne, then turned back to Mystra. "Very well. My listening will not corrupt the trial any further. I am certain the rest of the Circle has already been busy negotiating the outcome."

"Kelemvor and I have made a few inquiries, yes," admitted Mystra. "But Cyric has made no . . . arrangements of his own."

"Perhaps *he* trusts the process."

"You know better than that," said Kelemvor. "Cyric is planning something."

"He has the *Cyrinishad*," added Mystra.

"If you are certain of this, then you are a wiser god than I," Oghma replied. "I have not lifted my ban. How can you know that Cyric has the book when I have denied knowledge of the *Cyrinishad*'s whereabouts to all deities? And how can Cyric possess it, when he cannot perceive its location? He could walk into a room and pick it up and not know he held it in his hand. What you suggest is impossible."

Kelemvor scowled. "Whatever you say, Cyric has the book. That is the only reason he would be this calm."

"I see," said Oghma. "Not only do you know where the

Cyrinishad is, you know how the mind of a mad god works!"

"I know Cyric," Kelemvor growled. "I know him better than you ever could."

"You know Cyric the mortal," Oghma replied. "And we are speaking of Cyric the god."

"Oghma, I did not come here to argue circles with you," said Mystra. "I know better than that. So let us suppose that Cyric has the *Cyrinishad,* and that he intends to present it at the trial—as evidence."

Oghma furrowed his brow, then his eyes grew wide. "We would be obliged to hear it!"

The three were silent, for they all understood the power of the sacred *Cyrinishad.* They knew that upon hearing its truth they would fall to their knees and pay homage to the One, and they also knew the terrible retribution Cyric would take on them for the many affronts they had heaped upon him in the past.

Kelemvor broke the silence. "Good—we all agree. If Cyric brings the book, the trial is off. We destroy him on the spot."

At this, Oghma gasped and shook his head with such vigor that every sage on Faerûn lost the course of his thoughts. "No!"

"No?" Mystra gasped. "But the Balance—"

"Would be utterly destroyed," said Oghma. "Better to serve in Pandemonium than rule in a wasteland, which is all that would remain if we unleashed an all-out godswar! What you suggest would make the Time of Troubles look like a mere squabble."

"Never!" So fast did Kelemvor take his feet that it cannot be said that he rose; he was sitting one instant and standing before the next began. "I will destroy myself before I serve Cyric!"

Oghma's eyes grew as hard as diamonds. "The issue is not whether you would destroy yourself, Kelemvor, but whether you would destroy Faerûn. As a god, you must put your duty above disputes that linger from your life as a mortal. The fate of a world hangs on your every act, and you would do well to remember that." Oghma glanced at Mystra, then added, "You both would."

Six

The Night of Despair was upon me, for I had met my god, and he was the very Prince of Madness! At my best, I could not have done as he demanded, and I was not at my best, for I had suffered much at the One's hands. Half blind, half deaf, fully a bloodied fool, I saw only my coming failure and certain doom. I threw myself upon the portcullis and cleaved to the bars, and I wept as never before.

How could I save myself? I was too fat to squeeze through an arrow loop and too crippled to scale the tor. And even if such things were possible, I was too clumsy to do either without being caught. My god had asked an impossible penance of me, and now I would be delivered to his eternal enemy to suffer an unbearable destiny. I cursed Kelemvor's name, for he was a jealous coward who groveled in his city of bones and hid from Cyric's wrath and visited his hatred upon helpless souls like me. I also cursed the One, for in my misery I believed he had lost the *Cyrinishad* through his own folly, and that if I had relinquished my faith after enduring so much, it was more his fault than my own. This is a terrible shame to me now; I admit it only as evidence of the absolute truth of my account.

At length, there arose a clattering behind the gates, and the small wicket door behind the portcullis opened. Two monks bent down to peer out through the bars. Both were dressed for battle, with steel skullcaps on their heads and the bulk of their chain mail showing beneath their violet robes.

"Mukhtar!" exclaimed one.

The guards of the Low Gate called me Mukhtar the Mad, for in all my years outside Candlekeep, I had never given them my true name, knowing this to be the practice of all good spies. "By the Bard! What happened to you?"

I saw no use in lying. "I have been gored by a bull."

"Aye, and trampled too, judging by your looks," said one monk, whose name was Agenor. "But the Keeper thinks our enemy is playing a trick. We can't open the gate for you, Mukhtar."

I nodded, for I had expected no less. Indeed I was surprised they had not slain me already, but perhaps they did not know I had betrayed the *Cyrinishad*'s presence to the Caliph.

"Look at him, Agenor," said the other monk, who was known to me as Pelias. "He'll die!"

"We have our orders."

"We can raise the portcullis and let him crawl under. What can happen? There isn't a Cyricist within a league!"

"Remember what the Keeper said about wooden horses."

"Ulraunt has been reading too many epics," replied Pelias. "And what I remember is that Mukhtar is my friend."

"Friend?"

I was as surprised by this remark as Agenor. Pelias had shown me many kindnesses, but we had never spoken as I had with my friends in Calimshan, among whom it was customary to talk of the success of one's ventures and the importance of one's other friends. Yet I did not contradict him, for I sensed his words were sincere, and there might be some advantage for me in that.

Pelias was silent for some time. Then he said, "Yes, Mukhtar is my friend. We have broken bread together often enough, and what makes a friendship, if not that?"

Speaking thus, he stepped back and vanished from my sight.

Agenor followed at once. "Where do you think you're going?"

"To raise the portcullis."

Truly, Pelias's reply made my heart pound like the hooves

of the bull that had gored me. It had never occurred to me entry into Candlekeep might be mine for the knocking! Recovering the *Cyrinishad* would still be impossible, as it was certain to be well guarded, but perhaps my engagement with Kelemvor might be delayed if one of the citadel's healers looked after my wounds.

"Don't concern yourself, Agenor," said Pelias. I could hardly hear him, for both he and Agenor had stepped into the darkness. "I'll take the blame if Brother Risto levies any."

"He will," countered Agenor. "Don't forget that your friend is Mukhtar *the Mad*. And Cyric is the Prince of Madness."

No more sounds came from within; Agenor's words were having their effect.

"What do you think now?" asked Agenor. "Maybe Ulraunt hasn't been reading too many epics, eh?"

I had to do something or I was lost. "Pelias, Agenor is right!" I called. "You must not open the gate. I have seen Cyric himself upon the plain. He is the one who did this to me!"

"What?" Pelias and Agenor returned to the wicket door in an instant and eyed my bloody figure. "Cyric did that?"

"Not the goring, but all the rest." Among the many things my father had taught me about being a merchant, one was that it is always best to tell the truth, when convenient. "The first time he struck me, my eye shut fast. The second time he attacked, he did this." I raised my chin, displaying the gashes where he had raked my neck. "And the third time he hit me, my ear exploded."

"By the Bard! How many times did he hit you?" gasped Pelias.

"These three were the worst, though he also grabbed my shoulders and deeply pierced my flesh, and I am certain those wounds alone will be enough to kill me." I spoke softly and moaned to seem weak. In truth, neither my strength nor my pain had ebbed since the One had poured that vile stuff into my mouth.

"I am only a beggar and have but one thing in this life." I reached inside my cloak and withdrew the small dagger I always carry. "This is why Cyric has killed me. When you hold it in your hand, the gods speak to you."

I cocked my head, as though I were listening to someone even then—do not forget they called me Mukhtar the Mad— then I pushed the knife through the portcullis to Pelias.

"I want you to have it, my friend."

Pelias left the wicket door at once. There was great clamor inside, and the portcullis rose the span of three hands. I lost my grasp upon the bars and fell into the mud. Nor was this any pretense, for I was so delirious with my good fortune that I could not stand. Pelias himself crawled under the iron spikes and dragged me into the gloomy vault beyond. This was the first time I had ever passed through Candlekeep's gates.

Pelias and another man laid me on a litter and started up through the darkness, leaving Agenor and the rest of their number to lower the portcullis and stand guard against Cyric. Soon we passed out of the vault and into the moonlight, and I saw that already we had climbed a small height, for I could turn my head and look out over the plain. The knoll where Most High Haroun and His Deadliness Jabbar had died lay a thousand paces distant, once again blanketed by the feathers of Kelemvor's harbingers. Beyond that stretched a sea of waving grass so vast it made me dizzy.

The trail was narrow and steep, with many sharp bends. Still, my bearers ascended at a brisk pace, without the aid of lanterns or any illumination but the moon. They had passed this way countless times before and could have hiked it in a darkness as black as the Dark One's soul. I, on the other hand, had never been on the trail, and my left eye opened wide as I saw the sheer fall that lay over the edge of my litter. As we climbed higher, I could not bear to watch the ground growing more and more distant. I closed my eye, but the ceaseless shifting of the litter only confirmed my suspicion that I was in danger of sliding off.

Nor did the journey help my injuries. The constant pitching and swaying made my battered head throb and spin, which upset my stomach and caused the wound in my belly to burn with a cold fire. But the pain made me strong in a way I had never before experienced; the more I suffered, the greater my energy. I could have risen from the litter and walked up the path on my own, had I not wished to seem a dying lunatic.

We rounded the tor and traveled for a time far above the crashing waves of the Sea of Swords. When at last we came around to the plain once more, my knuckles ached from grasping the litter. Then I glimpsed the lights of Beregost flickering far in the distance and saw I would live through the night. This thought gave me no comfort, for Cyric's judgment, and my own, would come with the dawn.

I was tempted to offer myself to one of the gods who kept a shrine inside Candlekeep and thereby escape Cyric's punishment, but this was not practical. I was neither scholar nor sage, and so had nothing to offer that would make Oghma overlook my past. The same was true of the others who kept shrines there. Although I can write, my hand is so awful that only those who know its style can read it, and thus Deneir would not have had me; nor would Milil have taken me, for a bull camel sings more beautifully in his rut than I do in a fresh voice; and Gond would only have laughed at my hands, which are soft and unskilled at the building of anything but towers of coins. Seeing that I could not cheat Cyric of his due, I resigned myself to my destiny, swearing only to put it off as long as possible.

At last, the cliff above gave way to the mortared stones of a handmade wall. We rounded a bend and entered a small courtyard that hung like an eagle's eyrie upon the side of the tor. On three sides there was nothing but darkness and wind; on the fourth yawned the gaping mouth of the High Gate, with the jagged teeth of an iron portcullis descending from the roof of its entry arch. Arrow points and crossbow darts bristled from the many loops and watch portals of the gatehouse, and the harsh fumes of burning lamp oil wafted down from its murder holes.

Pelias and his helper carried me to the brink of the gateway and stopped, and I found myself staring up at the sharp teeth of the great portcullis. An iron plate clanged open behind a peephole in the wall, and a man asked, "Pelias, what do you have there?"

"Mukhtar the Mad," answered my friend. "He is grievously wounded and needs a healer."

"Not on my watch, he doesn't!" came the reply. "What's wrong with you? You heard the Keeper's order!"

"Aye, but you haven't heard what happened to Mukhtar. He was attacked by the Foul One."

"Cyric?"

"Who else?" Pelias started forward, guiding us toward a dark corner. "Why don't you fetch Brother Risto? I'm certain he and the Keeper will want to speak with Mukhtar themselves."

The iron plate slammed into place, and we waited in the shadows of the archway for a time. I felt many eyes watching me from the darkness and heard soft voices rustling down from the murder holes. I was careful to moan and cry out often, so they would know how grievous were my wounds and not think me capable of doing harm. Now that I was here on the very porch of Candlekeep, there arose in my breast a dim hope that I might find the *Cyrinishad,* and having found it, a fainter hope that I might recover it and escape the many torments awaiting me in the City of the Dead. This was foolish, but in his despair, a damned man will grasp at any chance.

After a time, there came a faint murmur behind the gate, which soon built to an officious drone. As I had heard a similar noise many times in the Caliph's palace, I knew that Ulraunt, the Keeper of the Tomes himself, was coming with his entourage. I prepared my mind with many fawning remarks, for I had heard the monks speak of him and knew he thought well of himself and that he valued those who did the same.

Two thumps sounded on the other side of the gate. When the wicket door swung open, I was set upon at once by an unpleasant odor. It was faint, yet it was also so foul and corrupt that it could have been the fetor of death pushing up through a grave. I was much amazed at this, for the monks were very clean and wholesome in their habits.

Pelias switched his grasp on the litter and passed through

the wicket door backward. He had to stoop low to avoid hitting his head, for the portal was constructed to allow a man passage only if he crawled or crouched upon his haunches. As soon as I was through, a veritable throng descended on us, trapping Pelias's helper against the gate. The crowd included not only monks, but warriors of the many companies that had come to aid Candlekeep. I recognized only a few of their insignias: among these were the Flaming Fists, the Hellriders of Elturel, the Silent Rain, and some others of lesser consequence.

I also recognized the black-veiled woman I had glimpsed that very morning, riding on a hippogriff and scanning the plain with her kohl-rimmed eyes. She made me most anxious, as she never looked away from my face, and I thought she might be a True Believer sent to watch over me. Then I glimpsed a pin she wore, a silver harp inside a crescent moon, and I knew her to be one of the Harpers, a band of meddling fools who send their agents far and wide to interfere in other people's business.

There was also the guardian of the *Cyrinishad,* the warrior who had almost killed me the night of the book's arrival. Of all the soldiers gathered there, only he was dressed in full armor, down to his gauntlets and greaves. I could tell that he recognized me, for his visor was up and he was scowling fiercely.

A bearded monk in a brown robe emerged from the throng. He pointed a gleaming black rod at my head. I averted my eyes, for the man was known to me as Risto, Keeper of the Portal, and I had learned to keep my distance when he came to inspect the Low Gate.

"Pelias!" said Risto. "What is the meaning of this?"

"I think we can see what the meaning is," said another man, who was dressed in a robe of palest blue. He stepped to Risto's side and stooped over me, taking in my many wounds. "This man came to the Low Gate seeking help, and Pelias ignored orders and let him in."

Although I had never laid eyes on the Keeper of the Tomes before in my life, I could tell by his cunning gaze and regal manner, and also by the diffidence with which the crowd parted to let him pass, that this was Ulraunt.

"Most Merciful Geyser of Knowledge, pray forgive my intrusion, for it was not my own doing," said I. "I did not come to the Low Gate seeking help, but to give it. I begged Pelias most sincerely not to take me in, but only to let me speak, that I might warn him *not* to raise the portcullis or to open the gate, for Cyric himself is lurking out upon the plain!"

Many in the throng gasped and inched back, but the Harper woman and the *Cyrinishad*'s bearer pushed closer and glared at me more intently.

Ulraunt laid a gentle hand upon my arm. "Don't worry, Mukhtar. We're not going to whip you for needing help."

This relieved me greatly, for I knew by his kind words that he would not lock me in a dungeon or tower, or some other place from which it would prove impossible to escape and go looking for the *Cyrinishad*.

Ulraunt glanced at Pelias, then also at Risto and said, "Nor will we punish Pelias for offering it."

"A blessing on your name!" I took care not to speak too powerfully, lest my host grow suspicious of my strength. "Truly, you are as full of wisdom and compassion as your many servants claim. When I pass into the next world, know that I will speak well of Ulraunt."

"As you should."

The man chuckled, but Risto sneered and the throng gasped. I sensed I had made a great blunder.

"But I'm not Ulraunt," said the man. "I am the First Reader, Tethtoril."

"*I* am Ulraunt." The voice, keen with resentment, came from someplace behind Tethtoril and Risto.

The crowd parted and expelled a short man with a bitter countenance, the sleep still in his eyes. He shouldered Tethtoril aside and glared at me, and I saw by the anger in his gaze he would hold my mistake against me. I had visions of being hurled from the eyrie outside High Gate or locked away to rot in some hole until I died and went to stand before Kelemvor.

"Now, what's this about Cyric?"

"He is out upon the plain," I answered. "I know this, because he is the one who did all this to me, save for the goring, which was done by a fleeing war bull."

As I said this, another man came to the other side of my litter. He wore the white shirt of Oghma's Chosen, and I saw by the many glyphs brocaded in his vest that he was a priest of no little power. His assistant came with a lamp, and I averted my eyes, lest the healer see the hatred I bore his thieving god.

As the priest prodded and poked my wounds, Ulraunt said, "I find it hard to believe someone such as you—" truly, he sniffed as he said this last word—"survived an attack by Cyric."

"Then it is good you were not there, for you would doubt your own eyes." This drew a snicker from Tethtoril and several others, which caused me no small concern, as I had no wish to anger Ulraunt more than I had. "I scarcely believe it myself."

The priest pushed a finger into my stomach wound and rudely stirred it around, doubtless to win favor with Ulraunt. I was seized by burning cramps and would have fallen off the litter, had Tethtoril and Risto not pinned me down. The priest spoke a word, then something he had placed in my belly burst open. It coursed through my body like a flaming demon, seeking out every injury wrought by Cyric and setting it afire. The world turned red and silent, and I felt myself falling.

When the fall ended, I cannot say. I opened my left eye to find the priest slapping my face and shouting in my good ear, and I saw that I still lay on the litter. The same throng pressed all around. My head still throbbed, my face still ached, and my neck and shoulders still burned with the same cold fever—but the pain in my belly was gone. The hole itself felt numb and full, as though the priest had filled it with a cork. The surrounding flesh was tender and hot; otherwise, my stomach hurt no more than being kicked by an irate camel.

"He's back." The priest sounded more relieved than I.

I noticed that the subtle stench I had smelled outside the gate had become stronger, though its source was not in this ward.

Ulraunt's face appeared above mine. "Don't do that again." I could not tell whether the Keeper was speaking to me or the priest. "I need to hear more about this meeting with Cyric."

"As you wish, Learned One," said the priest.

"How is it that you survived?" Ulraunt demanded.

"Not by my own doing, I assure you." As at the Low Gate, I was entirely truthful in this matter. "When Cyric could not find what he sought, he grew tired of his game and left me to suffer."

Ulraunt's eyes grew narrow. "And what he was seeking?"

I glanced at Pelias. Being much practiced in the appearance of madness, I knew it would be better to seem reluctant.

"Go ahead," Pelias urged. "Ulraunt can be trusted."

Though I already knew better than this, I nodded. I glanced around the throng and frowned, as though reluctant to talk before so many ears, then motioned for the Keeper to lower his ear to my lips. He did so, and I spoke thus: "He desires my dagger."

"Your dagger?" Ulraunt backed away from my litter.

"There's nothing to fear, Keeper," said Pelias. "He's given the knife to me for safekeeping."

Ulraunt scowled, and I saw that Pelias had made a foolish error in pointing out his superior's fear. From this time forward, my friend's life at Candlekeep would be difficult indeed.

The Keeper stepped back to my side, and when he spoke, his tone made it apparent that he had lost all interest in my story. "Now, why would a god want a beggar's dagger?"

I knew then I would be allowed to stay the night, as Ulraunt considered me a worthless beggar and would not trouble his men to open the gates and throw me out. Eager to reinforce this impression, I glanced at all the people around the litter, then motioned again for the Keeper to bring his ear near.

He was done with bowing and would not bend down. "You can speak freely. We're among friends."

I scowled once more, but Pelias nodded. So I said softly, "The dagger is magical. When you hold it, the gods speak to you."

The throng chuckled at this, but nervously. They knew the eyes of the gods were upon this place and that gods worked in strange ways. It was not beyond question that a deity would speak through a mad beggar's dagger. Ulraunt cast an eye upon Pelias and raised a brow.

"It—uh—hasn't worked for me, Keeper."

"Well, then." Ulraunt turned back to me. "If Cyric wanted the dagger, how did a simple beggar keep him from taking it?"

"I hid it." Truly, things were going as well as I could hope. "In my robe."

"And that fooled Cyric?"

"It did," I replied. "That was when he left me alone."

"I see." Ulraunt rolled his eyes, then scowled at Pelias. "Next time, Brother, do not be so naive."

"He isn't, Keeper," said the priest. "Being naive, I mean. Whatever happened to this beggar, he is telling the truth about his injuries."

"What?" It was the guardian of the *Cyrinishad* who asked this, and with remarkable swiftness he stood across the litter from the priest. "What do you mean?"

"Look here." The priest pointed at my stomach. Though my tunic was still torn and bloodied, the terrible hole in my flesh had been closed by his magic. "This wound was the worst by far, but it healed almost completely. Oghma's magic did nothing for these others."

"May the Binder protect us!" hissed Ulraunt. The Keeper retreated several steps, as did the rest of the throng, save only Tethtoril and the priest, the warrior and the Harper, and my litter bearers, who looked very worried indeed. "He was Touched?"

"Touched?" asked the Harper. "What do you mean?"

"I am close enough to Oghma that my hands have attained a certain . . . potency," explained the priest. "I could bring this man back from the dead, but I can't heal those wounds. He has been Touched by something very powerful—and very corrupt. That's why the Binder's magic struck him as it did."

"That, and because he is one of Cyric's!" The guardian of the

Cyrinishad grasped my waist and lifted me from the litter. "We must be rid of him at once!"

He ducked through the wicket door, and seeing what he meant to do, I twisted about and grasped the sides of the portal and would not let go, though the fingernails tore from my hands.

"Most Merciful Keeper, I beg you, don't let him throw me from the eyrie!"

The priest and his assistant rushed to my aid, grabbing my shoulders and pulling me back toward the ward, though my attacker retained his grasp on my legs and remained determined to drag me through the doorway.

"Gwydion!" cried Tethtoril. "Stop that—now!"

"This beggar has tried to steal the book once already!"

"Book?" I yelled. "I cannot even read!"

Pelias grabbed Gwydion's thumb and gave a twist, and at once the warrior's hand came free. The priest and his assistant fell upon the ground and I on top of them, and we all lay there while Tethtoril and Pelias interposed themselves between the guardian and myself.

"Gwydion, you are a guest here," said the First Reader. "If you cannot remember that, you will be asked to leave!"

Ulraunt, always quick to guard the prerogatives of his office, stepped forward. "That is for me to decide."

"I apologize." Tethtoril made room for Ulraunt but continued to stare at Gwydion. "I was merely stressing this to Gwydion, before he takes it upon himself to throw Mukhtar off the eyrie and deprive you of your interview."

Ulraunt scowled. "Interview?"

"You've been right all along, as this beggar's wounds prove," Tethtoril replied. "Cyric *is* out there, and only Mukhtar can tell us what he's doing."

My heart sank in my chest, for I had already told them as much of Cyric as I cared to, and it was said that Ulraunt's jealous mind made him a careful inquisitor. He nodded gravely at Tethtoril's advice and turned to look at me, and I saw at once I would pass the whole night in the Keeper's company and have no chance to search for the *Cyrinishad*.

It is fortunate that the Caliph suffers the mad to live in the streets of his city. On many occasions I have observed them and noted their strange habits—especially in the matter of fits, which can come upon some with the slightest provocation. Their eyes roll back in their heads until only the whites show, their limbs grow as stiff as clubs and shake and thrash about, they bite their own tongues and froth at the mouth, and when they are in this state, nothing in the world can reach them, whether they are tempted with beautiful women or burned with red-hot irons.

All this I did, even to the biting of my own tongue so blood would spray from my mouth in equal parts to spittle. I rolled about with no regard as to what I hit, and even crashed into Gwydion's legs so no one would think I had control over my movements. All the while I babbled in a strange gurgling tongue no man has ever spoken. I smashed my head upon the ground until it was covered with lumps and scraped my face over the stones until it bled. The pain this caused me only fed my peculiar strength, and my frenzy never wavered. Surely no man could have looked upon the spectacle and thought I was anything but mad.

After a time, I allowed Pelias and three others to seize my limbs and hold me splayed in the air. I continued to twitch and froth and babble, lest they think the fit had passed. The priest wedged a piece of wood between my jaws and bound it there with a leather strap, while Tethtoril pulled back the lid of my good eye.

"What has happened to him?" asked the Harper in the veil. She came and looked down upon my face, and in her dusky eyes I saw again the hippogriff's outstretched wings wheeling across the sun. "He looks like a camel dying of thirst."

"Then we should put him out of his misery," said Gwydion.

"No!" commanded Ulraunt. "Not until I've interrogated him."

"How can you?" Gwydion demanded. "Cyric has claimed him."

"This is not possession," said the priest. "It is a fit, caused by your attempt to kill the poor fellow. He will recover."

"When?" The question was Ulraunt's.

"Only the Binder knows," replied the priest. "The fit is already passing. After that, he'll sleep for a time. You can talk to him when he wakes. He'll have a throbbing head, but he should be able to answer your questions."

"Can't you do something?"

"You saw what my last spell did," answered the priest. "Another could kill him, especially if this fit has anything to do with Cyric."

The Keeper was silent for a moment, then asked, "What would his chances be?"

I bit the wood so hard that the blood in my mouth rushed up through my nose and spewed out my nostrils. In the same instant, I jerked three of my limbs free, dropped to the ground, and lay thrashing in mad abandon.

"Not good, I would say!" The priest tried to grasp my foot, which act I repaid with a wild kick that bloodied his lip. "Help me, someone! He'll hurt himself!"

"If he needs sleep, Loremaster, I can help."

The Harper stepped over near my head and reached into the sleeve of her robe. I tried to spin away, but Pelias recaptured my arm and pinned it down, stretching me out like an adulterer over an anthill. When the witch withdrew her hand from her sleeve, she had a small amount of yellow sand in her fingers, which she made to sprinkle in my good eye. I snapped the lid shut and turned my head away, but I was too late; the grains had already fallen, and she was already uttering her spell in a voice soft and sultry as a night in my own bed. I sank into a sleep deeper than the crashing sea, untroubled by any thought of my destiny in Kelemvor's realm or by any memory of the kind prince and my fortune and my wife, or by any dream of the sacred *Cyrinishad* rustling in its iron box.

A curse upon the Harpers! Why can they not mind their own affairs?

Seven

It is said every merchant has his bane, and this Harper was mine. Her name was Ruha. She had seen my face in a vision, and on that account alone she had sworn to make a hell of my entire life. Born to the desert nomads of Anauroch thirty years before, she had never led an easy or certain life, for her people feared magic and all other things they did not understand, which were many. Because Ruha had visions, her tribe cast her off at a young age and left her to the burning sands. She learned to go without drinking, until even camels craved water more, and discovered how to nourish herself upon anything, be it serpent, thorn, or bone. Seeing what a creature this girl had become, the Goddess of Magic guided her to a far oasis, where there lived an old harpy versed in the strange ways of desert sorcery. This hag taught her to fashion spells from sand, fire, wind, and water. In time, young Ruha could create any kind of magic at all with no more than the dust at her feet or the water in her mouth, and she became a witch in every sense of the word.

The time came when the Zhentarim sent a party to open a trade route through Anauroch. The Harpers, in turn, sent an agent to incite the desert people against this. Ruha glimpsed this man, and from that moment she wanted him. She cast an enchantment to make him love her, but he would not forget his mission and died in battle. Ruha made no lament, for jackals do not mourn the death of any man. Yet, having tasted the fruit of love, she had no wish to return to her oasis and live alone, so she stole the agent's silver pin and left Anauroch to find others like him.

And that is how Ruha came to the Harpers. What she did during the next few years matters little, save that she journeyed far and wide at the behest of her masters, learning the ways of Faerûn and spreading discord and destruction wherever she went. It was she who made Prince Tang renege on his bargain with the Cult of the Dragon, an act that caused the burning of half of Elversult! And it was she who kidnapped Duke Wycliff's daughter from the hill giants, halting a marriage that would have united two races in blood and kinship.

When word of Candlekeep's plight reached the city of Waterdeep, Ruha was there, handling a small matter of some children missing in Trollclaw Forest. Upon hearing of the conflict, her sight blurred, and she saw a haggard beggar—me—standing before a great host and reading from a book. Now, Ruha's visions were such that she never understood their meaning nor knew what to do about them, but she never allowed her ignorance to stop her from meddling. In this way, she was a perfect Harper. Leaving the children for someone else to find, she begged her masters to send her south with Waterdeep's contingent. So it was that she reached Candlekeep with the hippogriff riders, just as Haroun and Jabbar were about to kill each other.

I recount all this not to excuse what befell me at the High Gate; an apology never alters a thing. I only wish to make clear what a fiend was watching over me while I slept. I floated up from my slumber to discover the stench of corruption thick in my nostrils. At first I wondered if the witch herself or her foul magic were the source, but I soon realized the smell was more pervasive. Perhaps it arose from some infestation, for the odor was accompanied by a strange sound, an inconstant grating like mating insects. This rustling filled my head with such irritation that I thought my skull would burst, and though it seemed familiar, I could not recall hearing such a noise before.

I turned my head, and there above me loomed the kohl-rimmed eyes of the Harper witch. As always, she wore her veil, so all I could see of her face were two pools of fiendish brown. At once, I knew she had been studying me while I slept. My next thought was that she had used her magic to see into my dreams and learn of my secret and my purpose. And though I had never harmed a woman in my life, I knew at once I had to throttle her.

But the witch had anticipated me! My hands scarcely rose an inch before a leather restraint caught my wrists. I raised my head and saw that she had wound three straps across my body, binding me down at my chest, hips, and legs.

"It is for your own good," said the witch. "We didn't want you to hurt yourself."

"Myself?" My speech was thick and no doubt hard to understand, for my tongue was swollen and slow from the bite I had given it. "Why would I hurt myself?"

"She means by accident, Mukhtar." Pelias stepped into the light, his chain mail jangling beneath his robe. "You were having quite a fit. The straps are merely to keep you from lashing out and falling off the litter."

I looked away, as though mention of the fit caused me great embarrassment, but in truth I was hiding my relief. His warm tone meant the witch had not read my dreams—or told him if she had. I saw that I lay in a scribe's chamber, lit by the flickering light of an oil lamp and sparsely furnished. Two chairs had been positioned at the ends of my litter to hold it aloft, and on a desk in the corner sat Pelias's helmet and a copper water pitcher. The room also had a deep window seat, though the heavy curtain over the casement blocked my view outside. My heart began to beat faster, for I feared that dawn had come and I had awakened too late to find the *Cyrinishad*.

Pelias squatted beside my litter and laid a hand on my shoulder. "There's no need for shame, Mukhtar. How do you feel?"

"Well enough that there is no need for these." I raised my hands and pushed against the leather strap across my hips. I saw that with a little careful effort, I might pull my wrists up and free my hands. "And I am so very thirsty."

Pelias reached forward to release my bonds.

Faster than a lizard could dart, the witch caught his hand. "Leave him until we are certain the fit has passed, Pelias. Perhaps you should go find the Keeper. Did he not say to fetch him when Mukhtar awoke?"

"No, Pelias!" I shouted. If I was to have any chance of finding the *Cyrinishad,* I had to escape quickly—a thing that Ruha would certainly make more difficult. "If you love Oghma, don't leave me with the witch! I beg you!"

Ruha's brows came together. "Are you afraid of me, Mukhtar?"

I ignored her and fixed all my attention on Pelias. "She will kill me as I lie here helpless and bound!"

Pelias shook his head and took the woman's arm. "This is Ruha." He held her hand out toward me. "She won't hurt you."

I looked away from them both.

"Mukhtar," said she, "why are you afraid? I have caused you no harm."

I swung my head around so fast that I slammed my temple against the litter frame. "Then why did you throw sand in my eyes? And why I am tied here against my wishes, with a head that feels as if it could hatch an eagle?" With every word, I sprayed spittle from my mouth, hoping they would think me ready to have another fit. "Pelias, she has tried to kill me once already, and if you leave her alone with me, she will do it!"

Pelias wiped the spittle from his face and turned to the witch. "It would be better if you fetched Ulraunt."

Ruha's eyes grew narrow, and she studied me for a long time, and when she spoke, her voice was sharp with anger. "My spell did him no harm, Pelias. That dog has no cause to fear me!"

Pelias took her arm and led her a few steps away, but even with one bad ear and the rustle that filled my head, I knew what he whispered to her: "He needs no cause, Lady Witch. He's mad."

I felt her dusky eyes upon me and knew she was not entirely fooled by my pretense. Yet, neither did she understand what I was doing, and this made her as nervous as my words made her angry.

"As you wish, Pelias. I'll go for the Keeper." She made no pretense of whispering, but spoke loudly enough so I could hear. "But you mustn't untie him. This beggar plays a bigger role than we understand. It is best to consider him as dangerous as Cyric."

"As you wish, Lady Witch." Pelias probed a pocket in his robe. "You will need this token to enter the Keeper's Tower."

"I have my own. That is where I am staying."

With that, the witch left the chamber, making no mention of the vision in which she had seen me with a book. It was her custom to keep such things secret, for she had learned through unwelcome experience that most people would rather blame her visions for their trouble than thank her for warning them against it. Perhaps this stupidity is why the fear I feigned offended her so; this I cannot say, only that she was the first woman who ever took such an instant dislike to me.

After the door closed, I forced myself to count a hundred heartbeats. I was eager to begin my search, but I had to remain patient, lest my friend heed the witch's warning. Nor did it calm me much that it was Pelias who guarded me, for my escape would bring an avalanche of troubles down upon his head. I would have been a better friend to let him go for the Keeper and have the witch take the blame, but Ruha was more than my match. If I was to have any chance of avoiding Kelemvor's torments, Pelias would have to do me this one last service.

When I finished the count, I turned to Pelias. He sat upon the corner of the desk, watching me. The dagger I had given him was still tucked in the front of his sword belt.

I wrinkled my face to form a pitiful expression. "I am most uncomfortable, my friend. Won't you please undo these straps?"

Pelias shook his head. "If Ulraunt finds you loose—"

"What do you care of Ulraunt, my dear friend? He has already decided to make your life here most unpleasant. If you had any sense, you would leave and go home with me to Calimshan."

"Calimshan?"

There was no danger in what I had said. Though several companies from Calimshan had been conspicuous during the siege, I knew Pelias would discount my words as the ramblings of a madman. This allowed me to soothe my conscience with a genuine offer of assistance. "I am a personal friend of the Caliph of Najron," I boasted. "I could arrange a house for you, and fill it with women who suit your desires."

At this, Pelias laughed. "I am a monk, Mukhtar. I have all I desire here in Candlekeep."

"But not for long, I fear."

"Ulraunt is not so petty as you think. He's a wise man."

"Perhaps, but wisdom is not kindness."

Pelias's answer came more slowly than before. "All the same, if I can't have it in Candlekeep, I don't want it at all."

"And nothing can change your mind, Pelias?"

He laughed, as though we had been making jokes. "Nothing."

"Ah, well." I sighed wearily. "Then would you give me a drink?" On the side of my litter opposite Pelias, I bent my wrist back. "That terrible stench is making me sick."

"Stench?" Pelias frowned. He picked up the copper water pitcher. "What are you talking about?"

"Your nose is not offended?" Truly, I was amazed. "Then you must leave Candlekeep at once—you have been here too long."

Pelias laughed and brought the water to me. "The only thing that smells here is—well, never mind, my friend."

"Indeed? You cannot smell it? It is the fetor of the grave, rotting corpses and mold."

Pelias grimaced. "I think I'd notice."

I scowled. "And what of the insects? Does their rustling not drive you mad?"

Pelias raised his brow. "Insects? We don't allow them in Candlekeep, Mukhtar. They damage books. There are magic wards to keep them out."

"Indeed!" I gasped. Then it came to me where I had heard a

similar rustling before, and smelled a similar odor: the night Gwydion and the woman had arrived with the *Cyrinishad*. "No insects at all?"

"Not enough to rustle, certainly." Pelias leaned down to hold the pitcher to my mouth. Had my arm been free, I could have plucked my dagger from his belt. "Are you thirsty or not?"

I raised my head and saw that I had enough freedom to do as I planned, and then some. Pelias tipped the pitcher to fill my mouth with water, but I closed my throat and spat it all back at him and made a terrible coughing. At the same time I jerked my left hand from beneath the middle strap, freeing my arm to a point just above the elbow. Pelias placed a hand behind my head to support it, then poured again. "Swallow, Mukhtar!"

This I did. I also reached across my chest and grabbed Pelias by the shoulder. Through his robe, I gathered a knot of chain mail and jerked him down upon my body, and when his head came close to my face I seized his ear with my teeth and bit down as hard as a camel.

"Mukhtar!" He tried to pull away.

I held fast. Pelias couldn't free himself without tearing his own ear from his head. I jerked my right hand free of the strap, then reached up and fumbled at his sword belt until I felt the hilt of my dagger.

"Mukhtar, what are you doing?"

But Pelias knew what I was doing; this was obvious by the fear in his voice and the fierceness with which he struggled. He ripped half his earlobe off trying to pull free of my teeth, and he dented the copper pitcher on my head. Had he but known how this pain fueled my strength! He fought mightily to free himself and grab my dagger, and with only one hand and my jaws to restrain him, it was a difficult thing to hold him near. My blade scraped back and forth across his abdomen, finding no weak links in his chain mail. Still, the advantage was mine; he was fighting only to escape death, and I was fighting to escape damnation. Even as his torn ear poured blood over my face, I turned my dagger and drove the point through the jangling armor.

It plunged deep into his stomach. I worked the blade this way and that, twisting and turning, as did the Caliph's assassins to ensure that their victims grew too weak to give battle. Pelias howled; I pushed him away, and he collapsed to the floor, leaving me drenched in glistening blood.

Thus I repaid the kindest friend I ever had: with treachery and injury and agony. My heart should have been glad, for nothing delights the One like the betrayal of a friend, which is always a veneration of the day he killed Kelemvor. But I felt empty and unclean, a leper inside and out. At that moment I counted myself Faithless, and in my despair, I could not pay Cyric his due.

I cut myself free and went to Pelias's side. I removed his robe and his armor and bathed his wound in water, then bandaged it with a dressing torn from the hem of his robe. He suffered greatly, but he lived, and this was some small consolation. I filled his mouth with a gag and bound him securely, though I knew he was in too much anguish to move. I spoke soothing words, telling him that he would survive until the witch returned to save him. Whether he heard me or not I cannot say, for his eyes were closed and his breathing was fast and shallow.

In his Glorious Wisdom, Our Lord of Murder chose to overlook this insult and did not strike me dead on the spot. Certainly I deserved it. Aside from mocking the One, I was wasting time.

I went to the window and peered around the heavy drape. To my great relief, the moon still bathed the citadel in its pale glow, and the stars still burned in the purple sky. I studied the constellations to learn the time, then surveyed them again. Only an hour remained before dawn!

Hastily I looked out over Candlekeep, trying to guess where the book might be hidden. Below my window lay the fortress's great ward, ringing the entire span of the citadel. Along its outer edge rose more buildings than I could count—stables, temples, workshops, sleeping quarters—all standing tight against the massive outer walls, all crammed full of Flaming

Fists, Hellriders, and other defenders of thieving Oghma's monks.

In the center of the citadel rose an outcropping of dark basalt, terraced into many levels and mottled with thickets of trees, and laced by winding paths and cascades of steaming water. Here rose the fabled towers of Candlekeep, scattered hither and thither across the hill, each at the end of its own path, each as tall as a titan. And atop the mount stood the mighty Keeper's Tower, surrounded by a curtain of steam and looming above all the other spires.

At once, I knew where I had to go—not because the Keeper's Tower was the safest place to guard the *Cyrinishad,* and certainly not because Ruha had gone there only moments earlier—I had no wish to follow that woman anywhere. I had to go because a soft, sinister rustling was hissing down from the great spire, filling my ears with a murmur as relentless as it was gentle. The *Cyrinishad* was calling; the book was a living, sentient thing, and it could sense that I was near.

As I watched, a wedge of yellow light appeared at the base of the Keeper's Tower and shot across a drawbridge, silhouetting the veiled figure of the witch. She stopped to speak with the guard, and I remembered the token Pelias had offered her. Though the distance was too great to see if she displayed the emblem, I felt certain that only those bearing such wards were allowed inside the Keeper's Tower.

I returned to Pelias's side and rummaged through his robe until I found a small disk of bronze. My dear friend had served me yet again! I pulled the cloak over my head, then sliced away the bottom to avoid tripping on the hem, and then I felt the blood-soaked wool clinging to my stomach.

My hopes vanished in a breath. What sentry would let me pass with such a stain on my frock? And even if Tymora favored me and I somehow avoided the door guard, Ruha and Ulraunt would soon discover my escape and raise the alarm. And even if I found the *Cyrinishad* before they caught me, there would be Gwydion to deal with. Surely, he slept beside the book like a dog by its master. The moment I touched

Cyric's prize, he would leap up and slice me in half and send my poor soul on its way to Kelemvor!

Yet, I had no choice except to try. My desperation became my friend, for a hopeless man can try anything and lose nothing. I left with no clearer plan than this: to go to the Keeper's Tower in all haste, slip through its halls in complete silence, and deal with anyone who challenged me just as I had dealt with Pelias. If at all possible, I would find the *Cyrinishad* and do as the Prince of Madness commanded.

I left the building by a side-window and crept a third of the way around the ward, slinking warily through the shadows beneath the outer wall. Then I thrust my dagger into its sheath and started up one of the many paths that meandered toward the Keeper's Tower. Here I moved without hesitation; if someone observed me from a window, they would see only a monk walking along a trail.

Halfway up the hill, the path I had chosen bent in the direction of a lesser tower and ended there. I left the trail and went into the trees, and here the climbing grew much slower by virtue of the broken ground and the gloom beneath the low-hanging branches. A brook trickled across the hill, and in the confounding darkness I could not see whether it flowed left or right, or why it seemed to traverse the slope instead of rushing straight down. At once I lost all my bearings, and the world spun in the darkness. It tipped on its side, so that what had been up became merely forward and what had been steep became level, and the trees stood all about me at a slant, as though a stiff wind had battered them all their lives, and I remembered Cyric's mad words at the Low Gate: "It depends on me, of course. . . . Nothing is certain until I have beheld it and set it in place, until I have placed myself above it or below, before it or after," and I understood.

Then my feet grew light, and I rushed through the darkness, and not once did I trip or lose my wind. No longer was I climbing a hill. Now I was running across ground as flat as a beach, and I saw that this was a gift of Cyric's words, and that his words had also given me another gift far greater: the means to reach the *Cyrinishad* from an unexpected approach. Whether this was his plan I did not know, but it braced me up; I felt as fleet as a gazelle and as strong as the bull that had gored me.

I broke out of the trees and saw the Keeper's Tower looming up before me. At my feet lay a steaming moat, so hot that a flood of sweat poured down my brow and stung my eyes. The channel stank of brimstone and iron, and down beneath its white mantle I heard the water hissing like snakes.

I grew frightened, and the moat grew as wide as a river. The tower loomed like a mountain before me, its dark windows rising a thousand hands above my reach. I withdrew my dagger and felt Pelias's token in my pocket—perhaps it would be best after all to cross the drawbridge and seek admittance from the door guard.

From down in the ward came the witch's distant voice. "Alarm! Alarm!"

My dilemma vanished like smoke, for even with the token, no guard would let me pass now. I tucked my dagger back in its place, then closed my eyes and recalled Cyric's words once more.

"It depend on me, of course . . ."

I imagined the world as he had described it, standing on its side. I pictured the plain and the sea as one great precipice. The tor beneath my feet became a long, jagged spur upon the cliff's face—a nose, as it were. Then I imagined the moat as a ring of white clouds encircling the end of this nose, and the Keeper's Tower I perceived as a wart hanging on the tip.

When I opened my eyes, I saw what I had imagined. I grew dizzy and crouched down, clinging to the ground. My head whirled, for now the "ground" was the face of a cliff. To reach the tower, I would jump outward and down toward its curving walls, as if leaping onto a bridge whose end was anchored in a misty vale below. And then I would simply walk across that bridge! I pushed away from the cliff and dropped.

But I was not the One.

Everything did not depend on me. Indeed, all matters

seemed entirely certain of themselves, regardless of how I beheld them. In an instant the steam became so thick I could not see my own flailing hands. My skin itched and burned in the caustic mist, and the hissing of the water drowned out the rustling of the *Cyrinishad*'s dark truths. I was astonished to hear my own voice howling out, and more so because the name I called belonged not to Cyric, but to my wife. Then I splashed into the moat.

I could scream no more.

The water scalded me from head to foot, and no words can describe the pain. My skin turned crimson and peeled away in great sheets. Weeping blisters rose over my entire body, which puffed up and grew as tender as a rotten tooth. My lips cracked and bled, my eyelids swelled and burst, and surely I would have died but for the strength that had been mine since Cyric poured that swill down my throat.

In the next moment I found myself clinging to a dark wall, with no recollection of how I came there. I tried to blink and found my eyelids fused open, though one side of my face remained so swollen from Cyric's blow that I still could not see out of my right eye. My arms were red and blistered, and dotted with bloody patches. My hands were swollen and raw, with bits of skin hanging loose. My fingers were wedged between two blocks of basalt, and my feet were frantically scraping at the dark wall below. I bent my legs and felt my toes catch in a seam, and only then did I look up and see the high wall that soared into the heavens.

The Keeper's Tower.

Had I been able to speak, the word could not be repeated here. My luck had turned from foul to grievous. Below me, the tower wall dropped straight into the hissing moat. From above came the incessant rustle of the *Cyrinishad,* filling my head and drowning out all other sounds. I had no choice but one.

I placed my dagger between my teeth, then wedged my fingers in the next higher seam. And then I began to climb, moving one trembling limb after the other, never trusting my weight to a hold until its security was certain. When I reached a seam too narrow to welcome my fingers, I used my knife to scrape the mortar away, then continued on.

Thus I proceeded, driven by terror, pain, and a madness that most certainly matched my god's. A distant clamor rose in the ward as the monks and warriors answered Ruha's alarm. I dared not look down for fear I would grow dizzy and fall. Nor did I worry that an archer would pluck me from the wall, for the shadows on my side of the tower were as thick as ink.

When I had ascended to a height twice that of a fire giant, I stubbed my fingers against the underside of a sill. With great rejoicing, I grabbed the window and pulled my chest over the bottom edge. My head became tangled in a heavy woolen curtain, but I barely noticed. For many moments, I could do nothing but lie in darkness and feel my heart pounding against the ledge.

From the far side of the tower came many muffled voices. A valiant party was rushing up to save the *Cyrinishad*'s bearers from my murderous blade, but what did it matter? Gwydion would slay me the instant I neared the sacred book, and I was sure enough of my own abilities to know he would need no help.

Had there been any safe place to hide, I would have gone there and forsaken the command of my mad lord. But hiding was futile. My enemies were pounding across the drawbridge even now, and they would search the citadel stone by stone until they found me. Moreover, I had made it this far, into the very heart of Candlekeep, with nothing but my own wit and the strength of Cyric's elixir. Only a fool would have quit now!

I pulled the drape from my head and peered into the room beyond. It was black as a grave. I turned my good ear toward the gloom, trying to hear whether someone lay sleeping within.

Instead I heard the book, calling from above. The rustle of its dark truths grew louder, filling my head with the drone of a thousand hungry locusts. The stench of its ghastly parchment permeated my lungs; then a strange fever came over me. Nothing mattered but the book.

At once, I backed from the window and resumed the climb. A less truthful chronicler would claim that he chose this desperate path himself, knowing he would meet no one on the wall, while the stairs inside were packed with guards. I thought nothing of the kind. I only climbed, drawn upward by my obsession, and each time I pulled myself higher, the *Cyrinishad*'s touch grew more certain. My ascent became hurried and careless. Twice I slipped and caught myself with one hand, dangling by my fingers with my heart in my throat. Yet each time I pulled myself up and climbed even faster, determined to reach Gwydion's chamber before the warriors arrived to wake him.

I came to two more windows. Sensing that the *Cyrinishad* lay higher still, I climbed to a third. Here the book's stench was beyond compare. I reached for the curtain, and at once the rustling in my ears grew as loud as all the rasping throats in the City of the Dead begging for water. I drew the cloth aside so carefully that my heart beat a dozen times before I was done.

In this chamber, a candle sat flickering upon a table. By its light, I saw I had reached a small sitting room. There was a chair beside a table, and a shelf filled with books and fresh parchments. On my right, a small archway led into a second chamber, presumably reserved for sleeping. And beside this arch sat the *Cyrinishad,* still bound in its iron lockbox.

The *Cyrinishad*'s rustling quieted to a whisper, and I heard a small clink across the room. Gwydion himself stood facing the chamber door, staring at its latch! Perhaps the alarm had just reached his ears and he was not certain of what he heard, yet he already wore his full armor, down to his helmet and gauntlets, and I saw no sign of weariness in his bearing.

This puzzled me greatly—did the man never sleep? The answer, of course, was that he did not. I did not know this at the time—or I would never have entered the room—but Gwydion the Quick had been returned to life to watch over Rinda and the *Cyrinishad.* To assure the success of his mission, Kelemvor had blessed him with no need of sleep or of many other things required by common men.

I set my feet upon the floor and crossed the room as silently as a thief—or so I hoped. Gwydion heard nothing and reached down to open the door latch. I raised my dagger to strike, and he did not sense me until the last moment, when he glimpsed a strange shadow in the flickering candlelight.

He brought up one arm to defend himself and reached for his sword with the other. I leapt onto his back and, wrapping my legs around his waist, grabbed his chin from behind, pulling it high to expose his neck. My blade slipped up beneath his raised arm and found his throat, slicing at an angle down across the front. I pushed deep, cutting the many veins and arteries in his neck, opening the passage that carries air to the lungs and severing the strong muscles that hold the head in place.

A great rasp gurgled from Gwydion's throat, then he went limp and tumbled backward onto the floor. Though there was a small jingling of armor, my body cushioned the fall and the noise was not as great as it might have been.

From the next chamber came a woman's drowsy voice, still thick with slumber. "Gwy—Gwydion?"

The woman! Though I had expected some propriety, of course the trollop shared her chambers with the warrior.

"A thousand pardons." I made my voice as deep as a well. "I am an ox."

"Mmmmf."

I lay still for a time and listened. Through the door came the distant murmur of voices and the tramp of boots running up the stairs below, but the woman's room was quiet. I slipped from beneath the guardian and placed my dagger in my pocket, then lowered the drawbar across the chamber door. If I failed to notice that no blood had spilled from Gwydion's wound, it was only due to my elation. I had found the *Cyrinishad,* and now I would redeem myself in the eyes of my god!

I went to the iron box and laid my hands upon its lid.

At once, a vision flashed before my eyes. Inside the chest I saw a tome of raven-black leather, embossed with grinning skulls and dark sunbursts. From the center of the cover glared a head the size of a child's fist, with a stout silver chain stretched across its lipless mouth. The jaw began to work. A long black tongue darted out between its jagged teeth, but there was no sound. The book spoke in a way I alone could hear, by rustling its pages, rubbing them back and forth to beckon me near and release its terrible stench of decay.

The summons was almost more than I could bear. My knees trembled and my gorge rose until I could hardly breathe, and a terrible hysteria welled up inside me. My hands grew as numb as stone; tears poured from my eyes like rain, and, as a lamb before lions, I felt a wild urge to flee.

Then a sacred darkness hissed from the box and rose up to engulf me. The Flame of Knowledge burned my eyes, and the Dirge of Despair rang in my ears, and my tongue throbbed with the Perfect Anguish of Enlightenment. An icy fever coursed through my body, and I was struck by the full might of the Dark Truth, which is more than any mortal can bear. The marrow in my bones grew chill, and my stomach filled with cold nausea. I was seized by a dreadful revulsion, as though I had touched the living entrails of a man, and I grew so flushed and sick I nearly fainted.

This was hardly the rapture I had expected, but what did it matter? My god had commanded me to find the *Cyrinishad*, and now I had. All that remained was to deliver it.

I looked out the window and found the sky growing gray with the twilight that precedes dawn. Cyric's trial was only minutes away, but I needed only a moment to take up the iron chest and fling myself through the window, and less time than that to call the Dark One's name. I wrapped my arms around the box, which was as big around as a horse's belly, and lifted with all my might.

A great pop sounded between my shoulders.

Thinking someone had slammed a sword pommel into my back, I spun around at once, and this twisting only doubled my anguish. I collapsed onto the box and bit my tongue to keep from crying out. Only then did I perceive that no one was behind me, that I had caused this injury myself. A great knot of pain formed in the middle of my back, then spread around my chest in a band as wide as a sword belt and made every breath an agony.

The guards on the stairs sounded nearer every moment, and somewhere below them, the witch began to shout orders.

Seeing that I would never lift the iron box, I realized that I would have to open it instead. Biting my tongue against the pain, I rose and went over to Gwydion and searched his purse for a key to the locks.

There were only coins. Though I had once loved them as much as my wife, they meant so little to me now that I flung away the silver and copper and kept only the gold. Then I took the candle from the table, pulled my dagger from my robe, and crept into the other room.

The woman's chamber was a twin to the first, save that it had no door to the hall. The table had been moved to the window. On its surface lay a large book with a stiff leather binding, and also a fresh quill and an inkwell. There was no key.

The woman lay sleeping on a pallet in the far corner, squirming beneath her blankets. Her clothing hung beside me on a wall hook. I set the candle on the table and went in silence to search her garments. On my honor before the One and All, I swear I did this only to save time, and not because I was reluctant to murder her. If my hands trembled as I searched, it was only because Ruha's muffled voice echoed up from the tower below, calling out for Gwydion.

When I found no key in the clothes, I turned toward the woman. A long bare leg had slipped from beneath the covers, and a silver chain encircled her neck, disappearing into the shadowy cleft beneath the blanket's edge. I crept to her bedside and kneeled down beside her. Her dark, silky hair was spread around her head with beguiling abandon, and at that moment she smiled—perhaps she had sensed my presence in her dreams and took me for Gwydion. It occurred to me it might be wiser to let her live, as there could be some trap on the box she could warn me about.

Then a man's voice rumbled through the sitting room door and called upon Gwydion to remove the drawbar. The woman furrowed her brow, and I saw my folly at once. A servant of thieving Oghma would never help me recover the *Cyrinishad*. I pressed the tip of my dagger against the scribe's breastbone, and at that instant the voice of the witch voice filled the room.

"Rinda, open the door!"

Rinda's green eyes snapped open before me. Even in the candlelight, I must have seemed a fiend from the Abyss, with my boiled face and battered eye and burst lips. I started to clamp my ragged palm over her mouth, but already the scribe had pulled a knife from nowhere and was slashing at my throat.

"Gwydion!" she screamed.

Now all that follows happened in a whirl, and so swiftly that I can neither recall it in absolute precision, nor recount it with complete accuracy.

I threw myself backward. Rinda's blade slashed across my cheek, spilling hot blood all down my chest and leaving my face as numb as stone. Then the shrew leapt from her bed as naked as a beast and hurled herself upon me. Since my dagger was raised between us, she impaled herself to the hilt. She gave a great cry and lashed out once more, barely missing her mark. I saw that she wore no key about her neck, only the sparkling amulet of Oghma. I perceived then that the iron lockbox probably had no key at all, as its guardians never wished it to be opened.

A loud clanging arose in the adjacent room. This caused me some befuddlement, for it was certainly no door being battered down. I hurled the dead woman off me and scrambled toward the archway to see what magic Ruha had cast.

I met Gwydion in the doorway. There was no blood on him anywhere, which only made him more dreadful to behold. His head lolled about on the back of his shoulders, careening back and forth as he tried to swing it around so he could see to attack me. He had selected weapons for close quarters, holding a dagger in one hand and a hand axe in the other.

Apparently he planned to separate me from my limbs himself, as the guards were now battering at the door and he showed no interest in unbarring it.

I will not say what my body did then, as it was neither seemly nor important. I scrambled back into Rinda's room until I bumped into the edge of the table. Gwydion came after me, snapping his shoulders sideways so that his head swung around to leer in my direction. In the next instant, his axe was arcing toward my head.

I flattened myself atop the book on the scribe's table, knocking the quill and inkwell to the floor. My foe's axe struck the wall behind my head, knelling my doom. I rolled in the only direction left to me, into the window casement, then snatched up Rinda's book and held it before my face like a shield.

Gwydion's dagger struck the book with such force that it drove me out the window, and I found myself plunging down toward the steaming moat, still clutching Rinda's leather volume between my fists.

What could I say, except: "Cyric, the One, the All!"

Eight

In this much, gods are the same as mortals: those most eager for a thing arrive first. Long before Cyric's trial, Mystra manifested herself in the Pavilion of Cynosure and hid in a gloomy corner. There she lurked for a time, as still as a thief among the camels. The chamber looked the same as always to her, an alchemist's laboratory cluttered with braziers and glassware, but now it was dark and empty. She scanned every nook and shadow, and when she grew certain that no other god lurked there, she stepped from her hiding place to work her treachery.

The shrew worked quickly, first chiming a tin bell to make Cyric's voice ring false when he read the *Cyrinishad.* Then she wiped all the tables in the chamber with a living sponge, so the power would be drawn from the sacred words as they passed through the air. Next she summoned a serpent up through the floor and plucked its forked tongue from its mouth; this was to ward against oily words of persuasion and half-truths and promises of convenience, or lies of any kind.

When Mystra finished with the poor snake, she concealed her treachery by dropping a white veil upon the floor. The cloth had hardly touched the stones before the other gods began to arrive, Tempus clad in his armor, Shar cowering beneath her shadows, Talos haloed by an aura of flashing lightning.

"Kelemvor is not here?" asked Talos. The Destroyer's voice crackled with excitement, for nothing served his savage nature better than the annihilation of a god. "Surely he has not changed his mind?"

"Of course not!" said Sune, appearing in a swirl of red hair and flashing teeth. "Kelemvor has a steady heart." She glanced in Mystra's direction, then added, "Too steady, sometimes."

Moving quickly to deflect Sune's jealousy, Tempus dropped to his knees at her feet. "If there be battle anywhere on Faerûn today, it shall be for love!" he declared. The Goddess of Love was as fickle as a halfling in the desert, and she could be trusted to keep her promise only when showered with constant affection. "I am smitten by your radiance."

"And I am wild with lust!" Talos added.

To prove he spoke the truth, Talos set a crackling diadem of lightning in Sune's hair and circled her in a lewd dance. The goddess blushed and giggled, but she did not look away.

Chauntea and Lathander arrived together on a beam of golden dawn light, and old man Silvanus came striding down the ray behind them. Tyr appeared next, as always lacking both his right hand and his eyes. He took his place in the circle, then scowled at the number of spaces still empty.

"The trial was to begin promptly at Candlekeep's dawn."

At that moment, Kelemvor appeared at Mystra's side. His face was pale with fear, and he carried his sword on his belt. "I apologize for being late. But my full attention was required in the City of the Dead. Gwydion returned."

Gasps and murmurs filled the pavilion. Every god there knew who Gwydion was and what he guarded, and they were all as quick as cobras to see how Cyric meant to use the book against them.

"What of the *Cyrinishad?*" demanded Tempus.

Kelemvor's eyes went vacant, then he shook his head and shrugged. "I cannot remember."

This surprised no one, for each god knew the power of Oghma's enchantment. All eyes looked toward the Just One, and nine voices together demanded that he bar the *Cyrinishad* from the trial. Mystra spoke loudest of all, for she was much practiced in the art of deceiving men and knew that Tyr would suspect her treachery if she appeared unconcerned.

The Eyeless One raised the stump of his wrist, signaling for quiet. "We have dared to summon a fellow god to trial. If the verdict goes against him, we have it in our power to annihilate him—a penalty many are eager to levy." At this, he paused to turn his empty eye sockets upon Kelemvor. "It is only just to let Cyric defend himself as he wishes. If his words enslave us, that is nothing compared to the fate you have planned for him."

As the pavilion rumbled with outrage, Oghma manifested himself at Mystra's side, and his eyes were filled with dread. "Forgive me. All my attention has been turned upon the Fugue Plain. I can hear Rinda calling, but the amulet she wears prevents me from finding her spirit."

"What does Rinda's spirit matter?" thundered Talos the Destroyer. His fear sizzled through the pavilion in crackling white bolts. "Cyric has his book!"

The pavilion fell silent. Kelemvor reached for his sword.

Mystra caught his arm. "What are you doing?"

"I will not listen to that book of lies!" Kelemvor said this for all to hear. "Before I serve Cyric, I will rot in the Abyss!"

Tyr pulled a white-glowing hammer from the empty air and fixed his eyeless gaze upon the God of Death.

Before the Just One could warn Kelemvor against attacking Cyric, Mystra grabbed Lord Death's arm and asked, "What makes you think our only choices are rotting or slavery?"

"Tyr has decided—"

"You will not change Tyr's mind with your sword, and Tyr is the judge. You cannot defy him." Mystra pulled Lord Death's hand from his sword. "Ao would not allow it. Trust me in this."

Kelemvor scowled. Mystra held his gaze and did not look away, and finally his eyes lit with a secret comprehension. "As you wish. Perhaps I am being rash."

"Good." Mystra looked toward Tyr, then added, "No matter how much we hate Cyric, we must abide by the Just One's decisions."

Tyr nodded, for he was a buffoon, and buffoons are easily deceived by a woman's fawning words. He opened his hand and released his glowing hammer back into the empty air.

Oghma was not so easily fooled. He frowned and said, "I trust you mean what you say, Lady Magic. Remember, Ao knows all."

"Ao does not know all. If he did, he would have done something about Cyric before now." Mystra looked back to Tyr and said, "Since we must abide by your decrees, Just One, I ask that you hold Cyric to the same standard. I believe the trial was to start upon Candlekeep's dawn?"

"So it was," replied Tyr. "The charge is innocence by way of insanity, by which Cyric stands accused of failing in his godly duty to spread strife and discord beyond his own church. Since the Mad One is absent, who will speak against the verdict?"

It surprised no god present that the following silence was as deep as the Abyss. Tyr's eyeless gaze slid from one god to the next, lingering on each just long enough to observe a formality.

It was at this moment that Gwydion attacked me in the Keeper's Tower. His blow sent me tumbling out the window, still clutching the thick volume that had blocked his dagger.

"Cyric, the One, the All!" I cried.

Then I slammed down on something that felt like a log tangle. The air left my lungs in a burst, the book slapped my chest, and a skull's face eclipsed the brightening sky above me.

"You are late," rasped the One. He was as a giant to me. I lay in the palm of his skeleton's hand, with bony fingers as long as camel necks dancing beside me. He had eyes the size of wagon wheels and a jagged cavern for a nose and teeth that looked like two rows of ivory shields. One of his fingers curled down to tap the volume on my chest. "Hide that beneath your robe."

At first I did not understand. It seemed foolish beyond imagining that the One and All could mistake the plain ledger in my arms for the holy *Cyrinishad,* but Cyric closed his bony fingers about my body and began to squeeze.

"Obey!"

"But Mighty One, this is—"

"Do it now, Malik!" Darkness spilled from his eyes and poured over my body like a river, and I was swept into a sea of icy shadow. "The trial has begun."

How long I floated there is impossible to say. It seemed at once an instant and an eternity. I barely had time to tuck the book beneath my robe, yet a thousand thoughts drifted through my head. I recalled that while Rinda wore Oghma's diamond scroll about her neck, neither Cyric nor any other god could know the *Cyrinishad*'s location. I perceived that even if the book in my possession had been the sacred tome, the One could not have known it, and he certainly realized this. Then I saw Our Dark Lord's mistake: he believed that Oghma's enchantment had disguised the *Cyrinishad* as the book in my hands.

After an uncertain time the sea of icy shadow vanished, and we entered the Pavilion of Cynosure. I saw a dozen different places at once, a forest and a cavern and a golden sky and a battlefield and eight more, all in the same space. Each setting seemed as solid and certain as Faerûn itself, and each was filled with twelve shapeless, blinding radiances. Afraid of losing my sight, I covered my good eye at once—the other was still swollen shut—but the lights shone through the very thickness of my skull. They were a ring of fiery suns inside my head, burning in a dozen colors, and nothing I could do would shut them out.

"You are late, Cyric." Tyr's words filled me to bursting. "We have read the charges."

"You are mistaken as usual, No-Eyes," answered the One. "I am on time. You and the others are early."

Though the indignation that rustled through the pavilion was only a murmur to the gods, to me it seemed a rumbling earthquake. Cyric took no notice of it, but set me upon what was a stretching rack to him and a featherbed to Sune and a crypt to Kelemvor.

"But your hastiness hardly matters," said the One. "I know the charge, and I stand ready to refute it."

"How? By torturing that poor mortal to death?" asked

Mystra. A glittering stream of magic separated from her radiance and streaked across the room to douse me. At once, all my wounds and injuries vanished. "We all know you are cruel, Cyric. The issue is whether you are capable."

I saw at once that the harlot was trying to anger the One and get me killed, and so I cried, "What have you done? I have no use for a whore's kindness!" Next to the booming voices of the gods, my words were as a cricket's chirping, but I did not let this stop me. I spat toward Mystra's radiance, and I yelled, "A plague upon your Mysteries and your Order! They are as nothing to the Way of True Belief!"

A peal of Cyric's laughter knocked me from my perch and sent me plummeting to the floor, and as surely as this bruised my ribs, it also saved my life. In that instant, six lightning bolts from six different gods struck the bench where I had been standing. If none of these attacks came from Mystra, and if she did not revoke the magic that had healed my wounds, I am sure it is only because she feared the wrath of Our Dark Lord.

Still chuckling, Cyric plucked me from the floor and held me out on display. "This is Malik el Sami yn Nasser, and I will not have you killing him. Malik is my witness."

"Witness?" growled Kelemvor.

"Surely I am allowed one witness." Cyric addressed this to Tyr. "He will be my only defense."

"By all means," said Tyr. "Anyone you wish may speak."

"And this time no one will interrupt?" Cyric asked. "Especially with lightning bolts?"

"Any witness speaks under my protection," Tyr promised. "No harm will come to him. Is that clear, Talos?"

A crackle of reluctant consent sputtered from Talos's radiance. Then he began to drift about the pavilion, wreaking destruction across all twelve forms of the chamber's existence. Kelemvor's radiance drifted closer to Mystra. Sune slipped over behind Tempus, and Shar's luminous shadow began to shrink in on itself. They all knew of the book hidden beneath my robe, and like Cyric, they all believed it to be the *Cyrinishad*.

"There is no need for the mortal to speak!" Sune's radiance moved so close to Tempus's that they became one. "Perhaps Tempus will reconsider his charges?"

"No."

"For me?" In her desperation to prevent the reading of the *Cyrinishad*, it is a wonder Sune did not offer to have him on the spot. "I would be most . . . passionate."

"Tempus, you would do well to accept her offer," urged Shar. "Pressing your charges will only make matters worse for us all."

No sooner had the Nightbringer added her voice to Sune's than Silvanus and Talos added their voices to hers, and then Chauntea and Lathander added theirs to the growing chorus, and I saw that it hardly mattered what was hidden beneath my robe. The book could have been *The Caliph's Guide to Love,* and still they would have withdrawn their charges.

But not Mystra, and not Kelemvor, and not Tempus. Together, they exclaimed, "No!" and a veritable wind swept the pavilion.

When it had passed, the Battle Lord added, "I will not withdraw the charges. I cannot." And this was true, for Tempus would not break his word to Mask.

"Nor do I ask it," said the One. I felt his smirk in the prickling bumps that rose on my skin. "Indeed, I demand the right to answer the charges. Malik, you will read from the ledger."

"Read, Mighty One?" I felt almost relieved not to have the *Cyrinishad* beneath my robe; after the terrible nausea I had suffered merely touching its box, I doubted I would have survived reading the holy tome itself. "Me?"

"You, Malik—now!"

As I pulled the ledger from my robe, a deafening murmur filled the pavilion. The radiances of Tempus and Talos and Kelemvor all drifted closer, and Tyr moved to cut them off. Such a lump formed in my throat that I could not speak, for I perceived that I would be annihilated in the coming battle.

Mystra stepped forward and caught Kelemvor's arm. "Wait! Let him read." Without awaiting a reply, she turned to me. "Go ahead, Malik. Start from the beginning. No one will harm you."

The harlot's reassurance astonished her fellow gods as much as it did me. Kelemvor stopped on the spot, as did Talos and Tempus, and even Tyr's radiance spun around to face Mystra.

"What?" cried Cyric.

"She said to let him read." Tyr's voice was thoughtful. He remained silent a moment, then his radiance slowly swirled back toward Cyric. "Surely, you have no objection to that?"

"Of course not, but if she changed the book when she cast that healing spell on my witness—"

"She did not tamper with your evidence," said Tyr. "I have checked. Now, will you let him read?"

"Yes." The smugness in Cyric's voice had been replaced by wariness, and when he addressed me, I could feel the cold suspicion in his words. "Go ahead, Malik."

I opened the book and saw that it was Rinda's journal, with a dozen blasphemies in the first paragraph alone. Knowing what a grievous mistake it would be to read such sacrileges in the presence of the One, I decided to replace them with the story of the ascension of Our Dark Lord, which every child in the Church of Cyric learns by heart.

But when I opened my mouth to speak, a great hissing filled my ears, and instead of *A Childhood in the Shadows,* a terrible sacrilege spilled from my unwilling lips. I could read only what lay before me:

" 'I first met Cyric in a parchment shop, where the putrid air reeked of bloody hides and offal-filled tanning vats. The stench of the place was overwhelming, yet also fitting; nothing could describe better my feelings toward the Prince of Lies.' "

I tried to stop reading. But as soon as my eyes rose from the page, that terrible hissing filled my head, and I found myself staring at the next line. I did not know it then, but Mystra's spell against lies had caught me. I had to read the story in the ledger—and once I had begun, it was impossible to stop! Imagine my horror as the blasphemies continued to pour from my mouth:

" 'This is the story of Rinda, a scribe of Zhentil Keep who was forced by the Lord of Corruption to write the *Cyrinishad,* a volume of vile lies lacking a single word of truth'—"

"Malik!"

Cyric's voice blasted me from the bench and sent me tumbling across the floor, and still I could not stop reading:

"—'and of how Wise Oghma helped her write a true account of the liar's life'—"

I saw a red ball separate from Cyric's dark radiance and come streaking toward me, then I tumbled one more time. My world exploded into searing fire. That should have been the end of this tale, yet the flames did not devour me. They did not raise one blister on my skin, nor singe a single hair on my beard, nor char any page of the book in my hands, and still I read on:

"—'which resulted in Cyric's ejection from the City of the Dead and the downfall of his worldly power'—"

"Silence!"

Though the roar of Cyric's voice drowned out my pitiful chirping, I continued to read. How could I stop?

"Obey, Malik! Obey, or you will live to see me burn your bones clean in boiling acid!"

"You will not!" boomed Tyr. "That would be interfering with a witness. Until this trial is done, Malik el Sami yn Nasser is under my protection and, through me, Ao's. Neither you nor anyone else may harm him."

Cyric fell quiet, and of course I filled the silence with another blasphemy. " 'He read his own book and was driven mad by his own lies.' "

"Enough!" Cyric yelled. For a moment, his radiance grew so dim I could make out his fleshless hands pressed to the sides of his skull. "I release him!"

With that, the shapeless radiances of the twelve gods went dark inside my head, and the twelve forms of the Pavilion of Cynosure vanished around me, and I plummeted back into the sea of icy shadow, leaving the One to stand alone against his accusers.

The chamber fell silent in my absence. The thoughts of the gods turned inward, first to their relief that the book beneath my robe had not been the *Cyrinishad,* then to the strange compulsion that had kept me reading in the face of my god's anger. Mystra saw the questions in their eyes, and she knew that soon even her magic would not prevent them from seeing the truth.

"Did your thief steal the wrong book, Cyric?" she asked. "Or perhaps you find the impressions in Rinda's journal flattering?"

Many gods chuckled, but not Tyr and not Oghma. The Wise God furrowed his brow and turned to gaze at Mystra. "Lady Magic, why do you suppose the mortal kept reading?"

Mystra made no answer, for if she spoke at all, her own spell would compel her to reveal all she had done to guard against the *Cyrinishad*'s power.

Oghma pressed for a response. "Clearly, Malik knew his god was displeased."

"Most displeased." The One fixed his black-burning eyes on the Goddess of Magic and watched her most carefully. "Well?"

When Mystra still made no answer, Sune stopped preening and said, "The little man was in awe, of course. Twelve gods! What mortal would not be?"

Oghma bit his lip against an impatient reply, then said, "I fail to see how being in awe would cause him to defy his god. The effect would be quite the opposite, I would think."

Sune lifted her chin, then glared at Oghma. "It is impossible to say what mortals will do when they are awestruck—they are so flighty. You should know that. You are the God of Knowledge, are you not?"

"Indeed," Oghma replied.

"The mortal's reaction hardly matters," Kelemvor said, seizing on Oghma's pause. "He read nothing we did not know already."

"But it would matter," said Tyr. "In the Pavilion of Cynosure, everyone must be free to speak his own mind—including mortals, if they are important enough to be here at all."

"You said it would matter," observed Oghma. "Does that mean he was not compelled?"

"Not by magic or thought, not that I could find with Ao's power," replied the Eyeless One.

The reason for this, of course, was the veil Mystra had dropped before the trial. Tyr might have use of Ao's power, but Lady Magic was the mistress of the Weave itself, and she could do more things with magic than the Just One dreamed.

Thus acquitted of suspicion, Mystra felt safe enough to break her silence. "Now that Cyric has had his say and everything seems in order, the time has come to call for a verdict."

"Call for what you like, it does not matter to me." As Cyric spoke these words, he grew as translucent as a specter and began to fade from the pavilion. "I am above your verdicts."

"Not quite," said Tyr. The Eyeless One pulled a loop of chain from the empty air and tossed it in Cyric's direction; the chain vanished before it hit the floor, but the One's form grew instantly as solid as stone. "Until this trial ends, Ao has given me the power to bind you over for judgment."

"What?" Cyric shook his hands, and the sound of a rattling chain filled the air. "Ao gave you rule over me?"

"Of course. You are so much mightier than we," mocked Talos. "He knew we would need it."

"And now the time has come to wield our power," said Tempus. "Let us call the verdict and get on with our real business: naming Cyric's punishment."

Only Tyr did not add his voice to the chorus of agreement. "Cyric has not yet retired his defense," said the Just One. "He still has the chance to state his case."

"To you?" Though Cyric's tone was disdainful, he ran his gaze around the circle and studied each god in turn, and he lingered longest on the faces of Mystra and Kelemvor. "How can I expect you to understand me? I have made myself; I am as different from you as dragons are from lizards."

"Nevertheless, perhaps you should try." Oghma spoke gently. "These particular lizards happen to have the power of life and death over you."

Cyric's eyes flared to twice their normal size and burned like black fireballs. Yet when he spoke, he did it in a civil tongue. "I am charged with innocence by reason of insanity?"

"That is the charge," affirmed Tyr.

"Ah . . . Perhaps you will allow me the leeway to prove the charges at least half-correct." Cyric glared at Mystra, then smiled and marched across the pavilion to stand before Kelemvor. "I ask Lord Death to be my witness."

"What?" Kelemvor's hand dropped toward his sword. "If you think I will—"

"Really, Kel." Cyric glanced at Kelemvor's sword hand, then added, "Even if you could pull it off, I suppose Tyr's protection extends to me as well as to my witnesses."

Kelemvor took his hand away from his sword. "I cannot imagine how you think I would help you."

"Of course you can't. I'm crazy," Cyric replied. "I only want to know if you would ever serve as my . . . inferior, shall we say?"

"Never!"

"I suppose not. After all, I have always treated you rather poorly." The One nodded and started to walk away, but paused and turned back to Kelemvor. "Then tell me, when you thought Malik had the *Cyrinishad,* why did you let him read?"

Mystra tried to catch Lord Death's arm and warn him to be silent, but Kelemvor, thinking to evade the question with a vague answer, had already opened his mouth.

"Because Tyr said . . . " Here he stopped, and a long choking noise rose from his throat. He shook his head to clear it of a sudden hissing, then went on, "Because when Mystra urged Malik to read, I knew she had done something to protect us."

This surprised no one except Tyr. "But I checked for magic!"

Cyric ignored him and turned next to Mystra. "Is Kelemvor right? Did you do something to annul the *Cyrinishad?*" He paused here and glanced toward Tyr. "I am sure everyone will understand if you have no wish to reply."

"I will answer." Mystra gazed past Cyric to Tyr, who had

drawn his glowing hammer and looked ready to use it. "I spun the Weave to shield us from the *Cyrinishad*'s corruption, and to prevent anyone in this trial from lying."

As soon as she said this, her magic veil appeared on the floor. Tyr stuck his warhammer in his belt and snatched up the cloth. "This was forbidden!"

"So it was," Cyric said. "But, as I am the injured party, I ask you to wait until I finish before levying your punishment."

"So be it." Tyr wadded the cloth into his palm.

"I have only one more question, Lady Magic." Cyric curled his lip as he spoke this, for he knew better than any god that Mystra was no lady. "Do you want to see me destroyed because you fear me, or because you favor what you call 'the Good'?"

Mystra's answer came at once. "Because I hate you." She closed her mouth and tried to hold it that way, but there was more truth to tell, and so her lips parted again. "And because I favor what is good for the mortals of Faerûn."

These words occasioned many whispers among the gods. It was Mystra's divine duty to maintain the impartial balance of the Weave, and her admission was a violation of that sacred duty.

Tempus stepped forward and pointed at Cyric. "A clever trick, Mad One, but we can deal with Mystra later. You are on trial here."

Cyric spun on his heel and faced the Battle Lord and almost danced across the floor to meet him. "I know, Tempus! I was not trying to distract anyone!" The One was almost chortling now, and the Battle Lord recoiled as a vizier does from a beggar. "But since you ask, can you hold me alone accountable for war's decline in Faerûn?"

"Why should I not?"

"You have not been listening, Slowhammer! How many bystanders have been engulfed by stray fireballs lately? How many towns have been razed by magic earthquakes?" Cyric whirled around and pointed a naked finger bone at Mystra. "And how many rivers have suddenly run dry when a party of refugees needed to escape their pursuers? How many ridges have sprouted thorn thickets to turn a band of marauders away from a defenseless village?"

Mystra could say nothing, for Cyric's charges were all as true as the words of the *Cyrinishad*.

After a moment's consideration, Tempus nodded. "All you say is true. Faerûn's war magic has been less than crushing of late, and when it does devastate, it always favors the virtuous side. Perhaps Mystra shares in the blame—"

"Wait!" Cyric interrupted. "There is more—or have you not noticed how the noblest warriors are losing all fear of death, while the backstabbers and cowards grow more cautious than ever?"

Again, Tempus nodded, but this time he said nothing and waited for Cyric to continue.

"We all know whose doing this is." This time, the One pointed at Kelemvor. "The Usurper rewards noble men so favorably that they cannot wait to die. They sacrifice themselves in the most ridiculous causes—while the more cunning are so terrified of his punishments they hardly dare to fight. Soon enough, there will be no war at all on Faerûn! All the brave men will be dead in their paradises, and the cowards will not step across their own thresholds for fear of being killed by a falling pot."

Kelemvor could say no more than Mystra, for the truth was just as Cyric claimed.

After the One finished, Tempus looked him up and down. "All you say is true, but if you think to trade your own life for—"

"Not at all!" Cyric said. "All I ask is that I be charged for my own . . . actions."

"The request is reasonable." Oghma's comment surprised Cyric more than it did Mystra or Kelemvor. "A case could be made that Lady Magic and Lord Death are more guilty of neglecting their duty than is Cyric."

Tempus's visored face swung toward Tyr. "Can I expand my charges to include the other two?"

Tyr glanced at the crumpled veil in his hand. "Done."

Mystra whirled on the Eyeless One. "How dare you!" she stormed. "I may have disobeyed you, but I am not like Cyric. Neither is Kelemvor!"

"We will decide that in a tenday," Tyr replied. "Use the time to prepare for your trial."

Nine

Even the darkness of the Shadow Sea could not save me from the power of Mystra's magic. Though Rinda's journal lay hidden beneath an icy blanket of murk and my eyes could not read a single letter, syllables spilled from my lips one after another and strung themselves into words. The words knotted themselves into sentences, which bound themselves into paragraphs, and I spoke the foulest profanities that had ever assailed my ears. Yet these words were nothing compared to the blasphemies that had poured from my mouth in the Pavilion of Cynosure. Soon Cyric would torture me a thousand ways, and I saw each in overwhelming detail. They all ended with bitter death, with me lying alone and forlorn upon the Fugue Plain with no god to claim me—no god except Lord Death, who would sentence me to an eternity of torments as terrible as those inflicted by the One.

Some uncertain time later, my stomach rose into my chest, and the sea of icy shadow melted into wisps of black mist. The wall of a great tower appeared before me, silhouetted against the golden disk of Lathander's dawn sun. Cyric had returned me to Candlekeep in the same place from which he had plucked me, and now I was plummeting down alongside the Keeper's Tower.

Favoring a quick death on the moat's rocky bank to a slow death in its boiling water, I kicked my feet up over my head. The leather journal flapped open in my hand, and even then did Mystra's magic compel me to read what I had glimpsed:

" 'The skin of my father, Bevis the Illuminator'—"

The outline of the stony bank emerged from the sulfurous vapor below. I thought my death would come quickly and at last still my blasphemous tongue, but Cyric's trial was not over. I hit the stones with a soft thump, then bounced into the air and tumbled down the slope. And such was Tyr's protection that I suffered only a dizzy head.

I came to a rest against a scraggly pine, then finished the sentence that had been on my lips when I struck the ground: "—'was used to make the parchment for draft 398, and I knew my own skin would be used for draft 399 if my words did not please Cyric.' "

The accursed journal still lay in my hands!

Dawn was full upon Candlekeep; the sun stood a hand's span above the ramparts, flooding the citadel with golden light and laying down long streaks of shadow behind trees and towers. From the ward below came the bustle of companies forming to receive unexpected orders, but the area near the Keeper's Tower seemed surprisingly deserted, with not a monk or soldier in sight.

The *Cyrinishad*'s fetor hung thick and cloying in the air, and I felt a shadow of the revulsion that had sickened me when I touched its iron box. The beckoning rustle of the tome's parchment pages swelled into a blaring drone, but no longer did the sound come from Rinda's window. Now it reverberated through the thick walls of the Keeper's Tower, growing deeper and more sonorous as it settled toward the lowest floor.

They were moving the *Cyrinishad!*

And though my greatest ambition remained the recovery of the sacred tome, I was helpless to rescue it from the thieves who had it now. Even had I been a mighty warrior capable of slaying a dozen men, Mystra's magic compelled me to do nothing but read from the accursed journal in my hands.

" 'Cyric had brought me to that rank parchment shop to begin his story because he was born there. It is a pity his mother didn't toss him into a tanning vat and forget what she had borne; certainly Faerûn would have been the better for it!' "

As this sacrilege gushed from my lips, a booming clamor erupted on the far side of the Keeper's Tower. A company of guards thundered across the drawbridge, and the rustle of the *Cyrinishad*'s pages became a deafening roar. Then that meddling Harper witch shouted some orders, which I could not understand on account of the noise in my ears, and a small band of warriors left their fellows to rush down into the ward. I knew at once that they were carrying the One's sacred book, for the sound that filled my head grew more distant and more shrill.

I gathered myself up and stumbled across the hill, thinking I might circle around and follow them from a safe distance. My eyes darted from Rinda's journal to the uneven terrain and back again, caught in a constant struggle between ground and page. I had gone only a few steps before the meddling witch came around the tower with more than a dozen men. They could not have been thirty paces away, yet they were mere silhouettes creeping along through the steam that rose from the moat, crouching down to peer through the sulfurous vapor and search the water's steely surface for my scalded body. Fearful of drawing their attention, I stopped and dropped to my knees and clasped my free hand over my mouth, but even that could not stop me from reading.

" 'Cyric spoke until dawn, though I will not offend my readers with all the lies and false words he spewed forth that first night, except to say that I returned home sick and weary. There I was greeted by the second god I had met that day, a mysterious figure who arrived with Lord Chembryl of the Zhentarim to ask me to write a companion to Cyric's tome of lies. So it was that I began the *True Life of Cyric* that same day.' "

Though my palm muffled these blasphemies, they rang as loud as bells to my own ears, and I was certain my foes would hear them too. I turned across the hill and placed the journal on the ground before me, then crawled forward on my hands and knees, reading as quietly as I knew how, watching between words for loose rocks that I might send tumbling down the hill.

The witch and her companions edged along the moat and stopped beneath Rinda's window, where the guards stirred the water with the butts of their halberds. Of course, they did not find my body.

"Lodar, get some hooks and line so we can drag the moat," said Ruha. The *Cyrinishad*'s droning had grown distant enough that I could hear her words. "Balas, go ask Zale to rouse the rest of his hippogriffs. If that little murderer did not drown, then he has flown away."

The two soldiers moved to obey, Lodar returning to the drawbridge and Balas starting down my side of the slope. I rolled into a shallow crevice where a nearby pine had rooted itself. This cranny was a little deeper than my body was thick, and just wide enough for my belly—an ideal place to hide, at least until I could finish Rinda's accursed journal and turn all my thoughts to the *Cyrinishad*.

After Balas passed by, I squirmed onto my stomach so I could watch my foes above, then surrendered to my compulsion. The journal contained nothing but blasphemies and lies, and yet these made as much sense as the truth, so that not only was I compelled to read Rinda's vile story, but also to give it consideration and search out the inconsistencies that proved it false. Unfortunately, these were exceedingly few and small, as she was the most accomplished liar who has ever written.

After that first day, when Rinda met Cyric and that other cowardly god who would not show his face, she wrote day and night, meeting Cyric at the parchment shop at strange hours, then returning home to slave an equal time on the profane *True Life of Cyric*. And while she did all this, Mystra and Oghma and many other jealous gods struggled against the One and his sacred plan, turning Zhentil Keep, which was Rinda's city, into a place of deadly intrigue and shadowy battles. The time came when her last friend perished in this struggle. She despaired of surviving alone, and, fearing the One's wrath in the afterlife, wisely decided to destroy her unfinished work on the *True Life Of Cyric*. Before she could act, the coward-god revealed himself to her as Oghma the Wise and promised to look after her and protect her from the One and All.

Rinda wrote with such a plain and honest style that I would have believed these lies, save for the contradiction in her story: only a fool would believe Oghma powerful enough to defy Cyric the Almighty, and Rinda was no fool.

As I read this, the droning of the *Cyrinishad* grew more distant and more shrill in my ears, but I could not answer its call. With Ruha and the soldiers still searching the moat above me, I would have been discovered the instant I sent a stone clattering down the slope.

A long stream of hippogriffs began to rise from their pens and fly off in all directions to search for me. Then Lodar and three more men returned with a tangle of ropes and hooks, and the soldiers began to drag the moat. They started beneath Rinda's window and worked their way around the entire tower, drawing forth old soggy mattresses and swine carcasses and many other vile things, none of which was my body. It was a great relief to see the witch rushing to inspect each new discovery. As long as this business kept her occupied, there seemed little chance she would interrupt my reading.

At last, the day came when Rinda finished her work. Cyric came to her house and read the *Cyrinishad* from cover to cover and saw that it was perfect, and he took great pleasure in ordering Fzoul Chembryl, who was a notorious Unbeliever, to peruse the book. At once, Fzoul acknowledged the omnipotence of the Dark Sun. Then Cyric ordered him to punish Rinda, for the One had found the *True Life of Cyric* hidden beneath her floorboards and knew how she had betrayed him to Oghma. Fzoul obeyed, stabbing her in the stomach so she would die slowly and in agony. This so pleased Cyric that he bestowed on Fzoul the honor of reading the *Cyrinishad* to the masses of Zhentil Keep. He also commanded Fzoul to destroy the *True Life*, a volume which the One found too loathsome to touch himself.

As I read this, a lone hippogriff came swooping over my head and stopped my heart—if not my reading—but the creature did not wheel around to pluck me from my cranny.

Instead, it raised its wings and settled to the ground at the summit of the hill. The witch rushed over to speak with the rider. She stood close to him, like a lover, and they spoke too softly for me to hear. The man shook his head and waved his hand at the sky. The meddling Harper glanced back toward the moat, which her soldiers had already dragged two times, then began to scan the hillside around me. Something inside my stomach wanted to leap up and flee, but my head knew better than to think I could escape while reading a book.

My eyes were drawn back to the page, where I read of the low treachery of the One's enemies. After Cyric left Rinda's house, the god Mask emerged from Fzoul Chembryl's body, where he had been hiding to shield Fzoul from the power of the *Cyrinishad*. The Shadowlord healed Rinda. Oghma appeared also, and he gave Fzoul the *True Life of Cyric* to read in the *Cyrinishad*'s place before the masses of Zhentil Keep. Then the thieving God of Wisdom bestowed his diamond scroll on Rinda and gave her Cyric's sacred chronicle to safeguard.

I glanced up from Rinda's journal to see the witch motioning her soldiers away from the moat. "He is not there, or you would have found him. Let us work our way down the hill."

The soldiers dropped their hooks and spread out along the slope. I looked back to Rinda's journal—I could not help myself.

Fzoul read the *True Life Of Cyric* at dawn the next morning, and the lies in the vile book so inflamed the masses that they rioted at once. Then, as soon as the One turned his attention to the disaster in Zhentil Keep, the harlot Mystra stirred up a rebellion in the City of the Dead, and Cyric was helpless to save himself.

I came very near to believing these lies, as they did much to explain how the One lost the Throne of Death. Fortunately, at the last moment I perceived the flaw in Rinda's words, which was the impossibility of the One being helpless in any manner.

Up near the Keeper's Tower, the Harper and her soldiers began to creep down the slope, peering up into the boughs of every tree and thrusting their halberds down into every crevice. I began to inch backward down the slope, my eyes still fixed on the page before me.

Although Rinda did not claim to see Cyric's failure for herself—a rare honesty for her—she heard later that Mask was overcome by the *Cyrinishad*'s power, and that during the rebellion in the City of the Dead he confessed his betrayal to Cyric. According to Rinda, the One grew so furious he lost control of himself and, in his attempt to kill Mask, accidentally freed Kelemvor's spirit. On this falsehood, there is no need to comment; we all know the One never has accidents. I spat upon the page and smeared my dribble around to smudge the ink.

Then the *Cyrinishad* assailed my ears with a tremendous hissing. The cold nausea that had assaulted me in Gwydion's chamber returned, and my nostrils filled with the vile stench of sulfur and offal. I knew at once that my foes meant to drop the *Cyrinishad* into one of the boiling cesspools below their latrines, where no mortal could venture and no immortal would. I was filled with a terrible longing to rush to the holy tome's rescue—and also with the dreadful fear of glimpsing again its Dark Truths.

I started to rise, but then I saw the Harper hag standing at the other end of my crevice, peering up into the pine boughs over her head. Fearing the slightest movement would draw her attention, I froze and fought to keep my gaze from returning to Rinda's book.

Despite my terrible predicament, I lost my battle. My fingers turned the page ever so quietly, and my eyes read the first line, and the words welled up inside me, and nothing I could do would keep my lips from whispering them:

" 'As for Cyric, now he sits alone in his Shattered Keep, lost in delusions of grandeur and absolute power, leaving his church on Faerûn to grow ever more fragmented and weak. Some say this is because the shock of losing the City of Dead drove him insane, but I know better. Cyric was the first to read the *Cyrinishad;* his own lies drove him mad.' "

This blasphemy was too much, especially since I had felt for myself the omnipotence of the *Cyrinishad*'s Dark Truths and seen with my own eyes the One's mad behavior—and also because I perceived how well Rinda's lies explained al! that I had seen. A red sea filled my head, and, forgetting my terrible situation, I rose to my knees and flung the book away like the profane thing it was.

"Filth!"

I recalled my predicament when my world became a white flash. A deafening crack split the air, then a terrific jolt flung me from my hiding place and sent me tumbling across the hillside, until I finally struck a tree trunk and brought a shower of pinecones down upon my head. None of this caused me the slightest injury. I staggered to my feet and found myself facing exactly the direction I wished to go, which is to say away from the meddling Harper and her helpers.

The instant I tried to run, my limbs began to tremble with a sickly ache. My thoughts returned to Rinda's vulgar journal, and especially to her claim about the cause of Cyric's madness. Surely, this was another of her foul lies! The cries of my enemies rang out from all directions behind me, but still I found myself spinning on my heel to charge back toward the journal—and even I did not know whether this was because of Mystra's spell or my own need to find the lie in Rinda's claim.

My eyes were greeted by a solid line of armored warriors, grasping every sort of weapon, all rushing toward me. The sight turned my knees to rags, yet I grabbed a rock from the ground and ran to meet them.

Perhaps it would make a good tale to say that my assault stunned them so badly I smashed through their lines with nothing more than the stone and recovered the book, but the truth is much different. A few of them raised their brows; then we were upon each other. The stone flew from my hand the first time it struck someone's head, and the soldiers' weapons flashed at me from all sides, filling the air with such a whistling and clanging that I nearly died of fright—which was the only way I could have perished, as I remained under Tyr's protection and could not have been killed if a dragon had swallowed me.

Still, my foes thought I was giving a good account of myself.

In their fury, they slashed with blinding speed and thrust with the weight of their whole bodies and chopped with enough power to cleave me in two. But their blades never failed to turn aside, and each stroke hit one of their own. Before long, half of them lay bleeding on the ground. A clear alley to Rinda's ledger opened before me, and I shot from the melee like a bean squeezed from its pod, whooping for joy and thinking myself invincible.

The witch's voice burst into incantation. I glanced up and saw her flinging mud, but why should that have worried me?

"Save your magic, witch!" I leapt the crevice where I had been hiding and saw Rinda's journal ahead. "No one can stop the mighty Malik!"

She finished her spell the instant I finished my taunt. I did not know how I could possibly outrun my pursuers while still reading from Rinda's accursed book, but this could hardly matter to an invincible warrior such as me. I stooped to scoop up the ledger—then my feet plunged into a mudhole.

I fell flat on my face, and such was my compulsion to keep reading that I reached out and found the journal lying just beyond the fingers of my outstretched hand. I tried to bring my legs up to crawl forward and could not, and when I looked back to see the reason I found my feet caught in a block of solid basalt!

"Anyone can be stopped, Mukhtar." The witch walked down and picked up Rinda's journal, then scowled over her veil. "Or shall I call you the Mighty Malik?"

Ten

Kelemvor sat brooding in his crystal throne, staring out across a crystal floor through a crystal wall into the anteroom of the Crystal Spire, where an anxious mass of spirits stood awaiting admittance to the Hall of Judgment. Already the crowd filled the chamber to overflowing, and the Escorts were packing in more souls by the minute; the stream of the False and the Faithless never ended, and it was Kelemvor's duty to choose a fitting destiny for each one. If he fell behind, he would never catch up. Yet how could he pass judgment on all these souls, when he himself stood accused of failing his office?

"Jergal!"

Hardly had Kelemvor called the name before a shadow-filled cloak appeared beside the crystal throne, rising and falling upon a wind that did not exist. The cloak's hood contained a gray oval emptiness with two bulging eyes and no other features. A pair of white gloves hung at its sides, unsupported by any sort of arm or appendage.

"I am here for you, as always." This was the seneschal's customary greeting. "How may I serve you?"

"You know I have been charged with neglecting my duties," Kelemvor said. "Am I too kind to the brave or too harsh to the wicked? Do the charges have merit?"

"That is not for me to say," Jergal replied. "I am no one's judge, least of all yours."

"I am not asking your judgment," Kelemvor said. "I am demanding your opinion."

Jergal's cloak fluttered beneath Kelemvor's harsh tone.

"I have no opinion," said the seneschal. "I can only observe that you are always kind to the noble of heart and harsh to the craven. Your predecessors did not concern themselves with such questions, but only whether a soul had been Faithless or False."

"My predecessors . . . "

Lord Death leaned forward, braced his chin in his hand, and fell into deep contemplation, for there had been a long line of death gods before him. Kelemvor had stolen the throne from Cyric, who had taken it after Myrkul perished during the Time of Troubles. Even Myrkul had won it in a game of knuckle-bones, and all this reminded Kelemvor that if he failed in his duties, he could be replaced easily enough.

A second shadow-filled cloak appeared at the hall entrance. This was also Jergal, for even he had once been God of Death, and he retained the power to manifest himself in many places at once.

"Lord Cyric has requested an audience."

This brought Kelemvor out of his reveries, for the mere mention of the One's name set him on guard.

"Cyric? I have nothing to say to that madman."

"But I have something to say to you." As Cyric spoke these words, a mighty throne of polished bones appeared in the center of Kelemvor's empty Judgment Hall, and in it sat the One and All. He turned the black suns beneath his brow in Jergal's direction. "I did not request an audience. I demanded one."

Kelemvor drew his black sword from the air, but he was too shocked to use it. Aside from Mask, no one dared enter a Great God's home without awaiting permission—and with good reason, as any god was at his most powerful in his own realm. Yet here Cyric was, not only uninvited, but sitting upon his own throne. It made Kelemvor's head ache just to believe what he saw.

A third aspect of Jergal appeared in the entrance of the Judgment Hall. "Lady Mystra."

The Goddess of Magic manifested herself before Lord

Death's throne immediately, for the Crystal Spire was always open to her.

"Come quickly."

Kelemvor manifested an aspect of himself in Dweomerheart, Lady Magic's palace of magic curtains, and he saw that Cyric and his bone throne also sat in Mystra's shimmering audience hall.

"He entered without permission," said Mystra.

"The same here," said the Kelemvor in the Crystal Spire. He pointed past Mystra's shoulder at the Cyric sitting in his Judgment Hall. "He demanded an audience."

Mystra spun around and saw Cyric sitting before her in the Crystal Spire as well as in Dweomerheart, so that all three gods were in both palaces at once. All that follows happened in each throne room at the same moment.

"Just like old times." Cyric's mouth gaped open in a kind of grin. "Summon Adon, and the party will be complete."

"Adon has better things to do," Mystra replied. "Why have you broken into our palaces?"

The One leaned back in his throne and steepled his finger bones before his chin. "Did I approach you?" he asked. "Funny thing, but I swear you came to me."

"If I had come to you, you would be dead by now," said Kelemvor. "You demanded this audience. What do you want?"

The One leaned forward. In Dweomerheart he stared into Mystra's eyes, and in the Crystal Spire he stared into Kelemvor's.

"I have decided to take you two under my wing."

In both palaces, Mystra and Kelemvor exchanged puzzled looks.

"Come now," said Cyric. "Is this so hard to understand? We three must stand together. The others are conspiring against us."

"What are you talking about?" Kelemvor demanded.

"The others are jealous," the One explained. "And frightened. We have made so much of ourselves already."

"They are frightened of you," Mystra said. "With Kelemvor

and me, they are only angry—or have you forgotten how you used Tyr's aggravation against us?"

Cyric frowned at this. "Me? Tempus levied the charge!"

"At your prompting," Kelemvor noted. "Otherwise, we would be in trouble, but Tyr—"

"Tyr is as frightened as the others!" Cyric rose from his throne, and in the Crystal Spire he pointed a bony finger at Kelemvor, and in Dweomerheart he pointed one at Mystra. "Do not believe that rubbish about blind justice. He means to turn them all against us."

Mystra rolled her eyes, and Kelemvor shook his head.

"Sooner or later, you will join me. Do it now, and I promise you each a quarter of the spoils." The One shook his finger at the two lesser gods. "Imagine, the three of us ruling Faerûn!"

Mystra's jaw fell. "Can you really be that mad? You must know we would rather die!"

"We have listened longer than you deserve, Cyric." Kelemvor rose and pointed his black sword at the One. "Now go, before I save Tyr the trouble of trying any of us."

Cyric stared at the two gods in silence, then his teeth clacked together and he slumped back. "Fools! I was willing to forgive you." His throne faded into nothingness, so that he seemed to be sitting in empty air. "Now you fall with the rest."

Eleven

Rinda's journal lay atop a table on the dungeon's far side, and there was nothing I could do to reach it. My hands were bound behind my back, and my feet were embedded in a block of basalt as heavy as the Caliph's mother. For many hours now, Ulraunt had deprived me of food and water. He had ordered a pair of burly guards to hold my arms, then threatened to beat me with spiked clubs and brand me with hot pokers, and he even had an iron heating on a brazier now. Yet the only torture that frightened me was being deprived of the ledger. My need to read it grew more desperate with each breath, until I would have sold all my possessions at a quarter of their value just to glimpse one page. For this compulsion I reviled myself as a man does for any secret weakness, and I swore that even if Ulraunt held the book before my eyes, I would not read a single word.

Of course, this was an impossible oath. But I had yet to understand my affliction, and I did not realize Mystra's magic had caused it. I knew only that Rinda's journal made as much sense as the Dark Truth, and that her sacrileges explained what I had observed with my own eyes: namely, that the One's Church was tearing itself apart, and that Cyric had to be a lunatic to send a humble merchant such as me after the *Cyrinishad*. These thoughts were a great shame to me and more a reflection of my own craven nature than fact, yet they were as persistent as a hungry beggar, and it was to them I credited my obsession.

Ulraunt returned from the brazier with his glowing iron and held it before my eyes. I hardly gave it a glance, for my gaze was locked on the journal across the room, where the First Reader Tethtoril and Ruha stood with qualmish looks on their faces.

My inattentiveness angered the Keeper. "Look at this!" He slashed the iron back and forth before my eyes. "Do you know what I can do with this?"

"Nothing to me." By now, I knew this to be true, for I had not suffered a single bruise or blister from all the beatings I had taken before Ruha captured me. "I am under Tyr's protection."

"Tyr does not protect murderers! Hold his head!"

Though the rope binding my hands was as sturdy as a camel tether, Ulraunt's assistants were reluctant to release my arms, no doubt on account of the fierce reputation I had gained during my capture. One of the men slipped around behind me and locked his hands behind my elbows, and only then did the other guard release his own grasp and put me in a headlock. He was very large and strong; it would have been futile to resist, and I did not try.

Ulraunt waited to be certain his assistants had me securely, then stepped forward and brought the iron close to my face, so that I could see nothing but the glowing tip. He moved the poker forward, until it was so close my eyeball itched from the heat.

"I'll ask twice more, and each time you lie, I'll burn an eye out. I'm told it hurts very much."

"Ulraunt, this is not necessary," said Ruha. This was one time I was glad for a Harper's meddling. "He has already answered, and your own priest said he was not lying."

"This worm is immune to truth magic!" yelled Ulraunt. Such was the Keeper's anger that his own priest had left the room for fear of witnessing the torture of a helpless man. "No one can swim that moat. It will boil lamb!"

Ulraunt brought his iron close to my eye, and I saw that he meant to keep his vow and blind me. I wondered how Tyr would protect me from this, then the shaft of the poker turned as white as the tip. There was a low sizzling and the odor of burnt flesh.

Ulraunt cried out, then dropped the poker and grasped his hand. "How did you do that?"

I could not answer, for his big assistant was squeezing my neck so tightly that I could not move my jaw.

Ruha grabbed Ulraunt's shoulder and pulled him back. "You have had your chance. Now let me try."

Ulraunt scowled, then looked at his blistered fingers and shrugged. "If you like. But my patience is at an end. If he doesn't tell the truth, we'll execute him for what he did to Rinda and Gwydion."

The witch waved the assistants away, then watched as my gaze swung back to the journal. With each moment that passed, my compulsion to read grew twofold—and not only because of Mystra's spell. Rinda's claim about the cause of Cyric's madness was a terrible burden upon my soul, for I could not forget the cold nausea that had come over me when I touched the *Cyrinishad*'s box. Could the scribe be right? Could the Dark Truths of the sacred tome be so powerful they had overwhelmed even the godly mind of the One and All?

This horrid doubt was more than I could bear. I had to recover the journal and find the lie in her words and dismiss this blasphemous misgiving before it made me as mad as Cyric!

After watching me stare at Rinda's journal for several moments, the witch picked it up and brought it over, stopping just out of my reach.

"I will make you a bargain, Malik." She had already made me admit to my true name. "For every question you answer truthfully, I'll let you read a page from Rinda's journal."

"I must do the reading!" I blurted. Tethtoril cocked an eyebrow and Ulraunt frowned, and before either of them could object, I added, "I will tell you anything."

Perhaps this promise can be excused by recalling that I knew nothing of Mystra's spell. I perceived only that I had been seized by a strange compulsion to keep reading Rinda's journal; to my knowledge, I could lie as well as I ever had.

The witch nodded, then asked, "Did you come after the *Cyrinishad,* or this?" She raised the journal.

"The *Cyrinishad.*" There seemed no harm in admitting this much, as they had certainly guessed it already. "Cyric sent me to recover it for him, because he needed it for his trial, and Oghma's enchantment still prevents him from finding it himself."

This explanation seemed to spill from my lips of its own accord. I attributed my lack of self-control to my obsession and did not concern myself with it.

Ruha raised her brow. "Trial?"

I shook my head. "Page eight."

"Answer!" Ulraunt ordered, but the witch waved him off and turned to the proper page and held it up for me, and I read:

" 'As for what became of the *True Life Of Cyric,* I have heard that Fzoul Chembryl still keeps it in a safe place near the ruins of Zhentil Keep. Although I wish it were in the hands of a more trustworthy caretaker, I pray this is true. The *True Life* is the only way to unchain minds imprisoned by the *Cyrinishad*'s lies, and I fear the day will come when its plain truths are needed to save all of Faerûn. Gwydion and I are only human; someday, the *Cyrinishad* is bound to fall into the wrong hands.' "

Ruha lowered the journal, for the writing ended there, less than halfway down the page.

"Not fair!" I was nearly in a panic, for the passage had sparked the curious notion in my head that I might better serve Cyric by recovering the *True Life* and curing him of his madness, and I was anxious to find something to disabuse me of this thought before it became another vile obsession. "That was only half a page!"

"But everything written on it."

The witch closed the book and met my eyes, preparing to ask her next question. For the longest time she stared at me and said nothing, as though considering her words. Not once did she blink. I observed how silent the chamber had grown;

there was not the sputter of a torch flame, nor the rasp of a boot upon the stone floor, nor even the hiss of someone taking a breath. Ulraunt and Tethtoril stood as still as the Harper. My body grew damp.

"Mighty One?" I gasped. A foul taste coated my tongue.

The air chilled. A shadow oozed up between the stones of the floor and took the shape of an enormous man. He had a grinning skull's face and two balls of black fire where his eyes should have been, and his body was a mass of sinew and vein.

"Malik, you have failed me." He spoke in a thousand rasping voices, all edged with bitterness and anger. "You brought the wrong book."

"I—I could not lift the *Cyrinishad*," I explained. "It lay in an iron box, and I am only a humble merchant—"

"I know what you are! Do you still know where the *Cyrinishad* is?"

Truly, I did not want to tell him where they had dumped it. "More or less, Mighty One. They moved it, but I believe it is still in—"

"Do not tell me," the One snarled. He stepped over and braced his foot on the basalt block holding my feet, then grasped me by the throat. "We have one more chance, Malik."

With that, he began to lift. I grow longer and thinner, and also my chest, my abdomen, and even my legs, and I swear I grew as tall and lean as a gnoll.

"Please, O God of Gods, I am about to snap!"

"Nonsense, Malik. I could not hurt you if I wanted to."

The One jerked my neck up. An alarming crackle sounded from the floor, and as bones are weaker than basalt, I feared the worst. Then my knees sprang straight up and struck my belly so hard I coughed.

I opened my eyes and looked down. To my relief, I still had two feet hanging at the ends of my stout legs.

"You are under Tyr's protection." Cyric continued to hold me by my throat, so that my toes dangled above the floor. "And that is why my plan will work this time."

"This time?" My voice was but a gurgle, for the One's grasp

had all but closed my throat. "You still want me to read the *Cyrinishad* to your fellows?" Truly, I was astonished.

"See? Perhaps you are not so stupid after all. And now you have plenty of time. The trial resumes in a tenday."

And now I perceived that my god was madder than I had thought. "But the gods will never permit me—!"

The One closed his fist, pinching my voice off in the middle of my sentence. "Of course they will. Tyr has seen my glory. He is a True Believer now."

A shudder ran through my body, for I knew Our Dark Lord was deceiving himself. Tyr was determined to conduct a fair trial, but that was a far different thing than worshiping the One. If Cyric could not see this, he was doomed, and all True Believers with him. The passage I had just read in Rinda's journal returned to my thoughts, and with it the curious notion that the true way to help the One was not to recover the *Cyrinishad,* but to trick him into reading the *True Life Of Cyric*! If I could only return him to his right mind, he would not need the *Cyrinishad*—or anything else—to crush the other gods and bend them all to his will!

I perceived at once that this was what the Fates had always meant me to do and that I had interpreted my vision of the book too literally. My destiny was to unite the Church of Cyric not by recovering the *Cyrinishad,* but by finding a different book and curing the One of his madness! I cried out in joy, and Cyric, thinking me excited about Tyr's alliance, set me down.

I avoided looking in the direction of Rinda's journal, fearing that the One would guess my secret plan, but my compulsion won out. Before I knew it, I had gone over to the motionless witch and taken the journal from her hands.

I began to read aloud.

Cyric covered the page with a bony hand. "Must you?"

When I looked up to answer, it was with more shame than I have ever felt in my life. "I cannot seem to help myself."

Tongues of black flame shot from Cyric's eyes, but he did not chastise me in any manner. "Mystra's spell—damn her!" He glared at the book for several moments, then shook his head.

"There is nothing for it but to let you read the thing through. Destroying the ledger would only make you a greater idiot."

In response, I read a few lines describing how General Vrakk helped Rinda escape the destruction of Zhentil Keep. Then I drew the witch's curved dagger from the sheath on her belt and raised it over her heart, thinking to honor the One and rid myself of my bane in the same stroke.

Cyric's cold hand caught my wrist, then wrenched the blade free and tossed it into a corner. "Not now! I have enough to worry about without letting Oghma and Mystra know I am inside their precious citadel."

As the One said this, he pulled all the clothes off the Harper and pushed them into my arms, leaving her as naked as the day she was born. I will not tell you what passed through my mind then, for no man should have such thoughts about his enemies.

"Put these on."

I obeyed at once, placing the open journal on the table and reading about Rinda's dangerous journey through the Dales as I dressed. It is a fortunate thing that the witch wore her robes loosely and that she stood a little taller than I, for the extra cloth did much to hide my girth. The One himself wrapped the hag's scarf around my head and covered my face with her veil and lined my eyes with kohl from her pockets, but her silver belt was too small to clasp about my waist.

"No matter," said I, pausing after an account of how Rinda escaped a band of marauding frost giants. "As it is, the disguise will do well enough to help me escape."

"Escape?" echoed the One. "You need not escape. Just find the *Cyrinishad* and call me, as you did before."

I picked up the book and pushed open the dungeon's iron-clad door. "Of course, Mighty One."

And that is where I meant to leave matters, for I knew that escaping Candlekeep would be easy once I was outside. Disguised beneath the witch's head scarf and heavy veil, I could simply walk out the main gates and no one would think anything of it. But as I stepped out of the dungeon into the narrow stairwell, I felt the truth welling up inside me, and before I knew it, my foolish mouth was blurting it out.

"I will do everything to help you, Mighty One." Even as I said this, I slammed the dungeon door and dropped the drawbar in its locks. "But recovering the *Cyrinishad* will only make you more sick. I am going to cure you."

The One hit the door with such a terrific impact that it dented the iron and bounced me five steps up the stairway, yet the drawbar only bent and did not break. I snatched up Rinda's journal and ran up the curving stairs, and even then, with my frightened heart high in my throat, my obsession compelled me to read the story of how Rinda had awakened one morning to find Gwydion standing guard over her camp.

At last, a square of bright light appeared at the top of the stairs. I bounded up another step and paused to flip a page, and when I looked up again, a bloody wraith blocked my way.

Cure me, Malik? This time, Cyric's voices came from within my own head, for he had no wish to draw attention to his presence. *I am the God of Gods—if someone needs curing, it cannot be me.*

I stopped on the spot and let out such a shriek that my throat went raw.

Why so frightened? The wraith drifted a step toward me. *You know I cannot hurt you—not until the trial ends.*

I fell to my knees and touched my forehead to the cold step. "Please, Mighty One," I whimpered. "Let me explain—"

"Ruha?" Though this voice was familiar, it did not belong to the One. "Let me help you."

I looked up to see Oghma's priest rushing down the stairs in his white trousers and shirt. Although there was no sign of the One, the priest stopped two steps above me and gave a shiver.

Ten days, Malik. The One's thousand voices rasped inside my head. *The trial will be over in ten days, and then you are mine again.*

My belly turned cold and queasy, and my jaws began to ache with that terrible feeling that comes just before vomiting. Then I felt the priest's hand beneath my arm.

123

"Is Ulraunt actually torturing that poor beggar?" he asked.

My only answer was the sickly groan of someone battling his own stomach. I turned away and clasped my hand to my veil.

"No need to be embarrassed. Torture affects me the same way." The priest pulled me to my feet and began to guide me up the stairs. "Perhaps we'd better take you out to the eyrie for some fresh air."

Twelve

Gwydion the Quick squeezed free of the crowded ante-room, then strode across the empty Judgment Hall and knelt before Kelemvor's crystal throne. A red scar smiled upon the dead knight's throat, but this disfigurement was as nothing to the shame in his eyes.

"Rinda is dead." His gaze fell to the floor. "I let Cyric's assassin kill her in her sleep."

"You saved her a hundred times before that," said Kelemvor. "Look me in the eye, Gwydion. You have no cause for shame."

Gwydion raised his head and met Kelemvor's gaze, but his expression remained shameful. "It was that filthy little beggar! I should have killed him when I had the chance."

"How could you know? If you had killed everyone who might have been Cyric's agent, you would have slain hundreds for the sake of punishing the guilty few. Do you think that is why I let you return to Faerûn?"

Gwydion shook his head. "Of course not."

"Good." Kelemvor smiled sadly. "Then at least I can make this decision without doubting myself. You have performed your duty true and well, Gwydion, and so it is not my place to sit in judgment over your soul. Yet, before I release you to seek your place with Torm the True, I would ask a boon of you."

Gwydion nodded. "Of course."

"Rinda's soul lies somewhere outside the City of the Dead,

lost among the masses wandering the Fugue Plain. Oghma cannot find her while his amulet remains around the neck of her body, but if it is removed, Cyric will find the *Cyrinishad*."

Gwydion rose. "You want me to find her."

"And escort her to Oghma's palace," Kelemvor said. "He will not know of her presence, but I think Rinda's spirit will find comfort in the House of Knowledge."

Gwydion smiled, and now his customary pride chased the shame from his face. "It will be done."

Lord Death motioned with his hand, and Jergal's wraithlike form manifested itself next to Gwydion. "My seneschal will guide you to Oghma's palace and back to the Fugue Plain. Torm will come as soon as you call. I wish you a happy afterlife in his castle."

"Thank you, Lord Death." Gwydion bowed and then, with Jergal floating at his side, turned and departed.

But Gwydion left his shadow behind, lying upon the crystal floor. Lord Death started to call him back, then thought better of it and sat back, scowling and tapping his fingers upon the arm of his crystal throne. At length, a pair of white eyes appeared in the shadow's head; then it peeled itself off the floor and stood on two legs.

"I am glad to find you in a favorable mood, Lord Kelemvor." The shadow's limbs filled out and took the shape of a gloom-cloaked elf. "Perhaps you will receive my request as kindly as you treated Gwydion."

"I doubt it. I do not care for thieves." Kelemvor regarded the intruder with a hostile glare. Mask could pick any lock and steal even the most carefully guarded treasure, and for that reason he was never welcome in any god's palace. "Jergal!"

A pair of white gloves closed around each of Mask's wrists and stretched his arms taut. A shadow-filled cloak appeared on each side of the Shadowlord, and Jergal spoke in two voices at once, "I am here for you, as always."

Mask shifted his form to that of a helpless human female, but otherwise he ignored the seneschal and spoke only to

Kelemvor. "You dislike thieves? But you have stolen from me yourself!" The Shadowlord's wispy voice was neither male nor female. "Or perhaps you only made a mistake."

"Mistake!" Kelemvor leaned forward, but he was careful not to rise. To accuse a god of a mistake was worse than to say he had stolen something, and he saw that Mask would speak such words only to provoke a harsh reaction. "Explain yourself and be gone! I will not have Kezef chasing you through my city."

A shudder ran down Mask's murky figure, but he recovered himself quickly and continued. "You have passed judgment on one Avner of Hartsvale, have you not?"

Though many thousands of spirits had stood before Kelemvor since Avner, the memories of gods are limitless and perfect. Lord Death knew at once that Mask referred to a scofflaw orphan who had grown up in the streets of Hartwick, stealing from honest merchants and anyone else foolish enough to go near him. A firbolg named Tavis Burdun had taken pity on the boy and taught him to earn his bread by working, and Avner had turned his back on theft to become the most trusted scout in the kingdom of Hartsvale.

"Avner gave his life to save his queen's child," said Kelemvor. "I sent his spirit to Torm the True."

"And robbed me of my due." Mask's skinny figure began to thicken and sprout bulging muscles on its arms and chest.

"Your due?" Kelemvor scoffed. "Once a spirit enters the City of the Dead, it is mine to do with as I please."

"To punish as you please, not to pass along to your cronies!"

Mask's brawny shape grew as tall as a hill giant and strained at Jergal's grasp, but Kelemvor only sneered at the Shadowlord's blustering and said nothing.

"Avner was one of my False!" Mask continued. "He was happy enough to worship at my altar when the only way to fill his belly was stealing, but what homage did he pay me after the firbolg took him in? None! In the last year of his life, he did not steal a copper!"

Kelemvor shrugged. "Mortals are allowed to change their behavior—especially for the better."

Mask stopped struggling and shrank to the stooped shape of an old man. "Avner changed his behavior—but did he change gods?"

"Change gods?"

"Did Avner pray to Torm? Did he leave any offerings on Torm's altar?"

At that moment, one of Jergal's aspects appeared at the door. "Torm asks leave to enter the Crystal Spire, as requested."

"As requested?"

Mask's form changed into a perfect likeness of Lord Death himself. "I hope you don't mind." The Shadowlord's voice sounded exactly the same as Kelemvor's. "But I took the liberty. I am sure you want to work this thing out properly."

Kelemvor rose at once, but Torm had already manifested himself before the crystal throne. In his palm, the God of Duty carried a young sandy-haired man with steel-colored eyes: Avner of Hartsvale.

Torm stared at the two Kelemvors, then saw that the one being held by Jergal's aspects was an impostor. He bowed to the true God of Death. "I have brought the youth in question."

"I apologize for troubling you, Torm. But I did not ask you here."

"I did," interrupted Mask, now assuming the shape of a drow elf. "I just wanted to know if Avner of Hartsvale ever prayed to you."

The young man in Torm's palm grew pale, and the God of Duty answered, "No. He gave his life in the line of duty."

"But that is not worship, is it?" countered Mask. "Did he ever place any offerings on your altar?"

Torm frowned, glanced at Kelemvor, and reluctantly shook his head.

A white grin flashed across Mask's face. He took the shape of a certain six-armed goddess of destruction; with one of his extra hands, he reached into his gloomy cloak and withdrew a collection of sparkling objects, and these he held out toward the mortal in Torm's palm.

"Do you remember these, Avner?"

The mortal peered over Torm's hand and gasped in surprise. "I gave those to Diancastra!"

"But she is a giant's goddess, and you are a human." Though Mask's body remained that of the six-armed goddess, his face changed into the big-boned visage of the wily giantess, Diancastra. "Your offerings were to me—as you can see, I take many faces in many lands."

The mortal's jaw fell, and his mouth began to work up and down without speaking a word.

"Let us see; your regular tithe was one coin a week. How many do we have here? Seven hundred and ten?" Mask began to trickle copper coins from one hand to another. "And we should not forget the special offerings you made: a silver nugget, a brass comb, a scrap of linen. . . ." As the Shadowlord named each thing, he dropped it into his palm. "And this agate marble. As I recall, it was your first gift—"

"That is enough," Kelemvor said. "Those offerings mean nothing. The False are mine to do with as I please."

"That does not make them mine." Torm raised his hand and spoke to the frightened mortal. "Avner of Hartsvale, you died well and true, and if you had ever uttered a single word of prayer to me, I would be proud to keep you in Trueheart forever."

"But my life was—" The mortal caught himself, then bowed his head. "Forgive me, True One. I should know that you, of all the gods, cannot ignore your responsibility."

"Well said," replied Torm. "We shall miss you in Trueheart."

The True One turned to pass Avner to Mask, but Kelemvor stepped between them and thrust out his own hand.

"The False belong to me, and I can always use a loyal spirit such as Avner." Lord Death snatched Avner from Torm's hand, then retreated toward his throne. A pair of feathery black wings sprouted upon the youth's back, and Kelemvor said, "Avner of Hartsvale will be the first Seraph of Death."

"Seraph of Death!" scoffed the Shadowlord. "What will he do? Sing the glories of decay across the heavens?"

"Perhaps—or perhaps he will keep an eye on you. He can call the Chaos Hound whenever you start trouble."

Mask's eyes turned as red as embers. "I am glad to see you have a sense of humor, Lord Death." The Shadowlord's body melted onto the crystal floor, and Jergal's hands were left holding nothing but empty air. "Before we finish this, you will need it."

Thirteen

With Oghma's foolish priest holding my elbow and my veiled face buried in the sleeve of the witch's robe, we scurried out of the Dungeon Tower and down a path into the citadel's crowded ward, where hundreds of monks and warriors had gathered to hear news of my interrogation. They pressed in close to demand what we knew, but the priest cursed them and spewed dire warnings about the Binder's wrath. I kept my face toward the ground to conceal my eyes, which did not resemble those of the witch. I also made retching noises—this much was no act—and swung my head back and forth. The crowd cleared a path, and I scurried toward the High Gate as fast as I could. All the while I kept expecting someone to cry out that I was not the meddling Harper, or that there was a strange banging in the basement of the Dungeon Tower, but neither of these ever happened.

Rinda's journal continued to plague me. It was not enough that I had to keep reading despite the battle with my stomach; it pleased the Maid of Misfortune that I still felt compelled to speak the words aloud. I managed to hold them to a whisper, and so the priest kept pausing to lean close and ask, "What?" or "Did you say something, my dear?"

I could only shake my head and steal another glance at the vile book. No one discovered my disguise, and we reached the wicket door soon enough.

A monk, yielding to the urgency in the priest's voice, pulled it open, and I dropped to my hands and knees and crawled through into the shadowy passage beneath the gatehouse. The eyrie lay before me with nothing but sky and wind beyond. I jumped to my feet and rushed across the courtyard, thinking to hurl myself over the edge and trust Tyr's protection to save my life.

But I have never been that brave. As I neared the brink, my legs slowed of their own accord; by the time I reached the edge, they were hardly walking. I dropped to my knees and let out a sickly groan, more on account of Cyric's words in the stairwell than because of any fear of being recaptured—though this danger was certainly real enough.

In the sky ahead, a ribbon of black smoke snaked its way down to the knoll where Jabbar and Haroun had killed each other. There were dark flecks swarming all over the hill, dragging other dark flecks across the ground to a crackling bonfire. I did not need sharper eyes to know Candlekeep's defenders were burning all that remained of the Army of Belief.

The unholy sight was too much. My stomach surrendered its struggle, purging itself with a violence so great I pitched forward and found myself staring straight down the tor.

At first I took the fingers that caught my collar to be those of Tyr himself, but it was the priest's familiar voice that sounded in my ear. "Easy now, I've got you."

I allowed him to pull me back onto my haunches, then rested my hands on my thighs. I had made a foul-smelling mess of the witch's veil, but I scarcely noticed. The priest released my collar and kneeled beside me. I was quick to look away and pull my mannish hands inside my sleeves—and then I realized Rinda's journal was gone!

I dropped flat and peered over the edge, crying out in despair.

The astonished priest threw himself on top of me and exclaimed, "Ruha! What are you doing?"

I gave no answer, except to stare over the brink until I finally saw the book sailing around the side of the tor. It struck a rock halfway down and bounced. Then the wind caught its fluttering pages and carried it toward the coast.

I pushed away from the edge and slipped out from beneath the priest, who was so alarmed that he grabbed my leg and would not let go.

"Ruha, what is it?"

I waved my arm toward the edge and ran over to the path leading down to the Low Gate, and in my best woman's voice, I cried, "The book!"

I did not look back to see if this explanation satisfied him, but raised the hem of the witch's robe and plunged down the path at a dead sprint, and not only because of my strange obsession to finish reading her journal. I believed more than ever that the only way to help the One and All was to cure his insanity. And if there was any truth to Rinda's sacrileges at all—which I doubted most sincerely, of course—the only way to counter the *Cyrinishad*'s power was to read the *True Life of Cyric*, and the only way for me to find the *True Life* was to follow Rinda's journey back to where she had last seen Fzoul Chembryl.

As soon as the trail rounded the first curve, it grew narrow and steep, and sometimes it tilted away from the cliff, so that my feet slipped toward the edge with every step. Nowhere had the monks fixed a rope or chain to hold, for they claimed a treacherous path made a better defense, and I believed them. I kept my eyes fixed on the trail and ran as fast as I dared, all the while expecting to hear the peal of the alarm bell.

But the bell did not clang. The trail rounded the tor and hung for a time above the Sea of Swords' crashing shore, and I paused to peer over the edge until my eye caught the fluttering pages of Rinda's journal. The book lay thirty arrow lengths below, halfway down the stony bank that separated the grassy plain from the stony coast, and every time a gust flipped through its pages, the ledger slipped farther down the slope. There was no telling what would become of the journal if it slid all the way to the bottom; the shore was a snarl of old lava flows, tidal pools, and deep, jagged chasms roaring with trapped waves.

With no memory of how it happened, I found myself lying

on my belly and lowering my legs over the edge of the trail. At once, my fear of height filled my head with the pounding of my pulse, but my arms would not pull me back onto the path. I began to clamber down the cliff face, my fingers and feet trusting my weight to ledges and crannies as thin as a coin. This was the doing of my compulsion and not myself, for I knew the limits of my own courage and would never have attempted such a thing.

Twice my toe caught the hem of the Harper's robe and nearly pulled me from the cliff, and only Tyr's protection gave my hands the strength to hold me until I freed my foot and found a hold. I could do nothing about the clumsy robe except tuck the hem in my belt, but it always fell free and dropped back down. My foot tangled a third time. I grew so angry that I tore the witch's veil from my face and flung it away. In doing this I happened to look down and see that Rinda's journal had slipped down three-quarters of the bank. Even worse, much of the rocky shore had now vanished beneath the rising tide, and I had lived upon this coast long enough to know that in less than a quarter hour the sea would be so high that its waves would slap at the very place where the journal now lay.

I clambered down the cliff another few minutes, pausing every so often to glance at the book and at the rising tide. The uprush was just beginning to lap at the bank when the clanging of the alarm bell echoed down from the windy heights above, and I knew that Ulraunt and the witch had freed themselves. The shore lay perhaps twice a giant's height below me; if I could only reach it before my foes spied me clinging to the cliff, I would be safe.

The crashing waves had been tearing at the bank for centuries upon centuries, working even the tiniest fissures into small caverns. During my long winters outside Candlekeep, I had slept in a hundred of them. They were never very comfortable, but they kept the rain off, and there was even one grotto whose entrance disappeared at high water. Inside that cave, I could hide until the tide went out at midnight, then start my journey under cover of darkness.

The wind caught Rinda's journal and spun it around, and it slid down the bank until it was so close to the water that I saw the spray spattering the rocks around it. I closed my eyes and jumped and prayed that Tyr's protection would guard me against sprained ankles and broken legs, and most especially being caught in a wave's backwash and drowned.

Fourteen

In another ocean far from Faerûn, where the brine smelled as sweet as honey and the surf chimed like tinkling bells and the stars and the moon flooded the sky with light as lustrous as silver, Kelemvor and Mystra appeared in the glittering shoals near shore. In the distance ahead, Mount Celestia hovered above the horizon, its base lost in a swaddling haze of sea mist, its jagged peak hanging like a cloud in the air. Closer by, completely covering the rocky crown of a nearby island, loomed the immense white palace of Tyr the Just.

When Mystra and Kelemvor turned toward the island, they were astonished to see Oghma the Wise waiting. He stood on the stony beach beneath the citadel walls, wearing a yellow burnoose that soaked up none of the water lapping at its hem. A broad smile opened in his thick beard, and then he raised a hand in greeting.

"I thought I would find you here," he called. "You have come to ask Tyr to separate your trial from Cyric's, have you not?"

Mystra and Kelemvor waded toward the beach. "That is no business of yours," said Lord Death.

"Perhaps not, but you might have asked my advice."

"We saw no point in asking anything of you," said Mystra. "You seemed quite happy to see us charged alongside Cyric."

"True," replied Oghma. "But there is never harm in talking. It is through discussion that one gains wisdom."

Kelemvor stopped at the beach. "Then talk. We will listen."

Oghma dipped his head to Lord Death. "I have been told

that you sent Jergal and Gwydion to find Rinda's spirit; thank you. You have no idea how her cries have tormented me."

"That was out of fairness to her, not to win your favor. The Brave and True should not feel deserted by their gods."

Mystra waded out of the water and stood close to Oghma's side, then laid her hand on the Binder's arm. "All the same, if Kelemvor's service has caused you a change of heart, we would welcome your support at our trial."

Oghma's face grew sober, and he did not look at Mystra, but kept his eyes fixed on Kelemvor. "You are all accused together. If I speak in your defense, then I also speak in Cyric's. Surely you do not want that!" The God of Wisdom furrowed his brow. "Cyric has failed in his duties, and we all agree that is a terrible thing—even if we cannot decide what to do about it."

Kelemvor stepped past Oghma. "Shall we go, Mystra? He is no different from the others."

Mystra nodded and turned to follow, for Kelemvor spoke the truth. They had already visited the other gods of the Circle and received the same reply—even from Sune, who was always ready to change her mind. Save for Tyr and Cyric himself, the great deities were so determined to judge against the One that they would not speak in defense of Lady Magic or Lord Death. Kelemvor had begun to wonder if there might be another reason, but he kept his doubts secret. He knew better than to suggest to Mystra that the charges against them might have merit.

They reached the top of the beach and found the abalone gates of Tyr's citadel hanging open to receive them. Inside stood an honor guard of twelve paladins in gleaming armor, ready to escort Mystra and Kelemvor inside.

The captain stepped forward and bowed. "Lady Magic and Lord Death, please follow us. The Just One is expecting you."

"Is he?" Mystra glanced at Kelemvor and scowled, for she had not expected the God of Wisdom to oppose them so actively. "It seems the Binder has made some preparations."

"Not I," replied Oghma, joining them.

"Then who?" demanded Kelemvor.

"Perhaps you should see for yourselves." Oghma waved Kelemvor and Mystra through the gates ahead of him.

The three gods followed their honor guard up a long walkway and emerged in a huge plaza surrounded by edifices of many-pillared grandeur. The paladins cut straight across this square, clearing a broad swath through the throng of bustling clerks who stopped to stare at the passing gods, then halted before the grandest building of all. The portico stairs were as high as cliffs, and the columns so tall they seemed to support the sky.

Mystra and Kelemvor and Oghma entered the shadow of the first step, and then they were standing inside the great Tribunal Chamber of Tyr the Evenhanded.

The courtroom was shaped like a horseshoe, with high tiers of benches on three sides and the Just One's alabaster throne on the fourth. Next to this chair, leaning on the back as though he were Tyr's closest ally, stood a skull-faced wraith in tattered leather armor.

"Cyric!" hissed Mystra.

"The One and All," replied Cyric.

Though the court was filled with Tyr's faithful, who packed the benches day and night to bask in the wisdom of his decrees, now the chamber was hushed. It was rare that the gods themselves argued a matter in that chamber, and no ear wished to miss what was said.

"I am sure you will have no objection if I listen to your petition," said Cyric. "After all, it is sure to affect me."

"It is for me to decide what affects you, Cyric." Tyr craned his neck around to scowl at the One and All. "You may be certain that I would have summoned you if it was appropriate."

"But it is appropriate." The One went to the edge of the dais and glared down at Mystra. "Mystra and her boy have come to ask for a separate trial."

With a thought, Tyr increased the size of his throne, until he had risen high enough to peer over Cyric's head. "I would like to hear from Lady Magic and Lord Death why they are here."

Mystra nodded. "We have come to ask for a separate trial. We cannot defend ourselves as matters stand, since we agree with the charges against Cyric."

"And since no one will speak in your defense, as that would also mean speaking in mine," added Cyric. "I warned you about this. They are all so jealous of me!"

"Jealous?" snorted Kelemvor. "I think not."

Mystra raised her fingers to silence Lord Death, then ignored Cyric and spoke directly to the Just One. "Tyr, you have put us into an indefensible position. It is not fair to make us choose between defending ourselves and judging against Cyric."

"Lady Magic, I am not the God of Fairness. I am the God of Justice, and that is a very different thing." This drew a respectful murmur from the benches, which Tyr silenced with a single eyeless glance. "And if you find it impossible to defend yourself from the charges levied against you, then perhaps you should ask if it is because they have some merit."

At this, the benches burst into an applause, and Tyr did nothing to silence his admirers.

Cyric raised his skeleton's hands and looked around the gallery as though he had won a great triumph, and it is a testament to his mercy and patience that he took no offense at how quickly the ovation trailed off.

Oghma made use of the silence to step forward and speak. "Well said, Tyr. A little introspection might benefit both Kelemvor and Mystra." He glanced first at Lord Death, who bit his lips and looked away, then at Lady Magic, who only scowled and narrowed her eyes. The Binder returned his attention to the Eyeless One. "And there lies the crucial difference between them and Cyric, it seems to me."

Cyric leaned down from the dais and jabbed a weathered fingerbone at Oghma's face. "I warn you, Old Man—"

Tyr rose and caught Cyric by the shoulder, then jerked him back from the edge. "And I warn you, Mad One: my tolerance has its limits. This is my Tribunal Chamber, and you will not threaten any soul within its walls!"

Cyric's jaw clacked open. He whirled on the Just One, and the chamber grew still and tense. The two gods glared at each other for a time, until the One seemed to remember where he was and glanced around the court at Tyr's astounded worshipers. The fury drained from Cyric's blazing black eyes, and he closed his jaw and nodded as though granting a request.

"You may speak for yourself, of course. We must not forget, this is your palace."

"No, we must never forget that," replied Tyr.

Oghma cleared his throat, then spoke, "As I was saying, the charges against Mystra and Kelemvor cannot stand as they are."

"They cannot?" Mystra's voice cracked with astonishment. "But you said—"

"That I would not speak in your defense. However, I cannot allow you to stand trial on the wrong charge." Oghma turned to Tyr, and there was a glint in the Wise God's eye. "We have charged Cyric with innocence by reason of insanity—but Kelemvor and Mystra are neither innocent nor insane. We have asked them to prove a negative, which is both ridiculous and unjust."

Tyr nodded thoughtfully.

Before he could say anything, Cyric blurted out, "But Tempus has made his charge! They are as incompetent as I am!"

"That is for the Circle to decide," said Tyr. "But Oghma is right. The charge is amended to incompetence through humanity."

Mystra and Kelemvor turned to thank Oghma, but their appreciation was lost in the One's angry wail.

"Noooo!"

The chamber fell silent. All eyes turned toward Cyric, who was tearing handfuls of tattered leather from his armor and flinging them upon the floor. The instant they touched the stone, the scraps turned into steaming piles of fetor, filling the hall with such a poisonous stench that all of Tyr's Faithful rose and scrambled for the exits.

The Just One showed no sign of anger. "Cyric, what is the

basis for your objection?"

The One looked up from his hallowed labor. "Basis?"

"The reason," Oghma prompted.

Cyric removed his hands from his shredded armor and looked about the polluted chamber. Approving of what he saw, he clacked his skeleton's teeth together and turned to face Tyr.

"My reason is simple." The One spoke in a calm and pleasant voice, as though he had done nothing untoward in Tyr's courtroom. "Mystra has already tried to disrupt my trial once. If you separate our cases, what is to stop her from trying again?"

"I cannot deny what you say," Tyr said.

The Just One fell into silent thought, and as he considered Cyric's argument, his eyeless gaze fell on a pile of offal. The One, seeing where Tyr was looking, made a scooping motion with his bony hand, and the heap vanished at once. The Eyeless One's gaze wandered to the next pile, which Cyric promptly removed with the same scooping motion, and they continued in this fashion until the whole chamber was as bland and as barren as before.

Tyr smiled, then looked to Mystra. "The trials will take place at the same time." This drew a victorious chuckle from the One. "But the charges will be split; Cyric's verdict will stand separately from the verdict rendered for you and Kelemvor."

"What?" shrieked the One.

Tyr ignored him and continued to address Mystra. "I warn you, give me no reason to regret this. I shall be on guard against tampering of any kind. If I find it—"

"You will find no tampering," Mystra replied. Then, to make certain Tyr had not mistaken her pledge for a boast, she added, "I have learned my lesson."

Cyric ripped a handful of leather from his armor, but Tyr was quick to catch the One's arm.

"Your actions will not influence my judgments," Tyr said, "but I might present them as evidence at your trial."

"Traitor!" the One screamed. He opened his hand, and the scrap vanished. "Everyone has betrayed me!"

"So it seems." Oghma spoke softly, and Cyric had to stop yelling in order to hear the Binder's words. "You would do well to find out why—unless you want to lose your trial."

Fifteen

I left the cave with the midnight tide and made good my escape, creeping along the coast until Candlekeep's lights disappeared behind the horizon and the circling hippogriffs vanished from the sky. Then I climbed the headwall and crawled miles through the tall salt grass to a small farm with a pungent little barn. Thinking this stock shed a good place to rest and collect my wits, I opened the door and sneaked inside.

I was greeted by the shining eyes of five goats and a mangy dog, all peering out from beneath the belly of a swaybacked mare. I hissed a harsh warning for the beasts to keep silent, then turned to keep watch through a knothole—and nearly cried out myself.

Outside, silhouetted against a pink ribbon on the predawn horizon, a lone hippogriff was wheeling past the farmer's hut. The beast carried two riders, the man who held the reins and the cloth-swaddled figure of the Harper witch. Whether they had tracked me here or had only broadened their search, I could not say—but they were a terrible sight to see. Soon it would be morning, and if I fled, they would spy me running across the open plain. Yet I could not pass the entire day in the stock shed. There were certain to be scouts among the companies that had ridden to Candlekeep's defense, and the sunlight would make it easy for them track me here.

The hippogriff circled the farm and swooped less than a sword's length above the roofs, but it did not land. My foes were searching blind, hoping their mount would scare me out of hiding or else catch my scent—a thing that seemed impossible, given the stench of manure in the shed. I dared to breathe again but kept my eye to the knothole and thanked Tymora I was done with Rinda's journal.

I had finished it in the sea cave, by the light of a small fire struck from a pack rat's nest, which is always so dry and old it makes excellent tinder. The book was mostly an account of Rinda's wanderings with Gwydion and their many battles with Cyric's Faithful. In places, Rinda's words could have been my own, for she was as cut off from Oghma as I had been from the One during my vigil outside Candlekeep. Nor was Gwydion much comfort, as the same things that made him an excellent guard also made him a poor companion. He had little use for sleep or food, nor for any of the other things that men need, and this was a great sadness to Rinda, who was a robust woman with wants of her own. She often thought of her home in Zhentil Keep and of the lovers and friends she had known there and would never see again—but in this we were as different as night and day, for I was confident I would one day return to see my friend the prince and my loving wife and give them all they deserved.

The journal made no further mention of the *True Life of Cyric*, except to say she had heard that Fzoul Chembryl had fled for a time to a place called Teshwave, then returned to the ruins of Zhentil Keep to worship a new god named Iyachtu Xvim. It was a great relief to know my quarry was so important that people tracked his movements, as I had less than ten days to complete my journey and find him.

I was on a holy mission now, a quest to save my god—and if the One did not yet appreciate my efforts, I felt sure he would reward me all the more after he read the *True Life* and returned to his senses. The alternative was too terrible to imagine—though of course I could hardly keep it from my mind. If Cyric was insane when his trial continued, nothing would save him—or me. Compared to my punishment for disobeying the One, the torments of Kelemvor's city would seem heavenly delights.

The hippogriff circled the farm three times, approaching from a different angle on each occasion, and it was just swooping down toward the stock shed door when the mare nickered in fear. This occasioned several bleats and a growl from beneath the nag's belly. I spun around at once, bringing my finger to my lips.

"Quiet!" I hissed.

"Really, Malik, you are growing too cocky."

Though the thousand voices of the One were but a whisper, they filled my head as a roaring wind. My bones ached with a stinging chill, and I saw a man's shape blocking the gleam of the farm beasts' golden eyes. A gentle throb sounded outside as the hippogriff beat the air with its wings and flew over the shed. I fell to my knees and pressed my head to the stinking floor.

"Mighty One!"

Cyric's boots scuffed through the filth, and a bony hand grasped my shoulder. "Do not offer reverence you do not feel." The One plucked me from the floor and returned me to my feet. "It demeans us both, and you remain under Tyr's protection—for now."

"But—"

"Malik, there is no cause for worry. I only want to know why you betrayed me." He brushed off my robe—I was still wearing the witch's *aba,* as the dark cloth made excellent camouflage in the night. "Speak freely. Whatever you say, it will not aggravate your punishments."

I believed him, for I knew nothing could add to what he planned for me already. Yet it was impossible to do as he commanded. "Mighty One, I have not betrayed you. How can I ever betray the god of gods?"

The One clasped me by the throat, and I am certain that only Tyr's protection kept him from crushing my windpipe. "No lies, you mewling . . . !" He let the threat trail off, then removed his hand and patted me on the chest. He pulled the Harper's brooch from my robe and tossed it aside, and I heard the pin land in something moist and soft where it belonged. "I am trying to be patient here, Malik. Perhaps I could pay a visit to your wife?"

This, of course, was too great an honor to ask. "You would do that for me, Mighty One?"

"Of course, Malik." His thousand voices were as melodious and pleasing to the ear as a choir of eunuchs. "Just tell me what I want to know."

"But I have, Sacred One," I replied. "An *amil* does not betray his caliph, for he has too much invested in him. What hope but you do I have of regaining all I have sacrificed in your service? No other god will reward me for what I have done."

This, Cyric seemed to understand. A purple light suddenly filled the shed, drawing much snorting and bleating from the mare and her nervous goats, and the One fixed his blazing black eyes on my face and studied me a long time. The dog slunk into a corner and hid beneath a manger and lay there growling softly, but I could tell that the beast was not overly brave, or else it would never have lived to be so gray.

"Malik, can you really be telling the truth?"

I nodded. "Of course, Mighty One."

The One was not interested in my reassurances. He placed his bony hand in the center of my chest and began to push, and I stumbled back and kept stumbling back until I reached the wall and could go no farther.

"This may hurt," Cyric said, "but it will not kill you—not while you are under Tyr's protection."

My eyes dropped to the bony claw on my chest, and suddenly my heart was pounding like the hooves of a fine stallion. "Wh-what are you going to d-do?"

Cyric continued to push, and my sternum flexed inward. My ribs bowed out around his hand. A terrible crushing pain filled my torso, as though a giant were standing on my chest, and my breath stopped. My heart pounded harder than ever. Every time the organ expanded, I felt it touch my spine and my sternum at once, and I thought the One meant to crush it inside my own body.

Then his hand grew as pellucid as a ghost and slid into my

chest, so that all I could see was his wrist pressed tight to my sternum. My entire body grew cold and numb, and the pain vanished. His hand closed around my heart. With each beat, I felt the spongy muscles squeeze up between his fingers; each time they contracted, his grasp tightened.

"Stronger than I thought," he said. "That may not be good. Steadfast hearts are for Tempus and Torm, not me."

My knees buckled. I fell against the wall and slumped to the floor; there was nothing I could do. The warmth rushed back into my body, and a low boom-booming filled my ears, and I felt a strange void in the middle of my chest. The horse whinnied and the old gray dog ventured a bark, and even before I looked, I knew I would see the One holding my heart in his hand.

The sight was not as gruesome as I imagined. It reminded me of a small throbbing sponge, save that each time it pumped, the stuff that gushed from its pores was blood and not water.

"In the name of the One!" I was in no condition to think of what I was saying. "I am only a poor mortal! Put that back!"

"When I am ready."

Cyric did not even look at me, but stuck my heart into his mouth and bit a chunk from the side. I let out a great shriek, which should certainly have roused even the lazy farmer who did not rise before dawn to check his animals, then watched as the One spat out the piece he had bitten off.

"Aaarrgh! It's fresh!"

"But of course," I replied. "You took it from my chest."

"That is not what I mean." Cyric grabbed my collar and pulled me to my feet. My blood was smeared over his skeleton's mouth, and I could not bear to look at his face. "You are telling me the truth."

"I wouldn't dare lie—not to you!"

"Of course you would." Cyric propped me against the wall—I think he feared I would fall again—then he backed away, shaking his head. When he spoke, it was only in a single cackling voice. "It makes no sense. It makes no sense."

He looked toward the ceiling and answered himself in a demon's rumble. "Don't be a fool. You can see what's happening!"

Cyric spun on his heel and spoke next to the floor, this time in a soft woman's tone. "Malik has always been your most devoted worshiper." These are the exact words of the One and All, and I have not altered a syllable. "He is true to you. You have tasted that for yourself."

"But everybody has betrayed us!" Cyric's voice was now deep and angry. "Even Oghma said that!"

Yet another voice came to the One's lips. "He said it *seemed* that way!" He directed this to the dog in the corner, which only whimpered and crawled farther beneath the manger. "And he said we had to figure out why!"

With that, the One plunged his free hand into his own chest, and he withdrew a slimy mass of curd as brown as roasted coffee beans. It did not beat so much as slurp between his fingers, and nothing on Faerûn smelled stronger. The goats fell to their knees and rubbed their muzzles in the filthy dirt. Horrible choking sounds came from the nag's throat, and the dog crawled out from beneath the manger to do what I would have done myself, had I not been too frightened.

Cyric raised the putrid mass to his mouth and took a bite, and this he swallowed. "Rotten!" he announced, again speaking in a thousand voices, all of which seemed quite content. "Rotten to the core."

Having regained control of himself, the One pleased the horse and the dog by returning to my side of the shed. He raised his slimy heart toward my face. "Care for some?"

Of course, I was too stunned to reply. The number of mortals who have ever been invited to take a meal with their god can be counted on a man's hands, but what man has ever been offered such an honor as this? For a long time, I could only stare at the slurping mass and think of the many benefits a bite of the One's heart would surely bestow: unflagging strength, or a life free of disease—perhaps even immortality itself!

The organ was so close now that I could see it was threaded

with long white strands, and that these were writhing about on their own. These were the spirits of all the gods Cyric had slain in making himself the One, but I did not know this at the time, and I confess they turned my stomach. Nevertheless, I closed my eyes and opened my mouth, and I tried not to think of the stench as I lowered my head to partake of my god's manna.

But when have I ever been a strong man? As soon as my lips touched the quivering mass, my head began to spin. My vision blackened, and a deafening silence filled my ears and shut out the boom-booming of my own heart in his other hand.

When I opened my eyes, I sat slumped against the wall, with the One cross-legged before me. He was still holding both hearts, moving his hands up and down as though weighing the difference.

He looked at the slurping mass cupped in his left palm. "I thought not." Cyric shook his head, then raised his gaze. "Malik, what is Oghma warning me about? Is something wrong with me?"

Having been asked similar questions by many powerful friends back in Calimshan, I knew an honest answer was not expected. I dared to lay a comforting hand on the One's arm, taking care not to disturb the heart.

"Nothing," I said. I meant to stop there, but the truth welled up and spilled from my horrified lips before I knew what I was saying. "Nothing that can't be fixed, Mighty One. Your heart is rotten because you have betrayed your worshipers and your duties—that is what Oghma is trying to tell you."

Cyric's hand closed around my heart. I knew he meant to crush it, which would certainly be my death when Tyr's protection was lifted, yet I could not stop talking.

"You shut yourself in the Shattered Keep—"

"Castle of the Supreme Throne!"

"—and delude yourself into believing you play other gods like puppets. When they refuse to do as you command, you claim they are only jealous of your power, but even we mortals know they are laughing behind your—"

"Laughing!"

The force of Cyric's bellow slammed me against the wall, and I knew that even Tyr's protection would not save me from the One's anger. I bowed my head.

"Forgive me, Mighty One." My voice was as soft and shrill as that of a frightened child. "I don't know what came over me."

"Mystra's truth spell," he hissed. Then, one after the other, his thousand voices began to chuckle, and all at once they broke into a cyclone of wild laughter. "She saved me!"

"Saved you?"

The One dropped our hearts onto the filthy floor and grabbed me by the shoulders. "Mystra's magic was meant for a god, and you're just a mortal!" This was the first I had heard about her truth magic, but my runaway mouth made his meaning clear enough. "Even here on Faerûn, you can't lie!"

I groaned. This was not good news for a merchant.

"You had to tell me the truth!" Cyric guffawed. "And now the truth will save me!"

I looked away, for this was almost my plan.

After a time, the One brought his mirth under control and picked up my heart. As he brushed off the dirt, he asked, "So, what shall I do now?"

"You're asking me, Mighty One?"

Cyric nodded. "Yes—and give me an honest answer."

He burst into another bout of mirth, which gave me time to think, and when he stopped laughing, I had a good answer.

"My father once said, 'The camel fears her driver not because the driver wishes her to, but because she knows him.' "

The One looked at me, but there was no flesh over his skull's face and I could not see his confusion. Finally, he asked, "Malik, what in the Nine Hells are you talking about?"

"The camel does not fear the driver's switch; a whipping is nothing to a creature with such a thick hide. Rather, she fears the driver because she has watched him eat camel."

The One continued to stare at me, until I thought it necessary to explain. "You see, Mighty One, you are the driver—"

"I know, Malik. I *am* a god—or have you forgotten? You

mean I must to do something to remind my inferiors of how dangerous I can be."

"Yes."

"And I know just the thing." A red gleam appeared in Cyric's eyes. "Adon!"

"Mystra's patriarch?" I knew Adon's name from the journal, for he had done much to aid Rinda and Gwydion soon after the destruction of Zhentil Keep, and he had even arranged for them to rest a month or so in a tiny village named Tegea. "But surely, Mystra has placed many safeguards over—"

"You let me worry about that. You just go back . . ." Here the One hesitated. Oghma's enchantment was still doing its work, and already he could not remember where the *Cyrinishad* was hidden. "Go back to where you killed Rinda and get the *Cyrinishad.*"

"As you—" I was going to say "command," but I had forgotten about Mystra's spell; my tongue twisted itself and told the truth instead: "—must know, I have no intention of returning to Candlekeep. I'm going to Zhentil Keep."

"What? Zhentil Keep!" The One's roar set the dog to scratching at the shed walls. "What for?"

I said nothing, for I knew that if I spoke, it would be nothing but the truth.

"Well?"

Still I did not reply.

Cyric studied me a long time. I grew uncomfortable and looked away and watched my heart throbbing in his hand, and I wondered if I would ever get it back. The One followed my gaze and also stared at my heart, and after a moment he clacked his fleshless jaw.

"I see. You cannot tell me." He looked back to my eyes, which I carefully kept fixed on my heart. "Then what am I to do, Malik—trust you?"

"Whatever I am doing, it is only for your own good," I said, and Mystra's spell caused me to add, "and because it is the only way to save myself."

Cyric raised my heart to his mouth. I grimaced and looked

away, for I thought he would take another bite, but he only touched his long tongue to it and sneered with disgust.

"I suppose I must trust you. Your heart is true." He said this last word as a profanity. "That explains your failure in Candlekeep. Perhaps Rinda did not even have the *Cyrinishad!* What is it you merchants say? 'A thief steals the locked chest first?'"

I nodded, for this was indeed a favorite saying of my father's. It means a wise man does not hide his gold in an expected place.

"That is it! She was carrying a decoy!" Cyric jumped up and almost stepped into the slurping mass of his own heart, which he had left lying in the dirt. "And she hid the *Cyrinishad* in Zhentil Keep—is that correct?"

I clenched my jaw and was greatly relieved to note that I felt no compulsion to answer. The Harlot's magic forced me to be honest and complete when I spoke, but it did not compel me to speak against my own wishes. At least she had left me this much.

When I did not answer, Cyric cackled in delight. "Brilliant!" He reached down and plucked me from the floor. "But you will need help to reach Zhentil Keep before my trial."

"Then you'll carry me there?"

"You know I cannot, Malik. You would never find the *Cyrinishad.* Oghma's magic still keeps me from discovering it." He thrust my heart into my hand, then turned toward the old mare. She whinnied and raised her head and glared at him with her big round eyes. "But I can make sure you have a good mount."

"A good mount?" Under no circumstances could that swaybacked nag be called such a thing—though I had intended to steal her all along, as she looked like a beast even I might control. "If you'll just help me with the bit, Mighty One."

"Bit? For a spirited beast such as this?" Cyric went to her.

The trembling nag backed against the wall, and the goats fled to my side of the shed, and I snatched the One's heart up off the floor. Even when they are afraid, goats are voracious beasts that will eat anything.

Cyric grabbed the mare's mane and pulled her head down to his mouth. The poor beast grew so frightened she kicked a plank out of the wall, and through this hole, morning's golden light rushed in to mix with the purple glow the One had struck earlier. Our Dark Lord clamped his teeth over the horse's neck and bit into a vein, and her shriek was as shrill as a hawk's, save that it was a hundred times as loud. My ears rang, and the dog howled from beneath its manger, and the goats bleated and butted the door in their fury to escape.

Blood rushed from the mare's throat faster than Cyric could drink it, so that it poured out over his chin and cascaded into the dirt. The nag grew weak and began to sway, and still the One drank, forcing her to kneel in a steaming pool of her own blood. At this sight, my weak stomach threatened to betray me again, so I turned away and pressed my head against the wall. Through a crack in the planks, I saw an old man standing outside; he held a loaded crossbow in his shaking hands, but his mouth was gaping, and his feet seemed rooted to the ground in fear.

"Malik! Quit daydreaming. Get her harness."

I slipped my heart into the crook of my elbow, then took the bridle off a hook on the wall and carried it over to him. The nag had stopped struggling, and now Cyric was lying atop her, holding his slashed wrist over her throat. A sticky black syrup was flowing from his wound into hers, on which account she seemed to be growing healthier by the moment. Before my eyes, her swayed back straightened, her gaunt frame grew robust and strong, and her dull coat became bright and glistening.

Cyric pulled his wrist from her neck. Both his wound and the mare's stopped bleeding, and her eyes grew as blue as sapphires. Her lips curled back, revealing teeth as sharp and ugly as a shark's. She snorted clouds of cold vapor from her nostrils and raised her head to glare at me.

"She is waiting for her name." As the One said this, he took the bridle from me and tore out the bit, then slipped it over her head. "You are the one who must give it to her."

"Halah." I chose this name not because of its meaning, which was "nimble," but because she reminded me of my wife, whose beauty resembled the mare's in more ways than one. "I name you Halah."

Halah whinnied, and the sound was like the cold rattling of a captive's chains. She rolled onto her knees and rose, tossing the One off her neck as though he were nothing.

"Stand back," he ordered. "She is hungry."

I barely had time to leap aside before Halah sprang across the shed, trapping all five goats against the wall. She killed them in a flurry of snapping teeth and striking hooves, then whirled upon the whimpering dog. Seeing what was in her mind, the dog shot from its hiding place and vanished through the hole the horse had kicked in the planks earlier. The mare stopped short of crashing through, though I am sure she had the power to, and returned to the dead goats.

"Never stop her from eating," Cyric warned. "You can ride her day and night at a full gallop, but when she is hungry, do not even think of interfering."

I looked away from the goats, which she was devouring hoof, horn, and hide. "I doubt I could."

The One reached over and took my heart. "Certainly not with this. We shall have to give you something stronger."

"S-Stronger?"

"I will hold on to this one for you." Cyric's hand became translucent, then he slipped my heart into his own chest and shook his head as he had eaten something sour. "It might even help, if you are right about what Oghma says."

I looked down at my own chest, which had a hollow inside that felt as large as the stock shed.

"There is no need to worry, Malik. You can use mine until we finish." Cyric took his own heart from my hand, then plucked the writhing white threads from its slurping mass and dropped them into his mouth. "But it would hardly be wise to leave these with you, would it? No telling what kind of trouble they would cause."

I watched him pull out the last of the strings and swallow it, then I fell to my knees. "Please, Mighty One, I am not worthy! Let me keep my own heart."

Cyric grasped me by the shoulder. "Stop whining, Malik." He thrust his hand into my chest, and with it his fetid heart. "This is for my own good."

Sixteen

Talos was riding a storm in from the Sea of Swords, and he could see hippogriffs hurrying back to Candlekeep from all directions, their masters eager to reach shelter before a lightning bolt blasted them from the sky. Only a single beast, the big one that carried the Harper witch behind its rider, continued to sweep back and forth over the plain.

Today, the riders need not have worried. The God of Destruction would be hurling no bolts at them. Today, his fury was directed farther inland than they could see, toward a little rider on a fast horse who had already galloped farther than they could imagine. Though the protection of Tyr prevented Talos from causing the rider any harm, the Destroyer was determined to turn the ground into mud beneath the hooves of his swift mount.

As the storm rumbled toward shore, a great baying rolled from the clouds behind Talos. The sound was as deep and deafening as a thunderclap, and it sent a chill down even the Destroyer's spine. The Chaos Hound was coming.

Talos drew a handful of lightning bolts from the empty air and whirled around, determined to spear the beast the instant he saw it. The Chaos Hound fed on the marrow of the Faithful, and the Raging One had Faithful spread all through this storm, hurling bolts of lightning and pounding thunderheads and pelting the ground with waves of pounding hail. Another howl broke from the black clouds. Then a murky shadow came streaking out of the billowing darkness.

Talos hurled his first bolt, but the shadow saw it coming and dodged aside. The lightning streaked into a roiling cloud and blossomed into a flashing silver heart, and a tremendous crash rumbled through the entire storm front.

"Stay your arm, Destroyer!" Though the voice was wispy, it was as loud as the raging winds. "I mean no harm."

"No harm?" Despite his roaring, Talos dropped his lightning bolts and let them sizzle into the sea. "Then why do you lead the Chaos Hound through a gale of my Faithful?"

Mask trotted across the cloud top until he reached Talos's side. "Forgive me, but that was not my intention." The Shadowlord braced his hands on his knees, and his form shifted to that of a panting gnoll. "Kezef caught my scent as I entered the storm."

"Then leave."

Another howl broke from the depth of the tempest, and Mask glanced at the thunderhead behind them. "Soon enough." The Shadowlord kept the form of the gnoll, for he would need his strength to flee Kezef. "I want to talk with you about this trouble you have gone to."

"I make my storms where and when I wish."

"I have no argument with that," Mask replied. "But it seems a pity to waste so much effort on a mortal you cannot even kill."

"I have no need to kill him, only to slow him down."

Mask nodded. "Then we have reached the same conclusion. Malik is still chasing the *Cyrinishad*."

"I cannot know for certain." As Talos spoke, the storm began to roll over Candlekeep. With a thought, he instructed his Faithful to pound the thunderheads and sprinkle lightning bolts upon the shore, and then he looked back to Mask. "But I can think of no other reason for Cyric to give him such a horse."

"True, but this is so . . . obvious." Mask waved an arm at the length of the storm. "Even if Tyr does not stop you, Cyric is sure to counter with a measure of his own."

Talos shrugged. "I cannot help that."

"No, but perhaps something subtle would prove more effective—and also advance your cause against Mystra."

From deep in the storm came the screech of a soul in agony, followed by long, happy howl. Talos scowled and glared at Mask.

"Say what you have come to say and go. If I lose another of my Faithful, I shall forget you deserve the courtesy of a god."

"As you like." Mask pointed toward the Harper witch and her companion, who were still flying their hippogriff over the plain. "You see how determined the witch is to capture Malik. Perhaps she could use a little help."

"Help one of Lady Magic's worshipers? Never."

"You are angered that Mystra has weakened the magic of destruction?"

Talos made no answer, for the question did not deserve one. Magic had all but ceased to serve the forces of destruction, and the situation had grown so bad that the Destroyer often disguised an avatar as a new god and sent it down to spread the magic of wildness and havoc.

When Mask received no reply, he said, "The best way to beat a foe is not always to fight. Sometimes it is to steal."

Talos glared at the Shadowlord. "What do you care about my troubles with Mystra?"

"Nothing." A deafening howl sounded inside the thunderhead from which Mask had come. He shuddered, but kept his gaze locked on Talos. "I am after Cyric. Until I take back what he stole, I will never have the strength to chase Kezef off."

The Destroyer narrowed his eyes. "But the Eyeless One separated the charges. To find against Cyric, we need not find against Mystra and Kelemvor."

"Too late for me," Mask replied. "I have already laid a trap for Kelemvor, and I do not want Mystra taking vengeance after the trial. Unless they are both removed along with Cyric, I will be worse off than before."

Talos smirked and shook his head. "Was it not one of these plots that drew Kezef onto your trail in the first place?"

"This is not my fault! How could I know Tyr would split the

charges?" Mask was nearly shouting. "Besides, the verdict is more likely to go against Cyric if the Circle has already decided against Kelemvor and Mystra."

"As usual, you have snagged yourself in your own plot." Talos watched the Harper and her companion land their hippogriff and dismount; the gale was now rolling across the plain, and not even the bravest rider would fly through a thunderstorm. "I see no reason to entangle myself with you."

"Not even to be rid of Mystra?"

A tremendous howl broke across the cloud, nearly drowning out the Shadowlord's question. Kezef the Chaos Hound came bursting from a distant thunderhead. From his slavering jaws hung the flailing torso of one of Talos's Faithful.

Mask kept his gaze fixed on the Destroyer and did not turn to flee. "Even if matters go against me, no one will blame you. It will look as if you were only trying to stop Cyric."

Now Mask glanced at Kezef, who was sniffing back and forth across the swirling clouds—like any dog, he often relied upon his nose when his eyes would have served him better.

Talos considered the Shadowlord's plan, then instructed his Faithful to cast no lightning bolts in the witch's direction. "My magic is not the same as Mystra's," he said. "If I enhance Ruha's powers, she will know something is amiss."

The Chaos Hound let out another great bay, then tossed aside Talos's half-eaten worshiper and came bounding across the clouds.

"Let me worry about what Ruha knows." Mask stepped over to the cloud's edge and peered into the swirling darkness beneath the storm. "You just give her the magic to catch Malik."

And then he jumped.

Seventeen

Every god favors one mortal above all others, and for Mystra that mortal was Adon the Fop. He had been born to a wealthy family of Sembia more than thirty years before, and his life was one of sloth and excess until his fifteenth year, when a boy's normal obsession with the beauty of women grew so strong he entered the church of Sune Firehair. There he learned all the disciplines of love: the spells of enchantment and the art of good grooming and the skill of close combat. It was on account of these talents that Cyric and Kelemvor endured Adon's company and that he was present when they met Midnight, as Mystra was known then, and began their quest for the Tablets of Fate.

Early in the journey, Adon suffered one of the most terrible things that could befall a cleric of Sune the Fickle and Beautiful: a madman cut his face and left a hideous scar. Thinking the mark a sign of Sune's displeasure, the Fop lost his Faith and turned from the Church of Beauty. Yet he remained as loyal to his friends as a dog to its master, and in the many battles that followed, he and Midnight saved each other a hundred times. He was the one who stanched her bleeding in Waterdeep after Cyric stabbed her and took the Tablets of Fate, and when the lying Harlot persuaded Ao to make her Goddess of Magic, Adon was the first to declare his faith.

After that, he devoted himself to gathering worshipers for the Church of Mysteries. Mystra rewarded him with many special favors, not the least of which was naming him her patriarch. She also visited him in the sight of others, so that all would know Adon to be favored of the gods, and he became a much-valued guest in the homes of the powerful and the rich.

At no time was this more true than during the Rites of Joy. On account of the love between Kelemvor and Mystra, dying had become a time of wonder. If the departing one had lived a virtuous life and a cleric of Mystra was present at the instant of death, all manner of marvels would fill the air. Anyone who made a small wish would have it granted, provided the wish was a worthy one and for the good of another. Among those who value such follies as charity and compassion, the Rites were deemed a sure sign of the dead one's happiness in the afterlife.

Adon had taken part in a hundred such Rites over the last few years, but something in House Bhaskar made him uneasy. It could have been Pandara Bhaskar herself, who was not sitting with her dying husband like a good wife, but was hanging on Adon's arm and showing him off to her distinguished guests. There were more than a hundred of these, including Lady Lord Yanseldara and her good friend Vaerana Hawklyn, Prince Tang, Thunsroon Frostbryn, and a dozen others who had contributed most generously to the building of Elversult's new temple to Mystra.

So that all these guests could witness the moment of death, poor Nadisu's bed had been moved down to the banquet hall and placed on a dais, where he would be visible above the throng of musicians and dancing girls and acrobats and jugglers hired to keep the celebration lively. Nor would the guests go hungry waiting for Nadisu to die; the food piled on the feasting tables could have fed the poor of Elversult for a week—though of course Pandara had not invited a single beggar to the ceremony. Her husband had done so much for the poor in life, she had explained to Adon, that he deserved to die in dignity. The leftovers would be taken to the shanty quarter and given to the hungry.

It may have been the opulence of the celebration that made Adon uneasy, for he sensed none of the melancholy normal at even the most joyous Rites. Or it may have been only the itch beneath his star ring, a simple gold band set with an unpolished diamond. Mystra had given it to him to guard against Cyric's Faithful, who were always trying to win the One's favor by slaying the patriarch. Whenever an assassin came near, the diamond would sparkle like a bright star and the band would grow hot. But the ring had never itched; Adon did not know if this was a warning, or only an irritation such as men get beneath their rings.

Pandara pulled Adon over to a crowd gathered around a pair of scarf dancers, then stopped next to a guest in a gossamer robe. Of voluptuous proportions and sultry beauty, the woman looked the patriarch over and smiled. His ring finger began to itch more noticeably.

"Adon, may I present Usreena Juepara," said Pandara. "I believe she is . . . an *admirer* of your goddess."

"An acolyte, even." Usreena presented her hand for Adon to kiss. "Which is not to claim I am one of her favored."

"A pleasure." Adon bowed to Usreena, but did not take her hand. "You must visit the temple soon. It's nearly completed. Now, if you will excuse me, I must go to Nadisu. After all, this celebration is in his honor."

With that, Adon started toward the front of the hall. Pandara clutched his arm and dragged herself along behind.

"Really, patriarch! Do you know who that was?"

"I know *what* she was," Adon replied. He stopped and faced Pandara, and brought his mouth close to her ear. "And I must say that I am concerned about your husband's Rites. You have invited far too many people like Usreena."

Pandara pulled back. "What do you mean by that, patriarch?"

So shrill was her demand that nearby guests turned to stare. Among them were several people who had made large donations to Mystra's new temple, but Adon could not shrink from the truth.

"Something feels wrong here, Pandara." He fingered his star ring as he spoke. "The Rites of Joy honor the dying. They are not intended to impress one's friends."

Pandara's eyes narrowed. "How dare you! I am aware of how much Nadisu gave to build Mystra's temple, even if you are not."

"I am—which is why I must be honest with you." The whole banquet hall had fallen silent, and all eyes—except Nadisu's, of course—were turned toward Adon and Pandara. "The Rites of Joy are bestowed by Kelemvor and Mystra on those they deem worthy. I have no influence in the matter."

Pandara glanced around the room, then her face grew stormy. "What are you saying? You want more money for your temple?"

Adon shook his head. "Not at all. It would make no difference." He grasped Pandara's hands and spoke in his most comforting voice. "I am trying to tell you that something feels wrong. I'm receiving a sign. The opulence of the celebration may have offended Kelemvor, or Mystra may be reluctant to grant so many wishes. It might even be that Nadisu's time hasn't come yet. Perhaps he will recover as suddenly as he fell ill."

Pandara jerked her hands free. "Don't be ridiculous! Of course Nadisu will die! His face is as green as mold, and the circles beneath his eyes are as dark as a crow's belly."

Adon raised his brow. "You almost seem eager."

"And why shouldn't I be?"

Pandara's voice carried no love in it, and in a strange way, this relieved Adon as much as it stunned him. Perhaps her selfishness had caused his unease; it certainly would not be the first time a good person had married a wicked one.

"Nadisu will be happier in the afterlife, won't he?" Pandara asked. "Isn't that the point of the Rites?"

"The Rites don't do anything," Adon explained again. "They're only a sign—"

A ghastly wheeze sounded from the throne, followed by a sputtering groan. Nadisu sat up and gazed around the chamber in confusion. His head was the color of a green melon and as round as the moon, while his eyes were as dark and sunken as wells.

"Pan . . . dara!" he gasped. His dry lips cracked and bled. "Come . . . to . . . me!"

Nadisu dropped back and let out a long strangled gurgle.

Adon took Pandara's arm and started toward the dais, but the woman pulled free and shook her head.

"No—you go." The fear in her eyes was the first emotion she had shown concerning her husband. "I don't want to see him . . . like that, I mean."

"But he asked for you. It could be the last—"

"I don't want to!" Pandara covered her face and turned away, leaving Adon to frown at her back.

Yanseldara came to the patriarch's side. "I think the time has come. You should go to Nadisu."

Adon barely heard the lady lord, for his thoughts were completely absorbed by Pandara's strange behavior. Even if she felt nothing for her husband, she would want to keep up appearances.

"Pandara, what is it?" Adon asked. "Are you frightened of your husband?"

Pandara found the courage to turn around, and now she was crying. "No, of course not. I just don't . . ." She paused to glance at the dignitaries watching her, then wiped the tears from her eyes. "I don't want Nadisu to remember me like this."

Adon scowled at the lie; whatever the woman was hiding, it made his finger itch more than ever.

A long gasping rattle sounded from the bed, then a smiling servant girl came to the edge of the dais. "It's happening!"

Yanseldara took Adon's arm. "Shouldn't you go to him?"

Adon shook his head. "I don't think it will happen. Pandara's keeping something from us."

Yanseldara leaned close to Adon's ear, at the same time pulling him toward the dais. "Pandara's half-crazy," the lady lord whispered. "She lives in the Towers of the Moon as often as not, but Nadisu has never complained. And he has done more to feed the poor than any man in the city. I would consider it a personal favor for you to be at his side when he dies."

"As you wish," Adon sighed. "It will do no harm for me to be

164

there, as long as you remember that no one can buy—"

"Thank you, Adon." Yanseldara released his arm.

Given that Yanseldara's word was law in this city, and that she had personally given him the land for Mystra's temple, Adon could only hope the lady lord would not hold it against him if Kelemvor and Mystra withheld the Rites. He climbed the stairs and went to the dying man's side, acutely aware of all the eager eyes on his back. A terrible stench hung in the air, and the sheets were smeared with vile fluids seeped from the pores of Nadisu's bloated body. The dying man's fingertips had turned black and fallen off. The patriarch could not imagine what illness had seized the poor man, for the fellow had been as healthy as a horse just that morning.

Nadisu's eyelids fluttered open, but his eyes seemed only two dark holes. He raised his puffy hand. "Pandara?"

Adon sat on the edge of the bed and grasped the hand. Nadisu's skin felt scaly to the touch, but the flesh beneath was spongy and soft. "No, Nadisu. It's Adon."

"Adon?" Nadisu clutched the patriarch's hand and pulled himself upright, then turned his gaze toward the coffered ceiling. "Forgive me, my lord! Forgive my faithless heart!"

An astonished murmur rustled through the banquet hall. Pandara let out a little cry and sank into a chair, but no one paid her any attention. Everyone in the room, entertainer and servant and dignitary alike, kept her eyes fixed on the dais, and Adon's star ring grew hot. He tried to pull his hand free and failed, for Nadisu's grasp had grown strong as an ogre's. The diamond began to shine with its warning light, and shafts of silvery light shot up between Nadisu's fingers to dance across the ceiling.

Someone cried, "Look! The Rites!"

A hush fell over the hall as Pandara's guests made their little wishes, but Adon knew he was in trouble. His ring had grown so hot that he felt it scorching his flesh. He slammed his free hand into Nadisu's head.

"Hey!" someone yelled. "Is that part of the Rites?"

Nadisu's grasp remained as tight as before, and his gaze

shifted to Adon's face. "Cyric, the One, the All! Take me back!"

Though Nadisu spoke in a thousand voices at once, they were hardly a whisper, so soft that of all the people in the room, only Adon heard what was said. The patriarch reached across his body and awkwardly pulled his mace from its sling.

"What's he doing?" someone cried.

Nadisu's sunken eyes bulged from their sockets. They were as black as a grave and a thousand times as deep. As Adon looked into them, an inky darkness welled up from their depths to swallow him.

"Stop him!" someone yelled.

Adon swung his mace and felt it sink deep into Nadisu's bloated head. Then the gold of his star ring grew so hot it scorched the skin of his finger.

He cried out for his goddess. "Mystra!"

Mystra? Adon heard the word inside his own head, and the voice was sharp and hissing and cruel, one that he recognized from more than a decade before. *As you command, old friend— but I warn you, she has changed. My, how she has changed!*

The voice was Cyric's, of course. No sooner had he spoken than Mystra emerged from the darkness and rushed Adon, her long black tresses swirling behind her as foul and acrid as smoke. She wore a thin black dress that clung to her haggard body like wet silk. Her cheekbones jutted through the leathery skin of her face, while her lipless mouth gaped open to expose two rows of blood-crusted fangs. The hatred in her eyes licked out of her pupils in long writhing tongues, and when she reached for her patriarch, it was with gore-dripping talons.

Adon screamed and flung his arms up before his eyes, for he had seen Mystra's true face. Now he recognized her for the murdering trollop she was. She meant to slay him, as she slew all those who learned her secret, and to wipe even the memory of his existence from the face of Faerûn.

He stumbled back and fell off the dais, his head striking the floor with a sharp crack that silenced the entire chamber.

Now you see her as I do, chuckled Cyric. *Not so pretty, is she?*

Adon did not hear the One's words, for he lay on the marble

floor, curled into a tiny ball and clutching his bloody mace. The star ring had reduced his finger to a charred stump and fallen off somewhere, and his gaze was fixed far beyond the walls of House Bhaskar. He kept asking, "Why does she hate me? Why?" He did not notice the arm he had broken in his fall, or Vaerana Hawklyn pushing through the crowd to his side.

"By Torm!" She plucked the bloody mace from his hands. "He's lost his mind!"

Eighteen

The trail of the hell horse—for so Ruha had come to think of the beast she was tracking—ran into the Wood of Sharp Teeth as straight as an arrow. Even from the edge of the forest, she could see a hundred paces down the tunnel it had torn through the underbrush, and there was not a single turn in that whole distance. The horse always ran straight eastward, never veering more than a step or two off course.

Ruha turned away from the wood and went to stand beside her companion, a tall and handsome hippogriff rider named Zale. He was kneeling some distance back from the forest, in a crimson circle where the hell horse had made a kill. It had devoured its prey almost entirely, leaving behind only ten long claws, a pair of sharp fangs, and the blood on the ground.

"How long ago?" she asked, not stepping into the red circle.

"Six hours, at least." Zale crumbled a clot of crimson dirt between his fingers. "This can't be our man. We're riding a hippogriff! No one could be this far ahead of us."

"It is him."

Ruha fingered her Harper's pin, which now adorned the breast of her extra aba. After being drawn to the stock shed by a scout's signal fire, she had pulled the brooch from a pile of bloody goat dung and sworn vengeance, both for the disrespect shown to the Harp and the Moon, and for the death of the old man lying trampled in the farmyard. The witch and Zale had started after the hell horse at once, but the beast was so swift they had not even glimpsed it yet.

From the depths of the forest came a long howl, as ghostly as it was chilling. Ruha looked back toward the murky trail, then at Zale's hippogriff. The beast sat upon the ground in a pose of great nobility, massive wings folded against the flanks of its horselike body, huge eagle's head held high and proud.

"Can Silvercloud fly through the forest?" Ruha asked. "It looks too tangled."

"We'll have to go over and drop down to check the trail whenever there's a clearing." Zale glanced toward the west, where the sun was sinking behind the thunderheads that had been creeping behind them all day. "But we can't do it tonight. Silvercloud's exhausted, and if that storm catches us over the forest, we'll be in big trouble."

Ruha scowled, though Zale could not see it behind her dark veil. "If we wait, we will never catch that murderer. Already, he is pulling ahead."

"I know," said Zale. "And I want to catch him too—but not if it costs me Silvercloud. Capturing that little beggar won't bring back Rinda and Gwydion, or the man at the farm."

At this, a flash of sheet lightning erupted inside the distant storm, and a clap of thunder pealed across the sky, shaking the ground beneath their feet. Silvercloud screeched and spread his great wings and flattened himself against the grass. The glare he fixed on Zale made clear what hippogriffs thought about weathering storms in the open.

Another mournful howl sounded from the Wood of Sharp Teeth, but Ruha paid it less mind than she had the thunder. "Zale, all you say is true, but Malik is no ordinary thief. When Pelias brought him into Candlekeep, he looked as though a lion had mauled him, yet he swam across a boiling moat and climbed the Keeper's Tower. Then he killed Rinda and Gwydion both—something a hundred of Cyric's assassins have not been able to do."

"I know." Zale rose and went to hold Silvercloud's reins, for a constant rumble of thunder had begun to roll across the plain. "And then there's his escape from the dungeon."

This brought the heat to Ruha's cheeks, for Bedine women

were not in the custom of showing their faces—much less their naked bodies, which she had been greatly abashed to find on display. It was on account of this embarrassment that she was so determined to avenge the deaths of the *Cyrinishad*'s bearers, but that is not what she told her companion.

"Zale, this murderer is being helped by Cyric. That is the only explanation for all we have seen. And if he is being helped by Cyric, then there must be a good reason for what he is doing."

"What reason?"

Ruha shook her head. "I do not know, but he would not turn his back on the *Cyrinishad* without good reason. If we do not discover it soon, I am certain we are not the only ones who will regret our failure."

The witch did not tell Zale of her vision of me, for she had long ago learned that few people understood her curse. Either they blamed her for the ill foretold by her mirages, or they grew angry when she failed to warn them of some other catastrophe.

The mournful howl echoed again from the wood, and this time it sounded closer. Silvercloud raised his head and opened his great beak to hiss at the forest. Zale tightened his grasp on the reins and pulled the hippogriff's head back down.

"You may be right, but what difference does it make? Even if we risked the flight, we can't follow a trail in the dark."

Ruha raised her brow. "But you would take the risk if we could see the trail?"

Zale glanced at the approaching thunderclouds, then nodded. "I'll do it—but let's get on with it."

"You are a brave man, Zale." Ruha went over to him. "May I borrow your flint and steel?"

Zale dug the items from his saddlebags and gave them to Ruha, and she went over to stand before the hell horse's trail. She closed her eyes and sparked the steel, at the same time uttering the incantation of a fire spell.

The world flashed silver; then a deafening clap of thunder blasted her off her feet. The witch found herself sitting on the ground, her temples throbbing and her nostrils filled with the smell of scorched grass. A curtain of white spots danced before her eyes. Her ears rang with the clanging of a thousand bells, and she could not stop her muscles from quivering. The air seemed unbearably hot and full of smoke.

"Ruha!" Zale's voice was barely audible above the ringing in the witch's ears. "Are you hurt?"

The rider grabbed her beneath the arms and dragged her across the ground. The silver spots began to disappear, as did the quivering in her muscles and the ringing in her ears, and she saw the reason the air seemed so hot and full of smoke: her spell had shot a pillar of flame straight down the hell horse's trail!

The fiery column had set the forest ablaze on each side of the path. Now, two huge curtains of flame were tearing through the forest in opposite directions. The sky above the wood had turned black with escaping birds, and the air was filled with the crash and rustle of animals fleeing blindly through the undergrowth. Another mournful howl echoed out of the forest, closer and more eerie than before.

"Zale, what happened?" gasped Ruha.

"A lightning bolt," the rider replied. "It came down when you cast your spell."

"*I* did this?" The witch grabbed Zale's arm and pulled herself to her feet, then pushed him in the direction of his skittish hippogriff. "Quickly, get me some water!"

As the rider moved to obey, a woman's voice came from within the burning forest. "Do not trouble yourself, Zale." The words were both comforting and commanding, as powerful as thunder and as soft as a caress. "The fire will take care of itself."

A dark-haired woman of unimaginable beauty stepped from the smoke, her skin pale and radiant, her eyes as lustrous as ebony. She wore a simple gown of heavy black silk, clasped at the bodice with Mystra's sacred web. Ruha and Zale fell to their knees at once, their mouths gaping in awe.

Before they could utter a word, the woman said, "Speak no

names. We do not wish to draw our enemy's attention, do we?"

Ruha and Zale glanced at each other and said nothing at all.

A mournful howl echoed out of the forest. The woman cast a worried glance over her shoulder; no matter what shape the Shadowlord assumed or which god he pretended to be, the Chaos Hound was never far behind.

Mask stopped before the pair and motioned Ruha to her feet. "Our enemy has set his pet after me," the Shadowlord said, still speaking in Mystra's voice. "I cannot spare much time, but know this: what I have given you tonight, I have given you for good reason. Though it destroys a whole kingdom, you must never hesitate to use it. There is more in the Balance than you can imagine, and whatever you annihilate will be nothing to what you save. Do you understand?"

"Yes, My—"

Mask pressed his womanly finger to Ruha's veil, for he did not want the witch to draw Mystra's attention. "No names."

"Yes, milady."

"Good."

A savage growl sounded from just within the burning forest. Then there was a terrible crashing, and a huge, shapeless shadow came bounding out of the smoke. Mask laid one hand on Ruha's shoulder and the other on Zale's, then pushed them both toward Silvercloud.

"Go!"

The two mortals raced to their mount and leapt onto his back, and a terrible snarling broke out where they had been standing the moment before. Even before Zale had given the command, Silvercloud raised his wings and sprang into the air. Ruha pulled a pebble from her pocket and summoned to mind the words of a sand spell, but when they circled back toward the burning forest, she saw that Mystra had vanished as though she had never been present.

Now a huge mastiff occupied the spot, clawing and howling at the ground. The beast was as large as a draft horse, with a coat of slithering maggots and rot-crusted teeth as black as jet. Its yellow eyes gleamed with a profanity beyond human understanding, and ribbons of bubbling green poison ran from its lolling tongue.

"The goddess was right," Zale remarked. "Our enemy is a horrible one."

"And that is only a pet," said Ruha. "May the goddess forgive me, but I am glad it is chasing her and not us."

Nineteen

Mystra stood in the anteroom outside Adon's bedchamber, looking through a window at the placid waters of Hillshadow Lake and studying the reflection of her new temple. Though still six months from completion, it was already a sparkling edifice of alabaster spires and silver cupolas and crystal buttresses that did her great glory. When it was finished, she would ask her patriarch to make it his home; the lives of mortals were not endless, and Adon had already spent most of his spreading her worship from one end of Faerûn to the other.

Mystra turned from the window and found a handful of people kneeling on the marble floor, their hands clasped in supplication. Two men wore the scale mail of the Maces, Elversult's city guardsmen, and most of the others wore the simple robes of her own church. Only one man had not fallen to his knees; he had the yellow skin and black hair and slanted eye-folds of the Shou race, and he was dressed in a widesleeved silk tunic his people called a *maitung*.

He gave Mystra a slight nod, but made no other sign of obeisance. He was Prince Tang, eldest son of the Third Virtuous Concubine to the Emperor Kao Tsao Shou Tang of Shou Lung, and he did not bow to any god but those of the Celestial Bureaucracy. Mystra let the matter pass and stepped toward Adon's door, for she had no interest in explaining the Plurality of Being to the prince.

Tang intercepted her, placing himself before the great

copper-gilded doors that protected Adon's chamber. "Please let Adon rest."

"What?" Mystra did not disguise her irritation. "You dare—"

"I gave the honorable patriarch a potion to help him sleep," the prince explained. "He was most disturbed."

"Disturbed?" Mystra remained unaware of events in House Bhaskar, for her attention had been turned elsewhere when Adon called out, then he had actually closed his mind to the thought image she sent. She wondered if Tang's potion had caused the patriarch's strange behavior. "What did you give him?"

"Lasal-leaf potion. It stops troubling thoughts from—"

"I am aware of what lasal leaves do, Prince Tang." Mystra perceived the qualities of every herb or spice on Faerûn, and so she knew that lasal leaves were used to numb the mind. She also knew they caused confusion and trembling muscles, and that when used too often or too strongly, they destroyed the mind instead of numbing it. "I warn you, if you have harmed my patriarch—"

"I have helped him!" Tang insisted. "Adon is mad. He thinks you hate him, and he has even murdered a sick man."

"Adon? Adon is no murderer!"

Prince Tang continued to meet Mystra's stern gaze. "With my own eyes, I saw him kill Nadisu Bhaskar."

The goddess scowled, then looked to her kneeling acolytes. "Is this true?"

The oldest, a red-haired woman named Chandra, nodded. "There were a hundred witnesses. Nadisu was dying, and everyone expected the Rites of Joy—"

"This man asked a hundred people to witness his death?"

Chandra paled at her goddess's disapproval. "His wife did, and Adon was the priest . . ." She looked toward Prince Tang, then back again. "Well, even Vaerana Hawklyn says the patriarch went mad and smashed poor Nadisu's head with no reason."

"There *is* a reason, Chandra." Mystra's face grew as fierce as a sandstorm. "His name is Cyric."

The goddess stepped straight through Tang, which caused the prince to cry out, then went into Adon's bedchamber without opening the copper-gilded doors. The room was as majestic as the rest of the temple, with a ceiling of coffered oak and alabaster walls decorated with bas-reliefs of Mystra's miracles. But the bed in which the patriarch lay was as humble as that of any man, with only a plain wooden frame and a thin straw mattress covered by a blanket of gray cotton. It sat on the far side of the room, turned so that Adon could look out across his balcony and see the purple waters of Hillshadow Lake glimmering between the balusters.

The patriarch lay thrashing beneath his blanket, mumbling gibberish and trembling from the effects of the prince's potion. Mystra looked into his mind and found herself lost in a swirling lasal-leaf fog. She maintained contact with his thoughts and started across the room, gliding over the cool marble floor as silently as a djinn.

"Adon."

The patriarch's head snapped around to look at her. His red-rimmed eyes grew as large as saucers, then his sunken cheeks paled and he gave a piercing scream. Someone outside the room started to open the doors, but Mystra locked them with a thought and continued toward Adon.

He threw off his blanket and stood on the bed, pointing at Mystra as though his hand were a crossbow. She saw that the finger that had once worn her star ring was now a charred stick. Her heart sank, for she knew that only Cyric himself could have caused the gold to grow so hot.

"Stay away, hag!"

Inside Adon's mind, the goddess saw nothing but the swirling lasal fog. This raised her ire against Prince Tang, for the haze made it difficult to see what was wrong. "Adon, there is no reason to be frightened. This is me, Midnight."

"Midnight?" Adon lowered his hand.

"Yes. It is still me." Mystra gave him a reassuring smile.

Adon squinted, then rubbed his eyes. "Fangs!"

The goddess shook her head. "No, Adon. I have no fangs."

She reached out to embrace him. "Let me hold—"

Adon pointed at her hands. "Talons!"

The patriarch bolted onto his balcony, his head swinging to and fro like a wild animal seeking escape. He found none. The porch hung above the lakeshore twice the height of a giant, and there was nothing between it and the ground except air.

Mystra opened her hands and displayed her fingers. "Adon, I have no talons. Cyric is deceiving you."

"Fire! Poison!" Adon turned to fling himself over the rail.

Before he took a step, Mystra manifested a second avatar in his path. The patriarch slammed into her at a full sprint, but the impact did not even rock her onto her heels. She caught him up like a child, paying no heed to the blows he rained down on her avatar's face.

"This is Cyric's doing, and I forgive you for it."

Mystra carried Adon back into his chamber, and that is when she saw the blood bubbling up between her fingers. A half-dozen long gashes, each as deep and straight as any knife wound, had opened up where she grasped his shoulder and thigh. The goddess saw at once that her avatar's hands had caused these wounds, though she did not understand how. She laid patriarch on the bed. He shrieked and tried to fling himself from the mattress, and she pushed him down. Where her hand touched his chest, four jets of blood spurted up.

At that moment came a prayer from the Harper witch Ruha, asking for guidance in the use of her newfound powers. Too distressed by Adon's strange condition to give the matter much thought, Mystra noted only that Ruha begged a sign about whether to use all her magic against the killer of Rinda and Gwydion. The goddess cast a star down from the heavens to make plain she wished the witch to use every means at her disposal, then gave the matter no more thought, for she knew nothing of the lightning bolt that had blessed the meddling Harper with the power of destruction.

And as Mystra did all this, she sent her first avatar to the door of Adon's room to call for help. Prince Tang rushed in, followed closely by the guards and the acolytes, whom the goddess instructed to hold the patriarch's arms and legs.

"What happened here?" Tang asked, his gaze shifting between Adon and Mystra's two avatars. "Did he do this to himself?"

"No, I think I caused it." Mystra's second avatar left the patriarch's bedside and melded with her first, which was standing out of Adon's sight near the door. "I have become some kind of monster to him."

Tang furrowed his brow. "I do not understand."

"Neither do I." Mystra motioned the prince to her side. "The lasal potion prevents me from seeing inside his mind."

Tang stopped three paces from the goddess and eyed her suspiciously. "I apologize for the honest misfortune, but I did not know that you were coming, Venerable Goddess. I was only trying to be of service."

"You will be, Tang." As Mystra said this, she turned as translucent as a ghost and was suddenly standing at the prince's shoulder. "I assure you of that."

She began to slide into the prince's body, much as a person slips into a new cloak.

"No! This is not permitted." Tang tried step away, but Mystra only continued to invade his body. "I am an Imperial Shou—"

The last scrap of the goddess's robe vanished from sight, and the prince fell silent. He blinked several times, then stretched his arms as person does when rising in the morning.

"This will do." The voice was Tang's, but the words belonged to Mystra. She walked the prince's body to the bedside and bent over Adon. "Now, my dear friend, let us see what Cyric has done."

Adon eyed the prince's body suspiciously, but made no attempt to escape the acolytes restraining him. The two guards stood close by, cradling their maces and looking uncomfortable. Vaerana Hawklyn had told them to strike Adon down if he tried to escape, but they were loath to do this with the Goddess of Magic standing there.

Mystra took a diamond ring off Tang's finger and pressed it

between his palms. When the prince saw what she meant to do, he cried out inside her mind, *No! That is a magic Ring of Chameleon Power!*

Mystra continued to grind, believing in her arrogance that any magic was hers to give or take as she pleased. The diamond crumbled into powder, producing an acrid smell and a shrill chirp and a brilliant flash. The goddess ran her hands over Adon, covering him from head to foot in twinkling diamond dust; this was to dispel the magic Cyric had used to drive him mad.

"Poison!" Adon screamed.

His skin turned red and blotchy, then blisters of white ichor rose wherever the powder had touched. Adon wailed in agony and flailed about, tearing an arm and leg free. The two guardsmen raised their maces and rushed over.

Mystra glanced in their direction, and their weapons turned to smoke. She motioned the pair to Adon's side.

"Help hold him," the goddess commanded. Then she turned to the acolyte Chandra and said, "Wash him off, quickly!"

Chandra grabbed the water pitcher from the patriarch's dressing table and poured it over his body. Adon stopped screaming, but he stared at Prince Tang's body as though looking at his own murderer. His skin remained red and blistered, and he began to shake uncontrollably.

No one dared to ask what had happened, which was well with Mystra, as she had no answers. Adon's condition could not be magical in origin, or else her spell would have removed it—in such matters, only Ao had the power to defy her. She found herself growing angrier with Prince Tang about the lasal potion. It prevented her from seeing what was wrong, but attempting to clear the haze from Adon's mind would also destroy a good portion of his memories. Still, she was not ready to quit.

"Chandra, give me that." Mystra motioned at a silver starburst, the holy symbol of the Church of Mysteries, hanging about the acolyte's neck. "And open Adon's tunic."

The patriarch made no protest as Chandra obeyed. Mystra raised the holy symbol to Tang's lips and kissed it.

Adon's eyes grew wide, and he fought against his captors. "Fire!"

Mystra came very near to turning away, but then she thought of Cyric's infinite cunning and knew he would have foreseen her aversion to hurting her patriarch. What better way for the One to guard his curse than to protect it behind just such a shield of pain? With her kiss still fresh upon its metal, the goddess laid her sacred starburst on Adon's bare chest.

There was a sick sizzling sound; then Adon raised his head and let out a terrible scream. Mystra kept the starburst pressed to his chest.

"Take it away!" Adon looked into Tang's eyes, but Mystra knew he saw her. "What have I done to deserve your hatred?"

"Nothing, Adon," she replied. "I could never hate you."

Tiny tongues of yellow began to flicker up around the starburst, and Adon let out a horrid shriek. Chandra and the others gasped and stared at Mystra with wide eyes, but still the goddess pressed her symbol to the patriarch's chest.

Inside Mystra's mind, Tang asked, *Is killing your Esteemed patriarch the only way to remove Cyric's curse?*

The goddess ignored the prince and continued to hold the starburst in place. After a time, a circle of orange flame flared up around the amulet, and the patriarch stopped screaming. Mystra thought for a moment her plan had worked, but the flames only grew hotter. The stench of charred flesh filled the air, and Adon watched in horror as his skin grew black and crisp.

Mystra pulled the starburst away.

"Cyric!" The scream reverberated across nine heavens at once. "Now you have gone too far!"

Perhaps it is you who have gone too far, suggested Prince Tang. *That burn is most serious.*

Mystra slipped out of Tang's body, stepping back so that the prince's figure blocked Adon's view of her. "Adon will recover from the burn, Prince Tang, if he is cared for."

"We'll heal him at once." Chandra stepped around a guard, moving toward the head of the bed. "We have a dozen priests—"

"No, Chandra." Mystra waved the acolyte back. "Until I discover what Cyric has done, I fear our magic will cause Adon more harm than good." She offered the starburst to her acolyte.

Chandra glanced at the burn on Adon's chest and hesitated a moment, then overcame her fear and accepted the sacred symbol. It was as cool as when she had relinquished it.

"But if we don't heal the patriarch—"

"Adon will recover quickly under the prince's care." Mystra turned toward Tang, then added, "His lasal potion certainly proved effective."

The prince flushed, but nodded his assent. "I can heal the Esteemed patriarch's burns and rashes, but his madness—"

"Will be my concern—but no more lasal, at least not until I discover what Cyric did to him." The goddess turned to Chandra. "You will pray to me the instant Adon seems lucid."

Chandra looked surprised. "You won't be watching?"

"I will be busy." Mystra glanced at her tormented patriarch, then added, "And so will Cyric."

181

Twenty

First a roaring wind rose at our backs, then a wall of air slammed into us from behind. Halah stumbled and almost fell, catapulting me onto her withers, and I found myself clinging to her mane and sliding down her neck toward her flashing black hooves.

"Halah, wait!" It was an hour past highsun, and we were in the plain east of the Wood of Sharp Teeth, galloping toward the distant city of Berdusk at a dead sprint. "Stop!"

Halah surprised me by obeying at once. My fingers slipped free of her mane, and I hit the ground and tumbled more than a dozen paces into a ravine as deep as I was tall. For a moment, I lay there too dizzy to move, staring up at the sky and wondering at the power of the sudden wind. Then the roaring became a low, deep chugging, and leaves and sticks and screeching birds began to stream through the air above. I rose and peered over the rim of the ravine.

A stinging torrent of grit and gravel instantly assailed me, and I perceived this was no ordinary dust storm. The western horizon lay hidden behind a blowing curtain of dirt a thousand feet high.

"Halah, come here!"

Thinking I meant to take shelter, the mare trotted over and climbed down into the ravine. I took her reins and clambered out of the gully, for such was my devotion that I intended to ride straight through the storm.

Halah stamped her hooves and refused to follow me up the

slope. The storm continued to sweep toward us, and the closer it approached, the more deafening it grew, until my ears ached from the pulse of its roaring winds. The hair on my arms stood on end, and I saw dark shapes—branches and bushes and splintered trees—whirling around in the gray curtain.

I jerked on the reins. "Halah, I am the rider! Do as I say!"

Halah snorted in disgust, then raised her nose toward the storm. And now I saw another dark figure in the sky, soaring along above the top edge of the storm. It was shaped like a cross, with a blocky body and two feathery wings stretched out to catch the fierce winds, which were sweeping it forward so fast it doubled size in the span of a heartbeat.

And I knew, even before I spied the witch's cloth-swaddled head peering over the rider's shoulder, who was chasing me.

"Quick, Halah!" I leapt straight onto her back from the rim of the ravine. "Run like the wind!"

And she did.

Twenty-One

Kelemvor had changed the wall of his Judgment Hall into a mirror so perfect it revealed all the onlooker's flaws, whether of body or mind or character, and now he stood before this mirror, observing himself in its silvery depths. He saw a square-jawed man with a swarthy face, piercing green eyes, and a wild mane of black hair. He discerned no distortions or deformities of any kind, but neither did he perceive the resplendent reflection of a god.

"You will find no guidance there." Jergal drifted over to Lord Death's side, his disembodied hand dragging along one of the False. "Whatever a god does is perfect."

"If that were true, I would not be the latest in a long line of death gods."

In the mirror, Jergal was nothing but a gray eyeless face and two disembodied arms, the complement to the shadow-filled cloak in the chamber. The spirit in his grasp was reflected as a black rat with yellow eyes and a coat teeming with lice.

Kelemvor gestured at the gruesome reflection. "I have told you, I will not judge spirits until the trial is decided."

"So you have said. Judge this one anyway." Jergal did not wait for Lord Death's permission, but forced the False spirit to his knees. "Recount the tale of your life, Nadisu Bhaskar, and the God of Death will judge you."

Kelemvor turned to castigate Jergal for daring to order him about, and Nadisu Bhaskar, thinking the god's anger directed at him, clasped his hands before his breast.

"Have mercy on my wretched spirit, and I swear I shall make it worth your while!"

Lord Death cocked an eyebrow and glanced down at the brazen spirit. Nadisu Bhaskar was a round-faced man with ginger skin and the sly, dark eyes of a killer, and his words were such an affront that Kelemvor forgave Jergal's audacity at once.

"Nadisu Bhaskar, perhaps you could bribe the judges of Elversult, but that will not work here." Kelemvor turned to Jergal. "Will you begin? When Nadisu feels like making a free and honest confession, he may speak for himself."

"Certainly." Jergal pointed a disembodied glove at Nadisu. "Nadisu Bhaskar, you are the gutter-born spawn of a brothel sow. You learned to cut purses before you could speak, and you killed your first man at the age of ten. Because of this, Indrith Shalla recruited you to join the Cult of the Dragon. By the age of twenty, you were her top assassin and a loyal worshiper of Bhaal, Lord of Murder at that time."

"And that is when Indrith arranged employment for me in the house of Ganesh Lal." Seeing that Jergal was determined to cast his life in the most disapproving terms possible, Nadisu took over the narrative himself. "Ganesh's caravans had proved too effective in repelling the cult's bandits, and I was to kill Ganesh in manner that would warn others against his example."

Here, Nadisu paused to look up, and his expression was most earnest. "But then something changed my life. During the course of my duties, I met Pandara Lal, and we fell in love."

"*She* fell in love," Jergal corrected. "You merely thought it fun to get a bastard on your victim's daughter."

"Perhaps *I* fell in love later." Though Nadisu kept his eyes on Kelemvor, the rodent in the mirror snorted black steam at Jergal's reflection. "In any case, I convinced—"

"Indrith decided," Jergal interrupted.

"*It* was determined I would be more useful to the cult inside the Lal cartage company. Ganesh's life was spared—" Nadisu glanced toward Jergal, then continued "—for a time, and Pandara and I married. After a decent interval, Indrith ordered me to cut Ganesh's throat, but Ganesh had treated me so well that I smothered him in his sleep instead."

The False one tried a weak smile, thinking Kelemvor would approve of his compassion.

Lord Death looked back to Jergal. "So far, I see no reason to hurry the judgment of Nadisu Bhaskar. From what I have heard so far, I suspect he will find more mercy standing in line."

"Let him finish." Jergal's bulbous eyes swung in Nadisu's direction. "Say what occured after the Time of Troubles."

Nadisu continued, his voice too confident for one in his position. "After Bhaal died and Cyric ascended to godhood, I took him as my deity, and I continued to murder for Indrith Shalla. Then, when Yanseldara overthrew Raunshivear's cartel and made an honest city of the place, Indrith decided to plant an agent in her circle of friends. She ordered me to stop murdering and start contributing to charity, and soon my wagons were feeding half the city's beggars. Yanseldara took Pandara and me as her friends, and I started to enjoy helping others."

"You enjoyed feeling important," Jergal corrected. "Even Indrith did not know you were cutting your flour with sawdust."

Nadisu shrugged, then continued, "When I realized that Indrith never meant to use me as an assassin again, my offerings to Cyric grew smaller and less frequent, until one day I realized he was no longer as important to me as the people I was helping. I even opened an orphanage, and I never stole a copper from it."

Jergal nodded that this was true.

"But I should have known better than to think I could quit the One's church. One day Cyric came to me—"

"In Elversult?" Now Kelemvor was as interested in Nadisu's story as in his own trial. "How long ago?"

"Shortly before I died." The rodent in the mirror smirked, for Nadisu could see Kelemvor's interest, and he planned to use that interest to good advantage. "He possessed my body. Then he said, 'Telling the truth is good for the soul.' He made me beat poor Pandara and tell her how I had murdered her father and say that I had never loved her."

"And that last was a lie, was it not?" Jergal sneered.

Nadisu nodded. "Pandara was a silly woman, but she was also the mother of my children. Over the years, it seemed the softer I grew, the more I loved her. I would have killed myself before telling her I didn't love her."

"You would have done better to kill yourself before you killed her father," said Kelemvor. "What did Cyric do then?"

"He left me," Nadisu answered. "I fell deathly ill, and Lady Yanseldara herself suggested a party to celebrate the Rites."

"And Adon came to endorse them!"

"Yes. The instant he touched me, Cyric possessed me again."

"What magic did he use against Adon?"

In the mirror, Nadisu's rattish eyes gleamed with cunning. "It would be helpful if I remembered, would it not?"

"I have warned you about trying to bargain with me."

"Then why should I answer?" Though Nadisu's voice caught with fear, he looked Kelemvor in the eye and did not waver. "I will not ask much, and more on my wife's behalf than my own."

Kelemvor could not bear this insolence. "Jergal! Tell me what happened!"

"As you wish, Lord Death—but would you care to look in the mirror first?"

Kelemvor scowled and turned to look, and then he voiced such a gasp that all the vultures in Faerûn cried out at once. His reflection was covered head to foot in pitch, so that only his eyes and the great emerald on his belt clasp showed through. Lord Death recognized this image as the mark of a grafter, for he had lived many years in the kingdom of Cormyr, where it was custom to punish those who abused their office by painting them in tar.

"What is this?" Kelemvor demanded of Jergal. "You said whatever a god does is perfect!"

"And you said if I was right, you would not be the latest of many death gods," Jergal replied. "This is your own doing. You have made the rules by which you perform your office, and now you must decide whether to abide by them or break them."

"But I must know how this spirit died." Kelemvor pointed at Nadisu's reflection. "It is necessary for a proper judgment."

"Yes, but there is no need to tell Mystra what you learn," replied Jergal. "That would be violating the privacy of Nadisu's death, and you are the one who declared the dead deserve the secrecy of their graves. If you change your mind now, it is only because of your fondness for Mystra and her patriarch."

"What if I said he could tell Mystra?" Nadisu's voice was smooth and sly.

Kelemvor glared at the spirit. "In exchange for leniency?"

Nadisu smiled, thinking he had won Kelemvor's accord. "In exchange for a little forbearance and for keeping secret the true nature of my life. If my reputation is ruined, the high houses of Elversult will shun Pandara. She does not deserve that—not after the things Cyric made me say to her."

Kelemvor stared at Nadisu for a long time, then said, "I suppose a murderer and spy must have such nerve, but it will do you no good here."

Nadisu's eyes grew round. "You do not care about Adon?"

"I care. But if I am going to ignore my duty as God of Death, it will not be to spare you." Kelemvor looked to Jergal. "How did this man die?"

Jergal's yellow eyes swung back to Nadisu. "Cyric possessed his body again, then grabbed Adon and locked gazes with him. The patriarch tried to defend himself by smashing Nadisu's head."

"And what magic did Cyric use against Adon?"

"You are sure you want to know?"

Kelemvor glanced at the mirror and saw his eyes held open by sickles of ice. He knew this to be the mark of a traitor to duty, for in the cold land of Vaasa, such men were tied out in raging blizzards with their eyelids cut away.

"I want to know," Kelemvor said.

"Nothing," said Jergal. "Cyric used no magic at all. He only opened his soul and allowed the patriarch to look inside."

"And Adon saw Mystra through Cyric's eyes!" Kelemvor continued to stare at himself in the mirror.

"Yes, that is what drove him mad," said Jergal. "Adon's faith is remarkable, but it is no match for the mind of a god."

Kelemvor turned away and started out the anteroom door.

Jergal drifted after him. "Lord Death, where are you going?"

"Into the city," Kelemvor said. "A walk will help me think."

Jergal floated along at Lord Death's side, his disembodied glove dragging Nadisu across the floor. "And what of Nadisu?"

Kelemvor paused to look down at the False spirit, who had learned better than to beg for mercy.

"Nadisu Bhaskar, know that your reputation in Elversult will remain unblemished, for I have said that the secrets of the dead are their own. But you have lived a wicked life and a False one, and for that you shall suffer." Kelemvor pointed at the lice-covered rodent in the mirror. "What you see shall be your punishment. As long as any coin you ever gave in deceit is counted as money anywhere in Faerûn, you shall wander the streets of my city in that form."

Twenty-Two

If the Storm Horns are not the highest and coldest mountains in the world, then I do not know what mountains are. They are nothing but jagged granite teeth a thousand feet high, with no tree taller than a fire giant and a cold wind that blows down from the barren heights at every hour of the day and night. Yet barbarians will live anywhere, and some of them lived in a little village that straddled a treacherous goat path they stupidly called the High Road. In the heart of this village stood a small citadel, and by the starburst and skull discreetly carved in the top of the gatehouse arch, I knew this to be a temple of the One.

Despite my hunger and fatigue, I was reluctant to pound the gate. From inside the castle came a terrible wailing, and the air near the walls reeked of death; this could have been on account of the fresh kill Halah had snatched as we passed through the village, yet the underscent of decay and mustiness suggested otherwise. But even this was not as disturbing as the green fly roaring over the citadel; the thing was as large as an elephant, with black legs longer than spears and eyes as big as wagon wheels. This was not the sort of pet True Believers usually kept in their temples—at least not in civilized lands—and I found it difficult to believe what I saw.

I considered riding on. Certainly Halah was capable; she had already galloped a distance greater than the breadth of Calimshan, and still she was as fresh as the minute she burst from the stock shed. It was I who needed rest. The witch had been hounding my trail since her windstorm knocked me from my mount, and this was the first time I had stopped without spying her somewhere on the distant horizon. Whether she and her companion had finally ridden their hippogriff to death or merely stopped to rest, I did not know—but it hardly mattered. Even with the One's heart slushing in my chest, two solid days of riding had left me so weary that I had twice fallen off my horse. Only Tyr's protection had saved me from smashing my skull.

Halah tore a leg off her kill's carcass and began to gnaw at the thighbone, trying to get at the bone marrow. I turned away from the gruesome sight and studied my backtrail, as I had grown accustomed to doing. The River Tun snaked along the base of the mountains, as brown and murky as the plain beyond, and in the distance the sky was as blue as steel. When I still saw none of the brushfires or tornadoes or raging floods that always seemed to accompany the witch, I leaned over to knock on the gate.

The portal swung open before my hand touched it. An old priest in the silver skull-bracers of a True Believer peered out at me. His eyes were as vacant as a ruin, his flesh as gray and fixed as clay. If he noticed the flies swarming his ears and eyes and nostrils, he did not disturb them by twitching or blinking—nor even, so far as I could tell, by breathing upon them.

"Yes?"

"I am on a mission for the One and All." I had to shout to make myself heard above the roaring of the great fly above. "I need food and shelter and perhaps protection from my enemies."

He glanced at the bloody mess my horse had laid before the gate, then back at me. "Can you pay?"

"No, but you will if you refuse me."

I kicked Halah, and she grabbed her meal and pushed through the opening. The gatekeeper stumbled back with the stiff-legged gait of a sleepwalker, and it was then I saw I had been talking to a corpse. This did not amaze me much; it seemed but one more novelty of my draining journey through barbarian lands.

I dismounted. "What happened to you, old man?"

He shrugged the shrug of the weary, then glanced up at the great fly. "The Troubles," he said, as though that explained why he was not in the grave. He closed the gate and lowered the drawbar, then turned back to me. "Ours has been pestilence."

I glanced around the courtyard and noted how empty and unkempt it seemed, with flies swarming in the corners and crickets as large as cats chirping on the warm cobblestones. Though I was much amazed by what I saw, I had no wish to appear naive. And in any case, I was too weary to ask questions.

"I trust you can feed me."

The priest pointed toward a pair of rats fighting in an open doorway. "They are serving lunch, if you care to risk it."

"It is no risk for me," I answered, wondering what the old man was talking about. I passed Halah's reins to him. "See to it that she's combed and rubbed down. Feed her two goats and whatever else she wants, and let no children you like near her."

The walking corpse took the reins and started toward the stable, and he made no further mention of payment. His dead face did not betray whether this was because of my bearing or another reason; I only knew that my sacred pilgrimage and the god's heart slushing blood through my veins made me the most important person in the entire Faith. Now I understood how the Caliph's son felt when he rode his prancing stallion through the City of Brilliance, and why he did this so often. I crossed the courtyard and kicked the rats from the rectory doorway and went inside.

The room was customarily dim, lit only by a four-candled candelabra suspended beneath a vaulted ceiling. The air smelled of ale and meat, and in the center of the chamber sat a dozen murky figures, spread along a table that could have held three times their number. They made no sound except to smack their lips and clatter their mugs, and if any of them raised his eyes to see who stood in the doorway, I failed to notice.

I took a seat near the middle of the table. Seeing that none of my companions knew the use of silverware, I used my fingers to put a slice of musty-smelling meat upon a slab of stony bread and began to eat. The food was as foul as the company, but to one who had tasted only the dust of the road for two days, anything was delicious. I devoured the barbarous fare as though it were a honeyed partridge and helped myself to more.

As I began to sate my appetite, my thirst demanded its own attention. Seeing no empty mugs upon the table, I said to the figure across the table, "I have nothing to drink from."

A woman with hair as coarse as straw pushed her head close enough to scowl at me. "What you want me to do about it?"

I looked back at her. "Get me something." When she did not rise, I added, "I am on a mission for the One and All."

Her scowl deepened. Then she seemed to sense the One's presence in me, and her brow rose. She stood and went into a dark corner and returned with a wooden mug, which she filled from the pitcher on the table. The ale was sour and gritty with the dust she neglected to rinse from the cup, but after two days of drinking only my waterskin's foul contents, it was as refreshing as the elixir of life—and all the sweeter for having been poured by someone else.

I helped myself to a third serving of food, less to assuage my hunger than to enjoy my newfound prestige, and that is when something thumped onto the table.

"Pass some dog."

The airy voice startled the woman and all the other murky diners from their seats, and I looked down the table to see a circlet of yellow orbs glimmering in the candlelight. The globes were each the size of a man's eye, and they all sparkled like diamonds and swiveled in their sockets.

"Dog?" I asked. Behind the glittering eyes, I saw dimly eight hairy legs and a bulbous shape as large as Halah's rump. I glanced at the greasy meat on my bread. "This?"

"Do you expect me to eat rat?"

"Of course not." I carried the platter down the table and set the entire thing before the spider. I also slid a mug of ale over in front of it, then stooped down to peer into its eyes. "Is that you, Mighty One?"

"Congratulations, Malik." Now the spider spoke in the thousand voices of the One. "You shall soon be a father."

"What?"

"A father, Malik!" The spider curled one of its legs into a hoop, then used another to make a lewd gesture inside the circle. "You do know how a man becomes a father, do not you?"

"A father!" I dropped onto the bench. "But how? I have not seen my wife in . . . No! Say it is not so!"

"There has been a miracle." The spider hissed and chuckled. "Your wife claims you have been visiting her in her dreams."

My fist slammed into the table with such force that only Tyr's protection kept my hand from breaking.

"Really, Malik," said the One. "I would think you would be overjoyed. I suppose you want a son? I can arrange that—he might even look like you."

With that, the spider plunged its fangs into the platter of meat and began to slurp out the juice, and I laid my head in my hands and started to groan. What would my friends think? They were a cynical and suspicious lot, and they would never accept the miracle of my wife's pregnancy. No doubt, they were already calling me a cuckold and making little horns by their head when they mentioned my name.

"Stop sniveling, Malik," hissed the One. "What reason do you have to complain? Has Mystra been despoiling your temples?"

At any other time, this would have caused me to raise my head and curse the Harlot. But now, I could think only of my wife's good name, and of the many indignities she would suffer on account of this miracle. Not even the prince's favor would spare her reputation—or my business, since prudent men never associate with scandal. I slammed my forehead against the table.

"The Harlot's insolence is beyond belief!" growled the One, though of course he was speaking about Mystra and not my wife. "She ordered Kelemvor to keep my dead here on Faerûn, and then she snarled the Weave around all my temples."

I glanced at Cyric and saw him wave a pair of spider's legs toward the roaring fly outside.

"Now my Faithful are plagued by giant insects and cascades of boiling tar and singing rodents!" The One scuttled closer, then clacked his mandibles before my eyes. "Never involve yourself with a woman, Malik. You will be sorry every time."

"Indeed." I returned my gaze to the dark surface beneath my face. "Miracles are terrible things."

Twenty-Three

Ruha and Zale rode hard to catch up, and by dusk they were crouching in the shelter of a murky alley, peering out at Cyric's temple in the Storm Horns. Their mount remained tethered outside the village because of the green fly circling the citadel. Silvercloud had refused to go anywhere near the ugly creature, for hippogriffs looked upon anything with wings either as something they could eat or something that could eat them.

"That is where the little man went?" Ruha whispered, asking the question of a haggard man with red-rimmed eyes. When she and Zale had entered the village and asked after a pudgy rider on a horse from hell, the oaf had volunteered at once to lead them to the temple. "You are sure he is still inside?"

The man shook his head. "Can't be sure. There's too many sally ports and secret tunnels." His whisper was raspy and slow. "But no one's seen him or his horse come out, and that's the way he went in. You can still see my nephew's blood."

The peasant pointed to a patch of dark ground in front of the portal. Ruha studied the spot long enough to tell that it was covered with swarming flies, then glanced up at the gate-house. An old priest was standing watch as motionless as a statue. Four more sentries stood watch in the corner towers.

"Do they always post so many watchmen?" Ruha asked.

The peasant shook his head. "Only the gate guard, and he usually sneaks off to sleep."

"They're protecting something," hissed Zale. "And I'll wager it's our little friend."

196

"You are friends of this murderer?"

"Only in the sense that we know him well," Ruha said. "But you may be certain we are as eager to catch him as you are."

"I'm not eager at all!" said the peasant. "I have a wife and three children! But I would be happy if *you* killed him."

"That will be easier said than done." Zale looked to Ruha. "What do you think, Lady Witch? Sneak Silvercloud around the village and set an ambush on the road ahead?"

"It would be better to catch him sleeping. If we can keep him away from his horse, he will have less chance to escape."

Zale frowned. "We'd have to use magic to bypass the guards."

He did not need to say more, for every time Ruha cast a spell, she also spawned a whirlwind or earthquake or lightning storm, and the more she used her magic, the worse these disasters grew. Her last enchantment had sparked a downpour of hailstones that had leveled half the farmhouses outside Iriaebor.

As Ruha contemplated what even a simple spell might do to the village, Zale's visage suddenly blurred before her eyes, then grew round and pudgy, with thick fleshy lips and eyes that bulged from their sockets like a bug's. She knew at once whom she was seeing, for she had seen this handsome face in her visions a dozen times since the deaths of Rinda and Gwydion. As she watched, the bulging eyes grew as black as coal and began to burn with a fire as cold as the void. A long tongue of night-blue flame rippled from between the fleshy lips and began to wag, flinging little drops of sizzling poison in every direction.

Ruha closed her eyes and began to tremble, for she had never suffered so many visions in such a short time. Their frequency had to be a sign of her mission's great urgency, but in her exhaustion, the mirages were taking a toll on her nerves.

"Ruha, what's wrong?" demanded Zale. Though he had seen her gaze grow distant many times, she had never explained to him what she was seeing, and so he could not guess at the cause of her trembling. "You go rest; I'll keep watch."

Ruha shook her head. "We must attack now, Zale. You heard the goddess. Nothing is more important than catching our quarry."

Zale shook his head. "Not if there's—"

"Whatever you do, you'd better hurry." The peasant pointed at the gatehouse. "Look."

The guard was gone.

Ruha turned to the peasant. "Tell everyone to leave the village at once."

The man frowned. "Leave? But it's almost dark!"

Before Ruha could say more, Zale grabbed her arm. "Maybe the guard just went to relieve himself."

"And maybe he saw us and went to warn Malik! We cannot take the chance. If Malik escapes now, will Silvercloud have the stamina to catch him again?"

Zale shook his head. "It's a wonder he carried us this far."

Ruha turned to the peasant. "Go! Tell the others to leave, if they want to see the morning."

She pushed the man down the alley, and Zale drew his sword. They watched in silence until they heard the man banging doors. The citadel guards came to the front of their towers and peered out over the village. When none of them left to report what was happening, the witch knew the gate sentry had gone to alert her quarry.

Ruha gathered a handful of pebbles. "Do not waste your effort trying to slay Malik." She began to shake the pebbles. "Kill the hell horse if you can, and leave the rest to me."

The witch uttered a sun spell and hurled her pebbles. The stones streaked away in a golden flash and blasted the gate into splinters, and even Ruha did not expect what followed.

A deafening blast shook the dust from the citadel walls, and then a geyser of yellow steam sprouted in the center of the courtyard. The vapor was as foul as burning brimstone and so hot it scalded the flesh of any creature it touched. In less than an instant, the courtyard was filled with blistered rats and giant toasted crickets and screaming Believers—who quickly fled into the far corners of the temple and disappeared.

Ruha and Zale rushed across the street. By the time they reached the gate, the yellow vapor was billowing out in a great cloud. One whiff of the stuff caused the witch's throat to close and her eyes to water. A stream of rats, all bleeding from their eyes and nostrils, began to drag themselves out into the road. The giant green fly roared down out of the sky and hovered over the gate, glaring down at the witch and her companion with one of its bulging black eyes.

Zale ignored it and kicked at the fleeing rats. "Why aren't the Cyric worshipers coming out with the rest of the vermin?" He peered into the yellow fog, then said, "They must be leaving by the sally ports—and Malik with them!"

Zale pulled his tunic over his face and, before Ruha could stop him, vanished into the burning fog. The witch slipped her hands up beneath her veil and filled them with her breath, then uttered her spell.

This time, her magic shook the entire village. The gatehouse swayed, and the cobblestones in the courtyard clattered. From the streets behind her came the muffled crash of falling crockery and the strident cries of fleeing peasants.

Ruha turned her palms toward the courtyard and blew. A ferocious wind howled through the gate to carry away the poisonous steam. On the far side of the spewing geyser kneeled Zale, perhaps five paces from the stable. The yellow vapor had turned his cloak into a tattered rag, and wherever his skin was exposed, it was covered with yellow sores. He took a long breath of fresh air, then struggled to his feet and staggered toward the stable's open door.

Ruha started after him.

The geyser belched up a clap of thunder, and the yellow steam changed to fire, splitting the courtyard down the center. Zale glanced back; then a curtain of ash and molten rock gushed out of the fissure to separate him from the witch.

Ruha took her waterskin from around her neck and pulled the stopper, and at that moment, the green fly came over the wall and descended in front of her. The witch retreated, backing up a set of narrow stone stairs attached to the gatehouse.

And in the time it took this to occur, the fissure spewed out such a quantity of ash and fiery rock that when Halah and I burst from the stable doors, we found our way blocked by a wall of burning stone. Already the ridge stood as high as a man, with a frothing spray of molten rock spewing up behind it. I could see nothing on the other side except the wall of the citadel and the Harper witch on the gatehouse stairs.

"A pox upon that hag!"

I had been sound asleep when the gate guard roused me to report that someone was watching the temple, and I had gathered my things in a flurry and rushed to the stable half-awake, and so I was still clutching Rinda's journal in my hand as I turned to look for another way out of the courtyard. I did not even notice Zale until Halah reared and gave a menacing snort, and it was only out of fright that I brought Rinda's book around to shield myself.

Zale's sword bit halfway through the ledger.

Halah sprang forward, and the journal nearly slipped from my grasp, as it had trapped my foe's blade the way a log sometimes traps an axe. I dropped the reins and squeezed my mount with my legs and grabbed the book with both hands, and I found myself staring down the length of Zale's sword into his yellow-blistered face. He snarled a curse upon my father's name and tried to jerk me from the saddle, but Halah was dragging him across the courtyard. It was all he could do to keep his feet, and all I could do to keep hold of the journal.

The side of Zale's body suddenly turned as red as a tomato, and a searing heat stung my face. I glanced forward and saw Halah's head rising as she galloped up the ridge toward the frothing curtain of molten rock.

Why my foe did not release his sword is a mystery to me even greater than how I kept my seat when Halah sprang across the fissure. I saw the fire rush up Zale's legs; I smelled his charred flesh and heard his agonized scream. Then he became an orange flame and I saw the fires of Kelemvor's worst hell boiling in the chasm below. It took only an instant to cross, but it seemed an eternity. My skin burned. My eyes stung. My head ached, and my stomach turned, and my tongue swelled in my throat.

Halah landed on the other side and streaked toward the gate, her hooves burning as she splashed down a stream of molten rock. Zale's sword drooped over and fell out of Rinda's journal, but that did not prevent the pages from catching fire. I slapped the book against my chest and succeeded only in igniting the witch's aba. For a moment I sat there burning, holding a flaming book in my hands, wondering what to do. Then I heard Halah's hooves clattering on solid cobblestones and looked up to see the gate ahead, with the meddling Harper on the stairs above the giant green fly.

I saw the witch rub a pinch of dust off the gatehouse wall, and this frightened me out of my wits, as she had already proved that she could capture me. I pressed myself close to Halah and grabbed her neck with both arms, and the heat of my flaming robe made her gallop twice as fast as before. We were halfway to the gate before I realized I had dropped Rinda's journal.

Needless to say, I did not turn around. There were other ways to find Zhentil Keep.

Ruha raised her hand to cast her spell, but the giant green fly reared up to block her magic.

"What have you done here?" the fly demanded.

Though the insect remained as large as an elephant, its black eyes melted and became a pair of human eyes as dark and soft as the night. The long feeding tube shrank into a narrow nose, and the ugly mandibles came together to form a slender jawline, and the wings folded over the back to become a cascade of flowing black hair. Then its body slimmed into the figure of a shapely woman, and the air around it coalesced into a simple robe closed by a web-shaped bodice clasp.

"Goddess!"

Ruha dropped to her knees, but she could not help peering around Mystra's avatar to see what had become of the discarded ledger; perhaps the book contained some hint of her quarry's destination.

To her relief, the journal's pages had stopped burning when it hit the ground. It now lay smoldering just inside the gate, less than a dozen paces from the advancing tide of molten rock.

"Pay attention to me, Ruha!" Mystra said. "Answer my question—what have you done here?"

Ruha looked back to the goddess. "I was trying to stop Malik, as you instructed."

"I did not instruct *this!*" Mystra waved at the curtain of fire behind her. "You have knocked down a quarter of the village, and this lava flow will destroy the rest."

"But you said what I annihilate will be as nothing to what I save! You said I should do whatever is necessary to stop Malik—even if it means destroying a whole kingdom!"

Mystra's eyes grew dark with ire. "Do not be insulting. I would never say such a thing."

Shocked by her goddess's reaction, Ruha lowered her gaze and noticed that the journal now lay only nine paces from the advancing lava. "I thought you wanted me to stop Malik. I prayed for a sign, and you sent a shooting star."

This caused Mystra to fall silent, for she remembered both the prayer and what she had been doing when it came. "I sent the sign, yes—but that does not give you leave to destroy a whole village. What were you thinking?"

Ruha gave the only answer she could. "That you wanted me to catch him at any cost."

"That I wanted this? There can be only one thing that would excuse . . ." Mystra paused and grew thoughtful, then asked, "Is that it, Ruha? Did Malik recover the *Cyrinishad* after all?"

Ruha shook her head. "No goddess, it is still safe in—"

"Do not say it! There might not be much of this temple left, but it still belongs to Cyric."

Ruha frowned. In contrast to their first meeting outside the Wood of Sharp Teeth, Mystra was now using names freely. Perhaps the goddess no longer feared attracting the attention of her enemies—or perhaps there was another explanation.

"Goddess—"

"Not now, Ruha." Mystra turned toward the frothing curtain in the center of the courtyard. Already, the ridge of ash and molten rock had risen as tall as her avatar, and it showed no sign of abating soon. "At the moment, I have a village to save. I will talk with you later. Until then, the Weave is denied you."

"Denied?" Ruha stumbled and nearly fell down the stairs. "You are taking my magic?"

The goddess paused to look back at the Harper, and did not seem to notice when the lava began to swirl around her ankles. "For now, Ruha. Now go, while you can. I will be lucky to seal this volcano of yours before it engulfs the whole village."

Ruha bowed to the goddess, then turned toward the journal lying near the gate. The molten rock had closed to within three paces of it, but even without her magic, she could run that fast.

Twenty-Four

The citadel walls had turned orange and soft with the heat, and the rampart walkways had started to sag. A red-glittering portal in the empty gateway siphoned lava back to the paraelemental plane of magma, but not as fast as the molten rock poured from the ground, and already the ridge around the fissure stood as tall as the gatehouse. At each end of the crack kneeled an avatar of Mystra larger than any dragon, sweeping cinder and ash back into the rift by the armful, fusing the seam closed with her magic breath. Yet volcanoes are mighty things, being the much-favored toys of Talos the Destroyer, and even this small one was filling the citadel faster than the goddess's avatars could seal it. Liquid stone lay in the courtyard as deep as a man's chest. Any moment, it would melt through the citadel walls and send a tide of fiery syrup rolling down upon the village.

But Mystra could manifest no more avatars there. The volcano was only one of a thousand matters troubling her at that moment. She had two avatars trying to win support for her upcoming trial, and one more investigating their lack of progress. Four more were attending to the troubles she had started with Cyric, for her attacks had left the One with no choice but to assail her temples in kind. At any given moment, she was tracking the Worm of Gloom through the caves of Mt. Talath, or battling a gigantes at Elventree, or hunting a kraken in Hillshadow Lake, or defending her temples in any number of places too many to name.

And regardless of anything else in the heavens or on Faerûn, one avatar stayed in the House of Knowledge, searching Oghma's library for the spell that had turned Adon's mind against her—as though the One needed to look his tricks up in a book!

So, when one of Kelemvor's avatars rose out of the fissure's boiling lava, she was grateful for the help. His avatar was almost as large as the ones she had manifested, so that although he stood in the molten rock from the waist down, his shoulders rose above the brink of the fiery rift.

"Kelemvor, you pull the cinders back into the fissure, and I will seal it closed behind you."

Kelemvor was so browbeaten that he actually reached up to obey, then he remembered himself and brought his hands back. He brushed some beads of lava off his glowing chain mail, as though that was what he had intended all along, and stared into the boiling stone.

"I have no wish to involve myself in this. It is one thing to deny Cyric's dead leave to depart Faerûn and quite another to destroy his temples. If you are not careful, you will start the godswar Oghma fears—and then Ao will cast you both out."

Both of Mystra's avatars dropped their jaws, and the one facing Kelemvor paused to glare at him. "If the only reason you came here is to issue warnings, you have wasted your time." Mystra waved her arm at the orange lake that filled the courtyard. "Do you think I asked Ruha to do this? I am not even sure how she did."

Kelemvor scowled, for it seemed strange that a lava fissure would just happen to open at the moment of Ruha's attack. "Perhaps this is Talos's doing."

Mystra's avatar resumed her work. "I have thought of that. It certainly has the mark of his magic, and he has as much reason to delay Malik as we do."

Kelemvor nodded. "And speaking of Malik, why did you let him go? It would have been a small matter to stop him."

"Interfering with Cyric's witness would have been a breach of my promise to Tyr not to interfere with the trial. Besides,

Ruha assures me he is not chasing the *Cyrinishad*."

"If you are worried about your promise to Tyr, why send Ruha after him in the first place?"

"I did not *send* her—the truth is, I have been avoiding her. How can Tyr blame me for what she does of her own free will?" Mystra sealed a section of fissure with her magic breath, then raised her gaze. "Are you going to help or not?"

Kelemvor looked toward the citadel's front rampart, which at that moment was tumbling down into the lava, and shook his head. "If this is Talos's doing, it is not the place of the God of Death to save the village."

"What?" This time, both of Mystra's avatars stopped to stare. "Do you mean these people deserve what is happening?"

"I am saying that it may not be my place to prevent it," Kelemvor replied. "As God of Death, my concern is with their spirits, not their houses."

"And that concern prevents you from having compassion?"

The gatehouse collapsed into the courtyard and sloshed a great wave of lava against the wall, causing a section of stone to bow out into the High Road and disintegrate. At once, a slow-moving tongue of molten rock rolled into the breach. Mystra grabbed a handful of burning stone and flung it into the gap, filling it with another glittering portal to the paraelemental plane of magma.

"Kelemvor, if you are not here to help, then why come at all?" The goddess's avatars returned to filling the fissure.

"I came to tell you . . ."

Kelemvor had meant to finish by saying "how Cyric drove Adon mad," but the words caught in his throat. In his mind's eye, he saw himself standing before his mirror, gazing at the reflection of a tar-covered warrior with sickles of ice in his eyes.

"What?" Mystra swept an armful of cinders into the fissure and did not look up. "You wanted to tell me something?"

Kelemvor closed his eyes, and even he was not sure whether this was in shame or sorrow. "I came to tell you that I need to find Zale." He drew his sword and probed the molten rock around his waist. "There is something I must ask him."

Mystra frowned. "And you cannot do that in your own city?"

"I cannot wait that long." Kelemvor continued to probe the lava, and he was careful not to look up at Lady Magic. "Zale will travel through all of the elemental planes before his spirit stops burning, and I need to talk with him now."

Mystra shoved an armful of cinders down against Kelemvor's chest. "Then do it quickly. I will not wait to seal this."

Kelemvor backed away and resumed his probing. Before many moments had passed, he pulled his sword from the molten rock and held it up before him. A flame as red as blood danced on the tip, crackling and wailing as it writhed.

"Zale Protelyus!"

The flame spun on Kelemvor's sword, then stopped wailing and kneeled on the steaming blade. "Lord Death."

"Zale Protelyus, why did you allow your foe to drag you into this fissure? Why did you cling to your sword when you could have let go and saved yourself?"

"To. . . stop . . . the . . . murderer!" Zale's words seemed to come with great effort and pain.

"But when you saw that you would die and fail anyway, still you held on. Why?"

"Nothing to fear . . . in death." Zale kept his blazing head bowed toward the sword. "Brave man in life . . . sure to receive reward in death."

"But you are Faithless! Who will reward you?"

For the first time, Zale raised his fiery head. "You . . . Lord Kelemvor! Trust your justice . . . before any god . . . who demands flattery . . . and offerings."

So stunned was Kelemvor that he shrank until his chest sank into the boiling lava. "Can Cyric be right?" His head barely reached the chasm brink. "Have I been too fair?"

It was then that Kelemvor perceived the infinite cunning of the One and All. To win Faerûn for himself, Cyric had only to step aside and do nothing. Lady Magic would do half his work, denying the Weave to any force that harmed her beloved mortals, and Talos the Destroyer and the Battle Lord Tempus and

Shar the Nightbringer would grow weak and start losing worshipers. Kelemvor would do the rest, treating the spirits of the noble and compassionate with such kindness that many would turn from their gods and trust to his justice instead.

But most critical was this: the brave and courageous would lose their fear of death and sacrifice themselves in foolish causes, as Zale had done. Faerûn would be left to the cowardly and the corrupt. And when this was so—when all the other gods had grown weak through the compassion of Kelemvor and Mystra—then would the One rouse himself from his "madness" and call the wicked to his worship, and then would he drive all the other gods from his world.

All this Kelemvor perceived, and he saw that it was happening just as Cyric had planned. Still, he refused to think he had been doing the One's work. In his folly, he believed that every man strove for bravery and nobility, and he failed to understand that shielding the helpless encouraged laziness and dependence, and that treating the dead with compassion only made life all the more unbearable.

An avalanche of hot cinders crashed down upon Kelemvor's back. Another splashed down before him and covered his chain mail with hissing beads of molten stone.

"If you are finished there, I have a village to save."

"I am done in here, but I fear we are far from finished." Kelemvor lowered his blade and returned Zale to the lava. "I am sorry your journey must be so long and painful."

"And . . . my judgment?" Zale's figure began to melt into the lava. "What will I . . . find in the City of the Dead?"

"That I will not know until you get there."

Kelemvor reached beneath the lava to sheathe his sword, then pulled himself out of the rift. Though his chain mail had turned white with heat and molten rock fell from his body in globs, Lord Death hardly noticed. He was as immune to the ravages of fire as he was to every kind of agony, save that of displeasing Mystra.

Cyric's temple was completely gone, having melted into the lava pool and drained away to the paraelemental plane of magma. Only three small tongues of molten rock had snaked past Mystra's glittering portals and crossed the High Road, and Kelemvor saw that they would consume no more than a few huts before rolling to a halt. Lord Death could have stopped these flows with little more than a thought, but he turned away and raised his arm, extending his finger to form a perch.

"Avner!"

The seraph's dark-winged silhouette appeared high in the dusky sky and circled down like a great vulture. His wings were blacker than the night, so that they seemed more shadow than feather, and he was armored neck to foot in leather polished to an ebony sheen. He carried a bow as long as his body, double-curved for power and strung with a golden cord. A quiver of glass arrows hung on one hip, and a naked scimitar gleamed on the other. He wheeled around behind Kelemvor, then spread his wings and landed on the god's outstretched finger.

"At your command, Lord Kelemvor." His eyes looked like two steel balls, for they lacked either iris or pupil and were as gray as silver. "I am ready to serve."

"And so you shall, my seraph. Go and watch men die all across Faerûn. When you have witnessed a thousand and ten deaths, return to the Crystal Spire and tell me what you have seen."

"As you wish, Lord Death."

Mystra came to Kelemvor's side. "A handsome herald, Lord Death. Is he the harbinger of your newfound indifference to the helpless?"

"Perhaps. When he returns, we shall see."

Lord Death raised his hand, and the seraph took flight as silently as an owl. Kelemvor watched his messenger wheel out over the Tun Plain and vanish against the shadowy ground, then took Mystra's hand.

"I am worried, Midnight." He spoke without looking at her. "I think we have been making a terrible mistake."

"Mistake?" Mystra thought of the mistake Kelemvor had

made in refusing to help her with the volcano, but she had better ways to let him know about that than just saying so. "What mistake?"

Kelemvor turned to face her, and when he looked into her eyes, he saw the reflection of a tar-covered god. "A—"

Lord Death could not bring himself to say Adon's name, for he was as much a traitor as ever and valued his own conscience above the welfare of his old friend.

"A *what,* Kelemvor?" Mystra tore her hand from his. "You know how busy I am. Even as we stand here, Cyric has—"

"A mistake of conscience! And Cyric is at the heart of it."

Mystra raised her brow. "You have my attention. Go on."

Kelemvor shook his head. "I can say no more, except there is more to our troubles than we can see, and Cyric is behind them all. He has been behind them all along."

Mystra grew thoughtful, then locked gazes with Kelemvor. "This is about Adon. You know something."

Kelemvor nodded. "But I cannot tell you. The secrets of the dead are their own, and I will not betray the sanctity of the grave—not even to you."

"But Adon—"

"If I find Adon standing before my throne, I will treat him with all the respect he is due."

"Before *your* throne? Adon is one of my Faithful. When he dies, you must know I will make a home for him in . . . " Mystra let the sentence trail off, her eyes growing wide and wild as she perceived the meaning of Kelemvor's words. "No—I will not allow him to die without Faith!"

Twenty-Five

Becoming a father is always a shock, and this is even more true if a man has not seen his wife in years. I galloped north in a state of astonishment, so stunned I hardly noticed the peaks rising higher and higher around me, nor the great westward bend the High Road took before turning through High Horn pass. I could think of nothing except the unseemly timing of my wife's conception, and of riding straight home to rebuke her for being so unfaithful!

Such was my agitation that I hardly cared that I would be riding into the arms of the Harper witch, forsaking my sacred pilgrimage to Zhentil Keep and sacrificing all hope of finding the *True Life* and curing the One of his madness. Nor did I consider that I would be damning myself to Kelemvor's hell for all eternity; no torment of Lord Death's could be worse than the shame my own wife had brought on my head. Only my devotion to Our Dark Lord kept me from turning Halah around—my devotion, and also the thought of all my friends whispering behind my back!

Such were my thoughts as Halah galloped down the High Road along the brink of a sheer precipice, and I was so absorbed that I did not even notice when the shadow of a flying beast fell over me. The first I knew of my peril was when a huge talon struck my shoulder and jerked me from Halah's back and carried me out over the cliff's edge.

I found myself dangling thousands of feet above a forest valley, and I knew at once who had done this. "Witch!"

211

"Say it nicely, Malik—or you shall ride back to Candlekeep in Silvercloud's talons."

I realized instantly how the Harper had overtaken me—by flying straight across the mountains while Halah and I galloped around the great bend before High Horn pass—and I cursed myself for being so distracted that I did not anticipate her shortcut. I craned my neck around and saw the hippogriff's wings flashing silver as he climbed higher above the valley. Ruha's kohl-rimmed eyes peered down over his shoulder.

Not knowing that Mystra had denied the witch access to the Weave, my greatest fear was that she was preparing some spell to immobilize me. I reached into my stolen *aba* and pulled out my dagger.

"Malik, look how far we are above the ground!"

I did not look, for then I would not have had the courage to act. I drew the dagger back, twisting my arm around to aim it at Silvercloud's equine brisket.

"No!" Ruha yelled. "You will kill us both!"

"Not both of us!" I replied, and then Mystra's spell compelled me to add, "I am protected by Tyr's magic!"

And on account of these last few words, the witch had time to tap her mount's feathery neck. "Bite!"

My dagger shot forward, and in the same instant, Silvercloud's head darted down to attack. My blade struck his hooked beak and turned sideways, sliding along his upper mandible and sinking deep into his eye.

Silvercloud screeched and opened his talons, and I dropped away. My stomach rose into my chest, then the hippogriff and his rider became specks in the sky. I plummeted past the cliff top and looked over to see Halah galloping down the road. Then the valley rushed up beneath me, and I crashed through the billowing crown of a great oak, snapping a branch as thick as my body and tumbling down toward the ground.

Meddling Harpers!

Twenty-Six

In the foothills of the Alphrunn Mountains, a thousand Hlondethar footmen were carrying a hundred siege ladders up a boulder-choked slope. A steady drizzle of arrows and stones rained down from the castle of their enemies, and the wounded fell by the dozens. The closer the ladders came to the citadel, the fewer who remained to raise them. The baying of the war dogs was echoing over the fortress walls. The Seraph of Death sat watching from a spire of sharp granite, and six avatars of Tempus the Battle Lord were wandering the battlefield.

With their battered breastplates and closed visors and bloodied limbs, they all looked the same as they dashed across the slope, plucking arrows from fallen warriors and healing wounds and sending the injured back to the ladders as strong as before. And still the advance was slowing. The Hlondethar knew they would never take the citadel, and even the Battle Lord's presence could not convince them otherwise.

Mystra manifested herself beside one of Tempus's avatars, which happened to be reaching through a warrior's leather armor to pull an arrow from his lung. The man's face, normally the color of ginger, was as pale as mustard, and the sight of two gods kneeling over him seemed to stun him more than the shaft in his chest. He looked from one to the other, sobbing and cackling madly with laughter.

Mystra touched her fingers to his brow, and when he had grown calm she said to Tempus, "It seems strange to heal them and then send them back to be wounded again."

"It is the only way to keep the battle going." Tempus paused to raise his visored face, and Mystra's skin stung beneath his hidden gaze. "The Hlondethar are fond of their war spells; it is a wonder they attacked at all, with you denying their battle wizards any magic."

Mystra shrugged. "It is not my fault if their sorcerers neglect their studies."

"No mortal can study twenty hours a day." Tempus pinched the shaft between his fingers and pulled it from the man's chest, and the arrowhead had no blood or gore of any kind. "They would not have time to eat or sleep, much less make war."

"That *would* be a shame, would it not?"

"More than you know." Tempus placed his hand over the wound and spoke a mystic word. A circle of smoke shot out from beneath his palm, and the man screamed. "But you did not come here to learn the glories of war. What do you want?"

"Adon. Tell me what magic Cyric used to drive him mad."

Tempus cocked his helm and remained silent. Mystra's face prickled beneath his stare, but she could not look through his visor to see his expression. The war dogs began to bay more loudly, and an eerie howl answered from somewhere deep in the mountains. An arrow struck the goddess's shoulder and broke in two, and she felt this less strongly than the Battle Lord's gaze.

Tempus turned back to his patient and lifted his hand. A crimson palm print marked where the god had touched the man's armor, but there was no hole or other sign of the wound. Tempus stood the warrior up and pushed him toward the nearest ladder.

"Go, and make your maharani proud."

Despite Tempus's words, the warrior stumbled over the boulders at more of a crawl than a scramble. The Battle Lord shook his head in disgust.

"That will be one for Lord Death—though Kelemvor will never punish him as he deserves."

"There is no use changing the subject. Tell me what magic Cyric used against Adon."

Tempus did not answer, or even turn his visor in Mystra's direction.

She said, "So far, I have only made life difficult for your war wizards. Unless you wish me to deny the Weave to any spell-caster involved in war, answer me."

Tempus faced Mystra. "Why would I know anything about Cyric and your patriarch?"

"Because Cyric is behind this trial. He is in it with you."

"*With* me?" Tempus shook his head. "That is not so. He had nothing to do with my charges, except to receive them."

Mystra furrowed her brow, for it was not in the Battle Lord's nature to lie. Always one to choose an open fight over intrigue, he either spoke the truth or did not speak at all.

"Who claimed Cyric is behind this trial?" Tempus started across the slope, not clambering over the boulders like a mortal, but stepping right through them and walking upon the empty air between. "I do not like anyone lying about me."

"No one *claimed* that Cyric is behind the trial." Mystra floated along at his side. "I inferred it from something Kelemvor said: 'There is more to our troubles than we know.' "

The God of War stopped and kneeled beside an unconscious warrior, then slipped two fingers into the man's head and popped his dented skull back into place.

"There is more to your troubles than you know—but the cause is Mask, not Cyric."

"Mask?"

Tempus nodded. "He hopes to win back what Cyric stole."

Mystra's heart sank. Pressuring Tempus had been her best hope of discovering what Cyric had done to her patriarch, and Adon's condition was only growing worse. The last time she had looked in on him, he had been as frightened as before—and without the lasal haze clouding his mind. She had not dared probe his thoughts for fear of driving him completely insane.

Mystra fixed a stern glare on Tempus, who was pressing his hand to the man's head wound, and made a chopping motion with her fingers. At once, the magic faded from the Battle Lord's touch, and the fallen warrior remained unconscious.

Tempus raised his head, and his gaze stung Mystra's skin like a sandstorm. "You dare cut *me* off from the Weave?"

"To save Adon, yes. Your charges are distracting me at the moment. Perhaps you would withdraw them?"

"You cannot do this!" Tempus warned. "The Circle—"

"Will consider my actions at the trial. Until then, you will have to perform your duties without the Weave." Mystra glanced at the carnage strewn across the slope. "I wonder what Faerûn will be like after seven days without war?"

"Even you cannot stop war. It will survive without magic." Tempus's voice had grown more thoughtful than angry. "But perhaps we can make a bargain."

"What kind of bargain?"

There was another howl, and this one seemed to rumble up from beneath the hill itself. Tempus paid it no attention.

"You must agree to restore war magic to its full force, if I prove to you that war is good for Faerûn."

"You will never prove that."

"Nevertheless, I will withdraw my charges if you merely agree to consider—"

"But Foehammer!" protested a wispy voice. A black shadow rose from between the boulders at Tempus's feet, then assumed the shape of a Hlondethar footman. "What about our agreement? You promised not to withdraw your charges."

"Mask!"

Mystra's sharp tone drew the attention of the Seraph of Death, who spread his wings and flew over, swooping low past a company of Hlondethar footmen. More than fifty of them broke and ran for their own lines. Lady Magic hardly noticed, for her glare was locked on the Shadowlord.

"This has nothing to do with you, Blackheart."

"But it does." Mask continued to face Tempus and did not look at her. "It has everything to do with me, since Foehammer and I have an agreement."

"That agreement concerned Cyric," said Tempus.

"But it was not *my* doing that you expanded the charges to include Mystra and Kelemvor." Another howl sounded from between the boulders. Mask glanced into the crevice, then looked back to Tempus and spoke rapidly. "Nor that Tyr separated the verdicts—by then, I had made certain arrangements."

"Arrangements?" Mystra's eyes grew narrow. "If you are scheming against Kelemvor and me, stop it now."

"Or what?" Mask snorted. A shudder ran through his shadowy figure; then an extra face appeared on the back of his head. "Whatever you do to me will be undone after the trial. Already I have duped you and your paramour into proving your own guilt."

"You have?" Tempus demanded. This was just the sort of complication that he had feared when Mask came to him. "Did you not tell me you had overcome your weakness for intrigue?"

"This was not my fault!" A deep snarl rumbled up from the boulders beneath Mask's feet, and he started to sidle up the hill toward the besieged castle. "Besides, you have nothing to fear. Mystra and Kelemvor can save themselves no more than Cyric can."

Lady Magic sneered. "If that is so, Mask, what is there to stop me from destroying you now?"

It was Tempus who answered. "Tyr the Just." The Battle Lord's visor swung up the slope toward Mask's retreating form. "I will need to call the Shadowlord as a witness. It is only proper to disclose whose idea it was to make these charges."

Mask stopped on the spot. "But if Cyric finds out I—"

"You have nothing to fear from Cyric," Tempus said. "Not if everything goes according to your plan."

The Shadowlord withered to half his normal size, and at that moment a reek of foul meat filled the air. A pair of yellow eyes appeared in the shadows at Tempus's feet, and the Chaos Hound sprang from between the boulders. Before the beast could find him, Mask fled up the slope and vanished into the shadows beneath the castle wall. Kezef let out a low, baleful growl and raised his slime-dripping nostrils to sniff the air.

Mystra pointed up the slope. "There, Kezef."

Kezef cocked his great head, then let his muzzle fall into a sort of grin and bounded away over the boulders. He crashed through a heavy Hlondethar siege ladder and trampled the poor footmen who had been carrying it, then disappeared into the shadows after his quarry.

The Seraph of Death raised his wings and vanished into the sky. Mystra looked back to Tempus and shook her head.

"Foehammer, you should be wiser than to involve yourself in Mask's schemes. This will come to a bad end for you."

"Perhaps, but I have already given my word." Tempus glanced up the slope toward the reluctant Hlondethar advance. "Besides, you have left me no other choice. War cannot go on like this."

Twenty-Seven

Of all places in the City of the Dead, Rapture Round displayed most clearly the character of Kelemvor's reign. The Round was a vast circle of gardens where a dozen boroughs came together, and from Penance Hill at its center, Lord Death could see them all. In Pax Cloister, a vast region of high peaks and shadowy valleys, dwelled the spirits of peaceful hermits who had lived their whole lives desiring nothing more than solitude and quiet. Next to it stood the Idyll Hamlets, which were the villages of simple country spirits who valued family and good company above wealth or power. Flanking these were the Singing City and the Fruitful Forest, and to each of these Lord Death sent souls who would find happiness within; bordering these wards were others filled with kind and noble spirits who had either turned from their gods or never found one at all.

The vista behind Kelemvor was not so pleasant. In the Acid Swamp, the spirits of charlatans and swindlers gathered along roadways and bridges to beg help from passersby. Next to this, the Crimson Jungle was filled with murderers and torturers of every sort, all changed into ravenous beasts too busy devouring each other to escape. Beside these boroughs were the Maze of Alleys and the City of Cold, where Lord Death sent the spirits of thieves and panderers, and bordering these districts were homes for all the intemperate and pragmatic spirits who had made it their business to take care of themselves and no other.

"You know, Jergal, there was a time when every act I performed had to be a selfish one."

As Kelemvor spoke, the seneschal's shadow-filled cloak appeared beside him.

"Ah yes, the Lyonsbane curse: perform a selfless act, turn into a man-eating beast."

"Where would you have sent me?" Kelemvor turned and pointed at the Web of Snakes. "There? Home to the hopelessly confused?"

"I would not have sent you anywhere," Jergal replied. "Myrkul would have put you in his Wall of Bodies, and who can say what Cyric would have done?"

"I had a pretty good idea." The voice was Mystra's, and she appeared on the hill beside Kelemvor. "That is why I fought so hard to overthrow him before he found you."

Kelemvor dismissed Jergal with a thought, then turned to Mystra. "I am glad you saved me from Cyric's mercies, but sometimes I wonder about giving me his throne."

"I did not give you anything. The denizens of the city made you their ruler."

Kelemvor's eyes grew sad. "I have not forgotten. I think it would be easier to be a true God of Death if I could."

Mystra scowled. "Kelemvor, I do not like this 'thinking.' You are more suited to action, and I wish you would take some!"

Kelemvor recoiled as though struck, then raised his brow and squared his shoulders. "Maybe so. Is that what you came to say?"

Mystra shook her head. "No, I came to tell you it is Mask who started all this, not Cyric."

Kelemvor nodded. "I know. Avner returned to the Crystal Spire and reported everything Mask said."

"Including his claim that he duped us?"

"I fear it is more than a claim. He came to demand that I punish Avner as one of his False, and I stepped into his trap like a blind bear. I refused."

Mystra frowned. "But Avner died serving his queen."

"That would count for much, had he been one of Torm's

Faithful. But Avner worshiped no god except the God of Thieves."

"I see." Mystra bit her lip. "What does Mask have planned for me? I received no such demand."

Kelemvor shook his head. "I have no idea, but I can tell you there is only one way to counter his trap."

"And that is?"

"Reflect on ourselves. Make certain we are serving our nature and the Balance."

Mystra rolled her eyes. "I think we would be wiser to force our accusers to withdraw their charges. I will take care of Mask, but you must handle Tempus."

"Handle him?" Kelemvor's tone betrayed his wariness. "How?"

"Withhold death from the justified side in every battle."

"Withhold death?" Kelemvor was too stunned to say more.

"Nothing could bring all the wars on Faerûn to a swifter end. Tempus will be forced to do as we ask."

"You are as mad as Cyric!" Kelemvor shouted. Of course, this was not possible; Mystra was not smart enough to be even half as mad as Cyric. "Even if I could decide which side is justified—and that is Tyr's purview, not mine—Tempus would never break his promise to Mask."

"By the time I finish with him, Mask will beg Tempus to withdraw the charges."

Kelemvor cocked his brow. "I thought you promised not to interfere with the trial?"

"That was before Adon's affliction. More to the point, Mask was not part of the trial in the past, nor will he be in the future—there will be no trial, at least not for us."

Kelemvor took a breath and made no reply.

Mystra studied him. "You are not going to do this, are you?"

Kelemvor shook his head. "You are asking me to violate my duty as God of Death."

"But this is for Adon!"

"I know." Kelemvor closed his eyes. "But my refusal is for us. If you do this thing, you are lost."

Mystra staggered back. "What has happened to you?" She stepped off the hill into the empty air. "I will talk to you when your senses return!"

Kelemvor watched the goddess vanish, then looked back toward the Web of Snakes. "Jergal!"

"I am here for you, as always." The seneschal's empty cloak appeared at Kelemvor's side. "How may I serve you?"

"Did you hear what passed between Mystra and me?"

"Did you want me to?"

Kelemvor thought for a moment, then shook his head. "No, I suppose not."

Jergal's yellow eyes swung away, gazing down upon a bed of crimson lilies. "Then I heard nothing. Is there anything else?"

Kelemvor nodded, then faced his seneschal. "Mystra was right about one thing: it is time I started taking action." He stepped off the hilltop directly into the Crystal Spire's throne room, though the distance was farther than a camel could run in two days. "Jergal, I want you to prepare a list of all the judgments I have made since becoming God of Death."

The seneschal appeared at Kelemvor's side, his empty cloak waving like a banner in the wind. "All your judgments?"

"All of them. Avner will be returning with his report soon. If things go as I expect, we will have a lot of work to do."

Twenty-Eight

It required Halah but a short time to find me in the forest where I had fallen, for my hand was coated with Silvercloud's blood and she had a very keen nose for gore. Within minutes I was on her back, galloping along on my sacred pilgrimage. Aside from the strain my terror had placed on Cyric's rancid heart, I was none the worse for my long plummet. Though my thoughts remained much concerned with my wife's unfaithful miracle, I had learned my lesson and kept a careful watch over my shoulder. Apparently, the Harper's hippogriff had fared worse than I during our quick exchange. I saw no sign of the witch or her beast all day, and so it was that I rode into Arabel upon the supper hour, shortly before dark.

Although the One had graced the city by living there before the Time of Troubles, Arabel seemed no different than any other barbarian town, with dogs wandering loose and insects swarming out of the open gutters. The avenues were narrow and crooked and almost deserted, since most people were inside taking their suppers. The smell of roasted meat and warm bread filled the air. After my harrowing escape that morning and the hard ride that followed, I felt worthy of a good meal and a soft bed.

I guided Halah to one of the few people on the street, a burly guardsman standing outside an alley. As we approached, he turned to face us and angled his halberd across his body.

"Well met, traveler," said he. "How can I—"

223

Before I could ask him a single thing, Halah bit his halberd in two and nosed him back into the alley.

"In the name of Torm!" The guard dropped his useless polearm and reached for his sword. "Control your mount!"

The poor soul did not know the folly of what he asked. Before his sword could clear its scabbard, Halah bit off the astonished fellow's hand. There is little point in describing what followed, except to note that I was lucky enough to salvage his coin purse before my ravenous mount swallowed it whole. I retreated to the mouth of the alley and, by virtue of my dark *aba* and disheveled appearance, managed to look suspicious enough that the few passersby who came along crossed to the other side of the street. As I listened to Halah devour her meal, naturally my thoughts turned to my own empty stomach and to the soft bed I would enjoy afterward.

And the moment I thought of a soft bed, I also thought of my wife and of the unfaithful timing of her miracle. Bile filled my throat, my chest tightened, and I grew so angry about matters in Calimshan that I did not even notice the lanky figure in the hooded cloak until he was almost upon me.

I stepped out to meet him, thinking to distract him with the same question I had intended to ask the guard.

"Sir, can you tell me of a good inn?"

"Of course!" The figure spoke in a thousand voices, and when he raised his head, I saw Cyric's bony face. "But until you find the *Cyrinishad,* what use do you have for an inn?"

Mystra's spell compelled me to say, "I am hungry and tired."

"And?" asked Cyric.

I sighed, for I knew better than to declare I could not continue without rest. The truth was only that I felt sorry for myself and on that account did not want to go on, and who could tell what else I might blurt out?

"Malik, it seems your heart is no longer in your mission." The One tapped his chest to remind me how he knew this. "Perhaps you have been . . . distracted?"

"Perhaps," I said, and then the Harlot's spell compelled me

to add, "I can think of nothing except the shame brought upon my good name by my wife and the prince!"

Cyric smirked, which is a horrible thing for a skeleton's face, and said, "I thought so." The One looked away for a moment, then said, "You longer have any need to worry about your wife and the prince. I have eliminated that problem."

"Eliminated it, Mighty One?"

"Yes, Malik! You understand 'eliminated,' do you not? Do not let them trouble your thoughts again."

"Them?" I staggered back, for it was one thing to curse my unfaithful wife and quite another to know that it had been done. "Then my wife is . . . gone? I will never see her again?"

"Not in this life." The black suns beneath the One's brow flared to twice their customary size. "I am surprised her death troubles you. How can you think of your wife when I am on trial?"

"Because of the terrible shame she . . ." Here, my throat seemed to close in on itself, then another reply spilled from my lips: "Because I might miss her."

The One's jaw snapped shut, then he glared at me so long I thought he had turned into a statue. Yet, he could be no more surprised than I was, for I had not realized the truth of my words until they spilled from my mouth.

At last, the One shook his head. "I will not return her to life, Malik. She is too much of a distraction." He laid a bony arm across my shoulders, then pulled me as close as a brother. "But perhaps—if you ride very hard—I will hear her calling from the Fugue Plain. Then, after you recover the *Cyrinishad*, you can join her in the Castle of the Supreme Throne."

I did not know whether to rejoice or despair, as he had not mentioned how soon this might be. "That is more than I deserve!"

Cyric patted my shoulder. "Not so, Malik. If you fail me, you will join your wife in the City of the Dead—this I promise." The One glanced westward, toward the Storm

Horns looming beyond the city walls. "Now, think of your wife no more. You have other women to worry about."

I pushed myself away from the building and peered in the same direction. There, silhouetted against the crimson ball of the setting sun, I saw the distant figure of a hippogriff and its rider. "That witch is a demon from the Abyss!"

"No, Malik," corrected the One. "She is a Harper."

Twenty-Nine

When a man is seized by an unreasonable fear and knows it, he begins to fear his reason itself. He doubts what his eyes show and what his ears tell, what he smells and tastes, and even the thoughts that fill his head. He can be certain of nothing except that he is, and that something out there wants him not to be. This was the state of Adon the patriarch.

He lay in his humble bed, clutching the sides of his straw mattress, afraid to turn his eyes upon anything but the coffered ceiling above. When he looked outside, his gaze slipped between the balcony balusters and he saw Mystra's avatar on the shore of Hillshadow Lake. A cloud of hair floated like black smoke around her head, and her crimson talons were hurling lightning and fire at a many-tentacled monster thrashing about in the water.

But neither the battle nor Mystra's presence disturbed Adon so much as the certain conviction he was imagining the whole thing. The fight was as silent as a mirage; the lightning and roiling fire did not rumble or crash, and when the slimy beast opened its maw to roar, no sound came at all. This was because the goddess, having no wish to disturb the sleep of her troubled patriarch, had enclosed the combat within a curtain of silence. But Adon did not know this. To him, the fight seemed a dream, except that he was awake. And since he was awake, the dream could only be a hallucination, and since the dream was a hallucination, he could only be mad.

This thought was a great relief to him. Like any fool who

ever loved a deceitful woman, Adon preferred ignorance to betrayal; going mad was just the excuse he needed to ignore what he had seen in the eyes of Nadisu Bhaskar. Where before a heart full of adoration for Mystra had beat in his chest, now there was only a gnawing void he could not abide. He had felt such an emptiness once before, when he lost Faith in Sune after a madman's dagger slashed his face. For months afterward, he had felt hollow and sick inside, and he could not bear such emptiness again.

Yet the prospect was difficult to ignore. When he looked anywhere but the ceiling, he saw Mystra in all her horrible countenance. Her snarling visage was carved into every panel of the room's immense double door, and her dreadful form was portrayed in grisly scenes sculpted into every wall. Adon remembered choosing these scenes himself, though for some reason he had believed them to portray miracles instead of cataclysms. Had he been crazy then, or was he crazy now?

After several hours, Adon decided to test his madness by looking upon a relief he remembered well. On the wall opposite his bed was a portrayal of the goddess joining the hands of two rival kings. He had once viewed this scene as an illustration of Mystra's divine love. If he looked upon it now and saw anything else, he would know he had lost his mind. The patriarch tore his gaze from the ceiling.

The instant his eyes fell upon the carving, his vision blurred. He took a breath and squinted, forcing himself to see. He half-expected the goddess to start moving, but she remained as motionless as any piece of stone. His vision cleared, and he sighed in relief. There were no fangs or talons, no bare bones jutting through the flesh of her face.

And yet the carving was as smooth and white as Mystra's skin had been when she last came to him. The silky long tresses could have been the smoky hair he remembered, and who was to say whether the artist had envisioned teeth or fangs lurking behind her full lips?

Adon's breath grew fast and shallow, but he forced himself to study other scenes. Was the goddess turning back a fire, or spreading it across the fields? Was she stopping a tidal wave, or summoning it forth?

The patriarch shut his eyes and softly cried out in despair. He was careful not to scream, for he did not want an acolyte to come check on him. They all stank of the goddess's magic, and the smell made him retch and soil his bed.

"It is all so vague! Am I seeing these things or not?"

"What things, dear Adon?"

Though the voice was as quiet as a thought, the patriarch knew it had not come from inside his own head. He threw off his blanket and rolled onto his knees and spun around to search for the speaker.

The room was empty.

"That proves it." Adon cowered on his mattress. "I'm mad."

"Mad?" Now the voice came from behind him. It was soft, like a woman's, and sickly sweet. "Not at all, Adon. If you were mad, you would belong to Cyric. Do you think I would let that happen?"

"I am mad." Adon refused to turn toward the voice. "I am hearing voices."

A laugh followed. "But isn't that normal when a goddess speaks with her patriarch?"

Something rustled on the other side of the room. Adon turned toward the noise, but saw nothing. The sound had come from a bas-relief near the enormous double doors.

He broke into a sweat and stared at the scene. The carving showed Mystra dancing with a circle of horned fiends. The beasts were all about her, falling to the ground and writhing in ecstasy—or perhaps they were thrashing in pain. Adon could no longer see any difference; the scene depended entirely upon how he looked at it. The brutes could have been grinning or grimacing, as he decided.

Adon squeezed his eyes closed. "If you care about me at all, dear goddess, you will leave me alone."

"You have nothing to fear from me, Adon. I will cause you no harm."

The patriarch pushed himself across his bed, away from the

voice, and stepped onto the floor. He glanced out across his balcony and saw Mystra outside, still battling the kraken. This did not shock him, for he was sane enough to recall that gods can create more than one avatar.

A pair of stony footsteps echoed across the floor, as though someone had entered the room. Adon looked back toward the door and saw that Mystra's figure had stepped out of the wall carving. She was walking toward him slowly.

Adon crouched behind the headboard of his bed. "Stay back!"

The alabaster goddess was small, standing only as high as Adon's waist. Her hair floated about her head like pale smoke, and her eyes blazed with a fierce yellow light. Beneath the curve of her upper lip gleamed the tips of five little fangs.

The figure waved a white claw down her pale body. "How can you doubt what you see, Adon, when it is set in stone?"

Adon screamed, for what he saw was a fiend more wicked than any from the Abyss.

The doors to the anteroom swung open. Prince Tang entered, thrusting a square-tipped sword before him. "Patriarch! What is—"

The avatar swung an arm toward the intruder. "Leave us!"

At once the doors swung shut, knocking Prince Tang back across the threshold. He had no chance to withdraw his hand; his forearm became lodged between the great doors. There was a sharp crack, and his sword clanged to the floor.

The prince allowed a cry of pain to slip from his lips but quickly regained his usual composure.

"A thousand pardons, Goddess," said Tang, peering through the crack between the doors. Despite the unnatural bend in his arm, his voice betrayed no pain. "I did not mean to interrupt."

"Then be silent!"

Mystra fluttered her hand in the prince's direction. His eyes closed, then he slumped to the floor, his arm still caught between the doors. The goddess hardly looked at him; instead, she raised her alabaster arm toward Adon.

"Now come to your goddess and take comfort."

Adon could only stare at Tang's crooked arm. The Mystra he remembered would never have injured a mortal so callously.

Of course not, said a voice in his head. *You would have turned away if you knew the truth about her, and she needed you to start her church. Mystra was always good at such games—or have you forgotten how she played Kelemvor and me against each other?*

"Cy-cyric?"

The instant Adon gasped the name, Mystra's avatar jumped onto the foot of his bed. "Adon, come to me!"

The avatar's voice was so commanding that Adon found himself stepping around the headboard to obey.

No, Adon! If you go to her, I cannot protect you.

The patriarch stopped.

Call my name now, and I can save you.

"Save me?" Adon shook his head, praying that he was not yet mad enough to believe such a lie. "You would never save me."

Say my name, and I'll spare you her wrath.

The alabaster goddess sprang off the foot of his bed. "No, Adon, do as *I* command." She started toward him, and her lips drew back to show her fangs in all their painful glory.

Adon retreated into the arch that opened onto his balcony. "Keep back! Don't make me say it."

"Say what?" Mystra's little avatar stopped a pace away. The flesh had peeled from her cheeks, and the bone underneath was as white as the rest of her. "Adon, I want to help you."

"Then leave me alone!"

Mystra shook her head slowly. Her silky hair turned into black smoke and flowed into the room like bitter incense. "That I cannot do. You have gone mad, poor boy."

"But you said—" Adon gasped and rubbed his neck; the smoke had made his throat so dry he found it difficult to speak the words. "You said that if I was mad, I belonged to . . ."

The patriarch would not speak the One's name.

Go ahead, Adon. Say it.

Adon shook his head and continued to stare at Mystra. "You said that if I was mad, I would belong to him."

"I said I would never let that happen. And now the time has come to prevent it."

The statue stepped forward, raising her arm to strike.

Adon rushed to the edge of the balcony. Out on Hillshadow Lake, he saw Mystra's avatar walking across the water. She did not look up, for she was peering beneath the surface, stabbing at her quarry with harpoons of lightning. With each strike, the water rose like a curtain, and still none of it made a sound.

Say my name and let me save you!

"I'd rather die!" And this was true, for Adon feared Cyric's promises even more than he feared a Faithless death. "I will trust to Kelemvor's justice, but I will never trust you."

With that, he threw a leg over the balcony rail and looked down. Five stories below sprayed the Morning Fountain, surrounded by a stone terrace where the temple's Faithful liked to make their morning devotions. The court was empty now; the Faithful had all walked down to the shore to watch the silent battle between Mystra and the kraken. A few dozen townspeople had also gathered at the lake to observe the spectacle.

The goddess's avatar grasped Adon's arm. He tried to shove her away, but her talons were buried too deep.

Say my name, urged the voice in his head.

"I spurn you!" he screamed. "I repudiate both of you!"

Then Adon turned and flung himself off the balcony.

He was halfway to the fountain before he asked himself where he had found the strength to pull free from the grasp of a god, and by then, there was no time to recant—or to embrace the One.

Thirty

Mystra was still battling the kraken when she felt a pain in her heart and heard a body splash into the fountain beneath Adon's balcony. Her avatar reached the terrace before the splash faded from the air, but already she was too late. The patriarch lay floating in the pool, his dead eyes staring at the sky, a cloud of red blood billowing outward around his head. A crack had opened in the fountain wall where his skull had struck, and now a steady stream of water was pouring out upon the terrace.

The goddess pulled Adon's body from the pool and clutched it to her breast. Then she saw his spirit draining through the pool's cracked wall.

"Adon!"

"Forgive me . . ." The patriarch's words were garbled and prolonged. The red-clouded current had stretched his spirit into a figment from a nightmare, and his ghostly face was as thin as a snake. "Cyric tricked meee. . . ."

"Adon, how can there be anything to forgive? This was not your doing." Mystra kneeled beside the fountain and waited until her patriarch's spirit pooled on the patio in a shimmering blob. "Speak my name and I take you back."

Adon's face broke into a crackled pattern; the water was seeping down between the paving stones, and his spirit with it. "Say . . . name?" The shattered voice was shrill with fear. "That's what . . . he . . . wanted!"

"What he wanted does not matter!" shouted Mystra.

Already, Adon's face had become nothing but a pattern of ghostly lines. The goddess thrust a hand into the water to give his spirit something to cling to. "Call me to save you, and I shall return your spirit to your body!"

There came a strangled gasp, but even Mystra could not claim it for her name; the sound could have been a worm drowning as easily as the patriarch's voice.

Adon's spirit sank beneath the stones.

Mystra screamed, and there was such a surge of magic that spells misfired all across Faerûn. Now Adon would be lost to her until he reached the Fugue Plain, and that would be some time hence—after he found his way out of the elemental plane of water. The journey would not be as painful as Zale's passage through the paraelemental plane of magma, but it would still be difficult, and Mystra vowed to have her vengeance.

A swarm of onlookers arrived to gape at the corpse in the goddess's lap. Most were her acolytes, but a few were curious townsmen who felt no shame in invading the temple's privacy. They were all too stunned to speak, on account of both Adon's death and the miracle of seeing one Mystra on the terrace while another hunted the kraken in the lake. A few Faithful fell to their knees and opened their hands in the starburst sign of their goddess, and others ripped their cloaks in lamentation for the patriarch. But no one thought to offer any aid, or ask what had happened, until Prince Tang ran onto the terrace.

"Lady Magic, what has happened?" The prince cradled his broken forearm to his chest and carried his square-tipped sword in his other hand. "What have you done to Adon?"

Mystra scowled. "What did *I* do, Prince Tang?" As she spoke, her avatar grew larger and stretched forward, so that she was suddenly looking down on the prince. "I did nothing, except trust in you to guard him."

Prince Tang paled to the color of ivory. "Please forgive me, Lady Magic; I have made a terrible mistake. But when I saw your statue speaking—"

"My statue, Prince Tang?" Mystra stood, still clutching Adon's body in her arms, and now she was as tall as a verbeeg.

"Your statue from the wall carving." No sooner had the prince said this than he perceived how easily he had been duped and began to prattle on without a trace of his usual composure. "Your statue ordered me to go, then slammed the door on my arm so I could not, then it put me to sleep, and when I awoke—"

"That is enough, Prince Tang." Mystra spoke in a milder tone, for she was a weak-willed goddess who never punished her servants for a failure they were helpless to prevent. After Tang fell silent, she lowered Adon's corpse into the arms of four waiting acolytes. "Care well for your patriarch's body. He will soon have need of it."

"We shall." They took the corpse and started for the temple.

Mystra turned back to Prince Tang, then shrank to a height nearer his. "Now let me see to that break."

"That would be most kind, honorable goddess." The prince presented his twisted arm. "I regret my inadequacy in defending your patriarch, but before I realized what was happening, I was asleep and unable to call for help."

"There is no need to apologize."

Mystra took the prince's arm above and below the break, then pulled in opposite directions. The bone straightened with a soft pop. Tang's legs nearly buckled, but he was too vain to scream or faint, which any honest man would have done. The goddess placed her hands over the injury, then continued to absolve the prince of blame.

"You could not be expected to keep Adon safe from another god."

"Another god?" Tang asked. "You doubt it was Cyric?"

"Someone wants me to believe it was Cyric." Mystra made no mention of who that "someone" was, for she did not want to say the name before so many onlookers. "And when someone wants me to believe one thing, I am inclined to believe another."

Here, Mystra was thinking of the battle between the Hlondethar and their enemies, when Mask had bragged about duping her into proving her own guilt. She saw how it would serve the Shadowlord to start a fight between her and Cyric, and how Mask often favored such duplicity, and how the God of Thieves might steal Adon's sanity instead of using spells or curses to wreck it. She decided this was exactly what had happened and resolved to have her vengeance on the Shadowlord.

When Mystra removed her hands from Tang's arm, the swelling had gone, as had the purple color and every other trace of injury. Prince Tang flexed his fingers and smiled.

"A thousand gratitudes, Lady Magic." He bowed his head, but only briefly. "The arm has healed."

Mystra smiled. "Mending your injuries is the least I can do. Pass me your sword, and you shall have a true reward."

Prince Tang's eyes grew bright, and he passed the sword over at once. The hilt and scabbard were encrusted with rubies and sapphires and diamonds, but when Mystra removed the sheath, it was clear the weapon had been made for combat. The silvery blade gleamed with the legendary sheen of hundredfold Shou steel, which kept a better edge than any metal worked by mortals.

The goddess ran her finger down the blade, coating the edge with a film of her sparkling red blood, and spoke a mystic syllable. Her blood sizzled away in a wisp of brown smoke, and then a crimson light gleamed deep within the Shou steel. So beautiful was this sheen that the onlookers all gasped in delight.

Mystra slipped the sword into its scabbard. "This blade will slay any hound it strikes, whether the creature was born from natural or unnatural loins."

Though he was as inscrutable as any Shou prince, Tang could not keep his brow from rising. "Any hound, Lady Magic?"

"Yes, Prince Tang." A bewildered murmur rustled through the crowd of onlookers. Mystra ignored it and kept her attention fixed on the prince. "And while you hold it in your hand, no beast can follow your spoor, whether the creature be of this world or any other."

"Ah, yes . . . how very nice." Tang accepted the sword and lowered his brow, yet his eyes betrayed his confusion. Shou

236

princes were more accustomed to fleeing assassins than hounds. "This will be most useful. I am certain it will save my life . . . someday."

"It is but a small token of gratitude for the care you showed Adon. May it serve you well."

Mystra led Prince Tang back into the temple, leaving the onlookers to whisper among themselves. She could have heard every word if she wished, but there was no need; she knew her plan would work.

The thieves of the Purple Mask had been stealing sheets of alabaster and cartloads of marble from her temple since the day construction began, and their spies had certainly been among the onlookers who watched her bless Tang's sword. Those same spies would report the gift to their guildmasters, and the guildmasters would see at once how the weapon might benefit their divine patron. Before Prince Tang reached his palace, Mask himself would know of the weapon's special powers—and then Mystra would have her vengeance.

Or so the stupid Harlot thought.

Thirty-One

After my audience with the One, I took leave of Arabel at once and galloped north through Tilverton and Shadow Gap into Shadowdale, home to a nation of ignorant farmers and an irksome old twaddler named Elminster. Ruha, who had stopped in Arabel overnight to have a healer care for Silvercloud's injured eye, followed half a day behind, as unshakable as a bad reputation. Every so often, as I crested a mountain pass or crossed a vast bottomland, I glanced back and saw a speck in the southern sky and knew she was still there, dogging my trail as the Chaos Hound dogs Mask's. And then I cursed her for a hellhag and raised my eyes to the Heavens and asked what I had ever done to her, though of course I never received any answer. The truth was she hated me not for any wrong I had caused her, but on account of my place in the many terrible visions and dreams she had been suffering of late, and because she feared these mirages would drive her as mad as Cyric if she did not stop me.

But even had the witch been farther behind, I would have stopped no longer than it required to sate Halah's hunger. Cyric's visit had renewed the zeal for my sacred pilgrimage, as I had no wish to send my unfaithful wife to the City of the Dead— or to join her there, which would certainly be my destiny if I failed to recover the *True Life* and cure the One of his madness. With my holy devotion thus renewed, I rode day and night, giving no thought to rest or food or any need that could not be answered in the time it took Halah to gulp down her meals.

And such was my fervor that when I galloped into a muddy little village and saw the One's sacred starburst and skull openly flying from the flagpole of an imposing black fortress, I stopped only long enough to demand a meal for Halah and myself. As usual, the acolytes were at first reluctant to feed me when I said I would not pay, but this changed as soon as they sensed Cyric's presence in my person. Halah was shown to the goat pen, and I was taken into a great hall and seated at the head of a long banquet table. Like the rest of the temple, the entire hall was shuddering and trembling from the effects of Mystra's unjust assaults on the One, but I was too weary to let this trouble me.

As I waited for my food, two Believers came and stood at my sides, their hands resting on the hilts of their weapons. One, a brawny man with flinty eyes and a narrow face, wore a purple robe trimmed in black silver. The other, whose shoulders were as wide as Halah's, was dressed in armor of red leather, and it was he who addressed me.

"Who are you to come into Voonlar and insult Gormstadd"—here he jerked a thumb at his silk-robed companion, then continued—"by ordering his monks around in his own temple?"

I replied without rising. "I am Malik el Sami yn Nasser, and I am on a sacred pilgrimage for the One. It is a great honor for Gormstadd"—and here I jerked my thumb at the man in silk—"to aid me in any way he can."

This caused both men to raise their brows and remove their hands from their weapons, for like any True Believer, they were quick to sense the One's presence. Then a monk happened to arrive with a tray piled high with food and drink, and Gormstadd himself took the platter and held it out toward the red-armored man.

"Why don't you serve, Buorstag?"

Buorstag nodded, then set the mug on the table before me and filled it with mead from the pitcher. This did much to restore my spirits, as it reminded me of the great honor and power that would be mine after I saved the One.

"You look tired, el Sami," said Buorstag. With his own dagger, he cut a piece of bread for me, then smothered it in honey. "Perhaps you should stay and rest in Voonlar."

I shook my head. "I am being pursued by a Harper witch, and if I let her catch me, I will never cure the One of his madness."

I did not know whether it was my own weariness or Mystra's spell that caused me to add these last words, but as soon as I spoke them, I realized what a blunder I had made! Buorstag and Gormstadd scowled and stared at each other and dropped their hands again to their weapons.

I leapt up to flee. Gormstadd clapped a hand on my shoulder, and Buorstag grabbed my arm, and I thought they would certainly throw me in chains and denounce me to Our Dark Lord.

But such was their awe of the presence they sensed in me that either they thought it wiser to ignore my blasphemy or did not notice it at all.

"This Harper—can you describe her?" asked Buorstag.

I saw by his white knuckles that he liked meddling Harpers no more than I. "Of course. You will recognize her by the hippogriff she rides and by the veil she wears over her face."

"Good," said Gormstadd, pushing me back into my seat. "Finish your meal. Buorstag will make certain that Harper never catches you."

Thirty-Two

Prince Tang passed the day gathering his company of body-guards and riding home to the Ginger Palace, which lay about a half day south of Elversult. He finished the trip so exhausted that he commanded his servants to wash him and put him straight to bed. He did not stir until late in the night, when he was roused from a dead slumber by a strange and ghostly baying. The howl sounded at once distant and near, as though his bedchamber had stretched to a length of many *li*.

Tang thought of Mystra's gift and sat up. His bed formed its own room, covered as it was by a silk canopy and enclosed by lacquered panels depicting all manner of leering monsters. These were the guardians of his sleep, which prevented evil spirits from stealing his soul as he slumbered. When the prince heard no sound from his night servant, who sat beyond the panels at the foot of his bed, he wondered if the baying had been a dream.

Then came another howl, louder than before and so eerie that it sent a prickle up his spine. The night servant did not open a panel or make any other move to wake him, and Tang thought this strange. He reached under his pillow and withdrew a dagger of silvery Shou steel, then crawled to the end of his bed, wondering if the goddess had foreseen this when she blessed his sword. He wedged the tip of his knife between two panels and slid them apart, moving so slowly they made no sound at all.

The night servant lay upon the floor, her eyes dead and wide and fixed upon the little lamp she kept burning on the night table. The purple cord that had strangled her remained wound about her throat, and the murky shape of the assassin stood a few paces beyond, facing away from the bed. In the flickering light, the intruder's body seemed to curl and roll like smoke. He was staring at the freestanding sword rack where Tang kept his most cherished weapons. The rack resembled a ladder, each rung a bejeweled scabbard worth an entire caravan of frankincense. In the highest berth rested the *chien* Mystra had blessed.

Tang did not call for his guards; he guessed that the intruder had already killed them. Instead, the prince watched the dark silhouette in growing puzzlement. The thief was staring at the blessed *chien,* yet he seemed reluctant to take it.

Tang did not guess that the intruder was Mask. Nor did the God of Thieves sense Prince Tang's wakefulness; the Shadowlord was consumed by thoughts of the *chien.* Even through the scabbard, Mystra's magic radiated off the blade so strongly that it nearly blinded him. This made the thieving god more suspicious than ever, for he had known the instant he heard the guildmaster's prayer that the sword was bait in a trap. Still, he had come. A weapon that could keep the Chaos Hound at bay—or kill him—was worth any risk.

Kezef's plaintive howl sounded again in the distance. The Shadowlord shuddered, imagining what would happen if the hound's poison-crusted fangs ever sank into his tenebrous flesh. He reached into his cloak and withdrew a piece of raw venison, and this he tossed into a dark corner. Then he took a half-starved wolf pup from his other pocket and set her on the floor to see if the sword's magic would prevent the beast from finding her meal.

The pup looked around the dark room, then touched her nose to the cold marble and fell over dead.

Mask nearly screamed his delight, for the weapon was more powerful than he had hoped: it had killed the wolf pup without even touching her. All that remained was to find Mystra's trap and disarm it, a task that the sword's blinding aura of magic would render considerably more difficult.

From the same dark corner through which Mask had entered came another howl, this time so loud it rattled the lacquered panels of Prince Tang's bed.

Tang cringed, for he feared the sound would draw the intruder's attention to his hiding place. But this did not occur. The thief—and the prince thought him to be simply that—ignored the baying and also the soft rattle of the panels, and he paced back and forth before the sword stand. In the darkness, the figure looked like an elf at some times and at others like a man, and once it even seemed to be an orc. These changes Tang dismissed as tricks of the dim light.

The prince could not imagine why the interloper hesitated, but he wished the man would find his courage. The strange howls convinced him that Mystra had foreseen the need for just such a weapon, and as soon as the intruder reached up for the *chien,* Tang meant to attack. Unfortunately, it was beginning to appear the hound would be in the room before the fellow made up his mind.

Tang kept his eye pressed to the crack between the panels, watching the intruder consider the sword stand. Twice more the hound howled, and this baying disturbed even the thief, who shuddered like empty cloth and glanced toward the sound.

A low growl rumbled through the room; then a pair of yellow eyes appeared in the dark corner. The eyes began to grow larger, and the prince dared wait no longer. He pulled the panel aside and flung himself at the intruder, dagger raised to strike.

The silhouette did not turn so much as ripple, and the prince found himself looking into the damson eyes of a towering gnoll. Like all Shou nobles, Tang had mastered the art of mortal combat, and in a blink, he stopped himself short and delivered a kick to the gnoll's knee that would have snapped a ginkgo tree.

Nothing happened, save that the impact broke several bones in Tang's foot.

"Fool!" sneered the intruder. "Leave me alone, or I—"

The rumble in the corner became a blaring howl, and a sickening reek of spoiled flesh filled the chamber. Four sets of claws clattered across the floor, and the prince knew that if he did not retrieve his *chien,* nothing would save him now. He feigned another kick, then slashed at his foe's eyes and tried to slip past to grab his sword.

A murky arm swept down to block the attack, then flung the prince back toward his bed. Tang glimpsed an enormous beast loping beneath him, then crashed through a pair of sliding panels and found himself lying where he had started.

Though his body ached, the prince rolled to the edge of the bed and saw a creature as large as a horse. It was the most hideous hound imaginable, with a tail of bare bone and a haze of brown breath ringing its blocky head. The beast stopped and shook itself, spraying a cloud of wriggling maggots in every direction, then leapt at the thief. Tang gasped, for he knew the hound would turn on him as soon as it swallowed the intruder.

Seeing that Tang had robbed him of any chance of escape, the thief whirled and grabbed the sword, intending to complete the circle and attack the Chaos Hound in one smooth motion.

This was not to be.

A slender arm shot up from the *chien*'s supporting berth and wrapped itself around Mask's wrist. He tried to shrink free, but the smaller he made his arm, the tighter the hand grasped him.

"Mystra!"

Even as Mask hissed the goddess's name, the Chaos Hound tore into his leg and severed it at the thigh. A great blast of darkness shot through the room, shattering the panels of the canopied bed and smashing the furniture against the walls.

Kezef's poison surged through the Shadowlord's veins, filling him with a scalding weakness that seemed to consume him from the inside out. He felt his head shriveling into a wrinkled husk and his limbs withering into drooping stalks, and his spirit rushed out through his severed veins. In that moment, he knew the folly of angering the Goddess of Magic.

The Shadowlord shook his head clear and saw Kezef's great head looming above him. The remains of his leg dangled from the dog's slavering jaws, yet the hound made no move to attack. Instead, he kept his angry eyes fixed on the *chien,* for he could sense the blade's magic as well as its purpose, and it made him cautious. Mask looked back to the arm that had sprouted from the polished wood of Tang's stand.

"Mystra, wait!" the Shadowlord pleaded. All the swords except the blessed *chien* clattered to the floor. "Let me save myself, and I will tell Tempus to withdraw his charges."

"It is too late for that." Mystra's avatar flowed out of the sword stand and took shape beside it. She held Mask's wrist with one hand and Prince Tang's *chien* in the other. "After what you have done, you cannot buy me off with a mere boon!"

"I thought that was what you wanted!"

"No longer."

With a flick of her wrist, Mystra freed Prince Tang's *chien* from its scabbard. At once, the bare blade filled the room with a crimson glow. Mask's shadowy form lost all semblance to a body; it became a puddle of darkness upon the floor, and the goddess raised her arm to strike.

As the sword fell, a steel gauntlet appeared on Mystra's wrist and stopped the blow short. The goddess screeched as a second gauntlet appeared and wrenched the *chien* away.

"Is this what your word means?"

The booming voice shook the chamber so terribly that the prince's bed danced across the floor. In the next instant, even as the two gauntlets continued to hold Mystra motionless, a burly, one-handed warrior appeared before the goddess. His eyes seemed a fierce steel-gray for a moment, then faded to become black empty sockets. Never in his dreams had Prince Tang imagined such guests! Tyr the Eyeless now stood between Mystra and the Chaos Hound, pointing his stump at the goddess.

"You promised not to interfere with the trial."

"Mask was never in the Pavilion of Cynosure," Mystra

retorted, struggling against the disembodied gauntlet that still held her arm.

"Lady Magic, I will have none of your excuses!"

So angry was Tyr's voice that Kezef dropped Mask's leg and looked away in submission.

"I have been watching," Tyr continued. "Tempus told you he would call Mask as a witness, and still you did this!"

The Eyeless One waved at the quivering pool of darkness on the floor. In this moment of distraction, Kezef picked up the leg and skulked into the shadows, disappearing from the room.

"But Mask killed my patriarch!"

"I know what Mask did, and better than you." Tyr fixed his eyeless gaze on the empty space beside her, then commanded, "Hold the goddess until the trial. No one is to see her or speak to her, or to communicate with her in any way."

As the Eyeless One spoke, the gauntlet on Mystra's wrist jerked her arm rudely backward. The second gauntlet dropped the *chien,* then seized her other wrist and pinned both her arms behind her back. Only then did the goddess's captor reveal himself; he could have been an empty suit of plate mail, since that was the only form Helm the Vigilant ever assumed.

Although not as mighty as some other deities, the God of Guardians was as constant as he was heartless, and on this account he was the jailer of the immortals. After being placed under his charge, no deity could escape his care, or persuade him to forsake his duty, or overpower him in any manner.

Helm acknowledged Tyr's order with a nod, then pushed Mystra toward the shattered bed, where Prince Tang still cowered in fear. Lady Magic knew better than to struggle. With her own eyes, she had seen the Great Guard destroy the previous Goddess of Magic during the Time of Troubles, and she knew he would not hesitate to kill her now.

She turned to make one last appeal. "Tyr, how can you allow this? Mask is more guilty of interfering with the trial than I!"

"That is for me to decide."

"But the Weave—"

"You brought this on yourself," Tyr said. "And whatever happens to the Weave is your own fault as well."

Helm shoved the goddess onto Tang's bed, barely leaving the awe-stricken prince time enough to scramble off. At once, four fathomless walls replaced the shattered panels. The canopy changed into a ceiling of darkness, and the mattress became a void of soft emptiness, and Mystra found herself trapped in a cage of inescapable nothingness.

Helm removed the purple cord from the throat of Tang's servant and tied it to the leg of the bed. Then he took the line in his hand and vanished from the chamber, pulling Mystra's prison along behind him.

Tyr turned his eyeless gaze upon the quivering puddle that was Mask. "Quit your trembling, Shadowlord. The hound is gone."

The dark blob assumed the shape of a one-legged man. "What took you so long? Kezef nearly had me!"

Tyr shook his head. "You are lucky I came at all. If Mystra had not attacked, I would have let Kezef finish his meal."

So saying, the Eyeless One faded from sight, leaving Mask to reassemble his form as best he could. The Shadowlord melted again into a shapeless mass and writhed about on the floor. First he became an orc with three arms and no legs, then a gnome with three legs and no arms, then a spider with tentacles instead of legs.

Tang rose from behind an overturned couch and saw his red-glowing *chien* on the floor, next to the shifting blob of shadow. He rushed across the room to snatch the weapon up.

As soon as he touched the bejeweled hilt, a tendril of cold shadow shot from the puddle and caught his wrist.

"Not on your life, Prince!" hissed Mask. "I lost a leg for that sword!"

Thirty-Three

Every spy fears one place above all others, and for Ruha that place was Voonlar. The town sat just north of the Dales, where the Shind Road forked off toward Zhentil Keep and the Northride continued to Teshwave, and it was here the witch had first meddled in the affairs of others. The Harpers had sent her to take a position in the Swords Meet tavern, where she was to serve as a messenger for another agent and spy upon the Zhentilar who met there. This role demanded that she dress in the immodest fashion of a serving wench, which is to say without veiling her face or much of her bosom, and she was pretty enough to attract a man's eye. It was not long before a slave smuggler crossed her palm with a silver coin, and she accepted the coin with thanks.

Now it was true that Ruha was fresh from the desert and did not comprehend the meaning of the exchange, yet a bargain is a bargain, and she had no right to refuse the expected services. The smuggler grew angry and drew his dagger, and he would have slain her if his own man—who happened to be the very spy Ruha had been sent to aid—had not leapt to her defense. The two were forced to fight their way out of town, leaving the smuggler free to sell a hundred wretched souls into slavery. Since then, the Harpers have called this incident the Voonlar Debacle.

So it was with an anxious heart that the witch arrived on Silvercloud and circled low over the fork in the road, wondering which way I had taken. Her usual means of solving such dilemmas was to land and ask after a hell horse, for Halah never failed to leave the locals with good reason to remember her. But the witch knew better than to ask such questions in Voonlar, where the villagers were prudent enough to mind their tongues.

What was more, the witch had slept no more than five hours in five days, nor had there been much time to study Rinda's journal. And, despite the loss of his eye, Silvercloud had been on wing most of that time and worn himself down to feathers and bone. Ruha had no choice but to rest and make some discreet inquiries, trusting her veil to shield her identity and the strong ale of the local taverns to loosen the villagers' tongues.

The witch removed her Harper's pin and tucked it inside her robe, then landed at the edge of town. She led her mount past the Swords Meet, where she had failed so miserably as a serving wench, then onward to Voonlar's only remaining inn: the Sign of the Shield. The witch paid four silvers for a goat, hoping Silvercloud still had strength enough to eat, then told the liveryman to leave the hippogriff saddled. When she entered the tavern, she carried Rinda's journal tucked beneath her arm.

The common room was rough-hewn but clean, with panels of white daub set between open posts and beams. Nearly two dozen people sat drinking ale and awaiting the contents of the kettle bubbling upon the hearth. Ruha took a seat in a corner, where she could turn toward the wall when she lifted her veil to eat, then opened Rinda's journal in the hope of finding some hint of my destination.

As for Cyric, now he sits alone in his shattered keep, lost in delusions of grandeur and absolute power, leaving his church on Faerûn to grow ever more fragmented and weak. Some say this is because losing the City of the Dead drove him insane, but I know better. Cyric was the first to read the Cyrinishad; his own lies drove him mad.

The witch yawned. It was one thing to remain alert while riding a cranky hippogriff hundreds of feet above the ground—and quite another to stay awake in a warm inn steeped in the aroma of barley soup. The letters grew blurry and her chin dropped toward her chest, and when the heavy leather cover thumped down upon the tabletop, she did not even hear it.

Ruha would have dozed straight through the meal, had a familiar bellow not menaced her slumber.

"Give us some tankards, girl!" The man's voice was full of arrogance and spite, and even in her sleep the witch recognized its owner: Buorstag Hlammythyl. "And be quick about it! We've a thirst the size of the Moonsea."

The witch opened her eyes to see four men taking seats at the next table. Three wore the chain mail of the city guard, and the fourth, Buorstag himself, wore red leather trimmed in silver. He was the Bron of Voonlar, the elected ruler of the village and a notorious hater of Harpers. Though his back was turned and Ruha's face hidden safely behind her veil, the witch's pulse raced in her ears. Buorstag had always favored the Swords Meet; he had even been there the night of her debacle. She could not imagine what he was doing in the Sign of the Shield.

No sooner had the Bron taken his seat than a fifth man entered the tavern, this one dressed in armor of black leather and steel plate. A veritable giant, he stood two heads taller than anyone present. His dark beard and eye patch gave him a roguish look that caught the gaze of every wench in the room, though he seemed to have eyes only for Ruha. He strode to her table and sat down, his torso eclipsing Buorstag and the guards.

"Well met, Ruha," said the man. He spoke too loudly for the witch's peace of mind, as anyone nearby would hear his words without the effort eavesdropping. "You seem to have a problem. Perhaps I arrived just in time."

Though all the serving girls had been happy to ignore Ruha while she slept, a wench appeared unbidden, carrying the four ales for which Buorstag had called. Without taking her eyes off the newcomer's handsome face, she placed three mugs in front of him and gave the fourth to the witch, and neither Buorstag nor any of his fellows protested.

The stranger flashed a dazzling smile. "I lack even a copper."

The serving girl blushed. "That's all right. I'll pay meself."

She returned his smile, showing a mouthful of teeth as big as they were crooked, then whirled away to return to her duties. The stranger raised a tankard and began to gulp it down.

Ruha leaned across Rinda's journal. "Who are you?"

The man tossed the half-full tankard on the floor, where it shattered and left a dark stain. A few patrons glanced toward the corner, but as soon as they saw the big stranger, their scowls faded and they returned to their business. The fellow wiped his mouth on his sleeve and raised a hand to his eye patch.

"Come now. You know who I am." The stranger flipped up the patch, revealing an empty socket filled with whirling stars. "I am the one who has been helping you catch Malik."

Ruha gasped, for after Mystra's rebuke, she had guessed the identity of her benefactor. "T-Talos?"

The stranger nodded, then drained another tankard and hurled it against the wall. Again, no one objected.

"You tricked me!" Ruha said.

"I *helped* you—and I am willing to help you again, if you ask very nicely."

Ruha shook her head. "Mystra is angry enough at me."

"*Mystra* is no use to you now." Talos drained half a tankard, then looked around the room as though trying to decide where to throw it next. The inn's other patrons simply watched, their faces betraying different mixes of bewilderment, fear, and awe. "Tyr has locked her away until the trial—you do know about the trial? And after the trial is over . . ."

Talos shrugged, then flung the tankard against the ceiling behind him. It exploded into a shower of ale and pottery, soaking an entire table of patrons.

Talos tugged at his beard. "Shall we just say that after the trial, you will be calling on *me* for your magic?"

"And touch off a new disaster every time I cast a spell?" Ruha countered. "I would rather do without."

"Truly." Talos pointed at Ruha's tankard. "May I?"

Ruha pushed the mug forward and said nothing.

"Even if I am wrong about the trial, you need my help now." Talos lowered his voice. "I do believe those boys behind me know you for a Harper, and you understand what that means in this town. Without your spells . . ." The Destroyer sat back and raised his brow. "The odds are not in your favor."

Ruha glanced toward the door and saw that she had chosen a poor seat, for Buorstag and his men would cut her off before she reached it. Nor was the window a convenient exit. She would have to leap over their table to reach the casement, and then it only opened into the street, so that she would have to pass by the tavern's doorway to reach the stable. Still, hippogriffs offered some advantages to a woman in a hurry, and she knew the window was her only hope.

The witch looked back to Talos. "I see your point, but I must take my chances."

Tiny forks of lightning crackled in Talos's eyes—the empty one as well as the other—and his smile froze on his face. "You refuse me?"

Ruha nodded. "I am too old to learn a new way of magic— but if you still think it important to stop Malik, you could tell me where he is going."

"Why? You will not live long enough to catch him."

Talos raised Ruha's tankard over his shoulder and, without looking, poured the entire contents over Buorstag's head. Then he left, not vanishing in a flash of lightning so much as becoming one, and only a pile of smoking ash remained in place of the bench upon which he had been sitting.

Buorstag's deputies rose at once, blocking Ruha's route to the door, but the Bron himself merely wiped the ale from his face and turned to gaze at the witch. Ruha tucked her lip behind her teeth as Zale had taught her, then, praying that the tavern walls were too thin to muffle a whistle, gave a mighty trill.

Buorstag rose, but did not reach for his sword. "This Malik you are trying to catch—describe him."

Ruha's heart caught in her throat, for she could not imagine the very man she feared most would tell her which way her quarry had gone. Yet, she stood to lose nothing by answering.

"He is a pudgy little man with swarthy skin and eyes that pop out like a bug's. But you are most likely to recognize his horse: it is a magnificent beast with sapphire eyes and a monster's teeth."

Buorstag narrowed his eyes. "Your voice seems familiar." He scowled and stepped over to her table. "Why do you want to catch this Malik?"

Ruha replied without hesitation, for attempting to disguise her voice now would only heighten the Bron's suspicion. "He is a thief, and he has stolen something very important to me."

She had given the same answer in a hundred places, and it had always satisfied whoever was asking, but not Buorstag. He hated Harpers as much as he loved being the Bron, and he was only looking for some pretext to arrest Ruha that would not anger the inn's owner and cost him votes at the next election.

Buorstag glared at her, trying to unnerve her, but Ruha was accustomed to such games and returned his gaze in kind. The Bron looked away first, reaching down to seize Rinda's journal.

"What is this? Your diary?" He flipped the page and began to read. " 'As for what became of the *True Life of Cyric*, I have heard that Fzoul Chembryl still keeps it in a safe place in the ruins of Zhentil Keep.' "

"Of course!" Ruha gasped softly.

Buorstag paid her no attention and continued to read, still searching for some pretext to seize her. " 'Although I wish it were in the hands of a more trustworthy caretaker, I pray this is true. The *True Life* is the only way to unchain the minds imprisoned by the *Cyrinishad*'s lies, and I fear the day will come when its plain truths are needed to save'—"

Here, Buorstag quit reading. "What is this blasphemy?" And now his voice quivered with anger, for he was a loyal devotee of Cyric's temple in Voonlar. "Sacrilege is against the law here!"

Ruha did not answer, for she was too stunned by what she had perceived. Clearly, her quarry was on the road to Zhentil Keep; that much was obvious. But could it be that the crafty little spy meant to recover the *True Life of Cyric*, that he actually intended to cure Cyric's madness? The witch's mouth fell open, for she was much awed by the brilliance of this plan.

"Didn't you hear me?" Buorstag repeated. "This book is against the law in Voonlar!"

"Then you may confiscate it. It belongs to Malik."

This confused Buorstag for a moment.

Ruha started toward the door. "If you will excuse me—"

"Wait a minute! I know that voice." Buorstag reached across the table and jerked the veil from Ruha's face. "You!"

The witch tucked her lip beneath her teeth and whistled again, then feinted toward the door. At once, Buorstag and his deputies moved to cut her off. She spun around and rolled over her table, then leaped onto the next one and bounded across the room from tabletop to tabletop.

"Stop, Harper!" the Bron yelled. "Stop her!"

His command came too late. Ruha was already diving through the window and calling for Silvercloud. She hit the street and tucked into a roll, and when she returned to her feet, the hippogriff was flying over the stable gate. The witch did not command the beast to land, but threw up her arms and let him catch her in his talons. By the time Buorstag came scrambling out into the street, the pair was already sweeping over the temple of the Dark God Reborn and making for Zhentil Keep.

Thirty-Four

A line of dark ramparts rose up from the distant horizon, blocking the road ahead. The umber ribbon of the River Tesh oozed down from the west, and the gray Moonsea swept out to the east, and a pall of yellow haze hung low over the battlements, just as Rinda had described in her journal. At last, I had reached my mecca, the great Zhentil Keep.

I would have urged Halah into a gallop, save that she was already flying up the road at her customary dead sprint, and it was all I could do to keep from bouncing off her back. My long journey was over, yet the hardest part of my quest remained ahead. Now I had to steal the *True Life of Cyric* from Fzoul Chembryl and convince the One to read it, and I had only four days before the trial.

As Halah carried me nearer to Zhentil Keep, I saw that the One had punished the city terribly indeed for its betrayal. He had allowed the dragons and giants to reduce the barbicans and watchtowers to jagged ruins, and long stretches of pale stonework marked the many repairs necessary because of their attacks on the ramparts. Of all the city's buildings tall enough to rise above the walls, only a few retained their highest stories, and fewer still had roofs. It was difficult to tell more from a distance, for a huge round knoll stood on the far side of the river, and the details of dark shapes vanished against the craggy face of this strange hill.

When Halah and I drew close enough to see a cluster of shacks outside the gate, I realized Zhentil Keep was not the vast city Rinda had described in her journal. The whole town stretched but a thousand paces from east to west, and it could hardly have been a tenth that broad without spilling into the River Tesh, which separated it from the rounded knoll beyond. Such a tiny hamlet might have seemed a city to eastern barbarians, but it was barely more than a crossroads to a worldly merchant from Calimshan!

I reined Halah to a trot, then noticed that the hill across the river was made entirely of broken stone. It resembled a rubble pile, for among the rocks were many large slabs of mortared wall, which seemed carelessly tossed; had the mound not been so many times larger than Zhentil Keep itself, I would have thought it some sort of dump.

Halah trotted into the midst of the shanties outside the gate, and the strange hill passed out of sight behind the city ramparts. The gate stood open; two guards stepped out of the gatehouse and crossed their halberds across the road. Each was as large as a harem eunuch, and over their chain mail they wore black tabards emblazoned with the emblem of Zhentil Keep: a white, gauntleted fist surmounted by a jewel.

I tugged on Halah's reins, bringing her to a stop beneath the portcullis. At once, a mob of beggars filled the street beyond, ready to assail me the instant I was granted entry. Two men also emerged from the shacks behind me; one held a flimsy map in his hand, and the other was leading a rag-swaddled youth, whom he no doubt intended to pass off as a guide. Fearing Halah would make a meal of the boy, I waved these three away and fixed my attention on the guards before me.

"May I enter?"

"State your name and business in Zhentil Keep," commanded the oldest. From behind him came the acrid smell of burning peat and the gentle murmur of a city at work. "And show your coin, so we'll know you can afford to pay your way."

Now, any merchant who has visited as many cities as I have knows better than to show his money at the gate. If the guards are not thieves themselves, then they are certainly working with thieves, and even if they are honest, they are only trying to decide how much of a tariff to charge.

I made no move to show him anything. "Perhaps it would be better if you told me how much it costs to enter Zhentil Keep, and I will decide whether or not I can pay."

The guard studied my tattered *aba* and my magnificent mount, trying to decide whether I was a stealer of horses or the victim of highway robbers; his only interest in the matter was that he could charge the thief more than the victim. Halah snorted black vapor and eyed the two soldiers, and I prayed she realized how hard their chain mail would be on her teeth.

At last, the oldest guard decided I looked more the victim than the thief. "The tariff is a silver piece."

"A silver piece!" I cried. Having accumulated a small coin reserve from Halah's victims, I could have afforded ten times the price. But my father had taught me the wisdom of making any venture profitable, and so I shook my head. "I will be sleeping in the streets! I can give you this, and nothing more."

I reached into my *aba* for a copper, but Mystra's magic compelled my hand into the pocket where I kept my silver pieces, and it was one of these I flipped to the guard. He caught it and smiled in surprise. It was all I could do to stifle a cry of disappointment, as I felt certain he would have let me in for no more than three coppers.

I nudged Halah forward. She took two steps, then came nose-to-blade with the crossed halberds and bared her sharp fangs. The guards raised their brows, but not their weapons.

"Now state your name and business," said the younger of the guards, and I could tell he enjoyed this part of his duty more than his fellow enjoyed collecting the tariff. "We don't want no bad elements in Zhentil Keep."

"My name is Mu—" Here, Mystra's accursed spell caused me to choke on the lie I had meant to utter. "My name is Malik el Sami yn Nasser, and all you need to know of my business is that it is a private affair involving a resident of your city," and the Harlot's spell also compelled me to add, "Fzoul Chembryl."

I knew at once this was a terrible misfortune. The mapper

and the hired guide retreated to their shacks, and the beggars vanished into alleys, leaving only a straw-haired crone and two old men to assail me. I cursed the Harlot's magic for a pox, since I hardly wanted it known I had come to find Fzoul Chembryl.

Yet the oldest guard reacted calmly, lowering his halberd and motioning his companion to do the same.

He stepped to my side. "You'd be wiser not to mention the High Tyrannar's name too loud." As he whispered this, Halah casually swung her head around as though to watch the man, and had he not been cautious enough to move his halberd between his shoulder and her teeth, he would surely have lost an arm. "Fzoul's on Lord Orgauth's short list for the block."

"I see." Hoping to make the best of a bad situation, I leaned down to ask, "Can you tell me where to find his palace?"

"Palace? In Zhentil Keep?"

"Then perhaps the temple of Iyachtu Xvim. I have come such a long way—"

"You're one of the Faithful?"

The guard raised his palm and blinked twice with both eyes, and I, being accustomed to buying goods from certain people who use secret symbols, discerned the signal at once. I repeated it myself and nodded, thinking myself safe from the Harlot's magic as long as I resisted the urge to speak.

But then my mouth opened of its own accord, and these words spilled out: "I am Faithful to Our Lord Cyric, the One and All."

"A Cyricist?" The guard stepped away as though I were a leper. "A stinking, filthy Cyricist?"

Having been on the road for so many days, I was certainly all those things and more, yet I did not need to hear this from a lowly sentry. I kicked him in the chest and slapped the reins, and Halah sprang past the younger guard into Zhentil Keep. Now, in any other city, the guards within the gatehouse would have launched a flurry of quarrels after us, but instead it was only a single stone that came sailing over my shoulder.

"Cyric worshiper!" cried someone behind me.

I glanced back to see the young sentry and his older companion gathering more stones, and then a swarm of rotten turnips came sailing out of the gatehouse and landed wetly upon me. It would have been better if they had fired their crossbows, as then Tyr's magic would have protected me and I would not have been coated in rank-smelling slime.

The gate guards launched their stones. "Cyric lover!"

Puzzled by the strange alarm the guards were raising, I turned forward and saw the beggars rushing from their alleys. They began to fling all manner of garbage at me, and they were joined in this by well-dressed citizens throwing stones, and by masons hurling trowels of mortar. Someone in a high window even tossed out a full chamber pot, which shattered over Halah's head.

This was too much for such a proud beast. She reared up and snorted black steam from her nostrils, then whirled on our attackers and began to strike them down with her hooves. There was nothing I could do except keep my fingers twined in her soiled mane and hold on. I felt Cyric's heart grow angry in my breast, and soon my blood was slurping in my ears so loudly I could barely hear the insults of the crowd.

Halah's flashing hooves sent a burly mason crashing through the wall he was repairing, and I pointed at his bleeding head. "Fools! That is what awaits those who insult the One!"

Halah whirled on a silk-robed merchant and sank her teeth into his shoulder, then flicked her head and sent him sailing across the street.

I traced his arc with my finger. "Such is Cyric's wrath!"

At last, the crowd began to back away, leaving me a moment to look around. We were on a busy cobblestone boulevard lined by large, official buildings of gloomy-looking stone. Many were swaddled in scaffolding and surrounded by piles of rock, as the masons were still laboring to repair the damage done the last time Zhentil Keep insulted the One. At the far end of the avenue, which was no more than five blocks away, another gate hung open, revealing a half-constructed bridge arcing across the River Tesh to the strange rubble mound I had observed earlier.

The tramp of running boots brought my respite to a quick end. I glanced back to see a host of black tabards rushing out of the gatehouse. Although Tyr's protection would shield me from their halberds and crossbows, it would do little to free me from their dungeon if I let them catch me. I urged my mount toward the river gate, and that is when the straw-haired crone leapt into Halah's path. She was one of the beggars who had not vanished into the alleys when I mentioned Fzoul Chembryl's name.

The crone raised her hands. "Wait!"

Halah snorted black steam and reared up, and the beggar woman cringed and covered her head.

"Spare me if you love Cyric!"

Halah's hooves came down beside the crone, and the crossbows clacked behind me. Two quarrels struck me full in the back, but became entangled in my filthy *aba* and caused me no harm.

The crone's jaw fell. "In the name of the One and All!"

"Old woman, what do you want?" I glanced over my shoulder and saw the guards less than ten paces away. "I have no time."

"Then help me up." The crone raised her arm. "You'll be safe in the temple."

I grabbed her hand and pulled her up and spurred Halah into a gallop. "Cyric has a temple in this blasphemous city?"

"Turn left." The crone pointed down a side alley, then added, "There are those of us who know Zhentil Keep deserved the Razing. We are not popular—as you have seen—but Lord Orgauth fears the One's wrath and protects our temple."

We galloped twenty paces down a squalid lane so narrow my legs scraped the walls on both sides. In the space of that distance, Halah leapt two sleeping beggars and bowled over another, then the crone let go of my waist and pointed down another gloomy lane.

"Turn right."

We skidded around the corner, galloped another dozen paces, and burst onto a boulevard even larger and more crowded than the one by which I had entered the city.

"Left."

As I guided Halah around the corner, the mare made a detour to a street vendor's cart and smashed his chicken cage and snatched up a crowing rooster, which she devoured feathers and all as we galloped down the avenue.

Over my shoulder, I asked, "Can you help me find Fzoul Chembryl?"

"Of course. But you shouldn't have asked for him at the gate. He keeps spies there just as we do, and now he'll be watching for you."

"It couldn't be helped," I answered, and this was as true as anything I said that day.

After no more than a hundred and fifty paces, the crone guided me down a short side street, to the courtyard of a squat black building. Its condition was no better than most structures in Zhentil Keep. It lacked much of its second story and roof, and the city's blasphemous residents had defiled its walls with all manner of profanities blaming Cyric for the Razing.

Given the sacrileges I had witnessed so far, the One had shown the city more mercy than it deserved.

The crone slipped off Halah's back and began to pound on the copper doors of the temple. "Friar Fornault, this is Sister Svanhild!" She motioned me forward. "Open the doors and quickly! The One has sent us a savior!"

Thirty-Five

In a place as vast as Faerûn, many hundreds die each day, and so the Seraph of Death required but a short time to observe the final moments of a thousand and ten, as Lord Kelemvor had commanded. Now Avner stood in the Crystal Spire, recounting all he had seen. Lord Death sat slumped in his crystal throne, his face weary and dark as he listened to the report.

"In the Swamp of Nether," Avner continued, "a black dragon rose up beneath a punt in which Goodwin of Haywood was riding. The instant the wyrm opened its mouth, Goodwin drew his sword and leapt into its jaws."

Kelemvor raised his sullen eyes. "To what purpose?"

"None. The punt was already sinking, and his companions were either drowned or swimming for safety. There was no question of saving the treasure, and Goodwin might well have spared himself by diving into the water."

"And perhaps one of his drowning companions as well?"

"Yes. He was a good swimmer, and lightly armored." The Seraph of Death paused a moment, studying his god's stormy mood, then said, "Goodwin's death was the thousand and tenth. Shall I go and observe more?"

Lord Death gave no answer, for there comes a moment when even the blindest fool perceives the mistake of his ways. Kelemvor saw that he had made a poor God of Death—especially compared to Cyric, who knew in his infinite wisdom that humans are weak and selfish creatures who will always seek the easy way to do anything, except when they fear some incredible pain or anguish. On this account, the One had made his realm a place of bitter sorrows, to prevent the Faithless and the False from seeing death as an escape from their harsh and vulgar lives, and also to prevent the Faithful from turning their backs on their own gods. All this had Cyric done for the good of Faerûn's mortals, like a stern father who loves his children well enough to give them a harsh upbringing.

Kelemvor perceived these things at last, and he sat sulking for many long minutes; like any jealous child, it angered him that his rival should be right when he was wrong. He kept thinking the matter over and over, until at last he convinced himself that his error was due to a laudable concern for Faerûn's mortals, whereas Cyric's reign had been but the accident of a brutal and selfish nature.

When he had finally convinced himself of his righteousness, the God of Death fixed his gaze on Avner. "You could watch ten thousand and ten deaths. It would change nothing. If worthy men do not fear dying, they will leave life to the unworthy—and all Faerûn will suffer."

The Seraph of Death's black wings sagged. "But surely, it is not wrong to be fair to the dead?"

"It is not my place to be fair." Kelemvor shifted his gaze to the empty air beside Avner. "Jergal!"

The seneschal's shadow-filled cloak appeared at once, his yellow eyes glowing beneath the hood. "I am here for you, as always. How may I serve?"

"I have been remiss in my duties. Have you prepared the list of my judgments as God of Death?"

In Jergal's white gloves appeared a scroll as thick as a giant's waist. "I have."

"Good." Kelemvor glanced at his Seraph of Death, then said, "We will begin the difficult case of Avner of Hartwick."

Had Avner been alive, his knees would have gone weak and he would have felt sick to his stomach. As it was, he merely dropped a few shadowy feathers and did his best to stand up straight, determined not to embarrass himself by falling to his knees or begging for mercy.

If Kelemvor noted Avner's stoic acceptance of fate, he did not show it. "Bring me the list." The God of Death motioned Jergal forward, then took the scroll and began to scan names. "Now go and fetch the God of Thieves, if he will stop gloating over Mystra's imprisonment long enough to see me."

"He will not have the choice."

Jergal did not turn toward the exit; he merely began to float toward it. Avner stepped aside and let the seneschal pass, catching a glimpse of himself in the perfect mirror on the wall. Instead of the mighty Seraph of Death, he saw a sandy-haired orphan of ten years, doing his best to hide his terror behind a mask of cynicism and cunning. The narrowed eyes and fur-rowed brow did less to make the boy look dangerous than lonely. Avner lost his poise and began to tremble.

Kelemvor looked up from the scroll long enough to cock an eyebrow, then returned to his reading and left Avner to the horrors of his imagination.

Jergal appeared before Lord Death's throne. "Mask is in the anteroom, awaiting your summons."

"How kind of him. Show him in."

At once, the Shadowlord's wispy voice filled the Judgment Hall. "I am under Tyr's protection!"

A second Jergal appeared in the doorway, his disembodied white glove dragging along a tangle of writhing shadow.

"I warn you, Kelemvor!" Mask stopped squirming long enough to assume the shape of a huge firbolg; the warrior had both legs, but only one arm, and in his hand, he held the magical *chien* stolen from Prince Tang. The jewel-encrusted sword was barely as long as the firbolg's forearm. "If you want to share Mystra's cell—"

Kelemvor rolled his eyes. "Helm has his hands full guarding Mystra. But I have not called you here to assault you, Mask. There is no need to put on airs. They mean nothing to me."

To emphasize his point, Lord Death nodded toward the mirror. Mask's reflection was that of a little creature with a doglike muzzle and a pair of goat's horns on its scaly head. This kobold had two faces and seemed even smaller and more spindly than most, for there was only one leg beneath its hips, and the huge Shou sword in its hand was longer than its body.

Mask cried out and changed his shape to that of a burly minotaur; his reflection remained that of the kobold. The Shadowlord began to shift forms faster than a mortal could blink, becoming a Bedine sheikh, a Knight of Myth Drannor, and a dozen other noble warriors. The image in the mirror always remained that of a pitiful little kobold with a sword bigger than he was.

At last, the God of Thieves gave up and simply assumed the kobold's form, then allowed Jergal to drag him toward Lord Death's throne. "Is that what you brought me here to show me?"

"Not at all," Kelemvor replied. "I asked you here because I have been reconsidering the case of Avner of Hartsvale."

Mask glanced at the Seraph of Death, seeming to notice him for the first time. "Reconsidering?"

"Perhaps I was mistaken in refusing to return him."

"Mistaken!" Mask's tone grew angry; in his arrogance, the God of Thieves believed that Mystra's imprisonment had caused Kelemvor to fear him. He puffed his figure into that of a burly dwarf, then raised his nose and dared to place his foot on the crystal step beneath Kelemvor's throne. "It is too late to beg my forgiveness."

"I am not *begging* anything, especially from a craven little god such as you. What I *am* doing is offering to give Avner's spirit over to your care."

"My care?"

To hide his surprise, the God of Thieves scratched his scruffy chin and turned away. He began to look the seraph up and down, as any man might before purchasing a camel, but the Shadowlord was not trying to drive the price down. He was only buying time to think. If Kelemvor started acting like a proper God of Death, the verdict at the trial just might go in his favor—and then Mask would have yet another powerful enemy.

The Seraph of Death stood as straight as a rod and glared down at the Shadowlord's spindly silhouette. True, he had once worshiped the God of Thieves, but he had also answered the high call of duty and not flinched; nothing Mask could do would change what Avner had become in that moment.

At length, the Shadowlord twisted his kobold's snout into a snaggle-toothed smile, then turned to face the God of Death. "You expect me to take him back? After you have ruined him?"

"I do not expect anything. I only ask if you want him."

Mask shook his head. "Not now—not until he proves himself worthy."

"Proves himself?" Kelemvor leaned forward. "How?"

The Shadowlord tipped his snout up and scratched his chin. "Let me think. Something will come to me, I am sure." He made a great show of studying the ceiling. "I have it! Something you will appreciate more than I. He can free Mystra!"

"No one can do that," Kelemvor objected. "Not with Helm guarding her."

"Ah—well, I thought you might say that." Mask shrugged. "Too bad. If he succeeded, I was going to make him my Seraph of Thieves. As it is, I suppose you will have to change him into a rat and send him into the Maze of Alleys."

The Shadowlord shook his head as though disappointed, but when he turned to leave, his shadowy muzzle was grinning.

"I can do it."

Mask stopped on the spot, then whirled around and pointed his kobold's snout at Avner. "What did you say?"

"I can do it. Allow me to borrow a few things from this chamber, and I will free Mystra."

"Take anything you like, Avner." Now it was Kelemvor's turn to smile. "When you have succeeded, I am certain the Shadowlord will keep his word—will you not, Mask?"

Mask's first thought was that Lord Death had tricked him, but how could the God of Death have known he would insist on testing the seraph, much less foreseen the nature of the test? The answer was that he could not have; Avner's boast was nothing but the desperate attempt of a condemned spirit to escape his fate. Mask twisted his kobold's muzzle into a confident smirk, then looked up at the seraph. "Agreed. If you can free Mystra, then you are a better thief than I."

Thirty-Six

Time has no meaning for the dead, so when Adon found himself standing on the blinding expanse of the Fugue Plain, it was with no idea how long it had taken to get there. He recalled striking his head on the fountain and opening his mouth to scream, and then a great tidal wave had rushed down his throat to fill his lungs. His spirit left his body with less effort than it takes a man to slip from his robes. The cold waters swept him away, and Mystra's face appeared on the surface, blurry and rippling in the current, once again the beautiful goddess of his memory.

Then Mystra asked him to speak her name. The hatred returned to her eyes and the anger rose again in her voice. Adon cried out and sank into the depths of a black cold ocean, and the goddess's image shattered above him and vanished.

After that, his journey became at once endless and ephemeral. A swirling light appeared in the darkness ahead, and he swam in its direction until the waters thickened into a sea of slurping, sucking ooze. The swirling light became a distant glow, and he burrowed toward it until the mud hardened into a granite plateau. The distant glow became a radiance shining on the horizon, and he stumbled after it until his march became a numb and mindless trek. Then the radiance became a boundless white expanse, and the patriarch found himself standing upon the Fugue Plain with no certain memory of how he had come there.

The ground quivered beneath his feet like something alive

and restless, and the air buzzed with the drone of a million voices, and all around him the spirits of the dead beseeched their gods to come and rescue them from this empty wasteland.

Nearby, a matron cried, "O Chauntea, Great Mother, Golden Goddess of Grain, Merciful Giver of Life! Answer this, the call of your Faithful servant Gusta, who has borne fifteen children and planted a bountiful field each spring and prayed to you every day of her life. I beg you, take me into your garden—"

A shaft of golden light split the sky, and over Gusta's head appeared a winged herald bearing a yellow cornstalk. The harbinger lowered her stalk, and a flaxen beam shone down to engulf Chauntea's beseecher; at once, the cares and concerns of Gusta's life melted away, and her spirit grew so light that it floated up the flaxen beam into the herald's arms.

A short distance ahead, the spirits of a hundred warlocks and sorceresses had gathered into a great throng, all facing the same direction and staring at the sky. A low murmur rose on the far side and raced toward Adon and broke over him with all the force of a wave upon the ocean.

"Mystra!"

So loud was the cry that the patriarch grimaced at its volume; he could imagine it crossing the heavens and reaching Mystra's ears in her palace of shimmering magic.

"O Mystra, Lady of Mysteries, Guardian of the Weave, answer this, the call of your Faithful worshipers!" A hundred voices spoke at once, yet their words were clear. "When will you deliver us, we who have spent our lives studying your wonder, spreading the glory of your magic to every corner of the land? Hear the appeal of your worshipers, Lady Magic. Look! Here is Mandra the Mighty, who changed the Sea of Petark to wine, and here is Darshan the Dread, who filled the Chasm of Narfell with diamonds, and here is Baldemar the Brilliant, who . . ."

The prayer droned on, proclaiming the loyalty of Mystra's Faithful and the feats of each, and before five wonder-workers had been named, the patriarch saw the heralds of a dozen other gods appear and retrieve their worshipers. Of all the deities of Faerûn, only Lady Magic seemed content to ignore the pleading of her worshipers, to leave them gathered upon the Fugue Plain like a lost herd of cattle.

Adon ran over to the crowd. "Stop it!" He pushed his way to the center. "Mystra won't come! She cares nothing for us!"

The throng fell silent, and all eyes turned to stare at him.

"Forgive me." Adon turned in a slow circle. "Mystra deceived me, and so I have deceived you."

An enchantress as beautiful as any woman on Faerûn stepped close and looked the patriarch up and down, then shook her head in sadness and turned away.

"It is nothing," she said. "Only poor Adon."

Adon grabbed the woman's arm. "I have seen Mystra's true face! She is an evil hag! If she cared for us, why hasn't she sent a herald for us?"

"She will," answered another spirit, this one a tall black-bearded wizard. "We must believe she will."

"Why?" Adon cried. "Don't you see she has deceived us?"

"Poor Adon." The enchantress reached up and touched his cheek. "Poor, mad Adon."

Adon pushed the enchantress's hand away. "Listen to me! Mystra's eyes burn with hatred! Her mouth is filled with poison and fangs—"

"Enough!" The black-bearded wizard slammed a palm into Adon's chest, knocking him to the ground. "If we listen to the patriarch's madness, we will suffer his fate. He is Faithless!"

"Faithless!" gasped Adon.

"We must leave him." The enchantress backed away, forcing the other spirits behind her to do the same. "His madness will destroy us all."

As one, the throng drifted away, leaving Adon alone on the Fugue Plain. He watched them go, and when they were so far away he could no longer hear their prayers, he rolled onto his knees.

He clasped his hands before his chest and looked toward the heavens. "O Kelemvor, Lord of the Dead and Judge of the Damned, heed this, the call of your dead friend Adon. . . ."

Thirty-Seven

The Believers of Zhentil Keep were the strangest group of Faithful anywhere on Faerûn. All seventeen lived in the same hall of cold stone, and slept in the same crib of straw, and washed themselves in the same baths, and ate from the same wooden basin, and shared among themselves everything they owned without rancor or enmity of any sort. They said they did this on account of the many privations of their city and especially of their temple, but any fool could see they liked matters as they were. As we sat on the barren floor passing the gruel bowl from hand to hand—they did not own a single spoon—there was much joking and laughing and warm touching, and no one ever complained when he emptied the bowl and had to go refill it from the kettle.

Svanhild was standing by the fire, describing my entrance into the city. "And Malik said, 'I am Faithful to Our Lord Cyric, the One and All.' He didn't care whether the guard or anyone else knew he was a Believer!"

Svanhild no longer looked the crone, having washed her grime off in the temple baths. She had done the same for me—as I said, the Believers of Zhentil Keep share everything—and supplied us with the same flaxen robes worn by everyone in the temple. Hers fit just tightly enough to prove she was no more than half the age I had thought at the gate, but of course I had already seen this in the baths.

"He kicked the guard aside—" Svanhild pulled up her robe and raised a well-shaped leg to demonstrate "—and rode into

271

Zhentil Keep as proud as Lord Orgauth himself. Then, when the Believer's Shower started, Halah reared and began cracking heads, and Malik yelled, 'That is what awaits those who insult the One!' "

Svanhild pointed her finger at the floor and spoke in a voice deeper than my own, which drew many loud guffaws from her fellows. They were not laughing at me, but at the blasphemers whose skulls had been split by Halah's hooves.

" 'Such is the wrath of Cyric!' he yelled, and the guards fired their crossbows." Now Svanhild fixed her gaze on me, and I have never seen such devotion in the eyes of a woman. "The bolts didn't even scratch him. You should have seen the guards' faces!"

I felt the heat rise to my cheeks, for Svanhild had already hinted she wished to attend me after dinner. In truth, her advances had been so bold they filled the heart in my breast with a sense of godly due, and it was a wonder I had not enjoyed her already—especially after so many seasons away from my wife. Yet what were women to me when the *True Life* was at hand? I could think of nothing but stealing the book and curing the One's madness, and of saving myself from the City of the Dead, and of the great reward Cyric would bestow on me after he won his trial. Of course, I also thought of the four short days left to do all this, and of the difficulty of finding Fzoul Chembryl in a city as strange as Zhentil Keep, and of the chance that he no longer had the *True Life of Cyric*. But most of all, I thought of the terrible consequences for the One's Church if any part of my plan failed, and it was on account of this that I felt little interest in eating the temple's gruel or sleeping in its crib of straw, and certainly not in sporting with its women.

"Malik?" Svanhild shook my shoulder; I had been so lost in my thoughts I had not noticed her leave the fireplace. "Friar Fornault asked what spell you used."

"Spell?" I shook my head clear, then looked across the circle to Fornault Blacksun. The Friar, as they called him, was a snake-eyed man of fifty, as gaunt as his acolytes and far too ready with that lizard's grin of his. On his index finger, he wore an iron starburst-and-skull signet. "I know no spells."

Fornault creased his slender brow, and somehow that smile remained upon his thin lips. "You're not a cleric?"

"No, I am the Finder of the Book." I had told Svanhild about finding the *Cyrinishad* as she scrubbed my back. As there had been several other people in the bath, these events were already known throughout the temple. "I have never needed magic to serve the One and All."

Fornault's smile drooped at the corners. "So I have heard, but the Great Annihilator's spells are more powerful than my own." The Friar and his acolytes called Fzoul Chembryl the Great Annihilator, as he was the one who had read the *True Life* on the morning of the Razing and ruined Zhentil Keep's faith in Cyric. "You will forgive me for finding it strange that the One would send someone with no magic to punish our enemy."

The heart in my breast grew cold and spiteful, and I was seized by the urge to pull my dagger and strike this fool dead. I resisted this temptation, and not only because I feared his acolytes would never let me reach him. According to Svanhild, Fornault Blacksun was the only person in the room who knew where to find Fzoul Chembryl, and he had not yet parted with this knowledge. I forced myself to return the Friar's smile and tried to conceal my anger.

"I only asked you to help me find Fzoul Chembryl." I picked my next words carefully, on account of Mystra's truth spell. "I did not say the One sent me, or that I came to punish Fzoul."

Fornault's eyes flashed with anger, but his smile remained intact. "But you did not say otherwise. Perhaps you should tell us what you *do* want with the Great Annihilator."

Knowing I could not lie, and that neither Fornault nor his acolytes were likely to approve of my plan to cure the One, I clenched my jaw and said nothing. But neither did I look away, for the cold anger in my breast was making me bolder than I should have been.

The lizard's grin vanished from the Friar's face. "I am not

comfortable helping just anyone find the Great Annihilator." In any other temple of True Believers, such an explanation from the high priest would have been an unthinkable sign of weakness; in Zhentil Keep, it seemed as natural as the bricked-over windows. "A foolish attack is sure to bring swift retribution, and Lord Orgauth would simply stand by and watch. Nothing would please him more than to be rid of our temple without risk to himself, as only fear of the One's wrath makes him tolerate our presence."

Svanhild was quick to leap to my defense. "Malik is hardly some bumbling neophyte. He has touched the *Cyrinishad,* and he has spoken face-to-face with the One!"

"Or so he says." Fornault's eyes grew as dangerous as a cobra's, and he did not take his gaze off me. "But we have only his word. How do we know that he isn't . . . exaggerating?"

It was a strange temple indeed where Cyric's Faithful hesitated to call each other liars.

Svanhild thought for only a moment, then answered, "We know by what I saw at the gate. Crossbow quarrels do not bounce off the backs of normal men."

"And we also know because of Halah," added another sister of the temple, a raven-haired beauty called Thir. She pointed to the far corner, where my magnificent horse was devouring the temple's only milk goat. "How many horses eat flesh and exhale black fog?"

"That is a good point," replied a sister named Oda, and then a brother called Durin added, "I believe him."

This occasioned a general course of head-nodding and agreement. As I looked around the circle, I saw that all the sisters of the temple, and several of the brothers, were looking at me with the same expressions of yearning I had already noticed in Svanhild's eyes. No doubt this adoration had more to do with the god's heart in my chest than seeing my stout figure in the baths—at least, in the case of the men, I hoped so.

Fornault's expression flashed from shock to outrage to cunning, then settled on benign acceptance. This countenance looked as false on his face as a mask of brutish ferocity would have appeared on mine.

"Well then, it seems the matter is settled." The Friar clasped his hands together and rose. "Why don't I get a little surprise I've been saving? Then we'll sit by the fire and plan our vengeance on the Great Annihilator."

Svanhild frowned. "Surprise?"

"You'll see," Fornault replied. "Wash out the chalice, and I'll be right back."

Fornault lit a torch from the fireplace, then crossed the barren hall and disappeared into a dark stairwell. Though clearly troubled by the Friar's offer, Svanhild took the chalice off the fireplace mantle and went up to wash it out in the roof cistern.

As soon as they were gone, Thir came to sit at my side. She slipped her arm beneath mine, brushing the hilt of my dagger beneath my robe, and nestled up close. She brought her lips near to whisper in my ear.

Before she had a chance to embarrass herself, I patted her hand. "Forgive me, Thir, but Svanhild has already asked to attend me later." Here, the Harlot's accursed magic compelled me to add, "And even with her, I fear I am too consumed with Fzoul Chembryl to enjoy any sport—besides which I am a only recently widowed."

Thir frowned at this. "Widowed? What does that have to do with anything?" Then she leaned a little away from me. "Oh— look, I know you're one of the Chosen, but that's not what I—"

Fornault's steps rang out from the stairway, and Thir fell silent. She continued to hold my arm, but I could tell she was reluctant to make the Friar jealous, as she no longer pressed herself quite so tightly to my side. Svanhild returned from the cistern an instant later. She showed no irritation at seeing another woman sitting so close to me, but only came over and sat on my other side and pressed herself as close as Thir. What a pity my thoughts were so consumed with Fzoul Chembryl!

The Friar stepped into the middle of the circle and displayed his prize, a dusty bottle of scarlet liquor. I noticed at once that he had exchanged his signet ring for another, as no merchant with an eye as keen as mine would mistake tarnished silver for cold iron.

"The finest Mulmaster port money can buy," Fornault proclaimed. "Or should I say that a quick hand can steal?"

This drew nervous laughter from the acolytes, who seemed equally split between avoiding my gaze and casting furtive glances in my direction. Perhaps they thought I was selfish not to send either Thir or Svanhild away, or perhaps they knew something about the Friar's relationship with Thir I did not.

Fornault came over and made a great show of uncorking the bottle, then reached down to Svanhild. "The chalice, my dear."

Svanhild glanced at me.

"Sister Svanhild, hand it to me."

Her hand was trembling. She cast her eyes down, as if she might be jealous of Thir after all, then passed the chalice to Fornault. As he filled it, I leaned closer to Svanhild.

"You have nothing to worry about," I whispered.

Svanhild looked up with surprise in her eyes. "No?"

Fornault drank from the chalice and made a great show of swishing the port around in his mouth.

"I have already told Thir," I whispered. "I am too consumed with my mission for any sport tonight."

Svanhild wrinkled her brow, betraying her disappointment, and she hissed, "But, Malik—"

The Friar smacked his lips and pronounced, "A fine bottle!"

He refilled the chalice quickly, then swirled the contents around and passed it to me. Svanhild intercepted the cup.

"Svanhild!" the Friar said. "Don't you think we should let Cyric's Chosen drink first?"

Svanhild looked from me to her fellow acolytes. They all averted their eyes at her shameful behavior, yet she did not release the chalice. A bitter coldness began to fill my breast at this strange affront, for I had not tasted a drop of port, fine or otherwise, since leaving Calimshan.

Thir reached across my chest to take Svanhild's hands. "Let him drink." She took the cup and passed it to me, and I saw that her hands were trembling just like Svanhild's. "What harm can a little port cause someone as mighty as Malik?"

Now, had I not already raised the chalice to my lips, I might have thought twice about drinking. But as it was, the port was already upon my tongue and halfway down my gullet before I realized what her words implied. Even then I doubted them, for the port did not bear the slightest hint of bitter taste or mordant smell. Indeed I was not certain the Friar had poisoned the drink until my stomach grew strangely full and the soft mass in my chest began to gurgle and race.

I swallowed about half the contents of the chalice, then lowered the cup. The Friar's eyes were already as wide as saucers, and his color had gone from pale to ghostly.

"A fine port indeed, Fornault." My ears were filled with such a gurgling I could barely hear my own words, and my stomach felt as swollen as a woman's before she gives birth. Yet I could see by the Friar's reaction I should have been dead before I lowered the cup. "Now, will you tell me where I can find Fzoul Chembryl? Or would you like to finish what's left of the port?"

I stood and thrust the chalice back into the Friar's hands. He stared into the cup, trying to decide if his poison had failed or I was as great as Svanhild claimed. My head began to pound. A terrible coldness seeped from Cyric's gurgling heart into my breast, and this had nothing to do with the poison.

"Your decision?" I demanded.

The chalice slipped from Fornault's hand and clanged to the floor, spilling red port across the stones. He dropped to his knees and kissed the hem of my robe.

"I was only trying to honor Our Lord of Murder!" He was referring, of course, to the venerable act of killing an unsuspecting guest. "I didn't know you were Chosen!"

"I did not say I was." I could barely hear him over the gurgling in my ears. "Now, where will I find Fzoul Chembryl?"

His gaze followed my hand as it slipped beneath my robe and withdrew the shining blade of my dagger.

"Don't!" he pleaded. "I'll take you there myself!"

I shook my head, for I knew I was not strong enough to resist the cold yearning in my breast. "Tell me, or I will kill you now and let the One punish your silence in the next life."

This threat was too much for Fornault. "His old tower! My spies tell me that is where he worships Iyachtu Xvim."

I looked up and saw the eyes of the acolytes shining in eagerness, for the murder of a master venerates the One even more than the killing of a guest. Svanhild showed her approval by nodding excitedly.

"I can find the tower," she said. "It's in the Ruins."

I glanced around the barren hall, for I had thought we *were* in the Ruins, then raised my dagger high. Fornault closed his eyes, knowing he could not resist the Chosen of the One. The viscid mass in my chest squeezed slush through my veins, and I stepped forward to take my vengeance.

Then I imagined Fornault's spirit down on the Fugue Plain with my wife, calling for Our Dark Lord, and I knew by the cold lump in my chest that Cyric would never answer him. The poisoning had become a great sacrilege, distressing the One's heart as it had, and this could not be forgiven. The Friar would be hauled before Kelemvor and found to be ignoble as well as False, and then he would be sentenced to an eternity of torment.

My arm would not come down to strike the infidel.

I clenched my teeth and tried harder, and all that happened was that my hand began to tremble. How could I be so weak? It was a terrible impiety to leave Fornault's treachery unavenged, yet I could not strike, not even when I called upon Cyric's heart for strength. I cursed the Harlot's spell, but I knew I alone was at fault. I was so afraid of Kelemvor's tortures that I could not send another to face them.

Even now it shames me to admit such cowardice. I stood holding the blade aloft so long that all the eager faces turned to looks of puzzlement, and Fornault opened his eyes to gaze up at me piteously.

Svanhild frowned and stepped away from my side. "Well, Malik? Will you kill him or not?"

I tried again to bring the dagger down, but I was too weak—especially with my victim staring up into my eyes.

I shook my head. "No."

A startled gasp rose from the acolytes. I saw the yearning vanish from Svanhild's face—then Thir grasped my arm.

"Of course not! Malik has no need to prove his Faith." Thir took the dagger from my hand. "We're the ones who must prove ours!"

Thirty-Eight

The Caliph has a saying: *If it is not cruel, it is not punishment.* In service of this motto, his jailers have devised many implements of ingenious and splendid design. They have constructed machines that can bend the victim backward until his head touches his heels, and have forged little tools that can keep him laughing until he ruins his voice, and have built one hideous device that tightens around the prisoner's chest each time he exhales. Yet the Caliph would have traded all these treasures for the simple prison in which Helm confined Mystra, which was more brutal than all the racks and hooks in Calimshan.

The goddess sat on a bed of soft emptiness, cursing Tyr for a fate she alone had caused. So cramped was her prison that she could not lift her head without thrusting it into the cold void of the ceiling, nor lie straight without touching the unbreachable nil of the walls. Yet her agony was not physical, for the bodies of the gods can endure any torment with less pain than a mortal feels in bright sun.

What troubled Mystra was Adon. Her patriarch was down on the Fugue Plain, crying out in madness and confusion, his voice so full of anguish it muffled the pleas of all her other Faithful. "O Kelemvor, Lord of the Dead and Judge of the Damned, heed the call of your dead friend Adon! Take mercy on my soul and on all the poor souls who have ever worshiped Mystra, the Goddess of Lies! She is filled with hate and envy, and she deceives all who worship her! She has left us to rot, and I beseech you, the Fair Lord, the Kind and Merciful Lord, to take pity on our wretched souls and give us shelter in the City of the Dead!"

Mystra wailed in agony, for no torture could hurt more than this. She had heard Adon's treaties a thousand times, and each time she had tried to answer but failed. Helm's prisons existed outside time and space; any deity trapped inside was cut off from all godly powers.

That Lady Magic could hear the worshipers' voices was but a courtesy of her jailer, given in acknowledgment that the charges against her remained unproved. Mystra could have asked for silence, but she did not, for she believed Kelemvor would try to free her and wanted to be ready when the time came to escape.

Adon's plea to Kelemvor droned on for the thousand and tenth time. Mystra let out a great sob and swore that when she escaped, the first thing she would do was comfort her patriarch, then she steeled herself to hear the prayer again.

But Adon's voice fell silent.

Mystra's first thought was that he had lost all hope, and she ached to send a harbinger down to comfort him—then she realized that Kelemvor would have heard Adon's pleas as clearly as she had. Surely, Lord Death had sent one of his own escorts to answer the patriarch's appeal.

No sooner had Mystra consoled herself than an avalanche of prayers filled the hush left by Adon's silence.

" . . . of Mysteries, why have you deserted me?"

"Mother of Magic, I am alone and without guidance . . ."

" . . . answer me? Answer my prayers! Answer . . ."

These prayers came not only from her most devoted clerics, but from ordinary spellcasters as well. The desperation in their voices stunned the goddess. Even with her locked in Helm's prison, the Weave remained, and any devoted student of magic could still tap it.

" . . . frightened to use my magic . . ."

"My light spell blinded half the town! How have I . . . "

" . . . the sphere melted the King's favorite . . ."

Talos!

The name flashed into Mystra's thoughts like a lightning bolt. Three years ago, she had started to scale back the magic of devastation. The Destroyer had retaliated by beginning a quiet campaign to subvert her worshipers, secretly allowing the most destructive of them to use *him* as a conduit to the Weave. Seeing that it was easier to control a plot she knew about than one of which she remained ignorant, the Goddess of Magic had feigned ignorance and allowed Talos to continue.

It did not surprise Mystra to learn that the Destroyer had seized the opportunity of her imprisonment to further his plot, but she did not realize the extent of his success until she heard the prayer of the Harper witch Ruha.

" . . . sorry for my mistake, Goddess. But if you cannot forgive me, why do you allow Talos to steal your worshipers? I refused his offer, for I did not enjoy being a scourge to the land even when I thought it your will. But many others have not done the same. During the flight from Voonlar to Yulash, I had to avoid five savage whirlwinds, and one time the smoke from the burning forest grew so thick . . ."

Mystra rolled onto her hands and knees. "Helm!"

The God of Guardians made no response. Like any jailer, he was accustomed to much yelling and screaming from his charges, and he knew the wisdom of ignoring it.

"Helm, you must know what Talos is doing! You cannot allow it to continue!"

Still, there came no response.

"He is stealing the Weave! It is your duty to let me out!"

Helm stuck his head through the wall of nothingness. His visor remained down as always, and so he resembled a closed helmet hanging on a dark wall.

"How dare you presume to tell me my duty! My duty is to keep you here. If you had been doing yours, Talos would not have stolen so many of your worshipers. Even Oghma says that!"

"So many? How many?"

The God of Guardians shook his helmet. "I dare not guess.

But many centuries hence, I am sure this will still be known as the Month of Disasters."

"Helm, listen to me." Mystra clasped her hands before her. "You must let me out."

"I cannot. It is my duty to keep you here."

"You are the God of Guardians. Have you no duty to guard Faerûn?" Like any harlot, Mystra knew just the words to make a man doubt himself. "In the Time of Troubles, you were the one who kept the gods out of the heavens. Much of what they destroyed has never been repaired. Will you let Talos demolish the rest?"

Helm fell silent, though his visor hid what he was thinking.

"I am the only one who can stop Talos," Mystra said. "You know that."

"No! You are the one who neglected her duty, and you are the one who violated her promise to Tyr. If Faerûn suffers for that, it is on your head, not mine."

With that, the God of Guardians withdrew, leaving Mystra to the pleas of her Faithful and her bed of emptiness.

Thirty-Nine

In the Burning Gallery in the Crystal Spire, four of Kelemvor's avatars sat in four identical thrones, staring out over four endless lines of terrified spirits summoned from all reaches of the City of the Dead. The souls coughed and choked in the black acrid fumes that swirled off the walls of smoldering coal, and many of them murmured in soft tones, wondering why they had been called into this place of smoke and darkness. And when they reached the head of the line and learned the answer, some would cry out in delight and others would wail in despair, and they would fling themselves at Lord Death's feet and kiss his toes or clutch his legs, but he paid no heed to any of them. The souls would vanish and reappear in their new home, and Jergal would call the next forward and read his history, and Kelemvor would pronounce a new judgment, and the spirit would wail or rejoice and fling himself at Kelemvor's feet, and so the Reevaluation continued hour after hour, day after day.

In the Hall of Judgment, where the crystal ceiling had turned as brown and smoky as topaz, two more Kelemvors sat passing judgment on all the souls recently arrived in his realm. As these spirits heard their sentences, no laughing or wailing ensued, but only stunned gasps and long, sorry silences.

Out in the city, three more avatars reshaped the many districts and boroughs into ghettos better suited to the realm of the dead. Kelemvor blew a great breath over Pax Cloister, and the shadowy valleys and wooded mountains became a desolate land of howling dust and barren peaks. In the same moment, Lord Death let out a tremendous bellow in the Singing City, and the whole quarter fell as silent as a tomb. He waded into the Acid Swamp and seeded the quagmire with handfuls of pebbles, which swelled into stone islands where the charlatans and swindlers might find refuge from their soggy existences. No longer would Lord Death's judgments be decrees of eternal bliss or unending agony. Now the dead would make of their lot what they could, just as they had in life, except that they would dwell only with others like themselves, which was certainly enough to make any mortal stay Faithful to his god.

The last avatar stood at the city gate, rubbing the portal's alabaster face with his bare hand. Wherever his palm touched, the stone shimmered like quicksilver and hardened into a mirror like the one in his Judgment Hall, so perfect that it revealed all the flaws of any onlooker. Now, as the False and Faithless approached Kelemvor's city, they would see themselves from many paces away and have time to contemplate the flaws that had brought them to the City of the Dead.

It was to this avatar that Jergal brought the spirit of Adon, Mystra's patriarch. "I have the one you requested, Lord Death."

Before the God of Death could look away from his work, a voice screeched, "Kelemvor!" Two spindly arms wrapped themselves about his knees. "You have answered my prayer!"

Lord Death turned and plucked up Adon's wretched figure. The patriarch stood only a quarter as tall as Kelemvor, and he looked as demented as any lunatic. His cheeks were as hollow as bowls and his hair whisked into a tangled mess, and no bruise has ever been as purple as the circles beneath his eyes.

Kelemvor sighed at the spectacle. "Adon, what shall I do with you?"

"What you do with me doesn't matter!" The patriarch pointed across the white vastness of the Fugue Plain. "It is the rest of Mystra's worshipers you must save. They are out there praying, and she won't come!"

"She cannot answer her worshipers." Kelemvor made no effort to explain further, for he knew Adon's mind had been touched by Cyric, and that mere words could not undo the cunning of the One. "And it is not my place to aid the Faithful of another god. I sent for you only because your prayers have made you one of the Faithless—perhaps even one of the False, as you have tried to subvert the worship of Mystra. Before naming your punishment, I shall have to decide which one you are."

Adon gasped. "Punishment?"

"This is the City of the Dead, where the False and the Faithless pay the cost of their shiftless lives. You would not be here if you were not to be punished."

"But Mystra is a fiend!" Adon staggered back, then stopped when Jergal's disembodied gloves caught his arms. The patriarch paid his captor no attention. "I have seen her true face! She cares nothing for her worshipers!"

"Even if that were true, it would make no difference to me." There was a catch in Kelemvor's voice, and he avoided Adon's gaze. "As long as they remain Faithful to her, I cannot touch them. You, on the other hand, have placed yourself entirely in my hands, and you must suffer for it."

Adon's haggard expression changed from bewilderment to anger. "But you promised to be fair and just! You promised you would not torture the damned!"

Kelemvor glared down, his eyes burning red. "Neither your madness nor our past friendship gives you leave to speak to me as you have, and this is the last time I will warn you. As for my promises, I decide what is just, and there is no need for me to torture the damned. They shall do that themselves."

Adon's jaw fell. "What happened to you?" His shoulders slumped, then his face curled into a mask of lunacy. "I should have known! You always were Mystra's—"

"That is enough!" Kelemvor underscored his command with enough force to drive Adon to his knees. "I have warned you—"

Kelemvor was interrupted by a thunderous peal of laughter. "Your warnings mean nothing to Adon, Thronethief!" A huge, crimson-tinged skull appeared in the air. "In fact, I demand to know where you are taking him. Adon is one of my Faithful!"

The patriarch's eyes grew wide with horror, and beneath the One's head appeared a skeleton covered here and there by pieces of armor and patches of leathery hide. The avatar stood half-again Kelemvor's height, though of course size means nothing at all to the gods.

"Adon, is Cyric's claim true?" Kelemvor asked. "Have you ever prayed to him?"

"Never!"

Cyric smiled patiently and shook his skull. "*Tsk, tsk,* Adon. You must not lie. Only I can save you now."

Adon scurried to Kelemvor's side, dragging Jergal's shadow-filled cloak behind him.

Cyric reached down to take them both, but Lord Death lashed out and caught the One by the wrist. Then Kelemvor dared to lock eyes and grow just as large as the One and All, and Jergal pushed Adon through the city gates without bothering to open them.

"Give him back, Kelemvor!" hissed Cyric. "Call him out now, or I will see you locked in Helm's prison with your whore!"

"You have no claim on Adon," Kelemvor replied evenly. "If you did, he would have called you instead of me."

"Adon is mad!" Cyric exploded. "That makes him mine!"

"That makes him your victim, not your worshiper. Tyr will see the difference, if you care to call him."

Cyric jerked free and stepped back. From the wrist down, his hand remained in Kelemvor's grasp, but such things are of no consequence to the gods.

The One shook his stump in Lord Death's face. "You cannot cheat me out of my prize, Kelemvor! He is my proof!"

"Proof?" Kelemvor discarded Cyric's severed hand as though it were nothing but trash. "Proof of what?"

"Of my guilt!" The One's hand dragged itself toward its master, the bony fingers rising and falling like spider legs. "The charge against me is innocence by insanity. I am no innocent! Could an innocent steal Mystra's patriarch?"

Kelemvor shook his head. "You stole nothing except his life. Adon's prayer makes him False and Faithless to Mystra—not Faithful to you." He grew just tall enough to look down upon the One. "Adon is mine now. And so is this realm."

Cyric extended his stump, and in the next instant his severed hand flew to Lord Death's throat and clung there like a fiend. "You have not heard the last of this! Tyr is on my side!"

"Then get him." Kelemvor pulled the One's hand from his throat, tearing out his own larynx in the process, and thrust this whole mess at Cyric. "Until you do, leave me alone. I have much to do before the trial."

The wound in Kelemvor's throat healed as he spoke. He turned his back on the One, returning to his work on the perfect mirror, and watched Cyric's reflection vanish in a burst of black steam.

Jergal returned at once, dragging Adon's astonished spirit with him. "I await your command, Lord Death."

Kelemvor stared across the empty plain. "I wonder, will Cyric return?"

The shoulders of Jergal's empty cloak rose and fell. "It hardly matters. You were well within your rights."

"All the same, Lord Death," said Adon, "I thank you for not turning me over to him."

Kelemvor glanced down at the patriarch. "Do not thank me until you have heard your sentence." He turned his gaze upon the yellow eyes floating beneath the hood of Jergal's cloak. "Take him to the Crystal Spire and put him at the end of the line. See that he stays there."

Jergal's eyes flashed gold, then he bowed. "As you command."

With that, the seneschal split into two avatars. One pushed Adon into the City of the Dead, this time opening the gate first, and the other remained behind with Kelemvor.

"If I may have your permission to suggest it," said the seneschal, "I believe there is a solution to your quandary—one well within all these rules you have made for yourself."

Kelemvor cocked an eyebrow. "I am listening."

"Let Adon see Mystra through your eyes. Your perceptions should be powerful enough to counter those of Cyric."

Kelemvor sighed. "I wish it were that easy, Jergal, but love is not the same as worship. Adon must see Mystra as a goddess, and to me, she is still as human as I am."

Forty

Halah kneeled in the alley behind us, gnawing on a thigh-bone and making a dreadful noise. Fortunately, most passers-by only gave a start and scurried past without looking down the murky lane. But once, three burly guardsmen had stepped into the shadows to see what was causing such an awful snarling, and Svanhild and the other acolytes had been quick to guarantee that they would cause us no trouble.

Why Halah could not have stayed at the temple and finished her meal there was a mystery to me. After the Friar's death, I had demanded that we leave immediately to find Fzoul Chembryl, and the acolytes had led me to a secret tunnel. Halah had insisted on following, crawling through the cramped passage on her knees and hocks and dragging along Fornault's entire leg. Her companionship had forced us to traverse the length of the city through alleys and byways; even in Zhentil Keep, flesh-eating horses were a rarity, and we had no wish to alert Fzoul's spies to our approach. And now I stood watching the South Force Gate, wondering how we were going to sneak a blood-smeared mare past the sentries.

"What are you waiting for?"

Though the question came from behind me, I knew at once who had asked it; the alley had suddenly gone cold and it smelled of death, and a thousand voices filled my ears. I spun on my heel and found myself facing a bloody wraith in black leather armor. Cyric's bare jaws worked back and forth, grinding his teeth together and filling the alley with a terrible growl, and in the bony sockets beneath his brow, the black orbs of his hallowed eyes burned darker than ever. If he noticed the sixteen stunned acolytes kneeling behind him, he did not show it. Halah herself seemed unimpressed; she continued to gnaw on her bone and paid him no heed.

Cyric raised three fingerbones. "Three days to trial."

I did not answer, fearing the Harlot's spell would force me to say something unwise, such as the truth: *A thousand pardons, most honored god, but I cannot do as you ask because I am busy doing what you require; I am seeking a way to cure your madness.*

Cyric laid a skeletal hand on my shoulder. "Good news, Malik: I tricked Mystra into attacking Mask, and now she is locked in Helm's prison." Truly, it was a testament to the One's cunning that all the other gods believed this a result of the Harlot's own folly. "She will trouble us no more, but I need the *Cyrinishad* more than ever."

At mention of the hallowed book, Svanhild and several other acolytes raised their heads.

The One squeezed my shoulder so tightly my clavicle ached, then continued, "That pusdrinker Kelemvor stole my evidence."

"Evidence?"

"Adon's soul. I took him from Mystra."

"The Harlot's patriarch prays to you?" I was very excited, as I knew nothing at that time about the One's efforts to subvert Adon. "How wonderful!"

"He does not *pray* to anyone." The One released my shoulder, then looked down the street. A stream of filthy masons and dayworkers were pouring through the gate, returning across the Force Bridge to pass the night in the safety of Zhentil Keep. "That is my point. I drove him mad, and he disavowed Mystra, and now he never prays. If that does not make him mine, what does?"

"I don't know." I had let this slip before I realized I did know, and of course the Harlot's magic compelled me to say more than was wise. "I don't know why you think driving him mad makes him yours. If he prays to no god, then he is Faithless and belongs to Kelemvor."

In the next instant, I flew into the wall behind me and dislodged a dozen blocks and brought them crashing down on my head; without Tyr's protection, I would certainly have been killed on the spot. Though I did not see Cyric move, I suddenly found his bony hand pinning me to the fractured wall, and my eyes were staring down into the orbs of black ice beneath his brow.

"I am tiring of your honesty, Malik."

"As am I, Mighty One. I will try to do better."

"Just get the *Cyrinishad*," hissed the One. "Otherwise, you'll be joining Adon in the City of the Dead—and sooner than you like."

Cyric released me. My legs buckled and I dropped to my knees, and when I looked up, the One was gone.

The acolytes bounded to my side like a litter of puppies, kissing the ground where the One had stood and the cloth where he had touched my filthy robe and the stones where he had slammed me against the wall. Only Svanhild and Thir seemed less than thrilled by the visit of Our Dark Lord, but still they pressed themselves tightly against my body.

Svanhild proclaimed, "To speak to Our Dark Lord in such tones and survive! Malik must be very close to him indeed!" She made certain to look at each of the other acolytes as she said this, for the contest to replace Fornault had already started. "Aren't we fortunate I recognized him at the gate?"

"As long as the One does not blame us for his failure," countered Oda, who also wished to be the new Friar. She pushed her way forward and pointed an accusing finger at me. "If you wish to recover the *Cyrinishad*, what are you doing here? We sent letters to every temple in Faerûn saying Rinda had taken it and fled the city!"

How else could I answer, except to slap Oda in the face? I could hardly have said I was trying to cure the One's madness—she would have fallen to her knees and betrayed me to Cyric at once. So I did what I had to do and shoved her into

Svanhild's arms, and Svanhild's quick dagger was to thank for the rest.

By the time Oda's body slumped to the ground, Svanhild had whirled around to face her fellows. "I am sorry about Oda, but she had no right to question the Favored of the One."

Of course, this was only an excuse for eliminating her rival, but the acolytes were quick to accept the explanation—especially while Svanhild's dagger remained unsheathed. Oda's death seemed to upset only Thir, and she turned her wrath on me.

"Are you afraid to do your own killing, Malik? First I must slay Fornault for you, and now Svanhild must murder Oda! I am beginning to think you are an imposter!"

I slapped her as I had slapped Oda, then shoved her into Svanhild's arms, expecting the same speedy solution to my problem. This time, my ally's arms were too slow, and Thir sprang back at me with a thin stiletto in her hand. The weapon snapped the instant it touched my breastbone, thanks to Tyr's protection.

Svanhild pulled my attacker away, but this time she stayed her bloody blade. "Forgive her, Malik. Thir meant no harm. Oda was her closest friend."

I scowled at this, then looked into Thir's angry eyes. "I have enough to worry about. If I let you live, you must give your word on the One to make no more trouble."

"Oh, I promise." Thir's smile grew as sweet as her eyes were angry. "On my soul as a True Believer."

I was much relieved at this. I did not have the stomach to do as I had threatened, and I knew better than to think the rest of the acolytes would continue to abide someone else doing my killing. I nodded to Svanhild, who smiled and pushed Thir into the waiting arms of the other acolytes.

Then Svanhild glanced up at the sky, which was growing purple with twilight, and motioned her fellows out of the alley. "We must hurry, or the guards will close the gate."

The acolytes filtered into the street. I continued to stare at Oda's corpse, and I could not help thinking that if I became a problem, Svanhild would deal with me just as efficiently.

"Malik, are you coming?"

"Of course!"

I jerked my gaze away from Oda's body and saw that the other acolytes had disappeared into the crowded street. I stepped to the mouth of the alley, where Svanhild stood waiting, and Halah rose to join us, still gnawing on Fornault's thighbone. Svanhild took one look and shook her head in disgust, though I could not say whether this was directed at me or my faithful mount.

"Can't you do something about your horse?" This was a command, not a question. "With that bone hanging from her mouth, the gate sentries are sure to notice us."

I turned to Halah. "Halah, can you leave that behind?"

"You're asking her?"

"Halah is a very temperamental mare." In truth, I did not know what would happen if I tried to take the bone away, for I had never forgotten the One's warning to let her eat whatever she wished. "You have seen her power."

Svanhild scowled. "And you have seen how Zhents treat True Believers." She gestured at the workers flooding back into the city across the Force Bridge. "Do you really want to start a Believer's Shower as we go out to seek the tower of the Great Annihilator? Or perhaps you think Fzoul won't notice?"

I glanced at the mass of burly men coming toward us. Svanhild's plan called for us to take advantage of the deluge to leave the city while the guards were too busy to pay close attention; the sight of Halah chewing on a human femur would certainly make us conspicuous. Reasoning that Tyr's protection would shield me, I took a deep breath, then snatched the bone from the mare's mouth and threw it on a roof.

Halah whinnied in surprise, then raised her head to look after the femur. For a moment, she seemed ready to scale the wall after it, and her eyes grew as stormy as a thundercloud, then she lowered her head and snorted black vapor into my face.

"You should have—*aackhaw*—stayed in the temple!" I coughed. "Make no trouble, or I will have the One turn you back into the nag I found!"

I grabbed Halah's reins. A low purring growl rose up from her throat, but she did not balk or resist as I pulled her into the deluge of human flesh. There was no sign of the other acolytes; presumably they had already passed through the gate and crossed the bridge.

The street stank of sweat and lime and river sludge, and my skin crawled beneath the constant press of the workers' grimy bodies. It did not take long before Svanhild and Halah and I were covered with as much slime as everyone else. Whether this was part of Svanhild's plan, I did not know, but by the time we plowed our way to the gates, it was impossible to tell us from the filthy wretches pouring through from the other side. I pulled Halah past a sentry's nose, and all he did was say I was crazy to take my horse into the Ruins after nightfall.

Svanhild and I waited a few minutes for the flood of workers to slow to a rush, then pushed our way onto the Force Bridge. It was a long, arcing structure wide enough to allow three dray wagons to travel abreast. But a quarter of the way across, where it was undergoing repairs, it was encased in a skeleton of wooden scaffolds and narrowed to the width of a single donkey cart. Here, Svanhild and I mounted Halah and used her bulk to push our way through the flood of workers, and it was not long before we crested the top of the bridge.

Even with dusk falling, the sight ahead took my breath away. Before us loomed the rubble pile I had glimpsed upon entering the city, a veritable mountain of broken stone and splintered timbers. Here and there I saw the jagged remains of a tower, or a section of marble wall, or a thousand paces of straight furrow that had once been a street—but mostly, I saw a jumble of thousands upon thousands upon thousands of square-edged boulders.

"In the name of the One, what is it?"

Svanhild hung her chin over my shoulder. "The Ruins— what used to be Zhentil Keep."

"Then what is that?" I waved my arm at the city we had just left.

"That was the Foreign Quarter. General Vrakk and his orcs saved it from the giants when they destroyed the bridges. They were acting on the One's orders, of course."

"Of course." Mystra's spell compelled me to add nothing, for at the time I did not know this to be a lie.

As Halah descended the other side of the arched bridge, I noticed that a few blocks of the old city were being rebuilt near the river shore. The buildings all seemed fortresses unto themselves, with no doors or windows or portals of any kind on the first two floors. They could only be entered via a long set of wooden stairs that ascended three stories to a fortified drawbridge. This caused a shudder to run down my spine, for I could only imagine what creatures would warrant such precautions.

When we reached the bottom of the bridge, a spindly figure no taller than myself slipped out of the shadows and startled Halah. She reared, dumping Svanhild onto the muddy road behind us, then turned to lash the intruder with her hooves.

The spindly figure fell to his knees and covered his head. "In the Name of the One, don't kill me!" It was Durin, a brother of the temple. "And if you kill me, don't let your horse eat me!"

Halah set her hooves down without doing either.

"Where are the others?" Svanhild demanded, gathering herself up. "We were to gather here."

"Following the Great Annihilator," Durin whispered. He pointed into the shadows behind him. "Thir spotted him as she came down the bridge—and he was alone!"

Svanhild jerked Durin to his feet. "Then why are you still groveling? Show us the way!" She shoved him into the shadows, then raised her arm to me. "I can't believe our luck!"

I grabbed her hand and pulled her onto Halah's back. "Indeed, I cannot believe it either."

Forty-One

The Seraph of Death entered the heaven called Mechanus exactly where he intended, in the night sky over Everwatch Castle, the citadel of Helm the Vigilant. The fortress was a heaven unto itself, which made it larger than any kingdom in Faerûn. It consisted of five concentric wards of five sides each. Every few minutes, a great *clunk* would sound deep beneath the ground, then the entire realm would shudder and turn exactly one-fifth of a circle.

The innermost ward was larger than the entire City of Brilliance, which is very large indeed, and in the heart of this ward stood Helm's looming keep, Watchful Tower. The tower had five sides and rose five floors above any building in Everwatch. The uppermost story was ringed by an iron balcony and enclosed by walls of glass, and it was inside this glass room that Mystra's prison sat, with the Great Guardian standing watch outside on the iron balcony.

The Seraph of Death waited until Everwatch turned another fifth of a circle and carried Helm off to look in a different direction, then swooped down to within a halberd's length of the balcony rail. He hovered there, staring through the glass at Mystra's prison. It looked less like a black box than a square of emptiness, for that part of the chamber seemed not to exist at all—which was exactly the case.

A great *clunk* sounded below, and Watchful Tower turned another fifth of a circle.

Avner swung his shoulder satchel around to his belly.

Though the bag looked empty, it was filled with all kinds of equipment, including the items he had asked for from Kelemvor's Judgment Hall. The Seraph withdrew three silver hooks and hung them in a long line across the empty air. Then he reached into the pouch and grabbed a corner of the perfect mirror he had borrowed from Kelemvor's throne room. As he pulled, the mouth of the satchel kept expanding, and though the mirror was twice as wide as he was tall, he had no trouble withdrawing one whole end.

The gears clunked, and Watchful Tower turned again.

The Seraph of Death reached around behind the mirror and found a golden thread he had affixed to the back. He hung this line over the first silver hook, then he flew backward, pulling the mirror from the satchel and trailing the golden thread over the remaining two hooks. When he finished, the mirror hung securely in the empty air.

Watchful Tower turned again.

Avner flew around behind the mirror, then reached into his satchel and withdrew a small square of enchanted glass. He pressed this to the mirror's back, so he could see what occurred on the other side. Next, he removed a magic parchment and rolled it into a cone, then began gently flapping his wings to hover in place. He willed his breathing to slow and begged his heart to stop pounding so loudly and settled in to wait.

Avner had no wish to give up being the Seraph of Death—but Avner's wishes did not matter. Kelemvor had changed; no longer did he care for the plight of any mortal spirit. If Avner did not win Mystra's freedom and redeem himself with Mask, Lord Death would damn him to the same cruel punishment as that of any Faithless spirit.

Watchful Tower turned again, and Helm swung around to face the perfect mirror.

"Halt!"

In his surprise, Helm did not realize he was staring at his own reflection. The weary figure before him was a balding, long-faced warrior with shoulders drooping beneath the sadness of more than one world.

"Who goes there?" demanded Helm.

The seraph held the cone of parchment to his lips and spoke. "You know who." The words seemed to emerge from the mirror, for the lips in the glass moved with Avner's, and the voice sounded the same as Helm's. "If you cannot recognize me, it has been too long since you have raised your visor."

"What?" gasped the god.

The Vigilant One leaned across the railing and peered more closely at the figure. The armor matched his own, save that it was tarnished with age and battered with the dents of a thousand battles. The shield bore his sacred Gauntlet-and-Eye, and the sword hanging at the old man's side carried the same giant ruby in its pommel. Yet this knight did not hold himself square and proud, as did Helm; this knight let his shoulders sag and his back hunch, and he fixed his gaze on the ground at his feet, and he looked as lonely and dejected as any captive who had ever sat in Watchful Tower.

The gears of Mechanus clunked, and the tower swung away, carrying Helm off to look in a new direction.

The Vigilant One manifested a second avatar on the balcony, then realized he was gazing at his own reflection. He saw the rail in his hand, and the iron floor beneath his feet, and the glass walls at his back—but one thing he did not see, since Kelemvor had made the mirror to show matters as they truly were and Mystra's prison was made of nothing.

"This cannot be!"

The Vigilant One whirled around, then staggered back when he saw the black box still sitting behind the glass. He stared at it for a long time, then turned and stared at the reflection in the mirror for many moments more. The box appeared to be missing.

And during all these moments, Avner hovered behind the mirror worrying. He knew a god could create many avatars, but he had assumed Helm would simply walk along the balcony to stay before the mirror. Instead, the god had manifested a new avatar when the tower turned, and now the seraph had to deal with not one god, but two.

Everwatch Castle shuddered, and the gears clunked, and Watchful Tower turned again. Helm manifested a third avatar on the balcony. Avner stifled a groan; all he could do was wait.

The Vigilant One looked back into the mirror. The reflection of Mystra's prison remained absent.

"What spell is this?" Helm demanded.

"No spell—unless Mystra has escaped." Again, Avner spoke into the parchment cone, though now he found it difficult to feign a confident voice. "Only Mystra's magic could deceive you."

When Helm made no reply, Avner remained silent, allowing the Vigilant One to ponder the unpleasant choices: either Mystra had escaped and cast a spell to create the image in the mirror, or what Helm saw in the mirror was true.

He of the Unsleeping Eyes spent many moments contemplating how his own reflection could look so different. He saw that it might be an image of his true nature, for mortals and gods alike still bristled at him for obeying Ao's command during the Time of Troubles and confining his fellows to Faerûn.

And yet, the Vigilant One could not believe that he was the sad figure in the mirror. Like the mortals who venerated him, he took it on faith that those who performed their duty would always be rewarded. If this was not so for himself, how could he ask his worshipers to accept it for themselves?

On this account, Helm decided the image in the mirror was false. This comforted him; it meant he was still a proud guardian and Mystra still imprisoned in his tower—but then he remembered what such a deception implied. The Goddess of Magic could not be inside her prison, since only she could deceive him and she was cut off from the Weave by her prison's walls of nothingness. Yet how could she be anywhere else, since escape was impossible?

The gears of Mechanus sent a shudder through the castle. Watchful Tower turned once again, carrying Helm away from the mirror. He manifested a fourth avatar on the balcony. Then, while this one continued to watch the mirror, the other three passed through the glass walls and went over to Mystra's prison.

In a single voice, they called, "Lady Magic?"

Mystra made no answer. She had been listening to everything that had happened outside and, believing Kelemvor had come to rescue her, had no wish to help her jailer.

Avner reached into his satchel and withdrew a small shadow shaped like a bird, which was a memory he had asked of Kelemvor. He cupped it gently in his hands and puffed his breath upon it, causing the wings to rise and stretch.

"Mystra?" Helm's voice grew more cautious. Being much practiced in the art of jailing, he knew that a captive's silence could mean many things—and the least of these was that she had escaped. "Answer me, Lady Magic."

Avner opened his hands. The little shadow flew away and cried out the words that Kelemvor had once heard the goddess exclaim, after a pair of their heroes had destroyed a lich: "Goodbye and good riddance!"

At once, Helm manifested a fifth avatar in the empty air. He searched for the source of the goddess's voice, but the memory had vanished as soon as it fulfilled its purpose. The three avatars surrounding Mystra's prison drew their swords and prepared to look inside.

Avner prayed they would wait a few moments longer. The fourth avatar was still watching the mirror, and he knew better than to think he was quicker than a god.

The three avatars kneeled beside the box of black nothingness, each at a different side.

The gears of Mechanus clunked again, and Watchful Tower turned, carrying the fourth avatar away. Avner looked at the three avatars surrounding Mystra's prison, and he saw them lean forward to push their heads through the walls. He flew from his hiding place and was behind one of them in the blink of an eye. He angled toward the glass wall and crashed through, moving as swiftly as a stone falls from the heavens.

"This way, Mystra!" he shouted.

Before Avner finished his sentence, Helm's fourth avatar

rushed in from the balcony to intercept him. This did not matter. The seraph was still flying, and as the Vigilant One stepped in front of him, he lowered his head and crashed into the god.

Had Helm been standing with his sword firmly in hand and both feet braced on the floor, the seraph would certainly have bounced off his chest and perished beneath the god's gleaming blade. But the Vigilant One was still drawing his weapon and just turning to position himself. Avner's desperate attack unbalanced him and sent him crashing into another avatar.

This impact sent the unsuspecting avatar tumbling through the wall of nothingness, and Mystra saw at once what the mysterious voice outside had intended. She launched herself at the feet of the falling guardian, diving out of her prison through the same hole by which her captor was entering. The goddess saw Helm's fourth avatar looming above her, flying back at her from the force of the seraph's blow, and she thought she would be pushed back into the box of nothingness.

Then the avatar vanished, and she found herself lying on the floor next to the battered Seraph of Death. Mystra saw at once that she had escaped, for the instant Helm's avatar had fallen completely into the prison, the Vigilant One had lost all his godly powers and his avatars had disappeared. She leapt to her feet, knowing it would not be long before Tyr saw what had occurred and called upon Ao to free the Vigilant One. Before Avner could so much as moan, she dispatched eight avatars to Faerûn to answer the calls of her Faithful and undo the damage Talos had done to her church. She sent another aspect to visit Kelemvor in the City of the Dead, and only then did she kneel beside her broken rescuer.

"You have my gratitude, Avner." Mystra saw that when the seraph had struck Helm, he had snapped his neck and torn both of his wings and shattered one of his shoulders. As she spoke, she began to straighten all the breaks. "I shall tell your master of your bravery. Kelemvor will reward you well."

Avner shook his head. "No . . . Kelemvor is no longer . . . my master. Mask . . . sent me."

"Mask?" The goddess straightened Avner's neck, then enclosed it in her hands and allowed her healing magic to flow into him. "That cannot be. Mask has more reason than anyone to keep me imprisoned."

"Perhaps—but he did not expect me to succeed."

Now that his neck had been repaired, the seraph found it much easier to speak. As the goddess healed the rest of his injuries, he told her of how Kelemvor had decided to reassess all his judgments as God of Death, and Avner also explained how Mask had given him a chance to become the Seraph of Thieves by assigning him the impossible task of freeing her. When he finished, Mystra had healed all his wounds.

They stood, and the goddess said, "Avner, you should not be seraph to a low god like Mask. I shall intercede with Kelemvor, and you will remain the Seraph of Death."

Avner shook his head sadly. "I do not think so, Goddess. Lord Death has changed. The old Kelemvor is gone, and I fear even you cannot bring him back."

Forty-Two

Brother Durin led us through the shattered remnants of the old Harbor Ward Gate, then turned down a slippery river of mud that served as the main boulevard of the City Rebuilt. Dusk had fallen and plunged the borough into shadows as purple as the One's sacred vestments. The last of the masons and day laborers had vanished across the bridge, and now only the denizens remained, peering down at us from the arrow loops and third-story drawbridges of their fortress homes. The street stank of seaweed and fish entrails and all the other things anyone saw fit to dump into it, and so deep was this slime that Halah's hooves made sucking sounds as she carried Svanhild and me forward.

About a third of the way through the City Rebuilt, which is to say no more than a hundred paces down the boulevard, someone hissed at Durin from the shadows. He turned down a narrow lane between two buildings and vanished into the darkness. As I guided Halah after him, I thought of the burly guards who had perished in the alley where we had hidden earlier, and a shudder ran down my spine. *They* had died within the "civilized" confines of the walled city. Here in the Ruins, I doubted that even the One knew what might be lurking around any corner.

In this alley, the lurker happened to be Armod, a brother of the temple almost as gaunt and filth-covered as Durin. Armod led us through a maze of lanes so black I could scarcely see my hand before my face, and the whole time I kept thinking what a splendid place this was for an ambush. Yet nothing happened except that I felt many eyes watching us from above, and once a stray dog barked from a muddy alcove. Here Svanhild and I had to dismount and stand in the quagmire as Halah tried to make a snack of the dog, but her neck was not long enough to reach the back of his den, and after a few minutes we were allowed to remount.

We emerged from this maze of alleys to find Sister Kelda waiting behind the jagged vestiges of the Harbor Ward wall. She took Armod's place as guide and led us forward, and the gloomy citadels of the City Rebuilt were replaced by shadowy piles of rubble. The sound of Halah's hooves changed from a regular slurp to an unpredictable clatter, and the light of the full moon shone down to pave our way in glimmering silver.

The stench of the Harbor Ward vanished, and Svanhild grew less tense behind me. She leaned forward and brought her lips close to my ear.

"Why did you come to Zhentil Keep?" she whispered. "You must know the *Cyrinishad* is gone. We spent an entire year sending letters to important True Believers."

"You didn't send one to me," I retorted. "But I do know of the letter you sent my Caliph."

"So, why *are* you here?"

I held my tongue, for I had no wish to blurt out the truth to this woman. Fzoul might have stayed in his tower all day, watching and wondering when we would arrive—or someone might have told him we were coming at dusk, and that someone could be Svanhild as easily as any other of Zhentil Keep's acolytes.

"Well?" Svanhild pressed.

I craned my neck over my shoulder. "You ask too many questions, Sister."

Svanhild jerked back as though I had struck her, yet her arms stayed tight around my waist—the better to hold me when Fzoul sprang his trap, I supposed.

I furtively scanned the shadows, until it came to me I had little to fear from an ambush. With Tyr's protection to keep me whole and a mount such as Halah to insure my escape, no assault would harm me or my quest. Thus assured, I did a foolish thing: I leaned down to pat my faithful horse on the neck.

Halah swung her head around and bared her sharp teeth, and I barely had time to move my leg before her jaws snapped together.

Svanhild leaned forward. "What's wrong with her?"

"She is angry because the dog escaped." Mystra's spell compelled me to add, "Or maybe because I took her bone away."

"Who is the master?" Svanhild snorted. "You or Halah?"

"Who do you think? As I said, Cyric made her."

Kelda turned down a broad, rocky furrow that had once been a street. About fifty paces ahead, the path ended beneath a high, unbroken wall. There we found the rest of the acolytes. They were waiting in the mouth of a steep-sided trench where someone, or perhaps something, had tunneled through the rubble to create a narrow passage.

One of the brothers pointed down the channel. "The Annihilator went there. Thir is still—"

"Hurry!" Thir's voice sounded muffled and distant as it rolled out of the trench. "He's trying to escape!"

Kelda and the others rushed into the trench at once, but I held Halah in check and let them clatter through the dark alone.

"Go!" Svanhild commanded, kicking at Halah's flanks.

A snarl like a lion's rumbled up from the mare's throat, and she took a tentative step forward. I jerked the reins to stop her, and she in turn kicked up her rear legs, nearly dislodging Sister Svanhild.

"Malik! What are you doing?" Svanhild clutched my waist to keep from falling. "I thought you wanted to catch Fzoul!"

"As I said, you ask too many questions." Mystra's spell compelled me to add, "I did not get this far by being stupid. I see the ambush you are planning."

"Ambush?" Truly, she sounded surprised, and I realized how practiced she was at lying.

A loud crack echoed out of the narrow trench, then a silver flash bounced off its steep walls. Someone screamed in agony.

"See?" I exclaimed. "I am no fool!"

The acolytes cried out as one. A soft roar crackled out of the trench, then an orange glow lit the stones in its depths.

Svanhild took one arm from my waist, and something sharp pricked my back. "You wanted to find the Annihilator, and we have found him. Now ride!"

"Stupid woman—do you think I fear your knife?" Despite my words, I had nudged Halah into the trench, for I still meant to track Fzoul to his home. "You saw the quarrels bounce off my back when I entered Zhentil Keep. I am protected by Tyr himself!"

"Tyr?" Svanhild shoved her dagger forward, but the blade tangled in my robe and scraped past my ribs and did not inflict even a scratch. She spat on my neck. "Traitor! Tyr-loving spy!"

"Me?" I paid no attention to her attempt to kill me. "You are the betrayer!"

As all this happened, we rode half the length of the trench. I could have leaned out and touched the stones to either side, and the walls loomed so high above us they blocked the moonlight. Halah raised a terrible clatter as she stumbled through the darkness—but this hardly mattered, for a mighty roaring and a horrid screaming suddenly arose from the far end of the channel.

I looked up to see an imposing, long-haired figure twenty paces down the trench, trapped against a half-buried wall. A low curtain of fire burned between him and the handful of his attackers still standing; the rest of the One's acolytes lay rolling on the ground, screaming in agony and beating at the flames on their bodies.

My throat grew dry at the prowess of my quarry, but I had no time for wonderment. Svanhild pushed herself from Halah's rump and dropped to the rubble behind us.

She fell to her knees and raised her arms to the heavens. "O Cyric, god of gods, One and All, hear this, the prayer of your servant, Svanhild of Zhentil Keep."

"No!" I jerked Halah's reins around, but the trench was too narrow and rocky for her to turn quickly.

"Mighty One," continued Svanhild, "you have placed your trust—"

I pulled so hard on Halah's reins she reared and turned. Her front hooves struck the trench wall and caused a clattering rubble slide.

Svanhild shouted, "—in a traitor!"

"Lying trollop!" I drew my dagger and flung myself off Halah's back.

Before my feet touched ground, a silver flash sizzled down from the channel rim and struck Svanhild full on the brow. Her head vanished in a spray of blinding fire and bone, and I came down upon the headless corpse and drove it down into the bottom of the trench. For a time, I lay on top of the gruesome thing, too stunned to move and trying to blink the sight back into my eyes, gagging on the harsh fumes that rose from the place where Svanhild's face should have been.

"I trust she is dead." The words were so deep and resonant I mistook them for the One's, until I realized the man was speaking in a single voice instead of a thousand. "We cannot have her calling the Mad God, can we?"

I rolled off Svanhild's body and looked up. The speaker stood at the crest of the trench wall, high overhead, silhouetted against the pale night sky. With long, flowing hair and a high-collared cape stretched over a pair of broad shoulders, he looked eerily similar to the figure trapped at the end of the channel.

The man stared into the trench and lifted his arms high. "Rise up!" I thought he was calling to me, until he added, "Awaken, my children!"

A tremendous clatter arose along the entire length of the passage. Halah let out a startled whinny and at last wrenched herself around to face me. Behind her, the orange glow at the end of the trench had vanished, and now the rubble beside her began to churn. Halah bared her teeth and backed away.

"No, Halah! Come this way!"

Halah continued to retreat, then heard the stones behind her also stirring and stopped in her tracks. I stepped forward to grab her reins, but a pair of long arms suddenly shot out of the rubble between us. In the darkness, they looked like the branches of a gnarled myrrh tree, and I could see well enough to tell that one of these limbs ended in a deformed claw.

"Halah, come to me!"

The mare raised her head at my tone, then growled.

A head emerged from the rubble to join the arms that separated us. By the light of its burning red eyes, I perceived it to be the face of a corpse, long dead, with shriveled gray skin still clinging to its skull. The creature looked toward me and began to dig itself out of the rubble.

Of course the thing was not alone. The clatter of shifting stones continued to build along the length of the trench, and I glanced around to see dozens of pairs of red eyes emerging from beneath the rubble. I uttered a curse on Svanhild's soul, then looked back toward my mare, my only means of escape.

"Halah, now!"

Halah fixed a dark eye on my face, then snarled and sprang forward. The corpse between us lashed out and caught her foreleg with its twisted claw. She bit the arm off in midstride and stopped beside me with the gruesome thing still clamped between her teeth. I thanked the One for her loyalty and started to step around to mount her.

She reared up and planted her hoof in my chest and pushed me straight to the ground.

"Halah!" I glanced along the trench and saw a dozen red-eyed silhouettes shambling toward us. "Let me up! What are you doing?"

Halah growled and brought her face down close to mine. She rolled the corpse's filthy arm between her teeth and made a low, menacing nicker.

"Halah?"

The first corpse shambled closer, lacking the arm my horse had bitten off. It stooped down and grasped my ankle with its remaining hand. Halah allowed this, and I recalled the threat I had made before we crossed the bridge.

"Halah, I am sorry I interrupted your meal, but we had to leave the city." A second corpse came up, and she permitted this one to grasp my arm. "And I would never ask the One to turn you back into a nag. You know this."

Halah snorted in my face, just as she had done when I seized her bone, then took her foot off my chest and trotted on.

"Halah?"

I tried to rise, but the two corpses pushed me down. I grabbed a stone and smashed the skull of one, but this did not even loosen the thing's grasp. A third cadaver grabbed the rock and pinned my weapon hand to the ground.

"Halah!"

Her only reply was a mocking snort, now painfully distant. I kicked and rolled and tried to squirm free. Every time I moved a body part, another corpse arrived to pin it down. Within moments, I lay buried beneath a pile of rotting and writhing flesh, and my own limbs became more twisted and bent than Our Dark Lord's mind.

I cursed the One a thousand different ways. I called him a buffoon and an oaf, a fraud and a cheat and a miser, a maker of empty promises and a squanderer of borrowed wealth, a murderer and a liar and a thief, and a hundred names twice as scornful. Nor did I repent; I could think only of the great sacrifices I had made for the love of Cyric, and of how it would all come to naught because he had given me a horse so fickle she would betray me over a bone!

That the One did not strike me dead was but a testament to his limitless compassion, and perhaps to Tyr's protection. By the time I heard someone more graceful than a corpse skulking about near my head, my blasphemous fury had cooled. I fell silent, listening hopefully as this person stopped beside the pile and moved the limbs of a few cadavers away from my face, and then I saw my betrayer.

"Thir!"

She had changed the hemp robe of the One's temple for a silken cloak with a plunging bodice. Around her neck she wore a silver amulet shaped like a human hand, with a pair of emerald eyes staring out from the palm—the holy symbol of Iyachtu Xvim. Her face still bore the welts where I had slapped her.

"How nice to see you, Malik. It's a wonder the Banedead did not kill you." She smiled sweetly, then spit in my face. When I proved too helpless to wipe her spittle from my eyes, she turned away and added, "He seems harmless enough now, Tyrannar."

A pair of heavy boots crunched across the rubble, and then the imposing figure I had seen silhouetted against the sky peered down at me. He had a princely face with a square jaw and a drooping red mustache, and his pale eyes were as cold and cruel as the heart slurping in my breast.

"I am Fzoul Chembryl." He took a cloth sack from his belt and kneeled down to pull it over my head. "I hear you have been looking for me."

Forty-Three

The City of the Dead was a jewel losing its glitter. Kelemvor stood in the highest pinnacle of the Crystal Spire and watched a gray tide washing across his realm. As the dreary wave spread, the glimmering window lamps winked out, the shining street lanterns went dull, the sparkling candles flickered and faded to black. Only an ashen gleam remained, cloaking the city like the pall of a coffin, illuminating every corner with a pale, shadowless glow. Lord Death was extinguishing the lights of his domain. From that moment forward, no flame would burn within its walls, no sun would shine upon its streets. In the City of the Dead, there would never again be brilliant light or velvet black, only countless shades of gray.

"Kelemvor, I do not think much of these changes." As Mystra spoke these words, she appeared in the pinnacle beside Lord Death. "I hope you will forgive me for saying so."

"There is nothing to forgive." Kelemvor turned to face Mystra, revealing that he had changed more than his city. "I did not do it to please you."

Mystra gasped. She had seen at once that Kelemvor had changed his customary leather armor for a pearly cloak and charcoal hood, but that had not prepared her for what lay within the clothes. Her lover's rugged face had been replaced by the impassive visage of a silver death mask. His eyes had changed from emerald gems to drab gray orbs that lacked both pupils and irises, and his mane of wild black hair had grown as white and silky as spiderwebs. Even his brawny chest, now hidden beneath a tattered breastplate of scale mail, seemed sunken and hollow.

Kelemvor waved a hand over his new figure. "This appearance is more in keeping with my true nature."

Mystra raised her hand to her mouth and said nothing, as she could think of nothing gracious to say.

Kelemvor shrugged. "I see that Avner succeeded."

"Yes. Thank you for sending him."

"Mask sent him, not I."

"So Avner said." Mystra paused. "I wanted to speak with you about that. Avner does not deserve—"

"Avner is now the Seraph of Thieves. What's done is done, and you have no time to waste on things that cannot be changed." Kelemvor took Mystra's arm and guided the astounded goddess across the room. "The instant Helm is free, he will look for you here. Perhaps you should see what you came to see, then leave. You have much to do before the trial."

Though stunned by the curtness of Kelemvor's words, Mystra nodded at their truth. "Yes, Talos has been making inroads—"

"Forget Talos, Mystra. Answer the charges!" They reached the other side of the pinnacle, and Lord Death's tone grew more calm. "If you do not, we are both doomed. Tyr has not separated our charges."

"Is that your only concern, Kelemvor?" Mystra jerked her arm free. "I had not thought you so selfish. Perhaps you *should* fetch Adon, and then I will leave."

"I cannot bring him to you." Kelemvor pointed through the crystal wall, down to a huge crowd of souls awaiting judgment outside his palace. "Adon stands in line."

"Line?" Mystra pressed her face to the crystal and peered into the shadowless gray light of the City of the Dead. Even to a goddess, the throng was too distant to discern a single soul. "You're making *Adon* stand in line?"

"Of course. He rejected you in life; that makes him one of the Faithless. Moreover, he begged me to steal your worshipers from the Fugue Plain, and that makes him one of the False."

"But Adon is insane!" Mystra whirled on Kelemvor. "You understand that better than anyone."

"I must hold even the insane responsible for their choices." Kelemvor stared down at the throng. His eyes could see individual souls no better than Mystra, but he knew which speck was Adon: the one at the end of the line. "If I do not punish the insane when they turn from their gods, then half of Faerûn will go mad. Too many mortals are too lazy to pay their gods the proper worship."

Mystra spun Kelemvor around and stared into his empty gray eyes. "Have you gone mad yourself? Who are you hiding behind that mask? Cyric? Tempus? Mask?" She backed away, raising her hands to blast the imposter with raw magic. "You cannot be Kelemvor. He would never say such things."

"This is the same Kelemvor to whom you, Mistress Ariel, paid a very special price on the way to Elminster's Tower."

Mystra did not lower her hands. Many people knew that Ariel had been her true name as a mortal, Cyric among them. And Cyric also knew that she had revealed it to Kelemvor during the Time of Troubles, as a sort of payment for accompanying her to Elminster's Tower. But there was one thing Cyric did not know about the arrangement.

"What was the price, Kelemvor?"

He answered at once. "Your love."

"It *is* you." Mystra lowered her hands, then waved an arm at the dreary city outside. "But why, Kelemvor?"

"Because I am the God of Death."

"But where is your pity? To condemn Adon—"

"Pity is for mortals, not the God of Death. Adon will be judged according to his words."

Mystra's jaw fell. She stared out over the drab city for a long time, and finally turned to Kelemvor. "Then I want you to return him to life for me."

"Return a madman to life? Who would that serve but Cyric?"

"Who is not your concern," Mystra replied. "It is enough that I ask."

"No. That Adon will speak against you is your concern, but he has already dared denounce me for being your lover. I will not have him undermining the belief of my own worshipers."

"I am begging you, Kelemvor." Mystra stepped closer to Lord Death and took his hands. "In the name of our love!"

Kelemvor shook his head. "Not even for you. I must fulfill my duties as a god—and I warn you to do the same, or it will be the Circle taking your powers, not Talos or Cyric."

Mystra jerked her hands away. "How dare you lecture me! I did not become a goddess to turn my back on those who—"

Jergal's shadow-filled cloak appeared between Mystra and Kelemvor. "Excuse me, Lord Death, but Helm demands an audience."

"Kelemvor, return Adon to life!" Mystra's words echoed out of the empty air, for no sooner had the seneschal spoken Helm's name than the goddess had vanished. "Return him to Faerûn, or our love is done!"

"Then it is done already," Kelemvor replied, though even he could not tell if Mystra heard him.

"What is done?" Helm appeared behind Jergal, in the very place Mystra had been standing the instant before. "And I warn you, do not try to hide—"

"Do not threaten me, Coldheart." Kelemvor stepped straight through Jergal's body, so that he stood nose to visor with Helm. "I am not hiding the goddess Mystra. You may search my realm if you wish, but if you ever threaten me again, it will take Ao himself to save you."

Helm stepped back and bowed his head. "A search will not be necessary, Lord Death. Your word is sufficient."

Then the Guardian vanished as quickly as he had appeared—and not only to pursue his prisoner. Something in Kelemvor's tone had suggested that he was eager for blood, and Helm had no wish to test his prowess against that of a new Lord Death.

Jergal drifted to Kelemvor's side, and a white glove fluttered up to point at a line of shiny black beads rolling down the god's cheek. "What are those?"

"Nothing." Kelemvor's voice was strained. "All that is left of my mortality, I suppose."

"Well, I hope you flush it out soon." The seneschal moved away, as though Kelemvor were diseased and about to cough on him. "It is the oddest thing I have ever seen a God of Death do."

"Then do not watch!"

It was Kelemvor himself who turned away, and neither he nor Jergal noticed that each teardrop vanished as it hit the floor.

Forty-Four

The Great Fzoul and his handmaiden Thir bound me in chains and dragged me stumbling and staggering through the Ruins. The hood covering my head blinded me, and the short chain between my ankles hobbled me, but my captors pushed and pulled and grumbled as though they did not understand why I could not shamble more quickly. After hours of this abuse, we reached smoother ground, then we descended some stairs into a rocky passage, and the smell of damp stone and burning pitch filled my nostrils.

Fzoul tore the sack off my head, revealing a vast chamber cut entirely from rough-hewn rock. A few torches danced in the sconces upon the walls, filling the air with a smoke so black and bitter that it summoned a flood of tears to my eyes. The center of the room was empty, save for Iyachtu Xvim's symbol painted on the floor and a black altar at the far end. Along one wall sat all manner of strange furnishings, but in the dim light I could not discern what they were for.

After making this quick inventory, I began in the nearest corner and carefully gazed around the room, searching for an iron box or polished chest or any other container that might hold the *True Life of Cyric*. The gloom hung so thickly that I saw only strange outlines and vague shapes.

Fzoul started toward the center of the chamber. I shuffled along beside him, cursing the tiresome shackles upon my ankles and the manacles that held my wrists in front of my belly.

"The temple of Iyachtu Xvim." Fzoul waved his arm around the gloomy chamber. "Not as grand as you're accustomed to in the Church of Cyric—but then we in Zhentil Keep have had to make do since the Mad One smashed our homes to dust."

"The Razing was your own fault." I was not afraid to say this, for I knew Tyr's protection would shield me from harm. "If Zhentil Keep had remained Faithful—"

"Silence, swine!" Thir pelted me between the shoulders. "I have heard enough of Cyric's filth to last me a lifetime."

"No, my dear." Fzoul reached behind my back and waved Thir off. "Let Malik speak. After all you have told me, I wish to hear what he has to say."

"I have nothing more to say, except that you are a guttersnipe and a traitor for reading the *True Life of Cyric* to your city." Here, I watched Fzoul for any clue to the book's location—or whether he still had it at all—but the only thing that flashed through his eyes was anger. I continued, "*You* betrayed the people of Zhentil Keep, not the One."

Fzoul's hand tightened on my arm, but he showed no other sign of his ire. "A pity you feel that way, Malik. I certainly bear you no ill will." Fzoul stopped on the symbol painted on the floor, and I had the unpleasant feeling that the green eyes in the palm were staring up at me. "In fact, I want to help you."

"Help me?"

Fzoul nodded. "I wish to teach you the truth about Cyric."

"Nothing could be more wonderful!" I could not contain myself, for I believed he was threatening to read to me from the *True Life*. "I am ready."

Fzoul creased his brow, surprised by my enthusiasm, then shook his head. "First, we must cleanse your mind." He glanced behind me to nod at Thir, then added to me, "The truth will be . . . better . . . once your thoughts are pure."

I felt a knife running down the length of my spine. The blade caused me no harm, of course, but it did terrible things to my clothes. A damp breeze brushed across a region of my body that rarely feels such things, then Thir jerked my tattered robe from my shoulders, leaving me as naked as the day I was born.

"I thought you were going to cleanse my mind!"

"We will, Malik." Thir said this. "We certainly will."

She came around to stand in front of me, and I lowered my hands to cover the most private part of my nakedness. Thir slapped me in the face and grabbed my manacle chain and jerked my wrists back to my belly.

"You have nothing to hide from us!"

"All you had to do was ask!" And indeed this was true, for I have always had every reason to be proud in that regard.

Thir raised her hand to strike me again, but Fzoul caught it and shook his head.

"Don't be too hard on him. Malik has yet to understand." The High Tyrannar draped a burly arm across my shoulders and guided me toward the wall. "Thir tells me you never feel pain, Malik."

"Never!" I was only hoping to avoid a senseless waste of time for us both, but Mystra's spell compelled me to add, "Not in the past few days, anyway."

"No?" Fzoul grabbed my manacles and jerked them back to my belly, as my modesty had allowed my hands to drift south. "Well, there are many ways to cleanse a man's thoughts."

Fzoul stopped five paces from the wall. Before us, in the flickering light of a torch, sat a trio of large and elaborate devices. The Great Annihilator gestured at the first. Four copper balls were suspended above a table equipped with more straps than I could count. A narrow glass tube ran from the bottom of each ball, joining together at a little spigot that hung directly over a wooden neck pillow.

"The Drip Torment." Fzoul waved Thir forward. "Show him."

Thir stepped into the circle of light and turned the spigot. A bead of water dribbled from the nozzle, landing just above the pillow. The next drop fell a moment or two later.

This did not seem much of a torment to me. Compared to the wonderful machines in the Caliph's dungeon, it looked relaxing.

Fzoul guided me to the next device, which was a tilted chair with many straps. Before the chair sat a small round table holding a dozen ceramic pots, each topped by a hinged cap with a high barb at the center. Thir cranked something under the table. The surface rotated a twelfth of a turn, and one of the ceramic pots swung around before the tilted chair. A little bar sticking out from the chair caught the barb on the cap and tipped it open. At once, the room smelled as though a skunk had raised its tail.

"The Torture of the Smells."

I could not help but smirk. During my time outside Candle-keep, I had eaten things that smelled worse.

Fzoul guided me to the next device, which was little more than a tarnished copper tub full of dark water.

"The Eel Bath." Here, Thir lagged behind, and Fzoul had to wave her toward the tub. "Demonstrate!"

Thir's face grew pale, but she rolled up her sleeve and thrust her arm into the water. Something splashed. A soft sizzle reverberated through the tub wall, then Thir's eyes rolled back in their sockets. Her teeth clacked together, and her chin tipped up, and she began to tremble and fell over backward. When her arm came free of the tank, something black and flat untwined itself from her forearm, then slid back into the tub.

Thir's eyes grew glassy and vacant. When she tried to roll to her knees, her quivering muscles would not support her, but she showed no sign of pain. In fact, she showed no sign that she felt anything at all.

Fzoul slapped me, then pointed at my hands, which I had allowed to drift south again. When I raised them, he nodded his approval. "We would put you completely in the tub, of course."

"Of course." Though I tried to sound nonchalant, my words were but a squeak.

The High Tyrannar fell silent and gave a thin smile, so that I might contemplate what he had shown me. I perceived that he meant to do more than 'teach me the truth about Cyric.' To destroy my belief in the One's power, he had only to bring out the *True Life of Cyric* and read, and the power of Oghma's words would do the rest. But Fzoul wanted more; he wanted me to beg for the 'truth,' as that would be a greater insult to the One and a boon to his own god, Iyachtu Xvim. And I was happy to do what he wished, as I knew the last laugh would be Cyric's, and that nothing in the *True Life*'s pages could ever turn me away from Our Dark Lord—not while the One's heart slurped in my chest, and my own heart beat in his.

"You are wasting your time with this cleansing," I said. "I am ready for you to read me the truth now."

Fzoul shook his head. "It is not enough that you hear the truth, you must embrace the truth."

The One's heart nearly leapt into my throat, for Fzoul had fallen prey to a simple merchant's trick. The High Tyrannar had made no objection to the suggestion that he would read his truth, which was as good as telling me he still had the *True Life of Cyric*. Now all I had to do was convince him to reveal its location, and I saw that sterner measures would be required.

"The truth is that Iyachtu Xvim is a petty little god unworthy of the One's notice!" My plan was to make Fzoul so angry that he would forget about my cleansing and pull out the *True Life* just to silence me. "When you die, Cyric will take your soul from your pitiful little god and torment it for a thousand years in the dungeons of the Shattered Keep!"

Fzoul's face turned red with rage, and his hand flashed up from his side, cuffing my head so hard the blow knocked me off my feet. I crashed down on Thir, who had just started to gather herself up, then I rolled over laughing.

"Strike me again!" I staggered to my feet and shuffled back to Fzoul. "No servant of piddling Xvim can harm me."

The High Tyrannar raised his arm, then caught himself and brushed the dirt off my naked shoulders. "Forgive my outburst. I am here to help you." He turned me toward the torture devices. "Which shall it be, Malik? The Drip? The Smells? The Eels?"

My mouth went dry. The choice was obvious, as the eels would take less time than any of the other tortures. Yet I could not take my eyes off Thir, who still seemed so dazed and confused that she could hardly struggle to her feet.

"I choose . . ."

I choked on the words, and my gaze swung toward the Drip Torment. After my long ride, it would be nice to spend a few hours lying on a table. I might close my eyes and sleep for days.

And why shouldn't I, after all I had done on the One's behalf? For years I had lived like a beggar in the cold and the rain, and I had jumped into a boiling moat and fought guardians who returned from the dead, and ridden day and night across the breadth of Faerûn. And what had the One done for me, except give me a vile betrayer for a horse and slay my wife and threaten me with damnation if I failed him?

But as I thought all these things, the awful despair I had felt outside Candlekeep returned. I recalled how I had awakened amidst the carnage of the Ebon Spur and rejected Cyric in my misery, and how he had come to make me feel the terror of dying Faithless and returned me to the Way of Belief, and how he had given me a chance to redeem my wretched soul and honored me by exchanging hearts, and I saw I really had no choice.

"Which shall it be, Malik?" Fzoul stepped toward the eel bath, a mocking smirk on his face. "The eels?"

I nodded quickly, before I had time to lose my courage.

Fzoul raised a brow. "Truly? The eels?"

"I shall think of Iyachtu." I tried to sound spiteful, but my voice cracked with fear. "Even his name is slimy as an eel."

Fzoul's mouth twitched, yet he answered in a calm voice. "Strange, I had picked you for a Drip man." He studied me and saw that I could not take my eyes off the eel tub. "And yet, you pick the most enfeebling of the tortures? Why?"

I made no answer, fearing Mystra's spell would compel me to admit the truth.

Fzoul remained silent a moment longer, then got a cunning look and shrugged as though resigned to my choice. "Very well—the Eel Bath."

Thir, still quivering from her own treatment, came over to help lift me into the tub.

Fzoul raised a hand to stop her. "Not yet. I have given Malik what he wants. Now he must give me something."

"I shall give you the sweat beneath my arms!" I spat. "That is all any worshiper of Iyachtu Xvim deserves."

Thir's knee shot toward my exposed groin, but she slipped in a puddle of water and crashed to the floor. Whether this was due to Tyr's protection or her own quivering muscles, I did not know.

Fzoul scowled, but he continued to look at me. "Come now, Malik. I am only asking you to tell me who sent you." The High Tyrannar stepped closer and spoke in a reassuring voice. "There is no harm in that. I know everything already."

"You do?" Cyric's curdled heart oozed up into my throat, then I realized that Fzoul was either lying or mistaken. No one knew about my plans for the *True Life of Cyric*. "Then why do I need to tell you?"

"You must confess yourself. It is the way to love the truth. Tell me who sent you, and I will let you sit in the Eel Bath."

"Let me?" This was less incentive than he thought. "And I will let you lick clean the soles of True Believers in the time beyond the Year of Carnage!"

"I see." Fzoul's face grew as ugly as an orc's. He grasped my arm. "What is it you fear more than a vat of lightning eels?"

The High Tyrannar jerked me away from the tank and stopped before the Torture of the Smells. He flipped up three lids, filling the room with a melange of scents too vile to breathe.

"Decay? Death? Offal?" He watched me for signs of fear and when I showed none, he shook his head. "I think not. Being a Cyricist, you are accustomed to these things."

"Because we smell them so often on the bodies of Iyachtu Xvim's dead Faithful!" And Mystra's spell compelled me to add, "I have never smelled this myself, but I have heard it is so."

Fzoul dragged me to the next device, then grabbed me by the manacles and swung me up on the table and laid me down so that my neck rested over the wooden pillow.

"Water?" By the way Fzoul growled this, I saw that my plan was working. He twisted the spigot, and a single drop of icy water fell on my lip and ran into my nostril. When I made no complaint, he shook his head. "Or is time your torment?"

"You are a dog and the worshiper of a dog!"

Fzoul smiled. "Thir said you wouldn't spend the night at the temple." He leaned over me. "Are you in a hurry, Malik? Did Cyric give you a deadline? Is he that eager to see me slain?"

I raised my head and spit in his face.

Fzoul slammed me back to the table and pinned me down with one hand, then motioned to Thir. "Help me strap this weasel down. I must go before I kill him!"

"You're leaving?" I tried to roll off the table. Fzoul grabbed my manacles and tugged me back into place, and I cried, "You are a coward, as is your god!"

"That is enough!" He reached under the table and grabbed a crusty rag and stuffed it between my lips. Before I could spit it out, Thir laid a strap across my mouth and pulled it tight. Fzoul sighed in relief. "Silence has never been so golden."

My next insult was a mere grunt, but it hardly mattered. The Great Annihilator was already as angry as a wounded lion.

Forty-Five

At daybreak, when the dreary sun brightened the gray sky above the dilapidated towers of Zhentil Keep, Ruha and her hippogriff stood waiting on the road outside. She knew better than to pound the gate, for every city in the Heartlands kept its portals closed between sunset and sunrise, and no amount of knocking would convince a sentry that the sun rose any earlier than he said it did.

The witch waited nearly an hour before a heavy thud sounded somewhere inside the gatehouse and the portal swung open. Two bleary-eyed guards stepped out to greet her, each as large as a bear and reeking of ale. Over their chain mail, they wore black tabards emblazoned with the gauntlet and gem symbol of Zhentil Keep, a sign the witch had learned to despise long before becoming a Harper. Although she made no effort to move forward, they crossed their halberds before her veiled face.

"State your name and business in Zhentil Keep," commanded the oldest. From behind him came the acrid smell of peat burning in fireplaces, and the gentle clamor of an awakening city. "And show your coin, so we'll know you can afford to pay your way."

A few beggars drifted out of the alleys beyond the guards, but they looked too healthy to be paupers. Ruha reached into her robe and withdrew a small purse, then jingled the contents.

"I am searching for a thief," she said, extracting two silver coins. "Perhaps you have seen him?"

Each guard snatched a coin, but they made no move to uncross their halberds.

"There are many thieves in Zhentil Keep," said the oldest.

"This one is a pudgy little man with the eyes of a bug. And if you have seen his horse, you will never forget it. His mare eats flesh and breathes black steam."

The guards looked at each other, then the oldest one held out his hand. "We might have seen him. What do you want him for?"

"He stole something of mine." Being a foolish woman who believed that money had no value beyond what it could buy, Ruha placed two more silver coins in the man's hand. "I would like to see that he is punished for it."

The guard accepted the coins with a smile. "If you want to punish him, you'll have to stand in line." He passed one coin to his companion, then raised his hand again. "Could be, I can put your worries to rest."

Now, any astute person would have put her purse away and told the buffoon he had already been paid enough to buy every thought in his skull. But, as the witch was spending the Harpers' money and not her own, she withdrew two more silver coins.

"I do not need to put my worries to rest." The witch dangled the coins over the guard's palm. "What I need is to find this thief. I believe he will be searching for Fzoul Chembryl."

The older guard scowled. "What are you, another of Cyric's stinking assassins?"

"Never." Ruha continued to hold out the coins. "But I must catch this thief before he finds Fzoul Chembryl."

"You're too late for that." The older guard snatched the coins from her hand, then added, "But don't worry—your thief won't be going anywhere. Whoever stole of yours, he'll be punished for it more than enough."

"All the same, I would like to see this for myself." Ruha reached into her purse yet again, this time drawing out two gold coins. "Can you arrange it?"

"For that, I'll carry you there on my back!" The guard raised his hand to accept the coins. "But you'll have to wait until I'm off duty—and you'd better not be a Cyric worshiper!"

Forty-Six

Another drop fell out of the darkness and splashed my lip. The drops came in four kinds. This one nettled. It rolled into my nose and made me want to sneeze. I snorted it out. I sneezed anyway. Eighty-six thousand four hundred and—

Another drop fell from the darkness. I never knew when they would come. This one burned. It rolled into my nose and scalded my tender nostril. I snorted it out. The burning continued, and I wished I could sneeze. Eighty-six—no, eighty-four thousand six hundred and four—or was it five?

I waited for another drop to fall. I never knew how quickly they would come. Sometimes they burned, sometimes they chilled, sometimes they never seemed to come. I had tried to time them by my heartbeats, but Cyric's heart did not really beat. It surged and oozed, with no more rhythm than a dancing Amnian. I wondered what my own heart would be like when I got it back. I wondered if I would still want—

Another drop splashed my lip. It rolled into my nose and soothed the inflamed membranes. I snorted it out. A man could drown one drop at a time. Eighty-four thousand and sixty-four.

Another drop splashed my lip. They did not come in any order. This one nettled. It rolled into my nose and made me want to sneeze. I snorted it out. I was counting drops to keep track of the time, to count the seconds, and the days, so I would know how much longer I had . . . Eight thousand sixty-four and . . . a hundred?

I screamed.

I nearly choked on the rag in my mouth; I understood why it was called a gag.

I waited for another drop to splash my lip. I tried to remember whether the count was eight thousand one hundred and sixty-four or eight thousand six hundred and four, or—

"Malik? Are you still here?" Fzoul's voice rolled out of the darkness, and I was nearly blinded by the flickering glow of a torch. The High Tyrannar laughed. "Of course, you're here! Where else would you be?"

Another drop splashed my lip. How much time had passed? This was a cold drop. It rolled into my nose and tickled my sinuses. I snorted it out. Had Cyric's trial started yet? One drop every two seconds would be thirty per minute, three hundred every ten minutes, nearly two thousand every hour. Eighty-six thousand four hundred and one—or was it two?

I opened my eyes and saw two blurry silhouettes above me. One of them turned the spigot. The other loosened the strap that held my gag in place. One last drop splashed my lip. It rolled into my nose, and I snorted it out and spit the cloth from my mouth.

"A thousand blessings on your children!"

Fzoul chuckled. "Thir, didn't I tell you the Drip Torment would soften his tongue?"

The High Tyrannar patted my face dry. He used a smooth cloth, so that he would not crack my chapped skin and make it bleed. I dismissed any thought of trying to anger him again, both on account of his great kindness and out of fear that he would turn on the spigot.

Fzoul wiped the table around my head until it was as dry as my face, then wrung the cloth and spread it gently over my private parts. Though I had hardly recalled that I was naked until that moment, this seemed a great kindness.

"Thank you."

Fzoul smiled. "You can thank me, Malik, by taking the first step. Tell me who sent you."

I said nothing; if I spoke at all, I would blurt out the whole truth, and then I would never save the One.

"Come now, Malik." Fzoul nodded to Thir, and she began to undo my straps. "I must make certain you are ready before I reveal the truth to you."

"Truly?" I gasped. "You will read the truth to me—and all I need do is tell you who sent me? No more?"

Fzoul's mustache straightened above a row of perfect white teeth, and the resulting expression looked less like a smile than a jackal's sneer. "That is all."

Thir finished removing the straps. I sat up, thankful for the luxury of the cloth that now covered my private parts. After Fzoul revealed the *True Life's* location, I had no idea how I would steal the book and escape, but this did not concern me as much as how I would trick the One into reading it. Still, if my long service to the One had taught me anything, it was the art of charging blindly ahead.

I nodded to Fzoul. "Very well. I will tell you who sent me, and no more." I repeated this for my own benefit, as I hoped it might prevent Mystra's spell from causing me to reveal more than I intended. "No one sent me. I came on my own."

"Liar!" Thir slapped me across the face, then pulled the cloth away from my lap. "You can't hide anything from us. I saw Cyric appear to you with my own eyes!"

I ignored her and faced Fzoul. "He told me to find the *Cyrinishad.* You do not have the *Cyrinishad.* I know this for a fact, so it makes no sense to try to find it here. I have told you the truth about who sent me, and now you must read the truth about the One."

"Malik, what are we going to do with you?" Fzoul grabbed my manacles and jerked me off the table, then dragged me toward the Eel Bath. "Do you think you can lie to me?"

"But I am not lying!" I saw in my mind Thir's vacant eyes and trembling muscles after she had thrust but one arm into the tank, and I thought of the agony I had suffered beneath the Drip Torment, and I screamed, "I can't lie!"

"Not very well."

Fzoul pitched me into the tank, and I splashed into the

warm water. Something large and slimy entwined my leg, and another eel slithered around my arm, then a very large one wrapped itself around my belly, and for an instant they reminded of an experience I once had in the Caliph's Baths.

Then I made an unpleasant discovery: one does not need to feel pain to *know* pain. Every muscle in my body tightened around my bones, which certainly would have snapped were it not for Tyr's protection. The rumble of my grinding teeth reverberated through my head, and I swear a thousand-and-one banshees were screaming in my ears. My mouth filled with the taste of almonds and my nose with the smell of burnt onions, and my eyes rolled so far back in their sockets that I saw the inside of my own skull.

Some uncertain time later, I began to shiver, though I did not feel cold. Slowly I came to realize that I was sprawled on a stone floor, though I had no idea why. Then my sight cleared, and I recognized Fzoul Chembryl looming before me in his full regalia of priestly robes. He was holding a wooden pole, and when I saw the metal hook at the end, still dripping slimy water, and noticed the tub beside me, I remembered all that had happened.

"The eels!"

"You have no one to blame but yourself, Malik." Fzoul squatted down to look me in the eye. "How can I ask Iyachtu Xvim to accept you when you refuse to cleanse yourself?"

"Accept me? You want me to . . ." I could hardly believe what I was hearing, for Iyachtu Xvim hated Cyric as ice hates fire. I tried to shake my head clear; all that happened was that I sloshed the water in my ears. "You want me to convert?"

"It's your choice, of course. But the alternative . . ." The High Tyrannar shook his head. "Let us just say it would be better for both of us if you converted."

In my weakness, I forgot my sacred mission. I recalled the many hardships a man can suffer on behalf of the One, and saw how I might escape them in the service of Iyachtu Xvim, and I remarked to myself that Iyachtu Xvim had never thrust a slimy mass of curd into my breast, nor demanded that I do the impossible, nor threatened me with eternal damnation if I failed. All Iyachtu Xvim had ever done was offer me the hope of eternal salvation.

I asked, "What would be involved in this converting?" Here, my chest grew cold and tight, but this only made me more determined. "And how soon could it happen?"

"As soon as you confess." Fzoul smiled. "The truth will be your salvation."

"The truth? I have already told you the truth!" I would have been glad to tell him some lie that he liked better, but Mystra's spell prevented it. "You threw me in the Eel Bath!"

"Yes. And now you must tell me why Cyric sent you here."

"But he did not send me! The One has read his own book, and now he is as mad as a jackal with the staggers! He thinks he is as great as Ao, and he expects all the other gods to bow to his will, and he demands that I give him the *Cyrinishad* to make this so!"

A crushing weight settled on my chest. I gasped and clutched my breast, and a chill spread through my limbs, and in my folly, I grew even more determined to convince Fzoul of my honesty.

I waved a hand over my soft body. "Look at me. I am no hero! I found the *Cyrinishad* once and I could not even pick it up, and yet the One threatens to abandon me to Kelemvor's judgment if I fail." I had to pause and gasp for breath, as now my chest felt as though a camel were standing on it. "Forgive me, O Geyser of Merc—er—Malice—er—*aaaiee!*"

Mystra's spell would not permit me to speak the proper words of fawning. I grabbed the hem of Fzoul's robe and kissed it frantically, but the High Tyrannar's eyes were narrow and dark.

The great man plucked me off the floor as though I were an empty sack and threw me back into the tank. The camel on my chest became as an elephant. The enormous eels entwined me, but I did not fall instantly unconscious as before; this time I felt them pull me under. I pushed my face back to the surface and gasped for breath before I sank down once more. I felt something sharp and hard against my wrists; then my eyes rolled back and I felt nothing more.

When I awoke, only seconds had passed, or so I assumed, for the High Tyrannar had just dumped my soggy body on the floor and was withdrawing the hook from the chain between my manacles. Cyric's heart still felt like an elephant standing on my chest. My muscles trembled and my ears rang and my mouth tasted of almonds, yet my vision was clearer than after the dunking before.

Fzoul prodded me with his hook. "You owe me a confession."

"I confess that you are a bag of gleet squeezed from the purulent sphincter that is the mouth of Iyachtu Xvim!" He would not listen to the truth; what choice did I have but to return to my earlier strategy? "In the time beyond the Year of Carnage, your god shall empty the chamber pots at the Palace of Eternity, and you shall clean the garderobes!"

The crushing weight on my chest vanished at once, and I saw how blind I had been to seek salvation from any god but Cyric. He was the god of my heart, and I had no fate but the fate he decreed. I could only thrive in the shadow of his radiance, or perish in the darkness of his decline!

How stupid I had been to think I could escape my destiny. I fell into a fit of giggles, for I felt as idiotic as the Caliph's own harlequin, and he had always made me laugh until it hurt.

Fzoul was not so amused. He reached down and grabbed me by the manacles and lifted me off the floor, and he glared into my eyes with a murderous look.

"Why are you trying to anger me?" His breath was hot against my face. "Has Cyric warped your mind so much you enjoy this?"

And with that, he hurled me back into the tank of eels.

At once I ceased to laugh. The slimy things entwined me, and again their hideous magic burned my every sinew. My ears rang and my muscles tightened around my bones and the grating of my teeth echoed through my skull, but I never fell unconscious. This was less of a blessing than it seemed, for aside from the uncontrollable tremor, I could not move my own limbs. The eels drew me under. In wide-eyed horror, I watched the bubbles trail up from my nose, and I lay submerged for minutes, craving air and paralyzed with shock. Yet every time my yearning for breath overwhelmed me and I opened my mouth to inhale, my head always bobbed to the surface; through the mercy of Tyr my lungs filled, and then I sank again into Fzoul Chembryl's special hell.

After the fourth or fifth time I surfaced, Fzoul snagged my manacles with his wooden hook and fished me out again, ever careful to avoid the tank himself. I managed to stagger to my feet, and as I wobbled back and forth I discovered two new visitors to this chamber of horror. One was the old guard who had cheated me out of two silver coins at the city gate. The other was a slender woman dressed in a dark robe and veil.

"Well met, Malik," she said. "You are a hard man to catch."

My hands, still trembling and manacled, strayed down to cover my private nakedness. "Leave me alone! This is none of your affair, Harper!"

"Harper?" Fzoul exclaimed. Thir gasped as well, then the High Tyrannar turned to the guard. "You brought a Harper to my temple?"

"She didn't say she was a Harper!" The guard grabbed Ruha's arms.

The witch did not resist, but only studied me over her veil. "Well, Malik—did you find what you were looking for?"

Thir raised a hand to slap the witch silent, but Fzoul caught her arm.

Ruha continued to stare at me. "Or were you too late?"

"Too late?" I gasped.

The witch nodded. "Cyric's trial ended yesterday."

Ruha was deceiving me—but how was I to know? I had been strapped to a table for eighty-six thousand drops and thrown into the Eel Bath so many times my teeth buzzed, and I did not have even the beat of my own heart to mark the time. I slumped to the floor and beat my head against the tank.

"If the trial has ended, then I am lost!" I did not even think to ask what the verdict had been. I thought only of my eighty-six thousand drops and my three eel baths and the folly of all my useless suffering, and I threw myself at the feet of Fzoul Chembryl. "I will tell you all—only torture me no more!"

The High Tyrannar smirked, then turned to the guard. "Perhaps you should leave now. I'll send Thir if I have further need of you. And you can leave the Harper."

The guard scowled at his dismissal, but passed Ruha over to Thir and left by the tunnel that served as the temple entrance. Only after his steps had echoed away did Fzoul turn back to me. "Your confession must be true and complete—"

"A blessing on your name!" I wanted to add that he was also the most merciful and wise of men, but I could not lie. "What do you wish to know?"

"The same thing I have always wanted to know. Who sent you, and why?"

I groaned.

"Who sent you, and why?" The High Tyrannar pulled me up by my manacles and brought his face close to mine. "You must tell me the truth, or I cannot help you."

"I came on my own." My reply was weak, for I knew the High Tyrannar would believe nothing except that Cyric had dispatched me to kill him. "No one sent me."

"Malik!" Fzoul shook me so hard I thought my chains would fall off. "I am growing weary of your games!"

"I ca-a-me to ste-e-eal the *True Life of Cyr-r-ric!*" I bleated. "I needed it to cure the One's madness—"

Fzoul's face turned as red as henna, then he snatched me up and raised me over the tank. "Have it your way!"

"Wait!" Ruha cried. For once, I did not object to the witch's meddling, as I knew from my experiences in Candlekeep that she had no stomach for torture. "Tormenting Malik will change nothing."

Fzoul spun toward her, holding me by the manacles and shackles. "What?"

If the High Tyrannar's angry tone caused Ruha any fear, it remained hidden behind her veil. "Malik is telling the truth. He wishes to use the *True Life* to cure Cyric's madness."

This was more than Fzoul could stand. "You too? Enough lies!"

In his fury, the High Tyrannar hurled me clear over the tank. I crashed into the wall upside down and dropped from a height greater than my own body. My head struck the floor with a terrific crack, then I felt a terrible jolt in my neck and crumpled into a heap of chains and naked flesh.

I had grown so accustomed to Tyr's protection that it hardly seemed remarkable to escape the fall without a broken neck or cracked skull. I merely rolled onto my hands and knees and turned to beg my tormenter's mercy—and that is when I realized that Ruha had deceived me. Cyric's trial could not have ended, or the God of Justice would no longer be shielding me from harm.

I looked toward the witch and found my view blocked by the massive figure of the High Tyrannar, who had turned his attention from me to Ruha. I rose and rattled forward to glare at the meddling Harper.

"You lying sow spawn!" If this realization seemed a long time in the coming, it was only because of all I had endured in Fzoul's temple; otherwise, I am always most astute. "You black-eyed deceiver—"

"No more of your insults!" Fzoul whirled on me and made a pinching gesture with his thumb and forefinger, at the same time uttering the name of Iyachtu Xvim. "I have heard enough!"

The High Tyrannar twisted his wrist as though ripping out my tongue, and when I tried to explain that my insults had been directed at Ruha and not at him, my voice did not work. Fzoul ran his hands through his long hair and looked from me to Ruha and back again, then shook his head in disgust. He took a chain of keys from around his neck and passed it to Thir.

"Go fetch the *True Life* from my chamber." The High Tyrannar took hold of Ruha's arm. "The offering won't be as sweet as I promised, but perhaps the New Darkness will forgive us if there is twice as much."

"Offering?" Ruha tried to pull free, but Fzoul's grasp was too tight. "What do you mean, offering?"

Fzoul snatched her up. "What do you think I mean?"

I barely heard the exchange, for my ears were filled with the sloshing of the curdled mass in my chest, and my eyes were fixed on Thir. *She was going after the book.* Instead of leaving by the same tunnel as the guard, Thir took a torch from the wall and started across the chamber. I longed to follow, but even if Fzoul did not stop me, my shackles made me anything but quick or stealthy.

Still, the shadow of a hope began to flicker in my chest.

Behind me, Ruha screamed as she splashed into the eel tank. I kept my gaze fixed on Thir. She stopped on the far side of the altar and placed her torch in an empty sconce, then took the keys and lifted them to the wall. A trapdoor swung down from the ceiling, and she reached up to withdraw a sliding ladder.

"You've seen enough, Malik." Fzoul hooked my throat with his wooden pole and jerked me toward the copper tank. "Or would you care to join the Harper in a bath?"

I opened my mouth to assure him I did not, but no sound came out, for he had stolen my voice. I merely shook my head.

Fzoul laughed. He returned his attention to the eel tank's frothing water and used his wooden hook to fish out Ruha's head. Her veil had come off, but she did not look pretty. She had bitten her tongue, and her teeth were bloody and clenched, and her eyes had rolled up so that only the whites remained showing. And yet to me this was a beautiful sight, for the witch had fallen unconscious, just as I had the first time in the tank. My shadow of hope began to grow.

Fzoul pushed Ruha back into the tank and watched her thrash about. I waited. Cyric's heart sloshed madly, as if it sensed the clever treachery I had in mind.

By the time Thir returned to her master's side bearing a large leatherbound book, Fzoul was done with his fun. He hooked Ruha under the arm and backed away from the tank, dragging the unconscious witch half out of the water.

I ducked under the pole and thrust my hands into the water. At once, two eels slithered around my wrists. A terrible jolt shot up my arms, and my fingers dug into the creature's slimy flesh. My elbows locked, and my teeth clacked together, and the taste of almonds filled my mouth—but I did not fall unconscious.

"Malik!" Fzoul yelled. "What are you doing?"

I pulled my arms out of the tank, still clutching the eels in my hands. I swung first at Thir, and the slimy things caught her square in the face. The torch and the book slipped from her hands, along with Fzoul's keys, and her mouth opened as if to scream—yet no sound came. Thir's knees buckled beneath her, and before she hit the floor, I pivoted toward Fzoul.

The High Tyrannar dropped his pole, leaving Ruha draped over the edge of the tub. My arms kept swinging, bringing the eels against his flank. He went rigid and crashed to the floor and smashed his nose, spraying blood across the stones. I shook my manacles over his body until the eels slipped free and entwined themselves around his limbs.

Thir began to groan and struggle toward her knees. I thrust my hands back into the tank and caught another pair of eels, then shook them loose on her body. She fell silent at once. I had no idea how long the eels might live out of water, but I did know from my own experience that even a short jolt would leave Fzoul and Thir too shocked to move for several minutes.

I turned to find the witch still draped over the tub. By her quivering, I knew that at least one eel remained twined about her legs in the water. After all the trouble she had caused me, I should have pushed her back and left her to drown, but we have a saying in Calimshan: "The enemy of my enemy is my friend."

I decided to leave Ruha in the tank, confident that when Fzoul and Thir awoke and found me gone, they would torture the witch in ways even more horrid than those I had known.

I snatched the book up from beside Thir's dancing limbs. It was a huge gathering of pages bound in black leather, with dozens of dark suns and grinning death's-heads surrounding a

337

sacred starburst-and-skull. The adornments seemed strange
for a tome of Oghma's, but Rinda had written in her journal
that the decorations had been necessary so Fzoul could sneak
the foul volume past Cyric's priests. Still, I had a knack for
stealing the wrong book, and so I opened the cover to make
certain this was the one.

As I had hoped, the first pages were blank. Being an unskilled storyteller who did not know how to stretch a simple
sentence into three or four paragraphs, Oghma had written a
version of the One's life as short as it was false; to make the
True Life look as similar to the *Cyrinishad* as possible, Rinda
had filled the first part with blank pages.

In my hands, I was holding the object of my sacred pilgrimage, the relic for which I had endured so much: the *True Life of
Cyric!*

Forty-Seven

I could have called Cyric down at once, right there before the altar and symbol of Iyachtu Xvim, and attempted to cure the One's madness on the spot. But such an insult to the temple's proprietor would not go unnoticed. The Godson of Bane despised Our Dark Lord, and while Xvim's powers were paltry in comparison, a god is a god, and an angry god is worse. I did not need this complication, for even in the best of circumstances, it would be a delicate matter to trick the One into reading Oghma's book.

I snatched Fzoul's keys off the floor and removed my manacles and shackles, but I did not steal any clothes to cover my nakedness, as I had no wish to tangle with the eels twined around my enemies. Leaving Ruha to splash in the copper tank and Fzoul and Thir to thrash about on the floor, I extinguished all the torches in the room, save one that I kept to light my own way, and turned toward the passage by which the witch's guard had left the temple.

No sooner had I started down the tunnel than I heard a distant chanting and the sound of many footsteps coming my way. Now, while Xvim's followers were all fools in their Faith, most were cunning enough to stop a naked man carrying a book such as the *True Life*. I retreated at once to the ladder Thir had pulled from the ceiling, then climbed into the rocky tunnel that led to the High Tyrannar's private room.

This was no easy thing. I had to cradle the *True Life* in the crooks of my elbows and hold the rungs with one hand and the torch with the other. More than once I slipped and had to hook my arm around the ladder, bringing the torch so close that its flame singed the hair off one side of my head. Only Tyr's protection spared my face a terrible scorching. I soon reached the top of the shaft and thrust my head up into a dark, musty-smelling room.

My flickering torch revealed a chamber of stone walls and rough-hewn floor planks, with a bed and a desk and some other furnishings lurking in the shadows. The only sound was the sputtering of my torch, and the room had the leaden chill of a place that never sees light. I laid the *True Life* aside and clambered onto the floor, then rose to seek a door.

To my dismay, I did not see one. While an old doorway lay just beyond the desk, the opening had been bricked over. I stared back down the ladder, thinking I might simply jump and take my chances in the other passage, but there was still the problem of the temple guards.

Then Fzoul began to groan softly in the chamber below. Whether the eels had slithered away or died for lack of water, it was too late to go back. I shut the trapdoor and secured it with a drawbar. Then, without a thought to my own nakedness—are we not all naked before the gods?—I opened my mouth and exclaimed, *"Cyric, the One, the All!"*

Not a sound greeted my ear.

The next thing I mouthed was just as silent, though much more profane. I had forgotten the spell Fzoul had cast to silence my tongue. The heart in my chest dropped. How could I call the One if I had no voice?

I fell to my knees and clasped my hands before me. Surely, Cyric would hear my silent prayer—he was, after all, a god!

Cyric, Prince of Murder, Lord of Strife!

Nothing happened, except that Fzoul's groans grew louder. A tide of anger rose up inside my chest. By what right had the Fates taken notice and turned their favor against me, a helpless mortal who was but a flea in the affairs of the gods?

I began to clank around the room, searching for some means with which to signal the One. I discovered a chest of clothes, but I hardly bothered to rifle through them. Even if the garments had not been too large, I had no time for niceties!

Fzoul groaned again, then the witch moaned too. This gave me some hope; when Fzoul came to his senses, she would occupy him for at least a moment or two.

I shuffled toward the writing desk and found a quill and an inkwell beside a sheaf of parchment. Atop the parchment lay a dagger with an ebony hilt fashioned into Iyachtu Xvim's sacred palm-and-eyes symbol. I pushed the disgusting talisman aside and thrust my torch into a wall sconce, then dipped the quill in the inkwell and scrawled a note upon the clean parchment: *Cyric, the One, the All!*

Fzoul's voice rumbled up through the trapdoor, calling for Thir and vowing vengeance upon me. Ruha responded with something groggy, and Thir began to moan as well.

I scanned the room's dark corners for the ghoulish figure of the One and saw nothing but murk and gloom. I would have written his name in my own blood if that were possible, but thanks to Tyr I no longer bled. I dipped the quill back into the ink and wrote, *Cyric, Highest of the High*—another dip, *Lord of Three Crowns!* At the same time, I let these words echo through my head, shouting them the only way I could.

The chamber remained as empty as before, and Cyric's heart filled my chest with cold burning.

Fzoul and Ruha began to yell; I could not comprehend what they were shouting, but several thuds and sharp slaps vibrated up through the trapdoor.

I felt a terrible sinking, but I could not believe Destiny would drive me this far only to abandon me now. I grabbed the torch and rounded the fringe of the room, searching for some small passage that I might have overlooked. If I could escape, I would seek shelter in the Ruins until the High Tyrannar's spell wore off, and then I would call upon the One until my voice grew hoarse from screaming.

The only exit was the bricked-over door behind the desk. One glance at the ceiling dispelled any thought of leaving that way; the rafters were sagging beneath some great weight. My chest burned as though I had been drinking vinegar.

Ruha cried out and abruptly fell silent, then the High Tyrannar began to chant in a mystic tongue. He had the witch under control, and now he was preparing to find me. I returned to the desk and snatched up the dagger to defend myself.

The instant my hand gripped that vile hilt, I knew how to capture the One's attention. I thrust the torch back into its sconce, then pressed the dagger's ebony hilt directly over the One's heart.

The curdled mass twisted into a knot of cold, searing anguish as terrible as it was unworldly. A wave of bile bubbled up to scald my throat, as though the mere touch of Xvim's holy symbol had burst the One's putrid heart. I thought my breast would explode. I collapsed backward onto the desk, and it was all I could do to keep the dagger hilt pressed to my chest.

"Malik!" cried the One's thousand voices. "What are you doing?"

Before I could lift my head, Cyric grabbed my neck and jerked me off the desk. He held me up before his skull's face and fixed those black burning suns on my naked chest, and only then did I realize I was still holding Iyachtu Xvim's holy symbol over his heart. I opened my hands and let the dagger drop to the floor, and the pain in my chest faded at once.

"Well, Malik? Have you betrayed me?" He stepped on the ebony hilt and ground it to dust beneath his bony heel, and this caused such a rumble that I heard Fzoul cry out in astonishment. "You have but to deny it—I know you cannot lie."

No! I mouthed the word, but no sound came out.

"Then you cannot deny it?" Cyric's grasp tightened, and only Tyr's protection kept my head joined to my shoulders. "Even you, Malik? First Tempus betrays me, then Talos and Shar, and Tyr next, and now you? Faithless cur!"

The One flung me at the bookshelf, which splintered beneath the impact of my pulpy body. I tumbled to the floor amidst a cascade of tomes, then looked up to see Cyric stomping across the room. With every step, the chamber trembled, and a stream of dust sifted down from the ceiling.

"You think the verdict will go against me?" Cyric kicked Fzoul's bed aside and gave me no chance to shake my head. "You think Iyachtu Xvim will come for you on the Fugue Plain? How can you be such a fool, Malik?"

A beam cracked over his head, but Cyric did not appear to notice. "When the Harlot escaped Helm's prison, she sealed her own doom—and the Usurper's too!" He raised his skeleton's claw and curled his bony fingers. "Without Mystra's lies ringing through the Pavilion, I have the Circle in my grasp. They will bow down before me. They will kiss my feet, they will beg my mercy. . . ."

These words filled me with the same hollow sickness as the first time I heard Cyric speak them. His vision was born of his madness, for even I knew the gods would level Faerûn before they bowed down before the One. I gathered myself up and crawled across the floor, trying to reach the *True Life*, which I had left lying just beyond the trapdoor.

Cyric snatched me up and shook me as a mongoose shakes a snake. "You will rue the day you betrayed me, Malik!"

The One hurled me against the wall, and a mighty rumble shook the chamber and another loud crack sounded from the ceiling planks, and a steady trickle of splinters and dust showered down on my head.

"Do you think I fear this trial? I welcome it! The day is at hand when I will stand at Ao's side, and all the others will look to us as brothers!"

I gathered myself up and lunged for the *True Life*.

Cyric caught my ankle and jerked me to a halt. My face slammed into the floor, but my devotion to the One was too great to let him stop me now. I thrust out my hands and caught the corner of the book and pulled it into my grasp. As the One and All dragged me back across the planks, I flipped the cover open and began to leaf through the blank pages. Rinda had written that once a person saw the first word, he could not stop reading until he had perused the entire chronicle; if I could but whirl around and thrust the first page into the One's face, Oghma's foul words would do the rest.

As soon as Cyric saw the book, he stopped pulling. "What have we here?"

The tome lay about a third open, and the parchment was still blank. The One snatched it from my hands and closed the cover, scrutinizing the black suns and the death's-heads embossed around the sacred starburst-and-skull. He turned the book over to inspect the back, and his putrid heart filled my ears with such a nervous swishing I hardly heard him ask, "Malik, what is this?"

Of course, I could not answer. Instead, I sat up and reached for the book, intending to open it to Oghma's history. Vile as it was, I had to make the One read the account before the trial.

Cyric jerked the book away. "Is this the book you came for?"

Fearing that Mystra's magic would dispel Fzoul's and cause me to blurt out the entire truth, I did not even nod.

"You say nothing," said Cyric, "just as when you left on your quest."

The black orbs beneath the One's brows flared, and he stumbled back against the wall and sat down amidst the fragments of the shattered bookcase. Dust and pebbles rained down from the splintered ceiling, and the sagging joists complained with an ominous creaking, but he did not care. And why should he? Such things mattered less to him than to a mortal such as me.

"It bears no resemblance to the *Cyrinishad*, but how could it be otherwise? Oghma's magic would prevent . . ." Cyric let the thought trail off, then looked at me. "Malik, do you remain loyal to me?"

I nodded eagerly, for this was as true as ever.

The One let his bony jaw sag in a gruesome farce of a smile, then opened the book to the first page. "Blank!"

A great knot formed in my stomach, and I prayed to Tymora he would flip to the pages in back.

Instead, Cyric turned to the next sheet of parchment, and then the next, a single page at a time. "All blank—but how else would it look to me? Oghma's magic still works. If I could read the book, I would know that I held it in my hand." He turned the tome on edge and shook out the grit that had fallen into it from the ceiling. "You have assured my verdict, Malik! When you read this at the trial, even Oghma will bow to my brilliance!"

At the trial? I had to cure the One's madness before the trial or he would only anger his fellow gods and ensure that the verdict went against him. I shook my head and shouted a silent *No!*

Cyric closed the tome with great tenderness. "And we must do something about your voice. The trial begins in an hour."

I pounded on the floor and spread my hands as though they were an open book, then gazed at the One imploringly.

"We have no time for that now." Cyric rose and extended his skeletal hand. "Come along, Malik. I will let you bask in my shadow."

Forty-Eight

Mystra appeared in the temple of Iyachtu Xvim and found
Ruha lying spread-eagled upon the black altar, her limbs
stretched over the edges by four taut ropes. Over the witch
stood Fzoul Chembryl, wearing a twisted mask called the
Cowl of Hatred and waving a thin-bladed skinning knife. He
was droning a deep-throated dirge, and his Faithful were
singing chorus and dancing slowly around the ebony hand on
the floor. In the midst of their circle writhed a pillar of shadow
with flashing green eyes and a halo of mordant black smoke.

All this Mystra saw in the blink of an eye, and at once she
stood at Fzoul's side, towering high above his head. He cried
out and whirled on her, his weapon raised to strike.

Moving faster than any mortal eye could follow, Mystra
caught the High Tyrannar by the forearm and lifted him off
the ground. "Do not dare!"

Fzoul's mouth gaped open. The chorus fell silent and left
their pillar of shadow to writhe alone. Mystra plucked the knife
from the High Tyrannar's grasp, then closed it in her huge fist;
the dagger melted and dribbled onto the floor.

"This would not be a good time to make me angry. I am in a
hurry."

The green-eyed shadow guttered like a flame, then hissed,
"As you should be, Weave Hag! Leave my temple, now!"

"Or what?" Mystra turned her gaze on Xvim.

The pillar shrank, but the voice remained harsh. "Or I'll
fetch Helm."

"Soon enough, Iyachtu." Without taking her eyes off Xvim's nebulous avatar, Mystra flicked Fzoul Chembryl aside. "Until then, be silent—or I will embarrass you in front of your worshipers."

Iyachtu's acolytes gasped at this sacrilege and backed away, for they feared that a battle between gods was about to erupt. But the New Darkness knew better than to attack such a powerful goddess. He could do no more to show his outrage than fill the chamber with the stink of Gehenna.

Mystra cleared the air with a wave her hand, sending both Iyachtu and his stench back to the place from whence they had come. Fzoul's followers broke for the exits, and even the High Tyrannar himself retreated to a dark corner.

Mystra turned her attention to Ruha, whose skin was clammy and pale beneath the sacrificial tabard. The witch's shallow breathing betrayed the agony of having her limbs pulled back against their joints. Her muscles still twitched from her bath among the eels, and her purple swollen cheek and black eyes bore witness to the fight she had given Fzoul before being captured. And despite all this, her expression remained as stoic as ever.

"Goddess!" she gasped. "At last . . . you came!"

Mystra made no move to free the witch. "Do not thank me so soon, Ruha. I have yet to decide whether my purpose in coming to Zhentil Keep includes saving you—I have not forgotten that volcano in the Storm Horns."

"I do not matter," the witch said. "Malik escaped!"

Mystra scowled. "You said the *Cyrinishad* was safe."

"The *Cyrinishad* is! He came here to steal the *True Life of Cyric*." Ruha strained against her bindings. "That little scorpion is as mad as his god. He means to cure the Dark One's insanity!"

"What?"

"It may be too late already." Ruha pointed her chin at the ceiling, then gasped, "Cyric was up there . . . I heard Fzoul say this to his god."

Mystra glanced into the dark corner where the High

Tyrannar was hiding. "Is this so?"

Fzoul nodded slowly. "I don't know what he wanted with it, but that foul-mouthed little shoat stole the *True Life* and went upstairs into my private chamber." The High Tyrannar spoke in a tone at once spiteful and frightened, carefully calculated to placate Xvim's hateful nature and avoid offending Mystra. "Then I heard Cyric talking. He had a thousand voices, and they all sounded insane."

This news dismayed Mystra so greatly that her avatar shrank to the size of a normal woman. This was as terrible as any setback she had suffered during the past few days— Adon's death, Talos's plot to subvert her worship, even Kelemvor's betrayal. A sane Cyric might win a favorable verdict at the trial and start spreading his corruption over the world again. Moreover, with Lord Death too absorbed in his "Re-evaluation" to help her win the support of the other gods, the Circle seemed more likely than ever to find against her and Kelemvor and insist that they both yield their divine powers.

Mystra shook her head, much disgusted with both the trial and Kelemvor's strange willingness to believe the charges had merit. If she and he did not protect Faerûn's mortals, who would?

The goddess sent an avatar to watch the Shattered Keep and saw that Cyric had sealed every entrance and posted avatars around the perimeter. Seeing no reason for him to take such precautions unless he had already read the book and was preparing a special rebuttal for his trial, she gave up on the thought of stealing the *True Life* before he could read it.

All this took but an instant, and there was only a slight pause before Fzoul dared to urge, "Perhaps you should go, goddess. Iyachtu Xvim is searching for Helm even as we speak."

Mystra ignored the warning and continued her conversation with Ruha. "I have only a short time, so I will ask you directly. How did Talos persuade you to betray me?"

Ruha lowered her eyes, much ashamed. "I should have known better . . . But after the things Malik did in Candlekeep, it was easy to believe you wanted him caught at any cost."

"Me?"

"Yes. When it became apparent I would never catch Malik, you . . . someone I took to be you . . . gave me the magic to keep up with him and told me to use it no matter what destruction it caused."

"Then Talos deceived you?" Mystra sounded more relieved than angry, for proof of Talos's actions would do much to justify her escape from Helm. "He has been impersonating me, and using my own worshipers to subvert my control over the Weave!"

Mystra began to free Ruha, snapping the taut ropes as though they were threads. Fzoul started to protest the theft of his god's sacrifice, then thought better of it and remained silent, trusting that Helm would arrive soon to take the goddess away.

Ruha sat up, her face reddening at the folly of falling victim to the Destroyer's deception. "I learned of my mistake when you cut me off from the Weave, but I was not certain who had deceived me until Talos appeared in Voonlar and offered to restore my powers."

"And you refused him?" Mystra snapped the last binding. "You did not call on him even after Fzoul captured you?"

"His help carries a high price." The witch began to rub her wrists. "I would rather die than call upon him."

"I am touched." Mystra laid her palm upon Ruha's cheek, and her magic healed the witch's bruised face. "So many people have deserted me during these troubles—even Kelemvor. Yet you stand by me, Faithful even after the injustice I did you."

Ruha took Mystra's hand from her face. "I pray you will not be angry with me, but I must speak honestly before my goddess." The witch lowered her feet to the floor and stood on shaky legs, facing Mystra as best she could. "I did not refuse Talos for you. I refused him because I had already seen the terrible destruction that comes with his aid. And you did no injustice in denying the Weave to me. Whether it was you or Talos who gave me the magic to chase Malik, I was wrong to use it.

The Weave is there to use or abuse, and it is the choice we make that determines our fate. I chose poorly, and so I suffered."

Mystra hardly heard this last sentence, for the witch's words had already sent the goddess's thoughts spinning. "Ruha!"

The witch paled, mistaking the blast of Mystra's voice for a sign of anger. She dropped to her knees and clutched the hem of Lady Magic's robe. "Forgive me, my goddess. I did not mean—"

"No, Ruha." Mystra lifted the witch back to her feet. "You have done nothing wrong—but I *have*."

Iyachtu Xvim returned in a pillar of swirling black smoke. "Begone, you self-righteous shrew! Helm is coming!" The hateful god sent a wisp of sulfur-stinking fumes across the room to entwine Ruha. "And leave my sacrifice here!"

Mystra severed the foul strand with a pass of her hand, then looked into Ruha's eyes. "Close your eyes and think of Silvercloud."

The witch obeyed. In the next instant she was sitting on the hippogriff, back in the same dark stable where she had left him in Zhentil Keep, safe from Iyachtu Xvim and free to return, happily ever after, to her life as a meddling Harper.

"Thieving hag!" Xvim flicked his hand in Mystra's direction, and a cage of dark smoke rose up to enclose her, the bars turning instantly as solid as iron. "When Helm arrives, you shall pay for that insult, too!"

"I think not." Mystra walked out of Iyachtu's prison and did not seem to notice when the bars sliced her body into long strips. "But if I am wrong, you may tell Helm that I will be waiting at my trial."

Forty-Nine

To make it known he had tolerated the last abuse of his justice, Tyr had cast the Pavilion of Cynosure into the image he favored. Now every god would see it as he did: a round chamber of mahogany walls and marble floors covered by a luminous dome of milky alabaster.

Around the perimeter stood five bailiffs, all avatars of Helm. They wore full suits of plate armor and kept their visors down and cradled naked battle-axes in their arms, and on their belts they carried black manacles of nothingness.

In the middle of the room, the Greater Gods stood in their customary places—though they now waited behind a circular rail of burnished gold. Tyr, as usual, took the place next to the space left empty for Ao. The Just One carried his warhammer thrust into his belt for all to see, and in place of his customary leather armor, he wore a flashing suit of silver plate.

Cyric stood directly opposite the Just One. Our Dark Lord had also altered his appearance, assuming the form of a gaunt young man with white hair and flesh the color of chalk. The blood of countless murdered guests stained the sleeves of his ivory tunic, over which he wore a long hauberk sewn from the flayed skin of Tethyr's last king. Whenever another god dared meet his burning eyes, he glared at him until he averted his gaze.

Kelemvor wore his new attire, the same silver death mask and pearly robe he had donned when he doused the lights of his city. Mystra stood beside the Usurper, her ankles shackled together by one of Helm's black chains. She stared at the floor and never looked in Lord Death's direction; whether this was out of anger or shame, only the Harlot could say.

And what of Malik, savior of his god and all Faerûn? Now clothed in a crimson robe, I stood inside the golden ring with my eyes firmly shut, and even then I was nearly blinded by the naked brilliance of the gods. They were as large as giants, and their splendor shined through my eyelids as the hot sun shines through wax, and I saw everything in the chamber in a blinding kaleidoscope of light.

Beside me stood two other witnesses. Adon the Fop now resembled the walking dead, which in fact he was. The god Mask was also present, shifting his murky form like a child who cannot stand still, and every shape he took lacked a limb.

On a table before us sat the trial evidence: a gleaming chalice of gold, a shattered corner from Helm's prison, the black book I had risked all to recover, and a pulsing mass of yellow mold that had once been my heart.

This was not as I had planned.

The gods kept casting worried glances at the *True Life of Cyric*, then glaring at me. They believed the book to be the *Cyrinishad,* and I knew many of them would see me dead before allowing me to open it. And even if Tyr forced them to let me read, Oghma's lies would humble Our Dark Lord before his lessers—surely a fate worse than madness!

Lathander the Morninglord nodded to Tyr, and Tyr raised the stump of his wrist to signal for quiet.

"Dawn has reached the spires of Candlekeep." The Just One pointed across the circle to Cyric. "The Prince of Lies stands charged with innocence by way of insanity, by which he is accused of failing in his godly duty to spread the fruits of strife and discord beyond his own church."

Tyr turned his eyeless gaze toward Mystra and Kelemvor. "Lady Magic and Lord Death stand charged with incompetence by way of humanity, by which they are accused of ignoring their godly duties to show undue kindness to the mortals of Faerûn." The Just One glanced around the circle, pausing a moment upon the face of each god, then said, "Let the trial begin."

"I will speak first." My borrowed heart fell as Cyric spoke these words; he was far too eager to have me read. "I am first charged, and I shall be first absolved."

The outcry of protest nearly deafened me, and the gods cast nervous glances in my direction, and I feared I would discover what they had in store before I could escape my dilemma.

Oghma raised his voice above the others. "It is because you are the first charged that you must be last judged, Cyric." He was careful to avoid looking at the black tome on the table. "This trial began with you, and so it must end with you."

The Binder's logic escaped me, but his fellows were equally reluctant to deal with the book, and so they chimed a chorus of agreement.

To my relief, Tyr announced, "It is decided."

The dark suns beneath Cyric's brow shone blacker than ever, but he sneered and shrugged off his anger. "You must hear me sooner or later."

"And it will be later," retorted Tyr. He turned to Kelemvor. "Lord Death will speak first. How plead you, Kelemvor?"

"Guilty," replied the god in the silver mask.

An astonished murmur rumbled through the room, nearly shaking me off my feet. Kelemvor stepped forward, passing through the golden rail as though he were a ghost. I stepped back, granting his looming figure as much berth as possible.

The Usurper's voice was as somber as a dirge. "I have failed my duties in the past. I will not stand before you and say otherwise." He turned in a slow circle, facing each god in turn. "I have rewarded the brave and kind and punished the cowardly and cruel, and I am sorry for it."

Here, Kelemvor turned the impassive visage of his death mask toward Mystra, and at last the Harlot raised her lashes to meet the gaze of her forsaken lover. Only her glistening eyes betrayed her sorrow, for they were damp with tears.

Kelemvor continued his litany. "I judged men as if I were

353

yet a man. Good mortals have placed their faith in my fairness instead of in their gods, while the wicked have deserted their churches at the first sign of disfavor. My actions have undermined the worship of every god here, and I was wrong."

At this, Mystra bit her lip. Kelemvor faced the Battle Lord. "My offense against you, Tempus, has been greatest of all. By favoring courage over cowardice, I have invited brave warriors to hurl their lives away, and given cowards good excuse to hide in their holes. I swear, that was never my intent."

Tempus's face remained hidden behind his visor, but he lifted his bloody arms and opened his palms in a gesture of acceptance. When the Battle Lord started to speak, Lord Death raised a hand to silence him, then turned toward Tyr.

"In the past, I have been guilty of all this, but as I have changed myself, so have I changed my realm." Kelemvor waved a hand over his new attire. "I invite you all to send your avatars to see the new City of the Dead. Judge me not on my past, but on what you find there now."

As the Usurper spoke, he opened the gates of his city. Many gods did as he asked, though Sune turned around at the mirrored gates; the reflection of her slightest flaw was enough to convince her Lord Death had done all he claimed. The others continued on, swooping down ashen streets crowded with dull-eyed residents, passing whole boroughs of drab buildings and dead trees, crossing graceless bridges that spanned still waters the color of steel. They saw no cruelty or malice, but neither did they see joy; Lord Death's realm had become a domain of shuffling spirits and passionless shades, a place of neither punishment nor reward. And in the heart of this dismal city loomed the Crystal Spire, a soaring minaret of smoky brown topaz encircled by a line of sorrowful spirits, the False and the Faithless.

In the Pavilion of Cynosure, Mystra braced herself against the golden rail and let her shoulders sag. She stared at the floor in sadness, but it was Cyric who spoke first.

"Very convincing, Kelemvor." The One rolled his blazing

black eyes at the ceiling. "A nice show that can be undone as easily as it was done. Do you really expect us to believe you've changed so suddenly?"

Kelemvor's response was eerily calm. "I expect nothing of you, Mad One. You are incapable of learning from your mistakes, and so you cannot understand how others might."

"You learned nothing!" Cyric pointed a finger as long as a sword toward Adon. Mystra's patriarch was cowering at my side, looking away from the goddess he feared. "Even now, you are protecting Adon the Fallen!"

"I am protecting no one," answered Kelemvor. "Adon will be judged when he stands before me in the Judgment Hall."

"He is mine!" Cyric passed through the rail and started across the floor.

Tyr plucked his warhammer from his belt and pointed it at the One. "Do not touch the witness!"

Cyric continued forward, and all five of Helm's avatars stepped away from the wall in unison. For one terrible instant I thought Our Dark Lord would ignore Tyr's command, but he stopped abruptly, standing nose to nose with Lord Death's silver mask. Kelemvor remained as calm as a corpse.

"I stole Adon's soul!" Cyric spat. "You have no right to keep it from me."

"I told you before," came the steady reply, "you stole nothing but his life. He did not pray to you, and so he remains both False and Faithless."

Now it was Mystra who could not bear the Usurper's words. "How dare you call my patriarch Faithless—or False!" She passed through the rail, floating just above the floor to spare herself the shame of walking in shackles. "Adon would never have turned from me, had Cyric not driven him mad. You know this!"

Adon trembled and hid behind me. All three gods were as tall as trees and brighter than suns, and they stood a dozen paces away. I covered my eyes, but still their image burned in my head.

The fire faded from Cyric's eyes, and he asked in a voice

full of false forbearance, "Lady Magic, how can Kelemvor know something that isn't true? I did not drive Adon mad. You did." He flashed the Harlot a smug smile, then continued, "I let your patriarch see you through my eyes, and the sight of your true nature was more than any man could bear."

Mystra whirled on the One, and so great was her hatred that even I saw the gore-eating harpy of Adon's nightmare. "You profane canker of pustulation! I'll scrape you—"

"Hold!" Cyric raised his hands, still smiling. "You have no call to be angry with *me*, Lady Magic. Kelemvor knew what I had done. He could have saved Adon long before our old friend grew so troubled that he leapt to his death."

Mystra's face betrayed her surprise. She looked into the bleak orbs of Kelemvor's eyes, then shook her head in dismay. "It is true, is it not? You knew long ago, when you came to draw Zale's spirit out of the volcano—and you kept it from me!"

Kelemvor did not deny her claim. "The secrets of the dead are their own. That much has not changed in my city."

"But *you* have." Tears of sparkling magic welled in Mystra's eyes. "And I cannot love this new god as I once loved the man."

At this, Kelemvor dipped his chin, though he kept his gray eyes upon her. "No one should love Death."

As Mystra turned away, a single tear escaped her eye and rolled down her cheek. Cyric snatched the golden chalice off the table, then thrust it under the goddess's chin and caught the glittering drop. He all but squealed his delight, and I winced at his display.

Mystra pushed him away. "Stand aside, Foulheart." She floated back toward her place behind the golden rail. "You tempt me to forget where we are."

"As you wish." Cyric smiled compliantly, then returned the chalice to the table. "I'm done anyway."

Kelemvor looked on, but said nothing. The other gods shook their heads or rolled their eyes, and in my folly even I thought Cyric's behavior but another sign of his madness.

Tyr raised his stump at the One. "You may also return to your place, Cyric. We have heard enough about Adon the Fallen."

"And we have heard enough about the charges against Lord Death," added Oghma the Wise. "I say we find in his favor. We have seen for ourselves what he sacrificed for duty."

At this, the gods filled the pavilion with a general chorus of agreement. Only Cyric raised his voice against the verdict, and even he did not object too forcefully. This puzzled me greatly, until I noticed the cunning gleam in his ebony eye—and my puzzlement turned to concern, for there was clearly more to Cyric's plan than my reading of the *Cyrinishad*. I gazed at my heart and wondered if I might ever feel it beating in my chest again.

Tyr raised his stump. "The Circle has made its will known in the matter of Lord Death, but the charges against him have not been separated. He and Mystra stand accused together. If we find for one, we must find for both."

"Then let us hear from her," said Oghma.

Mystra addressed her fellow gods from her place behind the golden rail. "I, too, have learned from my mistakes."

"Your actions suggest otherwise," came Tyr's stern reply. The Just One pointed to the shattered corner of Helm's black prison. "You have shown little respect for the Circle's justice. And let us not forget why Helm took you into custody to begin with. You attacked a witness!"

Tyr gestured at Mask, who stood on the other side of the table a dozen paces from Adon and me. As usual, the Shadowlord was shifting from one murky form to another—none with all their limbs—and he still clutched Prince Tang's enchanted sword.

Lady Magic replied, "I have compensated Mask very well for his loss—unless he cares to return Prince Tang's *chien* and ask some other boon of me."

The God of Thieves folded the sword into a crease of shadow and shook his head, for being free of the Chaos Hound was worth more to him than he had lost.

Mystra continued, "And he is more than a witness at this trial. It was his scheming that convinced Tempus to lodge his original charge, and the Shadowlord told me outright that he had caused much of the trouble Kelemvor and I encountered in preparing our defenses."

Tyr turned his empty gaze upon Mask. "Is this so?"

The Shadowlord shrugged, then changed into the shape of a one-winged lammasu. "Admitting a thing does not make it so."

"It does in this trial," Tyr replied. "Tampering with the accused's right to defend—"

"Do not punish Mask on my account," Mystra said. "I find myself indebted to him. Without his interference, I would not have seen the injustice I have been doing to the mortals of Faerûn."

Her use of the word "injustice" was calculated to kindle Tyr's curiosity, and so it did. "What injustice would that be?"

"A despotism more terrible than any Cyric would inflict."

"As if you could!" The One raised his eyes to the ceiling.

"Tyranny of the flesh is nothing compared to tyranny of the spirit." Mystra turned her gaze toward Lathander and Silvanus and Chauntea, who all bore a greater love for freedom than it was worth. "In trying to deny the Weave to the destructive and the wicked, I have been attempting to choose Faerûn's destiny. This is not my place—and it is not the place of any god here."

"A choice has no meaning unless it is freely made," agreed Oghma the Wise. "It is for the mortals of Faerûn to make what they wish of their world. If we relieve them of this trust, the destiny of Faerûn will have no value to them."

"To them?" scoffed the One. "I did not make myself a god to let mortals ruin Faerûn."

"No, you became a god to ruin it for them." Sune flashed a dazzling smile at the One, then added in a voice of honey, "We all know what an ugly mess you would make of things."

"Beauty is in the eye of the beholder." Cyric's face had grown as red as Sune's hair. He could see that Lady Magic was winning too many gods to her side, and his plans for the new order had no room for Mystra and Kelemvor. He turned to the Harlot and asked, "What are you saying? That you will let me have free access to the Weave?"

Mystra met his gaze evenly. "Yes—and Talos and Tempus, and Shar as well."

At this the Destroyer snorted and looked up from the profanity he had been scratching in Tyr's gold rail. "In return for what? Supporting a verdict in your favor?"

"Not at all, Talos," the Harlot replied. "I have already reopened the Weave to you and your storm lords, and to Tempus and his war wizards, and to Shar and all her dark followers, and even to Cyric and his madmen. The Weave will remain open regardless of the Circle's verdict."

"Assuming that it remains in your power," Tyr reminded her.

Mystra nodded. "Assuming it does."

"It was only three years ago that the Circle censured her for denying the Weave to me!" It was a sign of the One's madness that he did not even wince after he said this, for everyone in the room recalled that Mystra had cut him off in an attempt to prevent him from making the very book they now feared so terribly. "I think we have heard this before!"

The voice of Shar drifted down to my ears like a blanket of whispers. "It would have been better if we had let Mystra do as she wished." The Nightbringer glanced at the dark book on the evidence table, then added, "I, for one, will accept Lady Magic at her word—if she will join me and some others in demanding that Tyr disallow any reading of the *Cyrinishad*."

"That cannot be!" the Just One stormed. "The accused has a right to make his own defense!"

"And we have a right to defend ourselves against his lies!" countered the Battle Lord Tempus.

As all this occurred, a sliver of shadow appeared beside the *True Life*. I glanced into the vaulted dome above our heads, expecting to see some source of light shining behind the translucent alabaster, but of course the Pavilion of Cynosure is beyond such mundane things as suns and moons. I lowered my gaze and happened to glance toward Mask, who stood only about half as tall as the enormous figures of the great gods. He was shifting from the form of a burly one-armed firbolg into that of a lanky one-armed verbeeg, and this arm was the only part of his body that was not rippling with change. The God of Thieves was reaching for the *True Life of Cyric!*

If any of the other gods also perceived this, they pretended to be too engrossed in the trial to notice. As for me, I kept quiet and debated the wisdom of letting the Shadowlord succeed, reasoning that I could always steal it back later—when I would not have to read it before so many of the One's inferiors.

While I watched the shadow creep up the edge of the book, the Battle Lord addressed Mystra. "Lady Magic, I once offered to withdraw my charges if you would consider the possibility that war benefits Faerûn. I cannot repeat that offer because of my earlier promise to Mask, but I do stand ready to assure a verdict in your favor—if you will guarantee to never again place such restrictions on the use of the Weave, and promise to stand with us against the reading of the *Cyrinishad.*"

Mystra removed the sacred starburst from around her neck, then tossed it across the chamber to Tempus. "Here is my guarantee; the Weave will not be restricted. But I cannot stand against the reading, even if it means my freedom." She turned to face Tyr. "I have already taken too many liberties with the Circle's justice; I must abide by Tyr's guidance."

Mask's shadow began to creep farther across the *True Life*'s cover. Still, I could not bring myself to act.

The Goddess of Beauty stepped to Mystra's side, bathing the Harlot in the blush of her flattering radiance. "I say we find in favor of Lady Magic. It would hardly be appealing to judge her by the past when we have already made allowances for Kelemvor."

Oghma nodded. "It is not the Circle's place to punish any god for past mistakes. Our only concern is the safety of the

Balance, and we may feel more assured than ever that Mystra will serve it well."

Again, a chorus of voices filled the pavilion, but this time Cyric was not alone in condemning the Harlot. Despite her pledge to keep the Weave accessible, Talos, Shar, and Tempus were making good on their unspoken threat: Mystra had refused to join them in opposing the reading of the *Cyrinishad,* so now they stood against her. Tyr spoke against Mystra as well; he had not forgiven the goddess for fleeing his sacred justice.

The Circle's vote was tied. And now only Kelemvor was left to break it.

"How say you, Lord Death?" asked Tyr. "Will you favor Mystra and spare yourself as well—or find against her and suffer the same punishment?"

There was a time when the answer would have been as obvious as it was quick, but Kelemvor did not reply at once. Instead, he turned his gray orbs upon the Goddess of Magic and studied her a long time. She met his gaze and did not flinch, though the sorrow caused by his hesitation was plain upon her face. And then even this sorrow faded.

Lord Death motioned Adon forward, then picked up the trembling patriarch and let him stand in the palm of his hand. "There is no need to fear. Look into my eyes, and tell me what you see."

Adon did as he was commanded. A pearly haze spilled out of Lord Death's eyes to engulf him, and deep within the fog, a silhouette appeared. She had long black hair as fine as silk and a clear radiant face with high cheekbones and full lips. Though her eyes were as dark and deep as the night, they sparkled with the warm light of a sacred starburst, and she was dressed in a flowing robe of twilight.

Adon whirled around to face Mystra, then fell to his knees in Kelemvor's hand. "Goddess! Forgive me, I pray you!"

"I never blamed you," Mystra replied. "Only Cyric."

Kelemvor passed the patriarch to his goddess. "Adon is yours by rights. Do with him what you will. I say you are as worthy a god as any who stands in this room." Lord Death's words bore no trace of fondness, as if he offered nothing but cold fact.

Mystra held her fingers above Adon's head and let a shimmering rain of magic sprinkle down upon his shoulders. The patriarch faded from sight, gone to await his goddess in her palace Dweomerheart.

Tyr declared, "The charges against Kelemvor and Mystra are repudiated."

"Fraud!"

So loud was Cyric's shriek that even the gods cringed, and I clasped my ears. Although the shadow on the *True Life* now covered nearly half the book, it quavered and looked as though it might retreat.

"Kelemvor has changed nothing but his face!" Cyric stormed. "He never meant to damn Adon!"

Kelemvor turned his mask toward the One. "I meant to treat Adon as any other, but those intentions are no longer relevant. Like you, I only allowed the mortal to see Mystra through my own eyes. If he prayed to her as his goddess, that was his doing, not mine."

Cyric looked to Tyr. "Rescind the verdict!"

"On what basis?"

"They cheated!"

The Eyeless One shook his head. "The Circle has spoken, and now the time has come to consider the charges against you."

I stared at the *True Life*. Now the shadow covered all but a quarter of the book. I caught Talos eyeing the book as he scraped at the rail with his sharp fingernails, and when he quickly glanced away, I realized that he also knew what was happening. Perhaps he and Mask had even planned it.

After glaring at Tyr for a moment, Cyric shrugged. "As you wish, then; consider the charges." He shot a smirk across the circle. "In the end, we will do as I wish anyway."

A disgruntled murmur rumbled through the Pavilion, and I knew my time was running out. Cyric's own trial was at hand,

and he had already begun to raise the ire of his enemies. I found my courage, and my arm shot up.

"Thief!" I pointed at Mask. "He is stealing the book!"

Mask's shadow left the *True Life* before I had spoken my second word, but even he was not quick enough to escape the Great Guard. In a blink, a pair of matching Helms had seized the Shadowlord, one by his squirming arm and the other by a writhing leg. A third Helm now stood at the evidence table, prepared to strike down anyone who dared reach for the *True Life*.

Talos shot me a look that said I would do well to be wary of lightning for the rest of my life. Tyr stepped over the golden railing—it would not have been right for him to ignore any aspect of his own courtroom—and strode forward to confront the God of Thieves.

"Explain yourself!"

Mask assumed the shape of a hook-nosed troll and shrugged. "I am the God of Thieves. You cannot fault me if I steal."

"But I can banish you from this court." Tyr looked to the Helm holding Mask's arm. "Take this thief outside. I will summon you if he is called to witness."

"I am more than a witness in this trial!" Mask objected. "I have a stake in it, too."

Tyr looked doubtful. "And that would be?"

"Intrigue." A shudder ran down Mask's troll form, and then he became a one-legged ogre pointing in the One's direction. "When you strip Cyric of his godhood, I demand dominion over intrigue. I have earned it."

Forgetting in his anger to make his body insubstantial, Our Dark Lord stepped forward and crashed through the golden rail. "After the Circle confirms me as its leader, I will strip you of your very life!"

The One hurled a bolt of dark-clotted energy at Mask's form, but Helm raised his axe and caught the attack on the flat of the blade. The weapon withered into a twisted twig, then dissolved into smoke.

Tyr stepped between Mask and the One. "We have not confirmed you yet, Mad One. Go back to your place, or I will find you incompetent to speak in your own defense."

Cyric's eyes flashed at the threat, but he knew no other god would ask me to read the *Cyrinishad,* and so he did as the Just One requested.

Tempus the Battle Lord straightened his shoulders. "We may dispose of Mask's request quickly enough. When he came to me with his scheme, he assured me he had learned better than to let his plots spin out of hand." The Foehammer waved his gauntleted hand at Mystra and Kelemvor, then at the evidence table. "If that were true, he would not have interfered with the defenses of Lady Magic and Lord Death, nor would we be faced with listening to Cyric's vile book of lies in the first place. No matter the trial's outcome, I say Mask has no claim on intrigue. Let him be happy with his stolen sword and being free of the Chaos Hound."

When no one objected, Tyr nodded. "So be it."

Helm's avatar vanished with Mask in his grasp, and then Tyr turned to the One.

"Cyric, you know the charge: innocence by way of insanity. What have you to say for yourself?"

The One smirked at Tyr and his other accusers, then turned his burning gaze upon me. "Read, Malik."

"Now, Mighty One?"

Cyric glared at me, and a black pit of pain took root in my stomach. Cold beads of sweat rained down from my brow. My moment of truth was at hand, and my knees nearly buckled as I stepped to the evidence table and reached for the *True Life*.

As soon as my fingers grasped the cover, a white flash split the air and a mighty crack filled the chamber, and a hot bolt struck my chest. I flew across the room and smashed through the golden rail, and I would certainly have crashed through the pavilion wall if I had not hit one of Helm's avatars first. I dropped at his feet, still clutching the *True Life*.

I looked up warily. Talos the lightning-shooter was pointing his finger at my chest. Another half-dozen gods came striding toward me—Shar and Sune and Lathander and more, their radiance merging like a raging fire. All had magic crackling in their fingers, and all were determined to keep me from reading the book. Silvanus flipped the evidence table aside and sent my moldy heart rolling across the floor toward Kelemvor's feet.

I raised my trembling hand to ward them off. "No, wait—"

"Quiet, child!" It was Chauntea who ordered this. No sooner had she spoken than my tongue swelled in my mouth, growing so thick I could hardly breathe, much less speak.

Tyr and four of Helm's avatars stepped out to intercept my attackers, and then the Nightgoddess Shar raised her hand. The room went as black as a grave, and I lost sight of my heart.

"Stand back!" Tyr ordered. "The witness is under my protection."

"We mean him no harm." As the Morninglord spoke, a beam of golden radiance struck my eyes, so that I became at once the only visible thing in the room and totally blind. "It is the book we want."

From somewhere off to my side, Sune's dulcet voice called, "Shove it over to me, Malik, and you shall have the love of all the women you desire."

Now, I could name a dozen women whose affections were worth more than a good stallion, and the adoration of any one of them would have been worth more than the unfaithful love of my own wife, whom Cyric had placed so far beyond my grasp. And yet, I considered Sune's offer for no more than a breath or two, as I was too loyal a servant to betray the god of my heart.

I heard heavy feet closing in around me, and I prayed that none would trample the pulsing mass Silvanus had so callously pitched from the table.

Tyr said, "Let Malik read the book or face Ao's wrath!"

From somewhere beyond my attackers, Cyric added, "You have nothing to fear from the truth."

Talos snapped, "You would not know the truth if you spoke it, Wormbrain."

"And we fear Ao's wrath less than we fear joining Cyric in his madness," said Chauntea. "We cannot see how that would serve the Balance."

"Does a thing exist only because you see it?" countered Oghma. "It is abiding by a just code that serves the Balance; what you are doing serves only yourself."

"We have no interest in your sophistry, Binder. We have all agreed." As Tempus said this, he sounded closer than I would have liked. "Before we let the mortal read the Mad One's book, we will start a new Time of Troubles."

"That would be a terrible waste," said Mystra.

A shimmering sphere of magic appeared around me and lifted me into the domed vault, and I found myself looking down upon a room full of darkness. At once, my swollen tongue shrank to its normal size. I opened the *True Life* to the back and began to flip through its pages, searching for the start of Oghma's lying narrative.

"Let him read." As Mystra spoke, the darkness vanished from the Pavilion below and I found myself looking down upon the heads of the gods. This was less exhilarating than it sounds, for they were all staring up at me, more than a few with murder in their eyes. I spied my heart lying intact beside the golden rail, near Kelemvor's feet, and the Harlot continued, "No harm will come to us or the Balance."

"You cannot guarantee that." Kelemvor raised his hand and drew a silver scimitar from the empty air. "You promised Tyr you would not interfere with Cyric's defense."

Mystra stepped to his side and took him by the arm. "I have not broken my promise, but you must trust me."

"Not anymore."

Kelemvor shook her off, then raised his scimitar and grew tall enough to reach my magic bubble. At once, Tyr and all of Helm's avatars swelled to an equal size and moved to stop him, and I lost sight of my heart beneath their many feet. Tempus the Battle Lord drew his great sword, and Talos filled his hands with lightning bolts, and Lathander's fingers began to glow with golden fire, and they all moved to stand with Kelemvor. The One filled his hands with black, venom-dripping daggers and began to circle around toward their backs, and I found the page at last. My hands began to shake so badly that I could hardly make out the letters on the page, and my ears filled with such a terrible sluicing I would not be able to hear the words when I read them.

Oghma rushed in between the battle lines. "Wait! We cannot do this!" The Binder raised his hands, as if he really believed such a pair of bony arms could stop the coming carnage. "A war between us will destroy Faerûn!"

"Out of the way, old fool!" Tempus commanded.

When Oghma did not obey, Tempus smashed the hilt of his sword into the Binder's head and sent him sprawling to the floor. Cyric raised his hand to throw his first dagger, and I saw that in the coming tumult, my words would never reach the ears of the One. I could not allow all my efforts to be for naught.

"Wait, you witless jackals!" I yelled this at the top of my voice, and my audacity so shocked the gods that I could raise the *True Life* and yell, "This is not the *Cyrinishad!*"

A stunned silence fell over the pavilion and the gods stayed their hands for an instant, and it was only Cyric's astonished shriek that extended this instant into a moment. "What?"

The One snapped his hand forward, and in the next instant his black dagger sliced through Mystra's magic bubble. I am sure that it was Tyr's protection and not my own reflexes that raised the *True Life* in front of my face. The venom-dripping blade sliced through the leather cover and halted just a hair's breadth from my cheek, then my stomach rose into my throat and I plummeted toward the floor.

I did not even notice when I hit. I only shifted my gaze away from the knife and began to read:

"Though men may try to wrest the reins of their destiny from the gods, they are all born at the mercy of Nature, bound in a hundred ways to those around them. This is how the gods insure

mortals are tied to their world of toil and sorrow. Cyric of Zhentil Keep was no exception.

"In the hottest Flamerule to ever grip the Keep, Cyric was born to a destitute bard so lacking in skill she could not earn a single copper. . . ."

Cyric grasped his ears. "No!"

The force of the cry hurled me against the wall and made my ears ring with the shriek of a thousand banshees, yet I continued to read. Indeed, I could not have stopped if I wished; Mystra's spell compelled me onward just as mercilessly as it had when I stood in the same chamber and recited from Rinda's journal.

I continued to read, describing how Cyric was sold as an infant to a Sembian merchant and raised in a life of luxury, and how Our Dark Lord repaid the man's kind upbringing with betrayal and murder. When I came to the part about returning to Zhentil Keep in the chains of a slave, the One let out a bloodcurdling shriek, then raised his hand and filled it with black darts.

"Liar!" As he cried this, he brought his arm forward and hurled the darts. "Betrayer!"

One of Helm's avatars lowered his battle-axe before my face, catching the darts on the flat of his blade. Then two more aspects of the Great Guardian seized Cyric's arms and held him motionless.

I finished the tale, describing the Dark Sun's escape from slavery to a thieves' guild, his many adventures with Kelemvor Lyonsbane, and finally his quest to recover the Tablets of Fate during the Time of Troubles. Of course, every word I read was a sacrilege and a vile lie, but this endless string of blasphemies seemed to calm the One. By the time I reached the part telling how he stole the tablets from his old companions and used them to win Ao's favor, Our Dark Lord stood motionless in Helm's grasp. He glared at me with an expression more lucid than I had ever seen on his face and said nothing, and when I finished the loathsome account and looked up, he only shook his head.

I closed the cover and flung the foul book away, then hurled myself on the floor at his feet. "Mighty One, do not punish me! I only did this horrid thing on your account, so that you might recover your wits and defend yourself at this farce of a trial!" I embraced his huge foot and showered the boot with kisses. "I swear it gave me no pleasure, and you know I cannot lie!"

Talos sent a gusty snicker across the chamber, but Tempus the Battle Lord was quick to cuff the Destroyer's shoulder. "This is no time for mirth. Not when we have been standing at the very brink of the Year of Carnage."

Talos returned to his place in the Circle, and Tempus followed. As the other gods also returned to their places, the One shook me off his foot.

"I will deal with you later, Malik." He pointed at the wall, where I was much relieved to see my moldy heart still pulsing upon the floor. "Now, fetch me your heart."

I sprinted twenty paces across the pavilion and knelt down to cradle the precious mass. It smelled like rotten fruit, and on one side there was a brown bruise where some god had caught it with his boot, but this hardly mattered to me. I scooped it up in both hands and held it as close to my breast as a child. The mold was soft and velvety, and the heart itself seemed almost liquid inside its skin, and still I counted myself lucky. If anyone had stepped on it in this condition, it would have squirted over the floor like a crushed plum.

"Malik! I am waiting for my evidence."

In truth, I was a little reluctant to give up the evidence. But, as I could not reach into my own chest and return the heart to its proper place, I knew I would have to surrender it sooner or later—and better sooner than later. I jumped to my feet and did as the One commanded.

As soon as Cyric took my heart from my hands, it grew as large as an enormous melon, so that it looked like a pulsing yellow peach in his gigantic hand.

"This heart helped me see the truth of my condition."

Cyric raised the moldy thing so that all could see, then

369

lowered it to his mouth and took a great bite from the side. A flood of watery yellow juice ran down his chin, and I cried out, but no one paid me any heed.

"The truth is that I am *still* a more worthy god than any of you!" The One spoke with a full mouth, and he smacked his lips between words. "And that is why you are all jealous."

Thinking my plan had failed, I cried out in despair and flung myself to the floor.

But Cyric continued, "I must admit, however, that I am no more powerful than any of you." The One turned my heart over as though he would take another bite, then seemed to think better of it and thrust the juicy thing somewhere inside his hauberk. "That was a delusion of the *Cyrinishad*. A happy delusion—" here, the One glared down at me—"but a delusion nonetheless. We can all agree that I am better now."

"This is your defense?" scoffed Lathander. "That you are better now?"

The One whirled on the Morninglord as though to attack, then suddenly straightened and shook his head. "Of course not. It is a statement of fact." Cyric crossed the floor and retrieved the golden chalice, which lay on the ground. "My defense is this: even when I was mad, I was worthy of my duties."

"How so?" Tyr scowled as he asked this.

Before Cyric replied, he looked into the chalice and smiled, for the cups of the gods never spill. He carried it over to Tyr and swirled it under the Just One's chin. "Look inside."

Tyr saw two tears rolling around in the chalice, one gleaming black and the other sparkling silver.

"This is all that remains of the love between Mystra and Kelemvor, and it belongs to me now." Cyric began to round the Circle, swirling the cup beneath each god's chin. "It was my doing that turned Adon against Mystra, and it was Adon's Faithlessness that pitted Mystra and Kelemvor against each other, and it was that which destroyed their love. Not much remains, but here it is. I own it."

The One continued his circuit. When Mystra and Kelemvor looked into the cup, they betrayed no emotion, nor did they glance at each other or give any other hint of the feelings they had once shared for each other.

Cyric smiled a little as he left them, then finished his round and stopped before Tyr. He raised the cup high, then turned to face the rest of the Circle.

"If I can destroy the love of gods, then I can certainly fill the lives of Faerûn's mortals with strife and discord."

The One raised the chalice to his lips and tipped back his head, for the tears of brokenhearted lovers have always been his favorite libation. After the two drops rolled into his throat, he smacked his lips and smashed the chalice against the floor.

Then he turned to face Oghma. "How say you, Binder? Guilty and sane, or innocent and mad?"

"We must judge you by the same standards as Mystra and Kelemvor, and though you have also made mistakes in recent years, we must all agree you have returned to us as wicked as before." Oghma looked past the One to address the other gods of the Circle. "And we must all remember not to judge Cyric by his fiendish nature. That is the nature of strife, and he could not fulfill his duties if he were not evil. I say we find for Cyric—guilty and sane."

"Never!" Sune shook her fiery head, flinging gouts of flame across the chamber. She was the Goddess of Love as well as Beauty, and Cyric's actions had offended her deeply. "Not after what he did to Mystra and Kelemvor."

"I do find in Cyric's favor," said Chauntea. "For better or worse, he has returned to us whole."

"Guilty and sane." Lathander did not explain himself, for no one expected him to disagree with Chauntea.

Silvanus shook his antlered head. "Not I—sane or insane, he believes he is entitled to do as he pleases with Faerûn, and that I cannot abide. I find against him."

"As do I," said Shar. "He cannot be trusted to do as he must. I say we strip his powers and divide them among ourselves."

"Of course you do," said Tempus. "You would bring all of

creation under your black canopy if you could. But I say we could find none better to spread strife across the land—as long as he swears never to read the *Cyrinishad* again, nor ever to look for it."

Cyric raised his right hand. "I swear."

"If you believe that," crackled Talos, "you are crazier than Wormbrain ever was. I find against him because . . ." The Destroyer fell silent, then shrugged. "Because I want to."

"That makes the count four to four," observed Tyr. "And Cyric cannot vote."

The One's face turned from smug to shocked. "Why not?"

"Because that is the Code of the Circle," Tyr replied. "And I will speak against you now. You have never been a stable god, and I suspect you have been mad since long before you became one of us. You are insane, and therefore unreliable, and therefore a constant danger to the Balance."

"What?"

Cyric stumbled back against the rail and glanced at Mystra and Kelemvor, and I grew sick to my stomach and quivered with fear. In that moment, I knew all my suffering had been for naught, and I was ready to fling myself on the floor and beg Tyr's mercy. But not the One; the shock in his face changed to anger, and he whirled on Tyr.

"You backbiting viper! You honey-tongued hypocrite! You—"

"Cyric!" Though Kelemvor barked the word, his voice contained no emotion, neither anger nor anxiety nor eagerness.

The One raised his brow, then snarled at Lord Death, "Gloat if you like. I will be back to do the same over you."

"I know you will try," Kelemvor replied. "But what about now? Will you abide by the Circle's decision?"

The One looked around the pavilion, sneering at each god who had spoken against him. When his gaze returned to Kelemvor, he spat upon the floor and nodded. "What choice do I have?"

"None," Kelemvor replied. "I only wanted to see if you realized it; you do, and so I must find you sane."

"Guilty? You find for me?"

The silver death mask nodded grimly.

"Still frightened of me, are you?" Cyric's smirk returned, for he knew better than to think Lord Death had made his choice out of a sense of duty. "I will not forget this."

"I am sure you will not," said Tyr. "But we have not yet found you guilty. The deciding word belongs to Mystra."

Cyric's face froze, and I swear the blood in my veins stopped flowing. That Kelemvor had spoken in favor of the One was a thing destined to happen; I could see that now, for the Usurper was a coward and a fool who trembled before the very thought of Our Dark Lord's vengeance. But what of Lady Magic? She was almost as fearless as the One, and she never failed to press her advantage when she believed she had it.

Cyric turned his glare upon the Harlot and made no pretense of reconciliation, for he knew she would not believe it. Either she would be frightened of his wrath, like Kelemvor, or she would be a fool and attempt to be rid of him.

"Well?" the One demanded.

"Cyric, after what you have done, how can you ask? My hatred for you is greater than ever."

Oghma took her arm. "Mystra, you are a goddess now. It is long past time to put away this mortal—"

Mystra whirled on him. "I have had enough of your lessons, Oghma! Never again do you need remind me of my duty to the Balance, nor tell me how to carry it out!"

The Binder paled and released her arm, and I began to tremble as a child. The Harlot was anything but frightened; I glanced at Kelemvor's silver mask and consoled myself, for after the many changes he had made in the City of the Dead, my torments were not likely to be much worse than what I had suffered already in the service of the One.

Yet they call Mystra the Lady of Mysteries for a reason. She looked back to Cyric, and I saw him grin. Then I knew that in his infinite cunning, the One had seen what I could not.

When Mystra spoke, her wrath had softened. "But my hatred is not the issue here—a fact that Lord Cyric knows as well as I. If I bore him no hatred, he would be unfit for his duties. As Goddess of Magic, I am allowed my feelings." Here, Mystra gave Oghma the same look any person of sense reserves for meddlers, then she continued, "But as a guardian of the Balance, I must act on my wisdom."

"Mystra, think carefully," urged Tyr. "Once you speak, the verdict cannot be changed. You may come to rue the day you made this decision."

"I do already," Mystra replied. "But when the Circle found in my favor, I promised to behave as a god, not as a mortal."

The Harlot faced the One. "I find for Cyric."

Epilogue

Mystra had hardly finished speaking before the Circle of Twelve dispersed and I found myself alone with the One. At once, the Pavilion of Cynosure became an abhorrent den of iniquity, strewn with couches and pillows and filled with such a fog of sweet-smelling perfumes and bitter smoke I could hardly breathe. Cyric shrank to a size more nearly my own and sank deep into a settee of plush cushions. I dared to approach and prostrate myself before him. He let out a great sigh and tipped his head back and stared at the naked fiends on the ceiling.

I stayed on the floor for many minutes, until my knees grew numb and my joints began to ache with the cold, and even then I dared not rise. I had to be careful, for Tyr's protection had ended with the trial, and I was as likely to die as any man—perhaps even more so. Indeed, I thought it a small miracle the slimy mass in my chest had not killed me already and sent me on my way to find my wife in the City of the Dead.

At last, the One deigned to notice me. Without taking his eyes off the ceiling, he asked, "Malik, do you want something?"

"No, Mighty One!" And to my great horror, Mystra's accursed spell still compelled me to add, "Only one or two things, and they should not be difficult to grant for a great god."

I vowed vengeance on the Harlot, for I knew then that I would always be compelled to tell the truth.

Cyric tore his gaze from the ceiling and stared down upon me. "One or two things?"

"There is the matter of our hearts," I replied. "I am sure you would like yours back. And, while it was great honor to lend you my own, I will certainly have need of it later."

The One reached into his cloak, then pulled out my poor battered heart. Hardly anything remained of it. Most of the fluid had drained out, and now it was as flat as a shoe. "You want this back? It might not work."

This thought had occurred to me as well, and yet I was loath to keep the One's heart for fear of what it might do to the rest of my body. "Perhaps it could be fixed, Most High. I am certain you will want your own back."

"I think not, Malik." Cyric shook his head, then tossed my heart over his shoulder. "I can always find another, but you had better keep mine. You will need it."

This filled my stomach with a sick feeling. "I will?"

The One nodded, then patted the couch beside him. I rose and sat on the edge of the cushion.

"I have something very special in mind for you, Malik." Cyric draped his arm around my shoulders. The orange blood of my heart still dripped from his fingernails. "You are going to be my Seraph of Lies."

"Seraph of *Lies!*" I cried. "But I cannot lie!"

The One smiled. "That makes you perfect. I already have a task for you; but we will discuss that in a minute. You wanted two things. What is the second?"

I held up my hand and pinched my thumb and forefinger close together. "A small matter, Mighty One. I was wondering . . ." My trepidation grew so great that not even Mystra's magic could keep me from hesitating. "I was wondering what kind of reward—"

"Reward?" Cyric's hand pinched my shoulder, and it was a marvel that he crushed no bones. "After what you did?"

"What I did?" I leapt to my feet—I could not help myself. "I cured your insanity! I saved you from being found innocent!"

"True—but I commanded you to get the *Cyrinishad*." Cyric

pulled me back down and pushed me so deep into the cushions I feared I would smother. "You failed me, Malik—for that, I should send you to join your wife in the City of the Dead."

I began to tremble, as I knew now what I had only feared before—that if I ever saw my wife again, it would not be in the One's palace.

Cyric continued, "But you also helped me see that I am not the Prime Mover of the Multiverse, and so I forgive your failure." The One brought his face so close to mine that I did not dare exhale for fear that my breath would offend him. "But that can be changed, Malik. I have a plan—and *you* will play a part in it."

"Me, Mighty One?" In truth, I had been hoping for a somewhat smaller reward. "What kind of a part?"

"When the time comes, Malik . . . When the time comes, I will reveal all." The One grinned, then spun away from me and rose. "But first, you must do your penance."

"Penance!" I shouted—but I was also quick to add, "Whatever you command, Most High."

The One clasped his hands behind his back, then turned and strolled toward the wall of the Pavilion. "I want you to write an account, Malik—a chronicle of the search for the Holy *Cyrinishad,* so that my worshipers will understand the many trials their god endures on their behalf."

"Yes!"

I saw at once that I had been blessed, that the vision I had seen on the plain outside Candlekeep would come to pass, that I would stand beneath a stormy sky before a vast host of True Believers and speak to them in the thunderous voice of the One True Prophet and reunite the Church of the Faithful under my own banner!

In my excitement, I leapt up and followed the One toward the wall of the Pavilion. "It shall be a True and Faithful Chronicle of the Trial of Cyric the Mad, and I shall report all the things that happened from the time I found the *Cyrinishad* until we saved Faerûn from a second Time of Troubles!"

The One whirled with black fire in his eyes. "*We,* Malik?"

And so it was that Cyric the All gave his blessing to this humble account, that he renewed my Faithless heart and returned me to the Way of Belief and burned my eyes with the Flames of Glory and Truth, until I saw all that had occurred in the world and in the heavens since before the Razing of Zhentil Keep, so that I might set down in complete accuracy and perfect truth all the things done by men and by gods during the search for the holy *Cyrinishad.*

Praise be to Cyric the One, Most Mighty, Highest of the High, the Dark Sun, the Black Sun, the Lord of Three Crowns, and the Prince of Lies! All Blessings and Strength upon his Church and his Servants, who alone shall rule over the Kingdom of Mortals and Dwell Forever in the Palace of Eternity in the time beyond the Year of Carnage!

This is the book of the Seraph Malik el Sami yn Nasser, Favored of the One and the True Prophet of all Believers, in which I give a complete account of my Faithful service to Cyric the All in the boundless lands of Faerûn and beyond, and of the Great Reward I received for my Valiant Labors during the Trial of Cyric the Mad. Every part is true, and I swear that if one word is false, then they all are!